DISCLAIM

PAM GODWIN

FOR KIM -

HERE'S TO THE MONSTERS

WE DON'T WANT TO

ESCAPE.

Visit my website at pamgodwin.com

If you have not read books 1 and 2, STOP!

The books in the DELIVER series are stand-alones,
but they should be read in order.
DELIVER (#1)
VANQUISH (#2)
DISCLAIM (#3)
DEVASTATE (#4)
TAKE (#5)

For the victims of human trafficking—
You are in my heart,
In my mind.

Human trafficking is the fastest growing and second largest criminal industry in the world. It accounts for more than 32 billion dollars in illegal profits every year—more than Nike, Google, and Starbucks combined. Yet it remains an almost invisible crime.

There's approximately 27 million slaves worldwide. Only 0.4% of the victims are identified, and the average entry age into the sex trade is 12-14 years old.

Modern day slavery isn't made up for books and movies. It's real, and it's happening in every zip code.

What can you do to make the world less nightmarish?
Get the facts.
Spread awareness.
Tackle a campaign.

PROLOGUE

With a swing of the hammer, Matias pounded a steel tent stake into the arm pinned beneath his boot. A normal man would've flinched at the godawful howls of pain. The man he used to be would've puked out his guts at the feel of tendons snapping beneath the crude impalement. But focused fury was his internal companion, a ruthless beast risen from the ruins of his former self.

Hazel eyes, identical to his own, stared up at him in pleading agony.

He swung again, burying the spike into flesh. Shredded screams fused with the damp air of the shed as metal pierced muscle and tissue, finding purchase in the dirt floor.

Four stakes secured Jhon's arms and legs. The hooked heads protruded from bleeding holes, neutralizing any attempt to thrash free.

Matias removed the final stake from his pocket. The one that would end his brother's life.

Luring Jhon to the abandoned farm was easy. Beyond the open doorway, thick foliage cloaked the mountainside, rippling toward a tributary of the Amazon River below. The blue haze of humidity filtered the sunlight and blanketed the atmosphere in a wet sheen.

The remote site in the Colombian jungle indulged his brother's greed to expand cocaine production. The absence of witnesses made it an ideal place for Matias' revenge.

With shallow breaths, Jhon blinked slowly, fighting to maintain consciousness. "Don't do this."

The same words Matias uttered the night he was ripped from his home. *From Camila.*

He was a world away from the Texan citrus grove where he spent the first eighteen years of his life. A world away from the girl he'd tried — and failed — to protect.

He pressed the stake against the hollow of Jhon's throat, his voice an avalanche of gravel. "Why *her*?"

"She was —" Jhon wheezed past gritted teeth. "Something you cared about."

"She was family!" And so much more.

Speared to the ground, legs twitching against the spikes, Jhon hardened bruised eyes. "*I* am your family."

Only by blood, which stank of corroded iron and betrayal as it seeped into the soil.

Matias pushed on the stake, digging between corded sinews and breaking skin. "Where is she?"

Camila hadn't contacted him in six weeks. The moment his phone stopped ringing, he knew.

A malicious grin cracked Jhon's pallid face. "Sold."

Slavery. That much he'd figured out, but it didn't stop the torment from exploding anew and ravaging his veins with fire. "Where? Who has her?"

"She's dead, little brother." Jhon swallowed against the steel point, raising his chin to drive the stake deeper, taunting. "You're chasing a ghost."

A ghost with an invisible trail, likely smuggled to

the farthest corner of the world, to be used, broken, and disposed.

The truth resounded in the empty chasm of his chest, a painful splintering quickly snuffed out by the nothingness that consumed him.

He was wasting his time with Jhon. His brother was too cunning, too loyal to the organization, utterly single-minded, and willing to die to protect the only secret Matias wanted.

So be it.

He reared back the hammer and struck the stake, slamming ten inches of steel through Jhon's throat. The gurgling cough ended too soon. Just like all the others, his brother's glassy-eyed silence didn't soothe Matias' hunger for retribution.

Jhon's death was neither the first nor the last. In the months that followed, Matias sank deeper into the unforgiving armor of brutality. He belonged with the cartel, among the corrupted and the heartless, and used every resource available to search for her.

Obliterating men as despicable as himself provided an outlet for the rage he was unable to quiet. He understood the need to gut betrayers and decapitate adversaries, to torture for information, build stronger compounds, and effect armies. He became one of them, embracing their predatory existence and embodying a reputation that made the worst of his kind fear his name.

But it didn't bring her back.

It didn't bring back the citrus scent of her golden skin when she'd dozed with him in the grove. The way her shiny black hair whipped against her back as he chased her through knee-high grass. Or the spark in her brown eyes right before she launched a lime at his head.

Slowly, his memories of her decayed.

Twelve months after her disappearance, she'd become a mirage in his wasteland, distorted at the edges and flickering out of reach.

He lay on his bed in the newly renovated Colombian compound, hands clasped behind his neck, eyes closed, trying to forget, if only for a few minutes. The faceless blonde between his legs helped with that, bobbing her head and working his cock to distraction.

His lower body clenched, balls aching and tightening as he strained for release. "Faster. Suck harder."

She quickened her movements, the suction of her mouth hot and wet and—

A distinctive ring tone sounded from across the room. *What the fuck?*

"Did you hear that?" He jack-knifed into a sitting position and shoved her off his lap.

She dragged the back of a hand across her swollen lips.

The ringing echoed again, chiming a tune he hadn't heard in a year, waking a phone only one person had the number to.

He vaulted off the bed. "Get out."

With a racing pulse, he sprinted toward the dresser. Following the muffled bleeps, he dug through piles of weapons, papers, and clothes that scattered the surface. There! He grabbed it.

Unknown number.

His hand shook as he tapped the screen and accepted the call.

Dead air.

No, no, no. He missed it. Hitting the call back

button, he rubbed a hand down his face. *Come on, come on.*

The screen flashed. *Call failed.*

Vicious rage tore through his body, inflaming his muscles. He spun and found the blonde taking her sweet-ass time dragging on clothes, her gaze on his softening cock.

He grabbed a chambered .45 from the dresser, flicked off the safety, and aimed it at her head, his voice cold and lethal. "Get the fuck out."

Eyes wide, she snatched her shirt from the floor and shut the door behind her.

He set down the gun and returned to the phone, deafening in its silence and still plugged in since the day he left it on the dresser. *Call me back, goddammit.*

It was illogical to hope. Camila was gone. Anyone could've accidentally dialed him. But wasn't hope the reason he'd kept the number all this time?

He stared at the blank screen, willing it to come back to life.

A moment later, it lit up. *Unknown Number.* The cascading ring tone penetrated his chest, stabbing interior scars with excruciating precision.

Tempering his breaths, he answered. "Who is this?"

Silence. Then a soft exhale. "It's me."

He stopped breathing, every cell in his body screaming in denial. His countless enemies were insidious in their efforts to destroy him. How hard would it be to procure this number and impersonate her husky voice?

He lifted his arm, zeroing in on the white pockmark on the inside of his wrist. "How old was I when I got my first scar?"

"So paranoid." A sigh ruffled through the ear piece. "Guess that means you still work for them."

His jaw set, his tone clipped with suspicion. "How old?"

"I was…uh, six. So you were eight?"

He gripped the edge of the dresser, his rib cage tightening. But any one of their friends or neighbors could've been tortured for that information.

Relaxing his grip, he sharpened his voice. "Tell me how it happened."

"I hate your asshole games."

Exactly how Camila would've responded, and the lack of warmth in the voice was perfectly her. But he couldn't trust it. "Tell me."

She growled in frustration. "You slipped in a stream and punctured your arm on a rock."

That was the story they told their families, an innocent lie to protect a mangy dog. Only Camila knew the truth.

His hope crashed, burning in his stomach. "Wrong answer."

"Seriously? We swore to take that secret to our graves." She cleared her throat. "Rambo wasn't a bad dog. He just didn't appreciate you taking his bone. You deserved that bite."

Camila. All the air evacuated his lungs as his mind spun and wrenched apart his painfully constructed acceptance of her death. Convincing himself she was gone had been a grueling effort in self-destruction, reinforced with irreparable distractions. The business, drugs, women, blood… So much fucking blood.

He couldn't feel his legs beneath the grip of shock,

6

his mouth dry and acidic. "You're not dead."

"Nope," she said, casually. Too detached, even for her. "Did you look for me?"

Every damn day. "Are you safe?" He snagged a pair of jeans, his hands sweating as he shoved them on. "Where are you?"

"I'm safe, but listen, I just escaped a fucked up situation and need to lie low for a while."

Escaped? Impossible. No one *escaped* a highly-organized human trafficking ring. Especially not a seventeen-year-old girl. *Eighteen now.* She'd been in captivity for a fucking year. Did they beat her? Rape her? Take her virginity?

His insides boiled with murderous wrath and overwhelming guilt. They were supposed to be each other's firsts. She was only sixteen when the cartel came for him, and though he hadn't seen her since that night, he'd waited for her, holding on to an impossible dream through their secret phone calls. Until she vanished.

"You haven't asked what happened to me." Her tone hardened. "You already know, don't you? How?"

He couldn't tell her, not until he was certain she couldn't run from his answer. "I need to know where you are and how you escaped."

"Who do you work for?" she asked.

"You know I can't tell you, *mi vida.*"

"Don't call me that." A muffled rustle of fabric followed, conjuring an image of her pressing the phone to her chest. "Dammit, I want to trust you, but you have to give me something. Anything. What happened to the boy whose thoughts completed mine? What did they do to you?"

That boy was dead. How quickly they'd returned

7

to their exhaustingly endless argument, one he refused to feed. "Tell me where you are."

"Will you help me?"

"Always."

As she rattled off directions to an isolated reservoir in Texas, he scrambled for a pen and scribbled down the details. *Two hours outside of Austin.*

It would take him a day to travel there from the bowels of goddamned Colombia. "I'm on my way. Just...stay put."

"Oh, I'm not there." Her breaths quickened, as if she were walking at a swift pace. "That's where I left a body. I need you to get rid of it since, you know, you're still in the *business*."

His skin chilled with the ramp of his pulse. "What body?"

"The sick fuck who bought me."

The phone's power cord snapped from the outlet as he charged toward the shirt on the floor. "You killed him?"

"Doesn't matter. But I'm using his phone and need to toss it like yesterday."

Fuck! She's going to get herself killed. And now his number would show up on phone records for rival gangs, FBI, fucking anyone to track.

He paced the room as a year's worth of ruthless crimes caught up with him. "Who else have you called?"

A pause, filled by the rush of her breaths. "Just you."

Relief loosened his gait. "I have to kill this number." He gave her the number to his main phone and made her repeat it several times. "Only use burner phones, and *mi vida*? Don't try to contact your parents."

8

"Why the hell not?"

They were dead. Buried beneath the scorched landscape of the citrus grove.

He evened his voice. "You'll endanger them."

She made a despairing noise, a small thing, but it was a hint of emotion nonetheless. She was closed-off by nature, reserving her softness for the few who earned her loyalty. He'd been on the receiving end of that once, had forgotten what it felt like.

The reminder was a molten shock to his system, intensified by a combustible storm as he imagined what she'd endured in the clutches of her kidnappers.

Who had touched her? How deep were her wounds?

His hand clenched and loosened on the phone. "How many motherfuckers do I need to kill?"

"I'll handle it. Just deal with the body. I need to go—"

"Give me a way to contact you." So he could locate her. And reclaim her.

"I'll be in touch."

"Don't you fucking hang—"

She disconnected the call.

CHAPTER 1

Ten years later…

"Lower. That's it. A little lower…" Camila rocked her hips beneath the scratch of whiskers. "Right there, *churro.*"

Churro, my ass. This underweight stick of a man reeked of sweat, stale smoke, and neglect. Or maybe it was the mattress.

Not that she expected a pleasant experience. The man between her legs worked for someone vile. Someone who didn't deserve to live. Shame she didn't know who that someone was. But she was here to find out.

Bony hands curled around her waist, his wet mouth slithering across the waxed mound of her pussy. *Here we go.*

A purr vibrated her throat, her pleasure as fake as her role tonight. But damn if she didn't sound convincing. With her legs spread, back pressed against the mattress, and a hundred-and-fifteen pounds of athletic nudity on display, she could rob a man of all common sense.

As soon as she could seduce him into position, she'd take more than just his wits.

He shifted lower, curled his tongue inside her, and

Whoa! What the — A charged warmth of bliss shot across her skin and bowed her spine.

"*Mierda*, yes!" She turned her neck, hiding the shock on her face.

Holy hell, he knew how to give head. She melted against the suction of his lips, clinging to the tingling rush of sensations. As far as surprises went, she could roll with this one. She might even come.

With wicked flicks of his tongue, he peered up at her, his pupils bloated in the dim light of a floor lamp. "Condom?"

He wouldn't get that far, but he'd picked her up at the local bar under the assumption she wanted to fuck.

"Got it covered, baby." She grabbed his brown hair and held his mouth against her pussy. "I'm almost there."

An orgasm wasn't in the plan, but fuck it. He did things with his tongue no warm-blooded woman could refuse. Tenacious and sinful, he licked in and out and all around, reviving the ever-present ache inside her.

His unappealing looks didn't matter. Whenever she climaxed, it was always the same face behind her eyelids. Jet black hair. Dimpled smile. Sun-soaked complexion. Strong jaw. *Strong everywhere.* With eyes like ripe limes, golden in the center and ringed in deep green.

At least, that was her silly, childhood memory of Matias. The past twelve years — doing whatever unspeakable shit he did — likely marred his beauty. Time had certainly hardened his voice. Wrapped it in ice.

But she could hear his timbre in her head, sharp and incisive. *Come for me*, mi vida. *Come now.*

Heat bloomed low in her pelvis, gathering into a rhythmic pulse and tumbling her over the edge. She detonated on the stroking tongue, grinding and panting with abandon. *Damn.*

He raised his head and snaked a hand over her abdomen, his gaze hungry and full of intent. He could look at her however he wanted as long as his fingers continued their prowl upward.

Inching along her ribs, he teased each bone in his path toward her tit. His position was just…about…

Perfect.

She captured his arm, shifted it diagonally across her chest, and held it tightly against her. Tight enough to widen his eyes.

Strengthening her grip, she lifted her knees above his head and pinned his neck between his own shoulder and her inner thigh.

"The fuck?" He writhed and twisted, trying to jerk free.

His other hand swung toward her face, but she knocked it away and clamped her legs around his thrashing neck. Jesus, he was strong for a skinny fucker.

She yanked harder on his arm and adjusted her hips, maneuvering him into a restrained position.

Finally. Adrenaline surged through her veins, and her breaths came in short bursts.

Realization glistened in the stark white of his eyes, and he snarled like a rabid animal.

That's right, baby. I know who you are. You're so fucked.

He bucked his chest against the mattress, his teeth snapping too damn close to her stomach.

"I have kids." His sunken cheeks blanched, his voice a choked rasp. "I'm a father."

Good for him. She had a father once. And a mother

and sister. Her heart twisted, the loss as raw as the day she discovered their deaths. They would never know what happened to her. Would never know she made it out of that attic of shackles and horrors. She'd escaped a fate worse than death.

The same fate this piece of shit inflicted on others.

"You should've thought about your kids…" She hooked her foot beneath her other knee and squeezed her legs. "Before you stole someone else's."

The compression of her thighs and the pulling grip on his arm crushed his bicep against his throat, strangling his ability to speak. And breathe.

Her muscles strained to defend the position as he kicked and rolled his hips. Keeping his arm pressed beneath his chin, she swatted away his attempts to punch her with his free hand. Over and over, he flung his fist toward her face, fighting for blood, for air, wild in his desperation.

No bueno.

If done effectively, the chokehold would cut off the blood flow in the arteries on both sides of the neck. It should've been over within seconds. Why was this motherfucker still squirming?

She tightened her legs and cocked her head, studying the waning twitches in his body. Unconsciousness would come soon. She settled in and tried to steady her heartbeat.

Months of stalking Austin's worst criminals had led her to Larry McGregor. Mailman by day and slave trader by night, he spent his downtime hooking up with sleazy women at the local bar. Bet he regretted that vice right about now.

Her thighs tensed, burning to snap his neck. But

14

she needed him alive.

Surveillance confirmed he held a teenage girl in an abandoned barn twenty minutes outside of Austin. Knowing her team was extracting the girl at that very moment should've made it easier to breathe. But there were more Larrys, more enslaved girls, the trafficking network in Austin vast and well-funded.

The only way to stop it was to cut off the head. First, she needed to know how to find that head.

Larry's body fell limp between her legs. She waited a beat, pushing at his gaping jaw before slipping from beneath him and checking his pulse. *Slow and even.* Unlike her own.

From her purse on the floor, she unwrapped a maxi pad and removed the plastic cable ties she'd hidden in the cotton. How long before he woke?

Fuck, she was out of her realm here. She wanted to end him, but if she didn't secure the information she needed, another would take his place, and another, and another. This would be her first attempt at torture. Did she have the balls to do it?

She quickly zipped his wrists to his ankles and stuffed the maxi pad in his mouth, her fingers twitching through the movements. Matias would have a body to dispose of soon enough.

Matias. Every call she made to him brought a new line of questioning. His *and* hers. Neither would budge in their secrecy.

A sudden chill crept over her. Just thinking about him made her feel vulnerable and…naked. She slid on her dress and heels.

She hadn't seen him since he was eighteen, not since the day those hard-looking men led him out of the citrus grove. Over the years, he told her he was *obligated* to stay with them. Were they cartel? He refused to confirm her assumption, but he didn't deny it either. What was she supposed to do? Trust him? No way in hell.

He was a thirty-year-old…what? Grave-digger? Hitman? Underling for a drug lord? Whatever his line of work, he always got rid of dead bodies for her. The first was the man who intended to buy her. Followed by six more buyers and their bodyguards for her six fellow slaves. Her last call was four years ago. To collect Van Quiso's body.

She retrieved her phone from her purse and pulled up her contact list. A shudder raced through her as she stared at the last number dialed.

Van Quiso.

The man who kidnapped her when she was seventeen.

The man who imprisoned her for a year and trained her to be the perfect slave.

As it turned out, he hadn't died from that gunshot wound in his shoulder.

No matter how hard she tried, she couldn't parse her feelings about that. They ran too deep, too entangled and confusing, much like everything else in her life. So she detached from it, held herself at a distance, and focused on the goal. She had a slave trader to torture and kidnapped girls to save.

She tapped his name on the screen. As the call connected, her heartbeat roared past her ears.

Van answered with silence.

"It's done and ready for pick up." She steeled her breath.

"On my way." He disconnected.

She slumped on the edge of the mattress, her shoulders loosening.

Ironically, asking her kidnapper to help her take down other kidnappers wasn't the worst call she had to make. That special pang of dread was reserved for her impending conversation with Matias.

God, she missed him. Almost as much as she feared him.

A soon-to-be dead man lay hogtied beside her, eyes closed and mouth stretched around the balled up maxi pad. She could dispose of the body herself. At the risk of getting caught and sentenced for murder.

If she involved Matias, he would shield her from the law. At the risk of him finally locating her.

Then what? Whatever connection they'd shared as children was a distant memory. She knew nothing about the man he'd become.

If his overbearing, razor-sharp tone over the phone was any indication, he hadn't lost his protective ownership over her.

But she hadn't spoken to him in four years. What if he'd forgotten about her? What if he was married?

Her heart punched painfully, and she reached up to rub her chest.

There had been a time when he'd gallantly stood between her and anything that threatened to harm her. If he knew she was taking dangerous risks, would he try to stop her? She was so close to finishing this. So fucking close.

And maybe she was protective of him, too. Maybe she still cared for him against her better judgment. If that were true, she couldn't take him where she was going.

She needed to forget about him.

Except she couldn't. In the back of her fucked up mind, she looked forward to her next kill just so she'd have a reason to hear his voice again.

CHAPTER 2

Camila paced beside the floor-to-ceiling windows in Van's living room, her impatience burning a short fuse. She dragged a hand through her hair, fingers snagging in the shoulder-length, black strands. She needed a fucking haircut.

She needed a lot of things.

Sighing, she turned to Van. "Why won't he fucking talk?"

After a week of interrogation, Larry McGregor was a goddamn mute. Strapped naked on a table in Van's garage, he'd endured sleep deprivation, starvation, solitary confinement, and her endless threats of permanent disfigurement.

All he had to do was tell her who he worked for and where he was supposed to deliver the girl he'd kidnapped. Two simple answers and his suffering would end.

Van reclined on the couch and rolled a toothpick between his lips. "You need to up your game."

"Oh, please enlighten me." She narrowed her eyes, her voice edged with bitter resentment.

She'd spent an eternal year in Van's shackles, learning obedience one welt at a time. At least this house didn't have an attic. She didn't need any more reminders of him whipping her body and picking apart her mind. He probably would have taken her virginity, too, but the man who had intended to buy her wanted that sick pleasure.

Van never managed to break her, though. What made him think he could give advice on breaking Larry McGregor?

Tossing his chewed toothpick on the coffee table, he removed a new one from his pocket. "Threaten his kids."

As a father, Van knew all too well how effective that was. But she couldn't do it. Even if it were a hollow threat, she refused to stoop to that level.

"No innocents."

She'd been an innocent kid once, one of the reasons Van had captured her. Back then, he was a vicious son of a bitch. Still was. But the past four years had diluted some of his poisonous nature. Or maybe his wife had something to do with that.

Unfortunately, his wife had put a full stop on Camila's plan to chop off Larry's fingers.

"Amber?" she shouted toward the second-story loft, where the strange woman had vanished moments earlier.

Amber approached the railing upstairs, her brown hair cascading in curls around her model-perfect face.

How Van had been able to coerce a beauty pageant queen into marrying him was anyone's guess. He'd kidnapped her, for fuck's sake. Yanked her right out of her house and imprisoned her in this remote cabin, not to be sold, but to be used as his own personal sex slave.

The kicker was, he'd stopped his kidnapping and

slave trading after that. Amber forgave him, and they fell in love or some shit. Their relationship smelled like an epic mindfuck, but on the surface, it seemed to be working for them.

Amber fingered her curls as if ensuring each one lay exactly right. Then she brushed the front of her sundress, erasing imaginary wrinkles.

Yeah, the woman had issues, and loving Van wasn't the weirdest of them. She struggled with severe OCD and agoraphobia. When Van snatched her, she hadn't been out of her house in two years.

Lowering a hand to the railing, Amber stepped down the spiral staircase, one toned leg crossing in front of the other like she was walking the runway in a fashion show. "Did you need me?"

Camila met her at the bottom step. "I'll cover the garage floor with plastic. I promise I'll keep the mess…not messy."

"No. That's—" Amber clutched her knuckles, popping each one systematically. "The blood will splatter. I'll never get it off the concrete and—"

"Amber." Van appeared at her side, gripping her fingers and stilling her favorite coping mechanism. "Crack your knuckles again, and I'll tie you to the tree outside."

"Right," Amber said on a stiff inhale. "I'm good. We're good."

She stared at her husband for a long moment, each second stretching into something intimate and unspoken as her expression heated. Jesus, did she want him to tie her up? This was Van Quiso of all people, prince of sadism and non-consensual kink.

The four-inch scar that bisected his cheek was the

first thing any terrified girl would notice. Followed by his obscenely oversized muscles, tousled brown hair, and the saw-blade angles of his face. There was no denying he was insanely attractive. *Insane* being the quintessential word here.

Amber pulled her attention away from him, shifting it across the room, eyes squinting. Hard.

Camila followed her gaze to the coffee table, returned to Amber, then back to the table. Van's chewed toothpick lay alone on the dust-free surface. Knowing him, he probably left it there to fuck with her OCD.

"You guys," Camila said, shaking her head, "are seriously whacked."

Hands fisting on her hips, Amber straightened her spine. "Says the woman who wants to cut off body parts in my garage."

Touché. Bringing Larry here had been a matter of convenience. The closest neighbor was miles away, and Van kept the property locked down like a fortress. As for his willingness to help her? Well, maybe that was his way of atoning for being a former human-trafficking asshole. Whatever helped him sleep at night.

"Fine. No blood." Camila crossed the room and took in the heavily treed landscape beyond the wall of windows. "I need to increase the Krokodil injections."

Created by mixing codeine with paint thinner, gasoline, and a few other nasty ingredients, the drug was more addictive than heroin. She didn't cook it long enough to remove the toxic impurities, hoping that would speed up the side effects, such as gangrene and pneumonia. Eventually, blood vessels would burst, and the flesh around the injection point—where she deliberately missed the vein—would rot and fall off the bone in chunks.

"How do you avoid a lethal dose?" Van leaned against the windowed wall, gnawing on a toothpick.

"No idea." She wasn't a druggie, had never even smoked tobacco. "I'm going to check on him."

Passing through the kitchen, she took in the polished appliances and spotless countertops. Exactly what one would expect in a house occupied by someone with OCD.

There was nothing lavish about the cabin. The fixtures, the furniture…it was all simple. Practical. Made her wonder what Van did with his wealth or if he'd even kept any money from his trafficking days.

She opened the door to the garage and found Liv and Tate bent over Larry's nude body.

It was surreal seeing them here, willingly standing in the home Van shared with his wife. His *domain*.

Liv Reed was the first person he'd captured, his first slave, and the one he'd hurt the most. After he broke the rules and raped her, he got her pregnant and couldn't sell her. Buyers wanted virgins. That had earned Van and Liv matching scars on their cheeks, courtesy of Mr. E.

Mr. E, now dead, had run the operation, raised their daughter, and controlled Van and Liv by threatening the little girl's life.

It was impossible to look at Liv without feeling a torrential mix of nostalgia, pity, and gratitude. While Mr. E had forced Van and Liv to capture and train slaves — nine in total — Liv covertly and brilliantly killed the buyers each time she delivered a slave. She did that for *years*.

Tate looked up from the table, his dark blond brows pulling together as he scanned Camila from head to toe. He'd been the sixth one Van and Liv enslaved.

Imagining a strong-willed, masculine guy like Tate Vades being forced to suck Van's cock… Camila knew it had irreparably damaged him. But he hid his demons beneath a disarming smile.

"Doing okay?" He met her gaze, a thousand more questions swirling in his crystal blue eyes.

"*Muy bien.*" She really wanted to know how *he* was holding up, but if she asked, he'd give her a similar bullshit answer. "You don't have to be here, you know."

When she told her team a few months ago that she'd asked Van for help with this phase of her plan, Tate had blown a gasket. But if Liv could trust Van—enough to let him be part of their daughter's life—they could rely on him for this.

"Van doesn't scare me." Tate crossed his arms, the sleeves of his t-shirt straining across his biceps. "I'm not going anywhere, Camila."

He hadn't left her side since the day she rescued him. They lived together, worked together, his shadow always hovering like a protective brother. Except the way he watched her was more like a boyfriend. One who refused to have sex with her.

Maybe he kept her in the friend zone because of what they'd been through. Or maybe it was because of what she'd become.

"This is going to be unpleasant." She approached the table where Larry lay motionless, his arms and legs bubbling with sores. She gave Tate a stern look, silently reminding him she was going to break another law. Murder another man. Throw away another body. "You can go before—"

"Stop." He gripped her jaw and brought his mouth

to her ear, his voice low. "I owe you my life, so just…shut the fuck up about it."

"Fine." She turned her head, breaking his hold.

As the first slave to be freed, she spent years helping Liv extricate Tate and the others. That included dismantling Mr. E's operation, killing the buyers, and using her connection with Matias to dispose of the bodies.

The freed slaves could've gone back to their lives if they'd had families or something to return to. They didn't, instead joining Camila in her effort to take down a new trafficking ring — the one Larry worked for.

"He's still not talking?" She prodded at the gangrenous, pus-filled flesh on Larry's forearm.

"No." Liv frowned, the scar on her cheek wrinkling. "I have to leave in a couple hours."

"You have Livana this weekend?"

"Yes." The tightness around Liv's mouth relaxed, replaced with the warm glow of maternal love.

Van and Liv shared joint custody with Livana's adoptive mother. It was a strange arrangement, one they fervently protected. Which meant they kept their involvement in Camila's illegal activities to a minimum. Had it been Van's weekend with Livana, he wouldn't have permitted Camila and her team of ex-slave vigilantes anywhere near his house.

Larry flicked open his eyes and thrashed his head, his rotten flesh tearing beneath the cinch straps.

To think, addicts purposefully shot themselves up with this shit. Cheap ingredients, easy to make, and a *killer* high? Yeah, no thanks.

She touched the abscess on his arm, and a layer of skin the width of her hand slid free and splatted on

Amber's pristine garage floor. Her stomach revolted.

"Shit." Tate rubbed the back of his neck. "Amber's going to have a full-on seizure when she sees that."

Not if they cleaned—

Holy fuck, was that a bone shining through the hole in Larry's arm? Bile simmered in the back of her throat.

"What are you doing to me?" Larry groaned, his eyes clearing.

Good, he was lucid. She turned to grab a syringe, but Liv was already there, holding it out for her.

"This," Camila said, positioning the needle an inch from Larry's flaccid dick, "is Krokodil. It's been eating you from the inside out. Given the dead flesh on your arms and legs, I bet your guts don't feel very good right now."

"You fucking bitch." He shifted his hips, unable to distance himself from the syringe. "Get away from me. I need a fucking doctor."

"Sure." She sweetened her tone. "Just tell me who you work for."

He dropped his head back and fell still. Gaze-locked-on-the-ceiling still. Something seemed to settle over him, the tension in his body draining away. Resignation? The motherfucker better not be giving up.

"Whatever you do to me," he said, eerily calm, "*his* retaliation will be tenfold. You have no idea who you're fucking with, you stupid cunt."

Tenfold? Maybe so. Whomever he worked for would probably go after his family.

"I'm going to put maggots on this." She traced a finger around the rotted cavern in his arm. "Move along the whole zombie thing you've got going on."

Tate grimaced, looking as nauseated as she felt. Liv somehow managed a bored expression.

"Do it." Larry closed his eyes. "I don't fucking care."

Okay, forget the maggots. She jabbed the needle into the root of his dick.

His back flew off the table, the rest of him restrained by straps as he screamed and flailed.

Holding onto the syringe, she hovered her thumb over the plunger and waited for him to calm down. "When and where is the girl supposed to be dropped? Give me that, and I won't rot off your junk."

He shook against a full-body spasm, his eyes bulging as he stared at the needle stuck in his delicate flesh. "Ten at night." He spat out a month, a day, and GPS coordinates.

Oh, thank fuck. It was only two days away, but she was ready, having tracked and hunted this operation for four years. Her veins sizzled with the need to finish this.

As Tate left the garage to shout the coordinates to Van, she removed the syringe.

Larry cried out in relief then glared at her with bloodshot eyes. "He's going to kill you. You'll beg for it before he's done."

She tried not to let that threat worm its way inside her, but it penetrated her resolve and formed ice in the marrow of her bones.

Shaking off the dread, she turned and found Liv drifting along the wall where dozens of dolls and mannequins hung from hooks. Van's garage was a workshop. His little shop of glassy-eyed horrors.

She took a step toward Liv then thought better of it. "Hey, Liv? You okay?"

Liv stiffened, her hand lifting to smooth down her straight, black hair. "I used to hate these things. Part of me always will, you know?"

When Van collected slaves, he also collected freaky plastic people. Now he made dolls out of leather and gave them to homeless kids.

Still fucking creepy.

Liv relaxed her posture and strode back to the table, her graceful legs encased in black denim. Her moods were difficult to follow, switching on and off like the masks she used to wear.

"Did he tell you why he has a fascination with dolls?" Liv asked, tone silky soft.

Camila shook her head. She and Van didn't have a let's-share-stories kind of relationship.

Sadness etched Liv's slender face. "Maybe he'll tell you some day. It puts all of this" — she gestured at the wall of leather bodies — "into perspective."

Curiosity itched beneath her skin, but Van's doll fetish would have to wait. Liv held out another syringe, this one with a thicker needle, the tube filled with Pentobarbital stolen from a vet clinic.

As Camila reached for it, Liv pulled it back, her voice low. "Let me do this for you."

Liv had killed slave buyers with blades, bullets, and even her bare hands. She certainly had the stomach for it. But Camila had helped with some of them. She could do this.

"Thank you." She held out her hand. "This is nothing compared to what I have to do next."

"What are you planning, Camila?" Liv released the syringe, her expression a cold mask.

A shiver rippled through her. *That* had been the

tone Liv used when she held a whip, posed to strike. When Camila's world had been confined to four windowless walls in a soundproof attic.

Deep breath. She was here because she didn't want other girls to end up in chains, where they would learn how to beg for an orgasm, how to stroke a man's cock, and how to relax into the bone-rattling bite of a whip.

She forced her attention on Larry, his eyes closed and breathing even. Passed out. Maybe already on his way to death.

Aiming the syringe over his heart, she slammed it down and drove hard and fast. When his eyes flashed open, she depressed the plunger and held a finger over the pulse in his throat until his eyes closed and his heart stopped.

She stood there for a moment, waiting to feel something. Like what? Killer's remorse? Was that a thing? All she felt was purpose. It strengthened her backbone and energized her pulse.

"Got to make a call." She headed toward the door.

Liv caught her arm and swung her back around. "What's your next move, Camila?"

That was the tricky part. Liv, Tate, none of her team would like it.

"I'll fill you in." She pulled her arm from Liv's grip. "But I have to deal with the body before it stinks up Amber's garage."

Liv studied her face, probing too closely, too deeply. "You're carrying a torch, girl. The damn flames are burning in your eyes. Someday soon, it's going to devour you." Liv's expression softened. "You can't save them all."

"I know." But she could save a lot of them.

In the kitchen, she grabbed a new burner phone from her bag on the counter and headed toward the front door.

Van blocked her path, arms crossed over his chest. "Who do you call to deal with dead bodies?"

"An old connection." She trusted Van more than she ever thought possible, but she didn't trust him with this.

"What the fuck kind of connection? Liv said you did side jobs for some cartel. Are you bringing that shit to my front door?"

She might've mentioned something along those lines at some point. She didn't do anything for any cartel, but it was highly probable that her connection did. "I'll move the body off the property. They won't come anywhere near here."

His jaw stiffened. "The same thugs that were supposed to dispose of *my* body."

"Hey, man." She held up her hands and met his frigid gray eyes. "I'm not the one who shot you."

His gaze turned inward. He scratched his shoulder—the old wound hidden beneath his shirt—and the corner of his mouth twitched. "Good thing Liv missed my heart."

Was that a good thing? Maybe so. If Liv had aimed true, Van wouldn't have lived to help them in the most valuable way possible. Financially.

"The thing I can't figure out, though…" He narrowed his eyes. "How did you know I didn't die? Liv says this guy, whoever you're about to call, doesn't have a way to contact you. If he didn't tell you I wasn't there…" He tipped his head to the side. "Were you watching the house?"

"No, I…" *Jesus fuck, this is an awkward conversation.* "I went there to clean up the blood. Except you didn't leave any behind, and your car was gone."

He nodded absently, seemingly absorbed in thought, so she slipped around him and opened the front door.

"Camila."

Her breath caught. Christ, would she always flinch at the bark of Van's voice?

Standing behind her, he squeezed her shoulder and removed his touch. "I'm sorry."

For which part? Snatching her from her front yard? Tying her up? Spitting in her face? Shoving his cock in her mouth?

"For everything." His footsteps retreated, leaving her shaken and off-balance.

Dammit, not the best frame of mind for the call she had to make.

It had been four years since she'd spoken to Matias. Did his promise to always help her still hold true? What if his number was disconnected?

Only one way to find out.

Her heart hammered as she stepped into the chilly darkness and dialed.

CHAPTER 3

The vibration of the phone shattered the chilly stillness in the SUV. Matias glanced at the screen, and a smirk pulled at his lips.

There had been a time when a call from an unknown number had sent his heart rate into a frenzy. But that was years ago, before he'd invested in spies, surveillance, and drone technology.

Parked on a barren road in the outskirts of rural Austin, he stretched out in the driver's seat and met Nico's gaze in the rear-view mirror.

"You gonna answer that, *careverga*?" Nico dropped his head against the backseat and closed his eyes as if he didn't give a fuck either way.

The pompous ass had apathy down to an art. Nico could yawn through mass beheadings and play games on his phone during gunfights, but everything he did was calculated. His brutal intellect and mafia-style code of respect made him the most feared cartel capo in Colombia.

Matias knew the man behind the reputation, though. He trusted Nico, not only with his life, but with Camila's.

"She made me wait four fucking years." He held

the vibrating phone in one hand and a wide screen tablet in the other. "I want to watch her sweat."

Live video streamed on the tablet, transmitted from a drone that circled four-hundred feet above Van Quiso's cabin. The quadcopter's modified cameras, with high-powered lenses and night vision, provided a bird's eye view of her position on the front porch while remaining outside of her range of hearing.

His phone cycled through another burst of vibrations and fell quiet.

"Well done." Nico's voice, while monotone to an irritating degree, held a tinge of amusement. "If she doesn't call back, you'll be an unbearable *hijueputa*."

"She'll call back." Matias tapped on the image of her head, initiating the drone's active track feature.

The small, self-flying aircraft adapted to its surroundings, using sonar detection to avoid anything in its path as it followed her movements through the yard. The aerial footage flickered between nebulous and grainy, but when he magnified the picture, he could make out the pixelated curve of a hand as it raked through her hair.

Was she thinking about him? Wondering if he was dead or alive? Probably cursing him for not answering the phone. What would she do if she knew he was parked less than a mile away, watching her?

She paced a circuit across the front lawn, activating perimeter lights that illuminated her slender frame. She stopped, kicked at something in the grass, and raised a hand to her ear.

His phone buzzed again. *Unknown number.*

He found Nico's reflection in the mirror and arched a brow.

"Don't look so smug, *ese*." Nico loosened the knot on his tie. "She'll run the other way as soon as she learns what you've done."

Camila didn't run from anything. Not even when they were kids. No, she would look him dead in the eye. Then she would kill him.

He placed the phone on the dash, set the call on speaker, and answered the way she expected. "Who is this?"

"Hey. It's been awhile, huh?" Her voice was strong, confident, but in the video, she doubled over, a hand braced on her knee.

His insides constricted in sympathy, stirring up years of anguish. Did she resent the time and distance between them as much as he did? Not likely. If she did, she would've fucking called.

He seethed with the urgency to go to her, drag her into the night, and chain her to his bed.

Just like Van Quiso. Only worse. He would never let her escape.

She would seethe and snarl and fight every step of the way, and he would absorb her hatred because, in the end, it'd all be worth it.

His skin warmed despite the cool air blowing from the A/C. Adjusting the vents toward his face, he wrapped his voice in silken tones. "It's been four years, *mi vida*. Where are you?"

"You first." Her blurry image resumed pacing. "Where do you live, and who do you work for?"

He caught Nico's glare in the mirror, those notorious eyes sharp with warning. *Don't you dare.*

"Ask me something meaningful." He flicked his attention back to the screen. "What do you really want to know?"

"Hmmm." The drone lost her image as she stepped beneath a large oak tree. A moment later, she appeared on the other side, headed toward the sedan parked in the gravel driveway. "Are you…okay?"

His breath hung in his throat. It was an unexpected question, but one he could answer honestly. "I will be when you come to me." *Willingly.*

"How would that work? Would we meet at Starbucks, smile over the rims of our *tintos*, and take turns asking questions that go unanswered? Or would we skip the bullshit and jump right into fucking and fighting?"

"*No quiero café.* I want your smiles, your fighting, and your fucking." His cock jerked. "I want *you.*"

"If you wanted me, you would've found me. Unless you stayed away because…" She hummed, a husky, feminine sound. "You want me too much."

"You think I'm protecting you from myself?"

If only he were that selfless. His hands were bound. Not in the way he intended to bind hers, because dammit, she didn't have an excuse for avoiding him.

Outrage hardened his voice. "Why haven't you contacted me?"

"You tell me," she said, acid dripping from every syllable. "I don't know what you do, what you're involved in. I know your voice, but that's where it ends. You're a stranger. Would I even recognize you if I passed you on the street? For all I know, you're an undercover cop with a wife and kids in the suburbs."

He didn't blame her for being paranoid. Her hellfire mission to take down a very specific kind of criminal had led her to commit felonies that were punishable by death. But did she honestly believe he would betray her?

"You don't trust me." He squeezed the steering wheel.

"I trust you enough to ask for help."

"I see. And here I thought you called because you missed me." Except he knew she'd brought an unconscious man to Van's cabin. "You have something for me to get rid of?"

"Yep."

"But you won't be there when I collect it?"

Silence.

"How is that trusting me?" He watched the screen, mesmerized.

"I trust you with this." She sat on the hood of the car and lowered her head. "To stand by your word and not leave my package where someone could stumble across it."

The Austin PD never closed the missing person case on Camila Dias. The last thing he wanted was them to find her now and charge her with capital murder.

"Will the package be there this time?" he asked.

"Yeah. The last one" — she glanced up at Van's house — "was a slippery sucker."

Not that slippery. When he'd arrived to collect Van's body, the bastard was driving away from the house, bleeding from a shoulder wound and clinging to the steering wheel like it was the only thing keeping him alive.

The situation had presented two options. Shoot her kidnapper in the head as he drove by or follow him.

Following Van had been the best decision he ever made. A few weeks later, Van had led him to Liv Reed, who unknowingly took him right to Camila's front door.

That was four years ago. Four years of monitoring her impressive operation. He had the patience of a goddamn saint, but his intentions were far from benevolent.

He wanted her with a vehemence, but the timing was crucial. The agonizing wait was so very close to being over he could feel the adrenaline coursing through his system.

"Where am I picking up the package?" He knew she wouldn't send him to Van's property.

As she gave him an unfamiliar address, he mapped it on the tablet. Enclosed by farmland and dirt roads, the drop was only ten minutes away. Of course, she assumed he was out of town. Otherwise, she would've dumped the body before she called him.

This was the point in the conversation where she expected him to ask her shit like, *What are you involved in? Who did you kill this time? What have you been doing the past four years?*

He needed more from her. Something deeper, vulnerable. "Are you afraid?"

"No."

"Ah, but you answered too quickly. Have you forgotten I know when you're lying?"

Silence stretched, followed by her sigh. "Maybe I am."

"Afraid?"

"Maybe. Sometimes…" She jerked her head up.

Something moved at the edge of the screen. A man came into view, approaching her with a human-size bundle rolled up in a sheet. Terrible goddamn timing.

The camera angle shifted as she slid off the car and

walked toward the house. "I need to go."

"We're not finished." He tensed, unable to dampen the vitriol in his voice. "Do *not* disconnect."

"Slow your roll, sparkle. I'll call you right back." She hung up.

He slammed a fist into the dash, cracking an air vent and shooting a jolt of pain up his arm.

"Feel better?" Nico asked dryly.

"Fuck off." He glanced at the rear-view mirror and met Nico's eyes. "Did you get the address?"

Matias could make the call to have the body picked up, but the order carried more urgency when it came directly from the boss.

"*Sí, pendejo.*" Nico opened the back door and stepped out, his black suit made darker against the backdrop of the surrounding woods. Turning, he leaned back in and nodded at the tablet. "You need to put a leash on that. Fuck her ass into submission."

Hard to argue when fantasies of destroying every hole in her body had kept him in a hyper state of arousal for over a decade.

Nico shut the door and paced away from the SUV, his profile stark against the glow of the phone at his ear.

Neither of them had time for this side trip to Austin. Not with the heroin shipment arriving in Orlando tomorrow and the operatives they were currently moving across the Chihuahuan Desert. Smuggling drugs and terrorists into the States was a lucrative business, but risky as hell, especially with federal agents sniffing around the compound in El Paso.

Nico sure as fuck didn't want their resources allocated to an unprofitable cause like Camila Dias. But the man owed his power, his wealth, and every phlegmatic beat of his heart to Matias. Nico might bitch and argue, but he wasn't going to tell Matias *no*.

The drone changed course, following her as she helped load the body in the trunk of the sedan. That done, she turned toward the man at her side.

The video was too muddy to make out details, but the way he crowded her, standing too fucking close, gave him away.

Tate Vades towered over her by a foot, his shoulders twice the width of hers, and one of his arms was sleeved in black ink. His blond-brown hair, blue eyes, and muscled physique made him an ideal sex toy for a slave buyer with an appetite for strong men on their knees.

Tate's buyer, however, didn't live long enough to drive away with his new slave. Matias had collected the body himself, as well as the 5.7×28mm casings that had been left behind. Rounds that could've only come from Camila's FN Five-seven pistol.

Fuck him, but he couldn't get enough of her murderous spirit.

Apparently, neither could Tate. For the past six years, he'd become a permanent fixture in her life. Given their close relationship, it was no surprise when she reached up and placed a hand on his jaw.

Step away, Tate. Matias zoomed in on the sliver of space between their unmoving postures. His molars crashed together. *Step the fuck back,* hijo.

Tate raised an arm above his head, holding something away from her. She gripped his neck, her other hand swiping at whatever he kept out of reach. The car keys? Were they arguing over who would deliver the body?

The guy was eager. Eager to protect her and fight for her cause. But if he wanted his dick to remain attached to his body, he'd get eager to remove her hand from his fucking neck.

Their arm-waving dispute ended when Tate broke free and climbed into the driver's seat of the sedan. *Good boy.*

She watched him drive away with the body, a hand on her hip and the other holding her phone.

Matias flexed his fingers, cursing every second she delayed. *Hit redial, Camila.*

A heartbeat later, she did.

He accepted the call on speaker. "Are you afraid of me?"

"Which answer will change the subject?"

"I'll take that as a *yes.*"

She walked to the yard, prompting the camera to pan to the side. Stopping beneath the perimeter lights, she lay on her back in the grass. Her hair fanned out around her in shiny, black tendrils, like tributaries of the Amazon River at night.

The sound of her breaths marked the space between them. So close he could see her and hear her, yet still too far away. She was stalling, turning his nerves into a breeding ground for desperation, anger, and desire.

"All right. I'll give you this," she said. "I'm afraid the reality of you won't live up to the memory."

His heart stuttered painfully. Her confession was so fragile, bleak, and…inaccurate. But he'd thought the same about her once, before he started watching her. The tough girl from his childhood had grown into every bit the fierce, beautiful woman he'd imagined she would be.

"I miss…us," she whispered. "But I'm afraid, if we

met again, I'd find that the concept of *us* is just a jagged mote of a memory. I don't think I could handle that. I want that part of my life to remain real. Untarnished."

She had no idea how much of her childhood was a lie. But the thing between him and her?

"What we had...*have*..." He closed his eyes, fighting the impulse to snap at her for doubting them. "It doesn't get more real than that."

"People change. How can you be so sure?"

Over the years, his need for her hadn't faded. It had become a living, starving thing inside him, ruling his fucking world. There was something else, though. Something beyond his desire to take, overpower, and claim.

It felt like a dark, festering mass knotting around his organs, strangling him with nothingness. Did it have a name? He rubbed his forehead, searching for a way to identify the persistent, agonizing...what?

He opened his eyes. *Loss.* That empty feeling, the hollow pit in his soul, was her absence. He mourned her. Deeply and endlessly.

"Remember the shack on the north side of the grove?" He traced the edge of the screen, lost in the fuzzy outline of her lying in the grass.

"*Mierda.*" She laughed. "I was convinced a cannibal lived there."

"Not just any cannibal. A big, hairy one that buried bones—"

"*Children's* bones."

"—under the floorboards." He grinned.

"I didn't make that shit up." She sounded defensive, but a smile teased through her voice. "Or maybe I did, but I swear I heard their cries from my bedroom window."

"That was Lucia riding her boyfriend in the backseat of his car."

"Oh, God."

A heavy hush settled between them. He wasn't sure if she was thinking about her sister or the night she finally entered the shack.

"You were so determined to get me to go in there." She let out a ragged exhale. "I was horrified by the idea."

"Do you remember what I told you?"

"The fear will haunt me," she said quietly, "until I step inside and show it my teeth."

"You took that quite literally."

He hadn't known the true meaning of *painfully hard* until he'd watched her strut her sexy ass inside that dark shack, holding the flashlight like a weapon and baring her teeth.

The moment she'd realized there was no cannibal, no rotting bones, and that she'd well and truly conquered her fear, she aimed the beam of light on her stunning smile and said, "Wanna know who I love? That guy."

She'd turned the flashlight on his face, and he'd felt her blinding declaration like a magnetic pulse. It had electrified every inch of his body, lighting up his chest and settling at the base of his cock.

They were virgins then, her sixteen, him eighteen. In the months leading up to that night, they'd fumbled and groped without clothes on, learning how to make each other come with fingers and mouths. But the look she'd given him in that shack, her eyes aglow in the shadows of her defeated fears, he knew she'd been ready. For all of it.

He'd pinned her against the crusty wallpaper in

the shack's only bedroom and fingered her until she screamed her declaration over and over. Until his conscience had forced him to step back.

Glancing over his shoulder, he spotted Nico behind the SUV, puffing on a cigarette.

He turned back to the phone. "I should've fucked you that night."

"I should've let you."

His chest clenched. They hadn't wanted their first time to be in a smelly shack. So innocent. Foolish. He thought they'd have more time, more opportunities, a lifetime of them.

Instead, he gave his virginity to a prostitute in a smelly alcove beside a dumpster.

"I wish I'd known," she said, voice clipped, "that was our last time together."

Neither of them had known what the next day would bring. She still didn't know it was the Restrepo cartel that had led him away with a gun pressed against his ribs. Or why.

"When did you lose your virginity?" All these years, and he hadn't been able to uncover her sex life. Or come to terms with it.

"I could ask you the same thing, but let's not do this to ourselves, okay? The answers hurt too much."

The misery in her voice gave him comfort. Thinking about her with someone else ate at him like a sickness. With her knock-out body, lethal confidence, and fuck-me eyes, she could have her pick of drooling dicks.

In one of her nine phone calls to him since her escape, she swore Van did not take her virginity. Outside of that, however, she remained tight-lipped. She didn't discuss sex with her roommates, didn't bring lovers home, didn't publicly date.

If she fucked, it was in secret and beyond the reach of his cameras.

She sat up and looked at the cabin. "Before I go…" She climbed to her feet, her voice quiet, serious. "I told you what I was afraid of, but you didn't tell me. What haunts *you*?"

"You." He gripped the back of his neck, eyes fastened on the screen. "Your fear of *us*. When are you going to step inside and show it your teeth?"

"Will I need a flashlight? Or a gun?"

"Neither." He sharpened his tone. "Tell me when."

"Someday, maybe."

"Not good enough." He drummed his fingers on the console.

"Someday, later."

"No—"

She ended the call.

Fuck.

Someday was the right answer. She just didn't know how soon. Everything was finally falling into place, giving him the opening he'd waited years for.

He wouldn't be leaving Austin without her.

CHAPTER 4

Camila slipped into the cabin and kicked off her flip-flops. *What the fuck was* that?

Her hands shook, her skin fevered, and a deep ache pulsed between her thighs. Not just because she wanted him. Because she'd heard the desire thick in his breath.

As she headed toward the kitchen, muffled voices drifted from the direction of the garage. Christ, she needed to pull herself together before she went in there.

Curling her fingers into her palms didn't stop the trembling. Damn Matias Guerra to hell! Was it not enough that he'd abandoned her and taken her heart with him? Evidently, the prick wasn't finished tormenting her.

She could've handled the questions he used to throw at her, had been prepared to redirect and volley them back. But his *are you afraid* tactic? It was dirty and below the belt.

Only he knew how to dig through her tough exterior, grab hold of her fears, and force her to examine them. She shouldn't have called him back, but like a scab itching to be picked, her obsession with the past overruled her need to heal.

His gravelly timbre had rolled time in reverse, his words transporting her to the safety of the citrus grove. It was as if she'd been talking to *him*, the boy who showed her how to make a slingshot fork from an orange tree, how to swallow while kissing to avoid unwanted saliva, how to do so many unforgettable things, like fall in love, the *conchudo!*

She paused in the kitchen, brushed the dust off her jeans, and attempted to straighten out her thoughts. Eighteen-year-old Matias never kept secrets from her. But the man he'd become was a mysterious, unreachable black hole.

Maybe she was just as closed off as he was, but he at least knew what she was involved in. Since the day she'd escaped, she'd told him she was killing slave buyers while he told her *absolutely nothing*.

Was he still involved with the armed thugs who'd taken him away twelve years ago? Or had he moved on to something worse? Something so awful he wouldn't, *couldn't,* share anything personal with her?

"Why didn't you come back for me?" she whispered, gripping the edge of the counter.

Why did his secrecy feel like a betrayal? Like he'd chosen his sacred thug life over her?

If he loved her, he would've returned for her, taken her with him, and prevented everything that followed. The attic, the bone-deep bruises, the chains of isolation, and the darkness that still pervaded her thoughts, following her everywhere. No, not following. *Smothering.*

That was the rub, wasn't it? She'd trusted him to protect her, to always be there, and he'd deserted her, left her to her fate.

She massaged her temples. Why was she

wallowing in this quagmire of imaginary angst? It felt a whole lot like self-pity, a bullshit mentality she refused to subscribe to. She'd never been a victim, didn't need protection or rescuing, and sure as hell didn't need a dick to get herself off.

What she needed was a mind-numbing drink.

A quick sweep through Van's cabinets uncovered an impressive collection of tequila. *Praise Jesus.* Popping off the cap, she drank straight from the bottle. Ah, God, it was the good stuff. Smooth and crisp, the agave slid down her throat like peppery, sweet water.

A few sips turned into a few more. She drank until her tongue tingled and her nerves dulled. She drank until the front door opened.

It snicked shut, and footsteps echoed through the cabin. Tate emerged around the corner, eyed the bottle, and winged up an eyebrow.

"Trouble in Crazy Town?" He nodded at the garage door, where the murmur of their former captors filtered through.

"Nope." She capped the bottle and put it away.

"Your phone call?" His forearms flexed at his sides. "The body—"

"Will be taken care of." She shifted her weight from one foot to the other. Or maybe she bounced.

The alcohol buzzed through her veins at a nice, even keel. Not enough to make her stupid, but it was doing its job. Tate's judgmental scowl had zero effect on her giveafuckometer.

The front door opened again, and a moment later, familiar green eyes came into view. Black hair outlined a golden complexion, boyishly handsome features, and straight white teeth. No one smiled quite like Slave

Number Nine.

"Hey, you." Joshua Carter didn't waste time closing the distance and wrapping her in a hug.

"Hey." She laughed, arms clinging to the packed muscles beneath his Baylor University t-shirt.

The warmth in her cheeks wasn't from the booze. There was something about Josh, a rare kind of inner light that enabled him to focus on the good in every person and situation. Hell, he'd married Liv — *after* the woman had kidnapped him, beat him, and pegged him with a strap-on. Underneath his rock-hard, linebacker physique was an endearingly squishy and very forgiving soul.

Or perhaps he was just as fucked up as the rest of them.

He released her and scanned the cabin's open layout, his face growing taut. "Where's Liv?"

Camila tried not to let his preoccupation with his wife affect her, but there it was, pinching her chest. She didn't want Josh, but she envied what he had — someone to look for and be concerned about. Someone to love.

Maybe she'd misjudged her tequila intake. It had turned her into a sensitive little girl.

"Liv's in the garage." She stepped out of his way. "Thanks for driving Tate back."

As a high school football coach, Josh had a legit career to protect. But he'd offered to meet at the drop location so that Larry's car and the incriminating DNA inside it could be disposed with the body.

He and Liv were the only ones in their little circle of freedom fighters who weren't considered missing or dead. They had a relationship with his parents and Liv's daughter. A family to spend holidays with. In that regard, they had more to lose than the rest of the group.

"Wish I could help more." With a pat on her head, he disappeared into the garage.

Tate crossed the kitchen and leaned into her space, his arm braced on the wall behind her.

Her eyes fluttered closed as the scent of his skin permeated the inches between them. His masculine proximity charged her nerve endings and heated her blood. He smelled balmy like a summer afternoon in the grove. Like a breeze ripened with the aroma of lemons and loam. Like the Texan sunshine when it emblazoned his hazel eyes—

She looked up, her gaze colliding with Tate's icy blue glare.

"What's going on with you?" He bent his knees, putting them nose to nose.

A dull throb swelled between her legs, engaging her inner muscles. "I need to get laid."

She needed so much more than the fleeting relief of an orgasm, but she'd settle for a kiss from a man who cared enough to give her one.

His gaze fell, heavy with regret. He didn't have to read her mind to know what she really wanted. Hands bound, ass spanked, hard, brutal fucking—they'd discussed her desires in detail until it'd become a laughable tirade. But that only made the stricken look on his face harder to stomach. He knew how goddamn lonely and hungry she was, and still, he rejected her.

She knew he was attracted to her, but he shut down whenever she approached the subject. Maybe her tastes were too dark for him, too much like what he'd endured. Or maybe they weren't dark enough.

"We only have two days." She ducked around him

and headed toward the garage. "We need to talk about what happens next." A plan that was guaranteed to receive a concerted *fuck no* from him and the others.

After gathering everyone in the living room, she explained how she intended to use Larry McGregor's information to infiltrate the human trafficking network in Austin.

Anticipating the most resistance from Tate, she paced the edge of the room, eyes trained on his bowed head as she outlined the initial steps. He didn't move from the chair by the windows, his gaze glued to the floor.

Van didn't show the same restraint.

"You've lost your fucking mind." His entire body bunched and flexed as he balled his hands into fists. He probably would've leapt from the couch if Amber wasn't sitting on his lap. "You want me to sell you? As a *slave*?"

Liv and Josh sat side by side on the love seat. Their rigid postures, narrowed eyes, deeply furrowed brows— they looked like Bonnie and Clyde's disapproving cousins.

Camila pursed her lips. They didn't have to like it. They didn't even need to be here.

"We don't know who these people are." Van dragged a hand across the scar on his cheek, his tone harsh. "And you want me to just show up and hand you over? First off, they're expecting Larry McGregor."

"They're expecting a girl, tied-up and blindfolded." Camila lifted her chin, even as her insides rioted at the idea. "Larry could've sent anyone to deliver her."

"Okay, fine, but you're like...what?" Van sneered. "Thirty-years old? One look at you, and they'll laugh their fucking asses off. Right before they cut out your throat."

"*Despégala pues!*" Her face caught fire. "I'm twenty-eight, dickhead."

"He doesn't mean it," Tate said softly. He didn't raise his head, but his eyes drifted upward and locked on Van. "She could pass as eighteen, and you know it. Look at her. They'd pay double the asking price to get their hands on her."

A heavy feeling sank in her stomach. She wasn't surprised Tate defended her, but she'd expected a godawful fight from him. No way was he okay with her plan.

"They trade in untouched, *underage* pussy." Van folded his arms around Amber, taking her with him as he leaned forward, his glower carved from stone. "Have you forgotten how I know that, Tate?"

"Not one person in this room has forgotten who you are, *Van*." Tate bolted from the chair and faced the wall of windows.

Arms across his chest, spine stiff, Tate stared out into the darkness. Or maybe he was glaring at his reflection. She knew he hated the way he looked, but he hated Van more for capturing him because he was attractive.

Van closed his eyes, his expression unreadable. Amber curled tighter against his chest and whispered in his ear. Across the room, Josh reached for Liv's hand and pulled it into his lap.

They had all been Van's slaves once. And there were more at home — Ricky, Tomas, Luke, Martin, and Kate — all nursing their own invisible wounds under Camila's roof. She didn't spend as much time with Van as she did with the others, but the dynamic between him and his former captives was improving, slowly adapting into something a little less hostile.

Van had been the one to initiate a truce. The money Mr. E had collected—the payments from buyers who didn't live long enough to indulge in their purchases—totaled in the millions. Van could've hoarded that money after Liv killed Mr. E, and maybe he did keep some of it. But he'd given an ungodly amount to the nine people he'd abducted and tortured.

Camila's share funded her vigilantism. Did that mean she owed him her forgiveness? She wasn't sure she'd ever reach that level of acceptance, and she wasn't the only one.

Every person in the room fought inner battles, their fears birthed in the same attic, their perspectives cut by the same whip. Tragedy had shackled them together, but when the locks fell away, they remained unified in their soul-deep appreciation for freedom. They understood one another in a way no one outside their group could.

That intimate camaraderie was palpable now in the stillness that enveloped them. The silence didn't isolate her. It connected her to them, her fellow survivors, her fighters, her closest friends.

"Camila wasn't underage," Tate said, glancing over his shoulder at Van. "She was seventeen when you took her. When you *chose* her."

Not helping. Camila pinched the bridge of her nose. "Tate—"

"I didn't choose her." Van addressed Tate, but his eyes drilled into hers.

"What do you mean?" A chill hit her core.

"I was given your identity, location, and the

buyer's contact number for the delivery when I finished your training."

She looked at Liv for validation.

"You were our first transaction." Liv absently traced Josh's fingers where they tangled with hers. "The only one Mr. E set up for us. Van and I handpicked all the others."

Her hand slid up Josh's thigh, fingernails scraping across denim, teasing the curve of his groin. She might've picked Josh because he met the buyer's requirements, but in the end, she'd chosen him for herself.

"I'm sure your plan is one-hundred-percent vetted." Liv stood and folded her hands behind her.

The capped sleeves of her corset-style shirt accentuated her delicate shoulders. The tiny waistline flared over the curves of her hips, drawing the eye along the tight fit of black denim on her legs. She wore casual clothes like lingerie, as if every cinch of fabric and peek of skin was deliberately designed to tantalize and distract. If she hid a knife behind her back, it would go unnoticed. Until it was too late.

"You're fully prepared to walk into a nightmare. *Your* worst nightmare." Liv prowled toward Camila, her lilt hypnotic, seductive. "You've envisioned the vilest scenarios even as you know your imagination hasn't scratched the surface."

True, she'd mentally prepared herself, but it didn't stop her heart from racing. "Yes. Of course."

"They'll restrain you." Liv circled her, trailing fingers along her arms. "Humiliate you. Whip you."

"I survived it all before." She stood taller.

"They'll rape you." Pausing inches from her face, Liv glared with enough potency to summon goose bumps. "You haven't survived that."

Liv's fathomless brown eyes brimmed with tortured experience. Torture she'd both inflicted and received.

"I was trained how to submit." Camila rolled back her shoulders. "I know how to keep my head down and attached to my body. I'll survive."

As if she'd have a choice. She wasn't naïve. She could be raped, mutilated, *then* killed. But she wouldn't let fear put the brakes on this plan. At that very moment, there were girls, trapped and alone, suffering the exact things Liv outlined.

"Maybe so." Liv stroked a finger along Camila's hairline, her gaze following the movement. "But I can't let you return to that life."

"I can't let other girls—other people's *daughters*—endure that life without doing something about it. I'm not asking for your permission."

Liv closed her eyes. When she opened them, her resigned expression said she wouldn't fight this. Nor would she support it.

"Your daughter is waiting for you." Camila stepped back. "Go home. Keep her safe."

Closing the gap, Liv framed Camila's face with her hands and touched their foreheads together. With a brush of lips, she delivered a kiss, closed-mouthed but no less penetrating. "You *will* come back."

With that, she left. Josh lifted Camila in a rib-breaking hug then followed Liv out, leaving Camila alone with Van, Amber, and Tate.

"Liv's right," Van said after a long period of silence. "You survived *me*, but I'm not *them*."

"So you won't help me?" Her stomach knotted.

She'd chased this trafficking operation for four years, and this was the first time she'd petitioned Van for help — beyond his financial support and the use of his home. She needed him now to deliver her into hell, because he was the only one who could.

"I know you're not them." She approached him, hands at her sides.

He leaned back on the couch, his eyes flinty and cold as he stroked Amber's hair.

"I also know," Camila said through a dry throat, "you have the grit to drag me in there by my hair, force me to my knees, and leave me there without a backward glance."

Tate turned from the window, devastation rumpling his handsome face.

She would've rather asked him to play the part of the asshole slave trader. He might've been able to pull it off. Right up until it came time to leave her.

"Let's say I can fill that role." Van dug through his pockets and paused when Amber held up a toothpick. He bit it out of her hand, rolled it to the corner of his mouth, and looked at Camila. "You're not a virgin."

Her mouth fell open. "What? How would — ?"

"I was trained to spot these things, and you…" He waved an arm, gesturing up and down her body. "You're like a walking advertisement for fluid exchange. Hungry flesh and — "

"Van, take it down a notch." Amber smacked away his waving hand and turned to Camila. "What he means is you radiate sex. It's beautiful, really, how comfortable you are with your body and sexual appetites. You wouldn't be that way if you hadn't experienced pleasure with another — on your terms."

Okaaaay. That was weird and intrusive and… Good God, was she that transparent? She locked down her muscles, trying to shut off any and all sexual oozing. But now she was hyper-aware, and the heat of Tate's gaze roaming over her tight tank top wasn't helping.

"Whether your experiences were good or bad," Amber said, "you long for more. I can tell because your hunger, it…it sensualizes the way you carry yourself and how you interact with people. Like him."

She followed Amber's gaze to Tate.

Confusion stormed across his face as he stared at her. Had he assumed she was a virgin? She'd confessed her desires to him, but she never told him about the long line of nameless men, the years of meaningless sex, all her failed attempts to find something or someone that would touch the places inside her she couldn't feel anymore.

Camila refocused on Van. "So you have virgin radar. Congratulations. But it's been a long time since I've had sex." She'd given up on one-night stands over four years ago.

"Your hymen doesn't grow back, girl." Van smirked around the toothpick. "They'll check."

"You didn't."

"I didn't have to."

Right. All he'd had to do was beat her into submission. But none of that mattered. The purpose of this tangent was to make a point, one Van had walked right into.

"When they check me" — she hid her disgust beneath a lazy shrug — "they won't be able to sell me off."

"They'll kill you." Van grinned, the fucker.

"They'll keep her." Tate rubbed the back of his

head. "That's her plan."

"Bingo." She sat on the arm of the love seat. "They won't kill me, because I have a working vagina, and I'm not ugly."

"You're gorgeous," Amber said with a small smile.

"Thanks. So they'll take me to the head asshole. I'll cry and beg for my life. Of course, that'll just turn him on. He'll try to fuck me and…" She looked at Van, his gaze bright with curiosity. "I'm not the same girl I was in that attic."

"I know."

Was that pride in his voice?

She'd spent the past ten years in dojos, learning how to use her body like a weapon. "I may not be able to defend myself against a gang bang, but I know how to unman a dick when it's between my legs."

"Larry McGregor?" Van raised a brow.

"Triangle choke. Killing him would've been easier than knocking him out."

"Jesus, Camila." Tate's chest rose and fell. "What if you're outnumbered?"

"That's where the tracking device comes in. I know a guy. A dentist." She opened her mouth and tapped the molar that would cost her fifty grand to drill tomorrow. "I've had him on standby to do a special kind of dental restoration."

"A GPS chip in a dental filling?" Van rolled the toothpick between his lips. "Smart. But the battery life—"

"It'll last two weeks, sending a signal every thirty minutes. It only uses the battery when I'm moving."

Oh, the creative and illegal things one could buy on the web's black markets.

Van sawed his jaw side to side. Was he loosening it

up to snap at her? Or was he thinking through her plan?

He blew out a breath and looked her firmly in the eye. "I'll do it."

Amber gripped his hand as relief fluttered through Camila's veins.

"Tate." She met his frigid eyes. "You'll track my position through the chip?"

He blinked, nodded. "Two weeks…You'll most likely be in the belly of the operation before the battery dies."

She hoped. "If I'm successful, if I kill him, I'll contact you, and you won't need to do anything." She rubbed her slick palms on her jeans. "If you don't hear from me, you'll have the location of the operation and—"

"We'll save you." The conviction in his voice vibrated through her.

"No." She matched his tone.

She picked at her cuticles, forcing her shoulders to relax.

"You and the others…" *The freedom fighters.* She smiled at that, because she knew she could count on her team. "You'll finish where I failed."

CHAPTER 5

Two days later, Camila sat on Tate's bed, transfixed by the contours of muscle playing across his back as he dug through a mountain of dirty clothes. His sex appeal aggravated the nervous energy twitching through her, but she couldn't look away. There was something she wanted, something Tate could give her.

"I need to talk to you."

"I'm listening." He shook out a wrinkled shirt, sniffed it, and tossed it back in the pile.

Van would arrive in three hours—three hours until she surrendered her freedom. Maybe only for a couple of weeks. Maybe forever.

The gravity of *forever* had plunged her into hours of introspection, creeping paralysis through her limbs and gnawing at her resolve. She wasn't putting herself in chains simply for the cause of justice. There was a darker motive. A selfish desire to overpower the fears that haunted her. Her enslavement had wrought a deep dissatisfaction with her own life, and though her body had healed from the trauma, her bleeding soul demanded she do this.

With a roll of her tongue, she sought out the new filling in her molar. Indiscernible to the eye, the composite material felt foreign and obtrusive in her mouth. The GPS chip, however, instilled a sense of confidence in her plan. Seeing her movements on the software program and knowing Tate would be tracking her made her feel a little less alone.

She thought about giving Matias' contact information to Tate. If Tate didn't hear from her, he could pass along her last known position to the one person who might increase her chance of survival.

But she didn't want to go into this with that seed of hope. Didn't want to find herself tied to a bed in a pool of her own failure, waiting for someone who might not come for her. Matias had already abandoned her once. For that to happen a second time? The destitution that would follow might very well kill her. He was the only person from her past she had left.

Therein lay the root of her loneliness. Van had given her a taste of how depraved men could be. Matias had shown her how to turn innocent love into a lifetime of bitterness. The only sex she'd experienced had been quick, unsatisfying fucks.

She'd known Tate for six years, and now, in her final hours of freedom, she wanted to know him on a deeper level.

"I've never made love." She held her breath.

He paused with his hand in the pile of clothes and glowered over his shoulder, his eyebrows drawn together. "Wait…so you *are* a virgin?"

"No. I'm—" She straightened her spine. "I've never had sex with someone I know."

Strangers, all of them. No connection. No emotion. Just sex. She blamed herself for that. She didn't let people in, didn't trust anyone outside of those she lived with.

His lips pressed together in a grimace as he turned away.

Was he judging her? Self-righteous anger burned beneath her skin.

Digging at the bottom of the dirty clothes pile, he smelled another shirt and reared back with a pinched face.

"This one should work." He tossed it at her.

It landed on her lap, and a waft of mold and sweat hit her nose. Jesus, did he have a month's worth of wet towels in that pile? For a guy who was fussy about hygiene, he had some strange abhorrence to doing laundry.

He joined her on the bed, lifted a lock of her hair, and sniffed it. "You stink, but not enough."

"What?" She slammed her teeth together and immediately slackened her jaw, remembering the expensive electronics in her molar. "I haven't showered in three days."

She'd spent hours working in the garden and running outside, letting herself get sweaty and dehydrated. A glance at the mirror earlier confirmed she looked appropriately filthy and starved, like a girl who'd been locked in Larry McGregor's barn for a week.

"I'll smell straight-up offensive after I put on this shirt." She set it aside and met his eyes. "You're evading my question."

"You didn't ask a question."

No, she hadn't. She didn't want to demand it. "It's different, right? Better when you have sex with someone who cares about you?"

He leaned forward, elbows braced on his spread knees, and stared at her out of the corner of his eye.

As secretive as she'd been about her one-night stands, he was even more surreptitious, sneaking out at night and stumbling home in the early hours of dawn, refusing to tell her where he went. Maybe he was searching for something, too.

"You care about me." She looked for a flicker of affirmation, any indication of softening in his stony expression, and found none. Her stomach sank. "At least, I thought you did. I mean, I'm grateful you're not fighting me on this plan, but why aren't you?"

"Let's not do this, Camila." His gaze ping-ponged between her and the floor.

"Which part?"

"All of it." He rose, stepped away, then hesitated, changing direction mid-stride to stand over her, hands on his hips. "I won't ruin our friendship by muddling it with sex. Nor will I let you walk into" — he waved an arm, seemingly wrestling for words — "into a place resembling Satan's fiery asshole thinking you don't have my support. I'm here for you, and I'll be here when you return."

But what if she never came back? What if she died, forgotten and alone, having never experienced the kind of love that connected two people in the most intimate way?

He crouched before her and gripped the backs of her calves, his hands warm and welcoming on her skin. "Is there a chance in hell I could talk you out of this suicide mission?"

"No." Definitely not.

"So what's the point in trying? It's not like you need my approval."

His push back would've shown she mattered. Maybe she wasn't the center of his universe, but it would've been nice to feel…what? Commanded? Forced? Reined in by someone who loved her enough to care about her wellbeing? Maybe she just wanted to be fucked so hard she felt it emotionally, spiritually, instead of just physically.

A lump knotted in her throat, and she swallowed it down. She was letting her emotions run rampant, twisting her into a jumble of contradiction. Had he opposed her mission, it would've pissed her off.

She'd been chained up, beat up, kicked down, and held in the dregs of her weakest point. But she never stopped fighting, never gave up. She'd mustered what little courage remained and chose to live, to learn, to hate and kill, to do whatever it took to not just overcome, but to evolve.

He knew all that, and the intense gleam in his eyes said he was confident she'd do it again.

"I would've showered," she said with a soft smile, "if you wanted to tie me up and fuck me."

"If things were different, if *I* was different, I would've put you in the shower and never let you leave."

Warmth spread through her limbs. "You sure you're not gay?"

"Yeah." He laughed. "I'm sure." He cupped her face, his nostrils flaring with a deep breath. "I hope you find what you're looking for."

She imagined the moral corruption she would find—men who perceived women as nothing more than livestock to sell, fuck, and piss on—and the hairs on her neck lifted.

Tate pulled away and shot a longing look at the doorway.

"I'm not very good with goodbyes." He scratched

his neck, avoiding her gaze. "So…"

"Go on." She shoved his shoulder, blinking through the achy burn in her eyes. "Get out of here."

He didn't look back as he escaped. The sound of his footfalls quickened down the hall and faded in the distance. When the front door slammed, the bang ricocheted through her chest, releasing a stream of silent tears.

She let them fall, promising herself they'd be her last until she saw him again. Then she dried her face and changed into his pungent black shirt.

For the next three hours, she made her farewell rounds through the sprawling, ranch-style Austin house. She shared a bedroom with Kate—one of the last slaves under Van's reign—while the five guys took over the other four rooms. The attic was finished, but no one would sleep there.

They were millionaires, thanks to Van. They could buy seven estates, retire in luxury, and live anywhere. But they clung together in a modest suburban neighborhood not far from Liv and Josh, in a house they'd made their home.

Heaviness pressed against her breastbone as she recapped the plan with her roommates. No one cried. No one tried to talk her out of it. Their need for retribution darkened their eyes and strengthened her backbone.

When Van arrived, she followed him to his car, leaving her friends standing bravely stoic on the front porch.

Barefoot, wearing only a mid-thigh shirt and panties, and accompanied by Van's menacing silhouette, she looked like a woman begging for someone to call the cops. Thank God, the street was empty and shrouded in darkness, but the evening heat weighed heavy, making the atmosphere feel stagnant and dead.

A hint of smoke tinged the air. She glanced around, tracking the scent until she spotted the red flare of a cigarette bobbing in an alcove beside the garage. Tate only smoked when he was irate, but she knew it was him, a brooding sentinel in the cover of night, always watching.

She gave him a chin lift, the motion jerking with the anxious rhythm of her heart.

Van stopped beside his '65 Mustang GT and opened the trunk. The hood of his sleeveless sweatshirt cast his face in shadows as he removed a coil of rope and a black scarf.

When he turned toward her, the moonlight caught the opening of his hoodie, revealing an expression cut straight from her nightmares. His eyes, like steel blades, flayed her skin in an icy chill and bled her pores with sweat.

"Are you numb with terror yet?" He cocked his head.

"Getting there." She tightened her muscles, fighting against the violent tremors gripping her body.

"Good." He grabbed her hair with unnecessary force and shoved her toward the shallow, coffin-like interior of the trunk. "You should be petrified."

CHAPTER 6

Camila wasn't claustrophobic, but after a forty-five-minute ride in the trunk of Van's Mustang, the tiny space had morphed into a malignant presence. It pressed in from every direction, growing heavier, tighter, restricting her movements. *No room. Too cramped. Can't breathe.* She needed air. She needed *out!*

But I put myself here. Inhale. *I'm in control.* Exhale.

Except she wasn't. Blindfolded and pinned on her side, she'd already given up her freedom. And this was the easy part. If she couldn't endure a trunk, she wouldn't survive the rest.

I'm a slave again. She focused on breathing—in, out, repeat, repeat, repeat—while centering her mind on submitting and surviving.

Her eyelashes dragged against the scarf, and her wrists burned in the scratchy bindings at her back. Van had tied the rope so tight it cut off blood flow, turning her hands into unfeeling stumps.

But it was necessary. As necessary as the melodramatic show she would put on for her captors. She needed to appear crippled with fright, her mind so horribly wounded they would only see a quivering, harmless girl. They would carry their traumatized little

Trojan Horse past their security, and there, ensconced in the heart of the operation, she would strike.

The tires spun off the pavement and continued on bumpy ground, spitting gravel against the chassis. Larry McGregor's GPS coordinates put the rendezvous at the edge of a cotton field. This must've been it, the final stretch of the drive. Her lungs seized with renewed panic.

Too soon, the car slowed, stopped, and the engine shut off. The sudden silence mired into her bones, shoving her deep into buried memories of the night she met Van. His hand over her mouth, the stabbing pain through her head, the blackout, the wooden box…

The trunk creaked open, and a blast of arid air filled her lungs, bringing with it a resinous perfume. A hint of camphor. The approach of cotton harvest.

She licked parched lips, tasting the dusty drought of summer as she eased up on an elbow, hands numb and restrained behind her. The blindfold stole her vision, and given the hour of night, there would be no light seeping in. But amid the chirrup of nocturnal creatures, she heard him, his rustling movements closing in. She braced for a ruthless hand to yank her out.

"If you get yourself killed," Van whispered, shockingly close, his breath at her ear, "I'm going to hunt you in hell and blister your fucking ass. Hear me?"

"Noted." She swallowed.

He pulled her from the trunk by her leg. Her back banged against the bumper, her hands and eyes useless as she tumbled downward and crashed against the solid dirt.

Pain jolted through her thighs, and pebbles dug into her knees. She dropped to her hip, but his hand caught her under the arm, wrenching her up and dragging her backward.

She stumbled, pivoting in an attempt to blindly walk forward. Without slowing his gait, he swung her around and shoved her in the right direction. Then his fingers found her arm again, jerking her against his side.

"They're watching." He kept his voice so low it was barely audible beneath his breath. "Two Range Rovers. Fifty paces ahead. They're exiting now."

The slam of a car door sounded in the distance, followed by several more in rapid succession. Footsteps approached. Many. But how many?

Her chest heaved. She tripped over a rut in the dirt, and her bare feet scraped against sharp rocks. She let out a whimper for effect, but also because she wanted to scream at him to take her back. She couldn't do this.

Blood roared in her head, her breath catching, stacking, choking, her mind spinning. *I can do this. I can do this.*

Van didn't let up, playing the part with his bruising grip and ground-covering strides. This was why she'd asked him. Tate would've carted her out of there at the first sign of her distress.

She staggered alongside him, dragging her feet and stopping, only to get hitched forward again. She wheezed and mewled in pathetic intermittent noises. She couldn't have faked a full-body tremble, but it was there, attacking her with a force that chattered her teeth.

Oh God, what if she couldn't do this? Why the fuck did she put herself here?

His thumb dug into her bicep. Then it tapped one, two…five times.

Five men.

71

Why so many? Mr. E's operation ran for years with only two captors. Her blood pressure skyrocketed.

She wasn't counting the steps, but it felt like a lot less than fifty when Van suddenly halted. He didn't give her time to slow, using her momentum to thrust her to her knees.

Free from his grip, she lurched sideways, scooting awkwardly without her hands in a pretense to escape.

Van caught her neck with his sneaker and slammed her face against the brittle soil, holding her cheek to the earth with the weight of his foot.

"Whoa. Lower the guns," he said, and the press of his shoe vanished. "Don't worry about her face. It isn't her best feature."

Fucking cocksucker.

She shrank into a fetal position, cowering in the curl of her shoulders, and feigned a series of breathy sobs. What she really wanted to do was tug down the blindfold and take inventory of the men and their weapons.

"Which one of you Zorros is in charge?" Van asked.

Zorros. He was telling her they wore masks. *Clever.* She might see their faces eventually, but Van would walk away without their identities.

It'll be okay. I have the GPS chip.

"Call me *Jefe*," a man said from twenty-some-feet away, his voice soft and raspy. "She's a virgin?"

He carried an accent, a tincture of south of the border, where *Jefe* meant *Boss.* But there were a lot of Hispanics in Texas. He could've been her neighbor, her gynecologist, or the guy who bagged her groceries.

"She says she's a virgin, but I didn't check." Van's

sneakers scuffed in place. "I didn't want to go prodding around and break something."

Vile amusement slithered through his voice, but no one laughed.

Dumbasses. A girl could be a virgin without an intact hymen. Lots of things could stretch or tear it. Horseback riding, water skiing, doing the splits, vibrators…

"Where's the money, Jefe?" Van asked, all humor gone.

Gravel crunched beneath advancing footsteps. Something heavy landed beside her head, followed by the sound of a zipper.

"Pass along our gratitude to *Señor* McGregor," Jefe said, maintaining his twenty-foot distance. "We look forward to more business from him."

Sorry, ese. *Larry McGregor's doing business with the Chief of Hell.*

Van lowered, his breaths near, and she curled tighter into a ball as if his proximity had conditioned her to do so.

"It's not all here." Van huffed. "This wasn't the agreed price."

What the fuck was he doing? He had no idea what was negotiated.

The man who had approached with the money treaded away, only to return a moment later. A second bag dropped on the ground.

"My mistake," Jefe said. "Now take it and go."

Well played, Van. Had he not questioned the payment, they would've known he was a fraud. Her eyes drifted closed behind the blindfold, but her relief was short-lived.

The bags lifted, and Van's presence retreated. She clung to the sound of his diminishing footfalls, aching for him to turn around.

Don't go.

What if there were too many guards and the operation was bigger than she'd estimated? What if this was all for nothing? Her surveillance had uncovered dozens of low-life scumbags like Larry McGregor. Men living normal lives — when they weren't stealing young girls and selling them to…*who?*

She'd imagined an operation like Mr. E's. Small and efficient with a network of Larrys on one end and buyers on the other. But five men had been sent to collect her. Five! How many were waiting at her destination? They could be gangsters, snuff filmographers, drug lords, chainsaw massacrers…

Van's Mustang growled to life, and the tires skidded. *Leaving.*

She was alone. Outnumbered. She didn't know what they looked like, what they were armed with, or who they worked for. And now they owned her. They could do whatever the hell they wanted to her.

Sweat pooled beneath her braless breasts as the rumble of Van's car faded into silence. There was no turning back. It was done.

"He's headed your way," Jefe said.

Dread churned in her gut. Who was he talking to? Someone on the phone?

"No, let him pass," Jefe said. "Just make sure he gets on the interstate. We'll wait."

Van was smart. He would know if someone followed him, and he sure as fuck wouldn't try to come back for her.

Her stomach clenched. With her hands bound behind her and miserably numb, she couldn't remove the blindfold. Only slightly less bothersome were the strands of hair stuck in her mouth. She tried to spit them out as she tracked the creaking of leather, the fall of heavy boots.

She'd expected a gang of uneducated hoodlums to fall upon her with grabby hands and verbal threats. But they remained silent. Disciplined. Like an army of professionals. Somehow, this was worse.

She dragged herself to her feet, teetering on shaky legs. "C-can someone…r-r-remove my blindfold?"

Well, that sounded effectively timid.

The air shifted in front of her face. She stopped breathing. Someone was there, close enough to touch a fingertip to her forehead.

She recoiled, but the hand stayed with her, trailing over the blindfold, down her cheek, and freeing the hair stuck to her lips. Her pulse raced, and the muscles in her neck strained against the pressure to hold still. She burned to slam her head forward and break his fucking nose.

Give him a weak little girl. Let him believe you're not a threat.

"Please don't t-touch me." She bunched her shoulders to her ears and tucked her chin to her chest.

Brushing the strands from her cheek, his finger followed the line of her jaw, pressed beneath her chin, and forced her face skyward.

She didn't have to pretend to be scared. The reminder that this man bought and sold humans was enough to get her throat working, her fear bobbing in her exposed neck.

The finger on her face disappeared, and metal clicked behind her. She jerked. Too late.

A slim ring of steel snapped around her forearm. More clicks, and the manacle cinched tighter. *A handcuff.*

He slid it down her arm, securing it above the rope on her wrists. Where was the second cuff?

Her answer came when he gripped her arm and the metal on his wrist clanked against hers. Her pulse thrashed in her ears.

What kind of man was she handcuffed to? Was he young or old? Covered in scars? Did he fuck his victims after he killed them?

"Let me go." She raised her voice several octaves and pulled against the restraints. "I won't tell anyone. I haven't even seen your faces."

She shook her body, hoping her freak-out was believable. Inside, she was frozen with terror, but showing her emotions didn't come natural for her.

"I wouldn't fight him, *puta.*" Jefe's accent issued from farther away. "He bites."

An image flashed through her mind of an oversized man with a boar's face and dribbling tusks. *And I'm handcuffed to him.*

"Get away." She blindly kicked his legs, snarling as she clawed at the hand on her arm. "I want to go home. Please don't do this."

In a flash, he shifted in front of her and wrapped an arm around her thighs. Her feet lost contact with the ground, and she was lifted up, up, and over his shoulder. She landed upside down, her face against the cotton on his back, and her wrists locked to one of his behind her.

No amount of bucking and kicking would dislodge the hand on her ass or the other one attached to her wrist.

But she struggled anyway, which only worked her panties into her butt crack and hitched the t-shirt halfway up her back.

Blood rushed to her head, and hard-packed muscle flexed beneath her. Jesus fucking Christ, maybe he *was* an oversized boar-man.

He carried her a short distance, tossed her onto a long bench seat, and pulled her to sit upright. Leather stuck to her thighs, and rubber mats met her feet.

The boar sat beside her, his shackled arm tucked between her tailbone and the seat back.

"Let's go," Jefe said through the open door on the other side. Then he slid in next to her, his body pinning her against the boar.

Doors slammed shut, and the Range Rover shot forward, bumping along uneven ground.

With the t-shirt rucked around her waist, the cool air from the vent pebbled goose bumps across her thighs. She squeezed her knees together, hating how she couldn't use her arms—to pull down the shirt, to work the blood back into her hands, to stab her fingers in their eyes.

She'd chosen modest navy-blue panties because they resembled swimsuit bottoms. *I've worn less at the beach.* But it didn't make her feel any less exposed.

"Where are you taking me?" She tightened her arms against her sides as pins and needles penetrated the numbness in her fingers.

There were at least three men in the car. The driver and the two on either side of her. Yet no one spoke. As unnerving as it was, it made sense. If she escaped or was sold, their anonymity would protect them.

"I can't feel my hands." She squirmed between

them and amped up the spasmodic sound of her whimpering. "What do you want from me?"

Jefe gripped her neck and angled her face in his direction. "Shut up."

She considered throwing a spastic fit until the bite of cold steel touched her cheek. A knife? She made a noise in the back of her throat and squeezed her eyes shut, letting her body go limp in the collar of his hand.

The dull edge slid across her cheekbone, gliding upward and slipping beneath the blindfold. With a flick of his wrist, he cut through the scarf and pulled it away.

Her heart pounded as she squinted through the darkness and found Jefe's black eyes watching her from the narrow opening of a black ski mask.

There was nothing noteworthy about those eyes. Were they even black? Hard to tell in the shadows of the car's interior.

He tightened his grip on her throat, stopping her from turning her head. The mask covered his hair, face, and throat. A glance downward revealed an average-sized physique in a nondescript t-shirt. He could've been anyone.

Beyond the heavily tinted windows, murky fields blurred beneath a starless sky. Which direction were they headed?

His gaze flicked over her shoulder and locked on the other man. Then he shoved her head between her knees.

What the fuck? Bent in half, she got a good view of her filthy feet. They looked so tiny and sad between the men's rugged boots.

She turned her neck to get a glimpse of the boar, but the fall of her hair blocked her line of sight. Fuck.

Jefe touched the blade to her skin again, this time on her wrist. The rope?

"P-please." She sniffled then heaved a couple of shuddering breaths for good measure. "I can't feel my hands."

"Can you be a good girl?" Jefe trailed a finger down her spine.

"Y-yes. Please untie me."

With his hand holding her head down, he cut the rope. The instant it fell away, she snapped her free arm forward and shook out her hand. Ah, fuck, it was so numb. But as the sharp biting sensations rushed in with the blood, it really fucking hurt. The shaking didn't help, and her fingers refused to bend or move.

Her other hand, still attached to the boar, was pulled onto his lap. Jefe released her head, and she straightened, quickly shoving down the hem of the shirt and scanning her surroundings.

Instead of a mask, the driver wore a baseball cap that sat low on his brow. Brown hair? Caucasian? She couldn't tell.

A three-lane highway stretched out ahead, surrounded by black smudges of farmland. No road signs in sight. If they weren't heading back to the city, where the fuck were they going?

The boar's strong fingers massaged her shackled hand, and the cuff on his wrist scraped against hers. The tingling receded, and warmth rushed in. She stifled a sigh and glanced at the hand she was shackled to.

A tattoo peeked out from the cuff of his sleeve. It was too dark to make out the design, but the ink looked faded and old.

Keeping her head lowered, she took in the casual

recline of his posture. His legs spread wide, invading her space. He wasn't oversized or boar-ish. Nor was he average.

His muscled thigh felt like stone beneath her wrist. The coarse material of his fatigues cupped an impressive groin, and the waistband rode low on his narrow hips. His shirt had inched up his navel, revealing a dark dusting of hair and deep indentions of abs.

The bastard was honed like a damn blade. Hopefully, his brain wasn't as sharp.

She lifted her eyes, following the bulge of a bicep, the stretch of cotton over ridges of pecs, and…a ski mask. *Mierda*.

Despite the absence of light, the eyes staring back weren't black. Pale hints of color streaked into inky rings. Gold? Blue? Green?

He watched her without blinking, his intensity edged with thick lashes. Something flickered in the depths. An emotion. She was sure of it. Did he want to fuck her? Kill her? No, it was more complex than that. Whatever it was made her heart pump and her mind scream, *Look away*.

But she couldn't. Jefe might've been in charge of this team, but *this* man… He was up to something, and it lodged a boulder in her stomach.

The SUV stopped moving, breaking her trance. Beyond the windshield, the paved road ended at a field, and in the distance sat a small plane. The second Range Rover pulled up beside them and shut off the engine.

Guess I'll be leaving Austin.

Didn't matter. The GPS chip worked globally.

When the driver climbed out, the overhead lights remained off. Probably disconnected.

DISCLAIM

"Stay here." Jefe joined the driver outside, leaving her alone with the man who disturbed her the most.

"Do you talk?" She turned, intending to give him an impatient glare, then slammed her eyes shut.

You're scared and weak, remember?

She curled her shoulders forward, balled her hand on his lap, and stuttered, "What are…you going to do…to me?"

"Good question."

That voice… The blood drained from her face. *No, no, no.*

"What did you say?" She met hazel eyes and knew she was seeing things. *It's too dark.*

"What have you gotten yourself into, *mi vida?*"

The vibration of his voice was a strong hand massaging between her legs, so familiar and arousing she couldn't breathe.

She gripped the arm attached to hers and lifted it, using both hands to yank back the sleeve and expose the underside of his wrist.

Swirls of ink blackened his skin, but her focus narrowed on the pockmarked scar of a dog bite. No, this man was probably riddled with knife wounds. Did she even have the right arm?

"How did you get this scar?" She searched his gaze, and it told her nothing. And everything.

Dropping his hand, she went for the ski mask. As she yanked it up his neck, he didn't stop her. Instead, he gripped her hips and pulled her onto his lap to straddle him.

Her heart galloped frantically in her one-handed effort to bare his face. Shoving and tugging the material higher, she uncovered a chiseled jaw, a dusky shadow of stubble, a wide mouth with full lips…

Her throat closed up, and she jerked her hand away. "You're not him."

"I'm not?" His fingers dug into her waist.

With the mask gathered across his nose, she could almost convince herself he didn't look like an older, more distinguished version of Matias.

"He wouldn't be here." A sharp pain twisted in her chest. "He would never support sexual slavery."

A sinister grin curved his lips. *Not* a Matias smile. Except there, hiding in the corners…

She lifted her hand to trace the dimples. The same dimples she'd stared at every day for sixteen years. The same dimples that had flashed whenever he put a spider in her hair or peed on her mother's roses and always when he came in the stroke of her hand. They were the same dimples that had bored into her memories for the past twelve years.

Her heart slammed against her ribs as she yanked off the mask.

Thick strands of black hair fell across a smooth tawny forehead. Dark brows pulled into a *V* over eyes that would glow citrine in the sunlight. If she pressed her mouth against those firm lips, which memory would he taste like? The first bite of a juicy orange? The full-bodied smoke of a bonfire? A refreshing dip in the spring-fed stream?

He was so sculptured and masculine, all grown up, filled out, and sexier than she could've ever imagined.

And he'd come to save her. Whether she needed that or not, he'd actually come for her.
Somehow…someway, he'd discovered she would be here and wanted to help her.

She cupped his face, the scratch of whiskers so strange against her palm. "It's really you, *mi vida.*"

My life.

She raised her other hand to frame his face, but her arm caught. Shackled. Her vision clouded. *No.* Oh God, no, he wasn't her life or her goddamn savior. He enslaved women. Quivering anger spiked through her body. He was…

My captor.

CHAPTER 8

The falter of Camila's breaths, the heave of her full tits, everything about her intoxicated Matias' senses. She was here, *right fucking here*, filling his hands with her tight, trembling flesh.

His reaction to her had been instantaneous, darting a possessive jolt down his spine and thickening his cock. But evidently, she needed more time to adjust. After all, he wasn't here to save her, not in the way she was probably guessing.

Her initial shock at hearing his voice had softened into wonderment, loosening her shoulders and parting her heart-shaped lips. In that moment, she'd seemed lost, completely knocked off her stubborn axle.

Now she glared at him with liquid hatred in her eyes.

Christ, she looked so goddamn fuckable when she was riled. On his lap. Chained to him.

He tightened his fingers around her hips to stop himself from violating every inch of her body. The same discipline he'd exercised the last time he had her alone. *Twelve fucking years ago.* Not that he had anything in common with that dumbass eighteen-year-old boy.

He'd shed his innocence in exchange for power,

every last ounce of chivalry traded for brutal dominance. If he hadn't, he would've been gutted and eaten alive.

And the woman who had smuggled her way into his ruthless world, pretending she was there against her will? She now had the audacity to look deceived.

"Did you expect me to be here?" She shoved at him, stealing peeks at the men outside as her legs kicked to escape the intimacy of their position. "This is…it's just too coincidental. How did you know?"

"Don't waste your breath asking questions I'm not going to answer." He held her against him, chest to chest, with her thighs straddling his hips and her cunt pressing on his erection. Exactly where she belonged.

"Tell me you're not with them." Her expression paled in a rictus of angelic horror, her muscles edged with frozen tension as if wrestling to maintain her cover. She had no idea what he and the other men knew about her.

"You should be more concerned about who *you* are with." He held up their handcuffed wrists and gave her a taunting smile.

The bright flash of her teeth drew his attention right before she swung her free hand across his cheek. She reared back to slap him again, but he caught her arm and wrenched it behind her.

"You still hit like a girl." He worked his jaw against the sting.

"*Me lo chupa.*" She curled her lip and lowered her voice to a harsh whisper. "You bought an enslaved woman. You bought *me*, Matias! You know what happened to me when I disappeared, what kind of hell I escaped, and still, you do this?" She yanked her arm in the handcuff. "How could you?"

He could ask her the same question. How could she team up with Van Quiso? How could she let that cock-sucking pervert tie her up, toss her in the dirt, and sell her to a cartel? Damn her for being so fucking reckless with her life.

As she glared at him, her seductive eyes seemed to fight an internal war, demanding answers while begging him to tell her this was all a big misunderstanding.

He wouldn't tell her shit. Showing her over the coming months, one agonizing day at a time, was the only way they would come out of this whole and together.

What was taking the guys so long? Matias glanced through the windshield and spotted a rangy silhouette crawling under the turboprop. Must've been Chispa, their explosives guy. If there was a bomb on-board, he'd find it.

Camila slammed her head forward and bit his shoulder through the shirt.

He jerked her back by the hair, holding her face inches away as he scowled. Jesus, fuck, he wanted to rip into her.

She jutted out her chin, holding his gaze with a voracious amount of attitude while whispering under her breath, "Who do you work for?"

Right about now, she was probably more concerned about what the other men knew about her and her dangerous ruse. There was so much she didn't understand about her situation, and she wasn't ready to learn the depths of his role in it. Keeping her in the dark was the only way this would work.

And the things he would do to her in the dark… He imagined trussing her up on a suspension beam, burying his teeth in her perfect rack, and pounding his cock into the clench of her sinful body. *Dios mío*, she had a knockout figure, with curves to hold on to and toned strength to withstand his cruelest, most sinister appetites.

He ached to unleash the violence inside him, to spread her open and let her feel what the last twelve years had done to him.

Instead, he pinned her hands behind her back and crashed his mouth against hers.

She held her breath, lips pinched, but he pried them apart with his tongue and buried it in the wet heat of her mouth.

Growling against her lips, he thrilled in her struggle, in the way she sank into the kiss while twisting her arms to get away. She could fight her desire, but she couldn't disclaim their unbreakable bond, one that had taken root so long ago in the haven of their citrus grove.

A moan vibrated in her throat as she stretched her mouth and drew his lip between hers, sucking and licking, gnashing and biting.

Electricity surged through his groin and tightened his balls as he devoured the furious lashes of her tongue. She tasted like home, warm and sugary, nourishing and *his*.

The soft familiarity of her lips fueled his arousal while the rigid resistance in her body heated his muscles with aggression. Fucking hell, he got off on her torment, on the stiffness of her spine and the frantic rise and fall of her tits. It only made the slide of her hungry lips taste sweeter, more rewarding.

He ruthlessly ate at her mouth, and she gave it right back, her tongue seeking and whipping with all the mistrust, anger, and years lost between them. Her frenzied inhales quickened his own, their breaths crashing together as her fingernails scratched at his hands.

It had been twelve years since he kissed a woman, and she'd been only a girl then with gangly limbs and tiny breasts. Kissing her now blew away the memories. There was no more shyness, no restraint or inexperience...

Resentment barbed inside him, puncturing holes in his unraveling control. How many men had she kissed? Sucked? Fucked? His vision blurred in smears of red. He needed vindication and intended to take it from her pleading screams, from the give of her body beneath his thrusts. Pain and pleasure. Twisted justice.

Not yet.

He tore his mouth away and shoved her off his lap, gasping with the fury of his breaths.

Her gaze flew to the window. Confirming no one was watching? She looked back at him, lips swollen and eyes smoldering. "Fuck you."

"Careful, Camila. You don't—"

She launched at him, teeth bared and fists swinging.

He subdued her easily, wrapping her shackled arm around her torso with her back pressed against his chest.

"Let me go, you fucking traitor."

He covered her mouth with his palm, fingers gripping her jaw shut, as he angled her face toward the window. "You promised Nico you'd be a good girl."

She froze, attention glued to the back of Nico's shirt, and choked an indiscernible sound against his fingers.

He released her mouth.

"*Jefe* is…Nico…" Her free hand touched the glass, and her voice dropped to a whisper. "Nico *Restrepo*? As in capo of the Restrepo cartel?"

Of course, she knew the name, but not because her parents had been Colombian. Anyone who watched the news knew about the ongoing conflict between the notorious kingpin and law enforcement officials in the U.S. and Colombia.

What she didn't know was that the Restrepo cartel had played an instrumental part in her captivity eleven years ago. He needed to guard that secret until she was mentally and emotionally prepared to hear why he was still embedded in the crime family that had banished her to chains.

"Oh my God." She dropped her head in her hand, her expression veiled by the tangled mess of her black hair. "This isn't just some local slave ring."

Not even close. She was headed bowels-deep into Colombia's most powerful criminal organization.

"You work for the fucking *Restrepos*?" She twisted on his lap and searched his eyes. "All this time?"

He flattened his lips into a line, knowing she couldn't handle the truth.

"What's your position exactly? VP of Shipping and Receiving?" She jerked on the handcuff. "Director of Human Slavery?"

Her jaw set in the defiant way that had always made him hard. He dug his fingers into her skin and tried to ignore the roll of her hips over his agonizing erection.

"Oh, right." She tipped her chin up, wearing a corrosive smile. "Even now, those questions are off limits. But you knew I'd be here? You planned this?"

He rapped on the window, anxious to get her across the border and show her what he thought of her questions. He hadn't expected her to confess the reason she was here, but whatever scheming she was still doing in that gorgeous head of hers was pointless. Her fate was sealed.

Nico broke away from his conversation with the pilot, and she instantly hunched her shoulders forward, head down, quivering like the mousy little girl she wasn't. Nico opened Matias' door, concealed by his ski mask and casual clothing, all safety precautions to protect his identity—not from Camila, but from anyone who might've been watching.

"*Listo?*" Matias tightened his grip on her stiffening body.

"Ready for what?" Her voice cracked.

"Something came up." Nico glanced over his shoulder at the plane and returned to Matias. "We're modifying the route."

Wasn't uncommon. Transfers and layovers changed with the intel. Sudden DEA activity, rival gangs mobilizing, anything could've compromised their scheduled stopover.

"Chispa's done with his sweep." Nico stepped back. "She's next."

Matias didn't give her time to fight, hauling her out of the SUV and tossing her over his shoulder. She felt willowy in his arms, but not delicate, not like the tiny girl he used to hoist one-handed into orange trees.

Stifling the twinge of remembrance, he crossed the field, lifted her into the eight-seat Cessna's rear door, and set her on her feet. Inside, he pushed her head down, both of them ducking as he guided her past three rows of chairs and shoved her into the front seat.

She didn't glance at the stripped-down interior, the exposed cockpit, or the absence of anything that could be used as a weapon. Her glare was all for him.

"Where are we going?" She tucked her shackled arm against her waist. "This hunk of metal won't make it to Colombia."

No, but their connecting flight would.

Removing a key from his pocket, he knelt before her and trapped her shins with his thighs. Then he unlatched the cuff from his wrist and locked her to the chair's frame.

The tread of soft shoes sounded on the stairs behind him, followed by the scratch of a familiar voice. *"Dejamos en cinco minutos."*

Turning, Matias met the cloudy eyes of their most trusted doctor, Picar. The old man's hunched spine and stocky frame allowed him to pass through the cabin without too much bending. But his decrepit appearance was deceiving. Picar earned his name by the way he wielded a scalpel. *Chop.*

Matias shifted out of the way as Picar slipped by and settled into the seat across the aisle from Camila. A black bag sat on his lap, his gnarled hands rooting through it.

"Whose shirt is this?" Matias gripped the neckline hanging off her shoulder, gathering the foul-smelling material in his fist. "If you give me a name, I won't torture him before I kill him."

She averted her eyes to the window.

Van Quiso and Tate Vades were around the same size, but he bet it belonged to Tate. He didn't put it past that bastard to send her off bathed in his own stink.

He ripped the shirt from neck to thighs, baring round, perky tits and dusky nipples. His pulse kicked up, rushing a torrent of heat to his cock.

Her free arm shot up and hugged her breasts. "What are you —?"

"You wouldn't believe the places I find bugs." He battled her gaze, never looking away.

"Bugs?" Lines formed on her forehead.

"Listening devices, GPS chips, countermeasures... They hide in the tightest crevices." Matias clasped her inner thighs and spread them apart, relishing the quiver across her skin.

"You think someone shoved a mic up inside me?" She injected a squeak in her voice and blinked rapidly.

She might've been angling for the scared little girl look, but there wasn't a hint of worry in her eyes. That meant he wouldn't find a bug between her legs. Probably not a hymen either, but he'd wait until they were alone to check that.

"Some chips are implanted in the skin." He trailed his fingers over her panties, along her ribs, and paused at the undersides of her breasts. "Lower your arm."

She heaved out a breath and gripped the armrest, her other hand twisting in its locked position against the chair.

Wedging his hips between her legs, he took his time reacquainting himself with the velvety texture of her golden skin. She'd bloomed into flawless proportion, the firm weight of her tits perfect handfuls and peaked with taut nipples begging to be clamped.

There were no incision marks, no bugs, but it was the twitch in her eye that confirmed he was searching the wrong place. A twitch she'd tried to hide as a kid whenever he'd flirted with the older girls who worked in the grove.

She wasn't scared. She was pissed.

Curious how she hadn't applied the martial arts training she'd learned over the years. He'd given her plenty of opportunities to lock him in a leg choke. Maybe she was waiting to attack him when they were alone, when he wouldn't have back up. Or perhaps Nico was her only target.

Matias moved up her chest, hands roaming over the exquisite lines of her collarbones, along her neck, and paused at her pouty lips. "Open."

Her jaw lowered, but he didn't miss the half-second of hesitation or the flicker in her chocolate gaze. An anxious crack in her facade. After all this time, he could still read her.

He gripped her wrist and held it to the armrest. His other hand flattened her back against the seat.

"Picar." He nodded at the doctor. "*Dale pues.*"

She whipped her head around and glared at the syringe in Picar's hand. "What is that? What are you doing?"

"Something to help you sleep."

"No, I don't need that." Eyes wild, she bucked in the seat, going nowhere. "Don't you fucking drug me!"

Picar leaned over and pierced the needle into her pinned arm, his hands steady despite her thrashing and spitting. When the syringe emptied, he gathered his things and hobbled toward the rear of the cabin.

Her lungs pumped for air, her expression furious, but her body began to weaken, slumping beneath the weight of the sedative.

"*Se arrepiente de esta. Enorme* missst…take." Her

head rolled, and she snapped it upright. "I hate you."

"No, you don't. You hate that you fear me." He brought his mouth to her ear. "Step inside and show me your teeth."

"Youuu *chucha* mmmwotherfruck…errr." She blinked heavily, her tongue lolling in her mouth. "Ima gonna…*picar* yerrr bwalllz off…n'kwill…" Her chin hit her chest. "You…dead."

He buckled in her limp body, brushed the hair from her face, and sat back on his heels.

She'd vacillated between weak and pissed, scared and brave, as if trying maintain her ruse with Nico but falling off-kilter with Matias. He knew she was still uncertain about his role in this.

He sensed the little girl inside of her warring with the grown woman. The girl longed for him to be the boy she remembered while the woman knew the truth. But her reality was probably confusing the two, leaving her unbalanced, guarded, and consumed with hatred.

He'd anticipated all of this, and though her hatred felt like a thousand knives twisting in his heart, it was a necessary part of the plan.

If she thought she hated him now, God help her. She had no idea what was coming.

CHAPTER 8

Distorted sounds stirred at the edges of oblivion. A throb penetrated the darkness and hammered through Camila's skull.

Matias fucking drugged me!

She lay on her side, the surface beneath her hard and smooth. No longer on the airplane?

Shoes scuffed nearby, voices jumbled in and out of her awareness, and…

Was that a whimper? Another woman?

Her pulse echoed in her head as she wrestled through the fog of sedation. Her eyelids weighed a hundred pounds, refusing to open. She tried to move her aching arms, but they wouldn't budge in the cuffs behind her. Focusing on her legs, she gave each a lethargic twitch. No restraints there.

She could still defend herself. Maybe after she mustered the strength to open her eyelids.

Where was she? Was Matias with her? The dull murmur of voices continued, but she couldn't hear him.

She managed a few sluggish blinks, wincing against shards of light. The waxy scent of wood polish infiltrated her nose, and with it came traces of cigarette smoke and sweat.

Pushing down the impulse to struggle, she forced herself to remain still, listen, and take inventory. Movement rustled in front of and behind her, but without footsteps or clear voices, she couldn't pinpoint the number of people, who they were, or how close they stood.

The whimper had come from the floor behind her. Other captives? The smoke meant there were probably men present, but the scent wasn't overwhelming. Maybe one smoker?

Her bare thighs chilled in the air-conditioned room, and the bottom edges of her panties were parked uncomfortably high on her ass. At least, her shirt felt dry and clean against her skin. Wait... Matias had ruined her shirt.

Long sleeves covered her arms. If Matias had switched her top, what else had he done while she was unconscious? Her fingers curled, rattling the shackles.

Another whimper sounded behind her, lifting the hairs on her arms. Definitely a second woman. Maybe more. She couldn't think about what that meant. Not right now.

Holding her eyes open, she waited for the bright wash of pain to recede. With her cheek pressed to the ground, she took in the wood flooring that stretched out in front of her. A couple yards away, two sets of black boots and a pair of shiny loafers stood still, toes pointed in her direction.

The voices fell quiet.

A shiver swept down her back. Was Matias among them? Christ, why couldn't she lift her head?

Elegantly carved baseboards encircled the perimeter of the room, broken up by wide doorways bracketed with white pillars. Couches, chairs, and low tables sat off to one side in an array of straight, modern lines and monochromatic fabrics.

Bands of sunlight striped the floor and warmed the backs of her legs. She'd been unconscious the entire night? Long enough to be transported to Colombia, if that was where they'd taken her.

Panic rose, quickening her breaths. *The GPS chip!*

With focused concentration, she moved her sandpaper tongue against the molar and prodded around the edges of the filling. It still felt weirdly numb but…intact. Hope bottled up in her chest. He hadn't found it.

Maybe she wasn't compromised after all. If Matias believed she'd been captured and stripped of her volition, her plan was still viable. Except there was a nasty, decaying hole in that theory.

She'd asked Matias to dispose of Larry McGregor. Although she'd never given a name during their phone conversation, it was safe to assume Matias identified the body as the man who was supposed to deliver her. *Fuck.*

So he knew she was playing him. Did he tell Nico or was he playing his own game?

With a heave of determination, she rolled to her back, groaning as her listless body landed on her shackled arms.

Turning her head, she came face to face with a dark-haired woman on her knees. Mouth gagged with a black bandanna and tears streaking from her wide eyes, she couldn't have been older than thirty.

She's my age. Definitely not the prime age for sexual slavery. Maybe these fuckers weren't picky about who they chose to destroy.

Camila's breath emerged on a guttural growl. Her blood boiled, saturating her muscles with heat as she tensed to fight, to defend.

Too soon. She needed to get her bearings, gather her wits, and reevaluate her plan.

The woman wore nothing, her beautiful bone structure, swarthy skin, and full-figured curves on display for whoever was in the room. And she wasn't alone. Another Latina woman knelt beside her, and behind them lay a blonde curled on her side with her eyes squeezed shut. All three were naked, gagged, bound, and reeked with enough sweat and fear to sour Camila's stomach.

These women were human beings. They had names, birthdays, and favorite songs. Somewhere out there someone was missing their daughter, sister, friend. Hell, these women were old enough to have children.

And now, they would only have pain.

Camila shook with the force of her fury as memories broke open in her mind. The coarse bricks against her back as she hung from chains. The violet wand burning between her legs. The ring gag. Van's engorged cock. His come in her throat.

The musty stink of the attic adhered to her nostrils and coated her taste buds. She tried to hack it from her system, coughing and wheezing past the dryness in her mouth.

She touched the modified molar with her tongue. At least now, the people in her life knew her location. They would save these women if she failed.

Behind the women, the room spilled into a roofless inner courtyard. Lifting her head, she leaned up on her elbow to see more.

DISCLAIM

There were no doorways to block the view. The entire wall was missing. Spanish tiles wrapped around an Olympic-sized infinity pool that merged into the most breathtaking landscape she'd ever seen.

A dense jungle of broad-leafed tropical trees and heavy undergrowth stretched to the horizon, cascading upwards over sloping hillsides that rippled into mountain ranges that must've been hundreds of miles away.

She'd never been to the basin of South America, had never even ventured outside of Texas, but she was certain she was staring at the Amazon rainforest.

Dizziness sailed through her, threatening to rob what little strength she'd summoned. Running would be a wasted effort. The compound was likely swarming with armed guards. She wouldn't even make it out the door. If she did, she wouldn't survive a night in the jungle.

Didn't matter. She hadn't come here to escape on the first day.

Pushing up to a sitting position, lightheaded and nauseated, she turned away from the unfathomable view and the terrified women and focused on the enemy.

A man in a black suit stood a few feet away, his eyes inky and unreadable, with a promise of callousness in his resting scowl. In his mid-thirties maybe, he kept his beard and mustache trimmed as short as the black curls on his skull. He might've been attractive if it weren't for the menacing glare that deepened under the mantle of his thick brows.

"Welcome to Colombia." He didn't grin, didn't change his expression in any way, but his accented voice confirmed he was Nico Restrepo.

Matias stood a couple of feet behind Nico. Her

heartbeat quivered with both relief and disappointment. He would either help her efforts or try to stop her.

He wore black fatigues and a white t-shirt, with hands behind his back and his stance wide and confident. He didn't look at her, but his nostrils flared. He must've been aware she was peering at him through her lashes.

And she was wearing his long-sleeved shirt.

Why wasn't she nude and gagged like the other women? Was he protecting her in some way? If that was the case, why was she on the floor, bound with the others, as if awaiting sentencing?

Whatever was going on, she didn't want to give them a reason to muzzle her, so she kept her mouth shut as she sat taller and waited for Matias to meet her eyes.

When he did, he rubbed a palm over his thigh, his golden gaze unbending and infuriating. What was he thinking? Was he trying to give her a warning? A silent command? What? The longer she stared at him, the more something didn't feel right, but goddamn, she could stare at him for hours.

Whiskers shadowed his strong jawline. Muscle roped around his forearms and flexed beneath the faded ink of his tattoos. His broad chest, narrow waist, and powerful thighs drew her focus to the considerable package between his legs. If the kiss they'd shared earlier was any indication, she bet he fucked as hard as he looked.

Heat flooded low in her belly, and her nipples hardened. Why did he have to be so distractingly attractive? She pressed her lips together.

His face tightened, and he looked away.

Shit. She shifted her attention to the third man who stood beside him, and her breath strangled.

The corners of his pale mouth tipped into a smile that had been sewed together with heavy black thread. It was like something out of a Tim Burton film. His nest of wild black hair, ghostly complexion, and purple bruises beneath his eyes only made his needlework smirk more disturbing.

Were the stitches self-administered or some kind of punishment? Jesus, how did he eat? She shuddered. No wonder he looked deathly anorexic.

"You already met Matias." Nico lifted his phone and nodded his chin at the Goth guy. "This is Frizz. Don't let his youth fool you. He has a supernatural talent with sharp objects."

Her lips tingled as she imagined him attacking with a lightning fast needle. And what did Nico mean by *already met Matias*? Did he not know they grew up together? If Matias was hiding things from him, maybe she could use that to her advantage.

"I have an impatient buyer in the pipeline." Nico swiped the screen of his phone, wearing a scowl that bordered on boredom. "He's bald, fat, and looking for love." He rolled his lips. "Well, maybe not love. Let's call it *commitment*."

Who the hell was he talking to? Matias stared at the floor. Frizz's threaded grin was aimed at no one in particular. The three women behind her sniveled and shook in their chains.

Camila returned her attention to Nico, her pulse beating a frantic tattoo.

"I need to sell one of you." Nico cocked his head, his gaze flat, dead, as it rested on Camila. "I really don't care who, so you tell me. Which one?"

Her mind spun, trying to make sense of his

question. He wanted her to choose a girl to sell. A tremor bowled through her, rocking her body. No fucking way.

Nico snapped his fingers, and Frizz stepped forward.

Dread swelled in her gut as Frizz's emaciated frame ambled through the room. He twirled a finger through his crazy hair and — with the stitches just loose enough to pucker his lips — he whistled something eerily cheerful.

"You're not getting it, *niñita*." Matias lifted his head and met her eyes. "If Nico tells you to do something and you ignore him, he simply cannot let that slide."

The brown-nosing hijo de puta! How could he not see this as anything but horrifically fucked up?

She twisted around, her heart lodged in her stomach as she followed Frizz's movements. *What's he going to do? Oh God, what is he whistling?*

When he crouched next to the blonde behind her, his creepy tune cut off. With a sick stomach, she suddenly recognized the melody as the *Kill Bill* whistle.

Frizz wrenched the blonde off the floor by her hair and hauled her over his knee, face up. In the next breath, he held a curved surgeon's needle above her frozen nude body. Black string threaded through the needle's eyehole and ended at a knot that pulled tight against her lower eyelid, which he held pinched between his fingers and pulled away from her eye.

The woman screamed against her gag, her eyes bulging and her lashes batting against the taut thread.

Camila's stomach turned, and saliva flooded her mouth. How the hell had he pierced and threaded her skin that fast?

"Stop!" She swung back toward Nico, hands

jerking against the cuffs as she grappled for a way to stall them. "If you…you disfigure her, you can't sell her."

Nico lowered into an armchair against the back wall and lit a cigarette, scratching his trim beard.

"Lucky for us…" Matias approached her, his lean, arrogant stride twisting the hatred inside her. "Mr. Bald-fat-and-committed isn't a picky guy. He only requested tight holes. We can close up the slits he won't be fucking."

All three women burst into pleading, wailing sobs. She wanted to join them, to give in to the hopelessness burning up the back of her throat. But she couldn't. She refused to surrender.

"We'd love to keep all of you." Matias circled behind her.

She shifted to her knees, following him with her eyes.

"But we can't run a business without profits, can we?" Matias ruffled the hair on the women he passed and returned to stand before Camila. "Times are hard, and to stay competitive, we have to sell the merchandise. It's basic economics. Supply and demand. I don't make the rules."

Every word he said fractured something inside her. The demon in front of her wore a Matias-shaped mask, but beneath it lay the soulless reflection of pure evil.

She searched his eyes for a phantom echo of the boy she once knew and found no remorse. Not a hint of goodness in the fiendish smirk he so easily donned on his too-attractive face. It left her feeling more cold and alone than her darkest nights in Van's attic.

This wasn't him. Matias was gone.

Unbidden, a trail of fire crawled up her throat, and

her eyes blurred with tears.

"Deciding someone's fate can be taxing." He gripped her chin, squeezing painfully. "All those messy emotions get in the way. It sucks. But it's time to woman up and choose."

Her skin crawled where he touched her, and she jerked her head away.

Frizz held the blonde over his bent knee, his hand poised to finish the stitch over her eye. Fuck him to hell and back.

"*Ir a la mierda.*" Camila angrily rubbed her cheek on her shoulder, trying to erase the fallen tears.

"You need to shut down that hormonal shit." Matias rocked on his heels, seemingly at home in his despicable skin. "Like your *papá* used to say" — he laughed in a deep voice—"I'll give you something to choke on."

Her *papá* never said that, but it didn't stop the smoke from billowing through her chest and strangling her airway. She seethed with the vicious need to wash the floors with his blood.

Nico rose from the chair and strolled over to Frizz. He drew a long drag on the cigarette and, without a whisper of emotion on his face, stubbed it out on the blonde's stomach.

The piercing sound of her howls slammed Camila's heart against her ribs, and the aroma of singed flesh pervaded her inhales.

Frizz launched into his haunting whistle and turned his gaze to the needle in his hand.

"No, wait!" Camila scrambled toward Frizz on her knees, her arms useless weights behind her.

Matias yanked Camila back by her hair. "Choose."

Fuck fuck fuck. Her gut instinct was to volunteer herself, but if she did, she wouldn't be able to stop them the next time, and all the times after that. But how could she condemn another to a life of rape and brutality? She couldn't.

She raised her chin and spat the words. "I choose me."

"Too easy." Matias released her with a shove. "You disappoint me. I thought you were made of stronger stuff."

"Why are you doing this?" Glaring at him, she fisted her hands behind her, mentally squeezing his scrotum between her fingers and ripping his balls from his body.

Blood-curdling screams jerked her head toward the blonde.

Frizz had made two loops over her eyes and swooped in for a third.

Oh fuck, oh God, they wanted a decision, but this wasn't a choice at all.

"Her." Camila nodded at the blonde, her voice cracking as she blinked through the onslaught of tears. "Just…please remove the stitches."

Frizz stood and hauled the blonde to her feet. She keened loudly, her head swinging side to side as if trying to shake the threads from her eye. With a grip on her bound arms, Frizz dragged her out of the room and around the corner, trailed by the hiccupping sounds of her sobs.

An agonizing chill settled over Camila. So fucking cold. Her body was a vibrating cage, a prison of ice and violent tremors. The kind of shivering anguish that locked up muscles, sought out bones, and made her want to die. She couldn't feel the sunlight on her back or the wood beneath her knees. Was this what death felt like?

But she wasn't dead. She needed to fight for the blonde woman. For the women at her back. And for all the others bought and sold by these monsters.

"This is your life now." Matias crouched before her and lowered his voice. "*I* am your life. *Tu vida.*" He hummed to himself, a smile pulling at his wretched lips. "When I spread your thighs, you will let me in, because I own these legs and everything above, below, and in between them. You fight me, and I'll take it out on someone else." With a raised brow, his gaze shifted to the women behind her and flicked back. "Now I know you're a smart girl. Nod if you understand."

Her throat constricted. He wanted her to be his slave, to wear *his* fucking chains. Well, wasn't that perfect? She certainly despised him enough to endure that role with an appropriate amount of misery.

It's just a means to an end.

Her slave training kicked in, and she lowered her eyes, bowing her head on a nod.

She would outwit him, fool him into thinking she was intimidated by his threats and weakened by her restraints. Then she would confide in him, figure out his angle, and convince him to turn on his boss.

If he refused, she would kill him.

CHAPTER 9

Matias knew the instant Camila came to terms with her position as his slave. Her entire demeanor changed, her gaze falling to the floor, shoulders loosening, and spine straightening.

He didn't believe for one second that this was surrender. The betrayed look in her eyes wouldn't be going away for a while, and neither would the damn ache in his chest.

So while she would undoubtedly wear the role Van Quiso had taught her with mechanical perfection, she wouldn't embrace it emotionally.

To obtain what he wanted, what they both needed, it was his responsibility to show her what it truly meant to yield to her Master.

"On your feet." He stepped back and clasped his hands at his back.

She rose gracefully, head down and arms drawn behind her in the cuffs.

Tendrils of black hair fell in front of her shoulders and hid her face, but he was sure her eye was twitching. Good thing he couldn't read her mind. He'd rather not know all the ways she imagined killing him. She wouldn't succeed.

"Follow me." He gave Nico a nod on his way out of the living room without looking back to confirm she obeyed.

Crossing the white marbled floors of the circular foyer, he veered toward the glass causeway that would take him to the east wing.

"Are you going to rape me now?" She appeared at his side, voice devoid of emotion as she matched his strides on silent feet. "Or can I take a shower first?"

He swung around and clamped a hand on her forehead, snapping her face upwards as he stabbed two fingers in her mouth. Pressing down on her tongue while pinning her head back, he trapped her startled gaze with the hard warning in his.

After a few noisy breaths, her jaw relaxed beneath his hand.

Good girl. He released her and turned back toward the hall.

Truth was, he loved her verbal banter. It was one of the many reasons he hadn't gagged her...yet.

He held his arms behind him, mirroring hers, and led her out of the causeway, past one of the three kitchens, and through an open terrace sitting area.

The warm breeze filled his lungs with the scent of rich soil, vegetation, and sunlight. The aroma of *vida*. One of his favorite features here was the ability to fold back the walls in every bedroom and living space and create this indoor-outdoor atmosphere.

"I thought mosquitoes were a plague in the jungle." She squinted against the rays that filtered through the overhead trellis. "Or maybe that's the idea. Are itchy, swollen bites one of your many methods of torture?"

"The balconies are above the tree tops, too high for insects. Turn right here." He let her lead one step ahead and into the expansive library so that he could savor the exploratory shifts in her gaze as she took in the estate for the first time. "There are mosquito repelling flowers planted at ground level, and we spray when needed."

"You say *we* as if your ass is out there exterminating bugs." She pursed her lips. "Or is that how you started in this business? Did you leave Texas to become a liveried servant for slave traders?"

"I was never a servant." He clenched his jaw at her blatant attempt to offend him. "But we employ a full staff. The servants live"—he pointed at a building nestled beneath a canopy of foliage—"there."

"Is that where I'll be staying?" Her eyes lowered to his dick and quickly snapped away. "Or do you keep all the slaves in a basement dungeon?"

"No dungeons." The holding cells were in the west wing. "*Tu vida es* with me."

"How does your boss feel about that?" Her gaze swept across his face and returned to the landscape. "Does he always let you keep random slaves for your sick enjoyment?"

"We both know you're not a random slave."

She pulled in a breath. "By *both*, do you mean you and me? Or you and Nico?"

"Hmm." A smile tickled his mouth. He'd let her stew on that for a while.

"What about the slaves in the living room?" she asked. "And all the ones that came before them? Do you rape them, too?"

He grabbed her arm, stopping her forward motion. "I'll allow your questions as long as the conversation interests me."

She limbered up her shoulders and curled her lip.

"Matters concerning Nico and our business are off limits." He tightened his grip. "Before you open your mouth, be damn sure it's a response befitting your station."

She rolled her jaw as if warring with her words, her eyes huge and feral. Then she looked away.

"Yes, Sir." She lowered her head.

Wicked satisfaction zipped down his spine and coiled low in his groin, throbbing urgency along his hardening shaft. He needed to bury himself inside her and fuck her vigorously and thoroughly until they were both spent. Christ, he'd fantasized about it since the moment he started beating off in their grove.

The end goal was to earn her loyalty and gain her consent, an undertaking that would require weeks, months, maybe longer. In the meantime, he was under no delusions that he had the strength or the honor to wait around while she worked shit out in her head.

He was going to use her body in every way he imagined. She could cry, spit, and writhe in her restraints. Hell, she would definitely be doing all of that, and he would devour every explosive second of it while her pussy clamped around his cock.

Keeping his distance from her for the past four years had nurtured vicious cravings inside him, warping his tastes into an almighty need for painful, destructive sex. He was going to fuck her until they were both annihilated. Until their broken pieces scattered in an unholy tangled mess. And when they put themselves back together, there would no longer be hers and his. Only *them*.

He didn't have to look inside her to know what she wanted. She'd come here, *willingly*, as a slave. She could tell herself it was a mission to stop slavery, but he knew she was searching for something to sate that which she didn't yet understand, yearning to face a fear that haunted her since her abduction.

She put herself in a position to be raped and tortured because, deep down, this was her way of stepping inside and showing her teeth.

Dammit, he wanted to belt her for being so fucking reckless. But at the same time, she'd finally given him the opportunity to help her. To be there for her when he'd failed so spectacularly in the past.

It was a reminder of why he'd waited. As much as he wanted her, the end result had always been about her and what she needed.

Releasing her arm, he swiped a hand down his face and stared at the tent in his pants.

She needs food and a shower, you impatient bastard.

When he looked up, she tore her gaze away, face flushed. Probably a reaction she hadn't meant to make so obvious, but there it was. He affected her.

He reclaimed her arm and hurried her across a long balcony that served as an end cap for multiple bedroom suites and corridors that led to more bedrooms. Beyond the glass railing lay a deep valley of majestic Kapok trees.

"Who stays in those rooms?" She stared at the closed doors over her shoulder as she passed.

"There are dozens of guards and hired whores who live on site."

"Whores." Her voice tried for deadpan, but it cracked at the edges. "Is this where you've been living the last twelve years?"

"More or less." He tipped his head to the side and watched her eyes track a cloud shadow as it glided across the treescape. "This is our home base. The cartel's citadel." The sanctuary he always came back to.

How many times had he imagined bringing her here just to see her stand in awe of the place he called home?

Her blank expression offered zero fucks, but she wasn't fooling him.

Situated in the southern-most point of Colombia, the fortress was nothing short of spectacular. Bulletproof glass encased the exterior, presenting unobstructed, cinematic views of the self-contained enclosure of tropical rainforest. The kind of views National Geographic enthusiasts would jack off to from any angle in every room.

But security had been the central ethos that had led the construction of every square foot. Panic rooms, iris recognition scanners, tactical cameras, motion detectors, and fortified polycarbonate and ballistic steel building materials made the property virtually impenetrable.

On top of that, very few knew of its existence. Anyone idiotic enough to approach the perimeter wouldn't live long enough to beg for forgiveness.

She would be protected from outside threats, namely his enemies and anyone she might've pissed off in her war against slave traders. But it had taken an exorbitant amount of planning to relocate her here without adversely impacting his objective.

He wanted her completely — heart and soul. While that in itself might've seemed preposterous, his approach to winning her was even more outrageous. But he didn't have a choice. He was competing against a ghost.

His fists clenched. Her heart belonged to a boy who no longer existed. Well, fuck that motherfucker. That was the guy who didn't protect her a decade ago, who let her get kidnapped. That fucking guy failed her. *I failed her.*

He wouldn't fail her again.

"There's a lot of white." She stepped into another living room and nodded her chin at the flooring, walls, and furniture. "White, white, white. Not the best color scheme for blood stains." Her face tightened.

"Bleach is rather effective, but you already know that." Considering he'd disposed of fourteen bodies for her over the past ten years—slave buyers and their body guards. He'd dealt with the bodies, but she'd cleaned up the blood. "This way."

He reached the heavy wooden doors that barred entry to his personal space but didn't unlock them, his focus on the approaching heel-toe click of stilettos in the hall behind him.

"Welcome home, gorgeous," a familiar voice purred.

"Yessica." He turned to greet her, taking note of the way Camila stiffened beside him. "This is Camila." He twisted Camila around to face the other woman. "Camila. Yessica."

Despite the bottle blonde hair, Yessica's heritage oozed from every dip and curve on her body. Like most Colombian women, she had more of *it* on her legs and ass, a cola-shaped figure accentuated by a flat stomach and full hips.

"Aren't you a pretty little thing?" Yessica sashayed toward them, long legs stretching her red floor-length dress and heels tapping against the marble.

Camila looked up at him, eyebrow arched, giving him a delectable view of the twitch in her eye.

Maybe she was jealous, but despite the borrowed t-shirt, handcuffs, and knotted hair, Camila's natural beauty transcended that of every woman he'd ever seen, no matter how extravagantly primped, nipped, or tucked.

Not that Yessica had ever gone under the knife. Her tits were smallish, and she knew how to work them. But that didn't make her any less shallow. Her life's ambition was to be pampered by a wealthy man, and while there was revolution and poverty in Colombia, she refused to leave her homeland under the equatorial sun. So here she was.

"Are you keeping this one?" Eyes on Camila, Yessica trailed a blood-red fingernail along the neckline of his shirt.

"Have you checked your room?" He removed her hand from his throat. "I brought you some gifts from the States."

"Mmmm. I'm headed there now." She smoothed her palm over his shoulder and lifted up on her toes to press her lips against his ear. "Will I see you at dinner?"

"You will."

"Excellent." She turned to Camila. "Nice to meet you."

With a devious grin on her face, Yessica disappeared down the hall, exaggerating the movement of her hips and shoulders.

The ass shaking was usually for his benefit, but this one was undoubtedly meant to unnerve Camila. When it came to her competition, Yessica was one of those kill-em-with-kindness while stabbing-them-in-the-back kind

116

of women.

"How long have you been tapping that?" Camila didn't even try to hide the bitterness in her voice.

"I have an idea." He turned toward the computerized pad on the wall, leveling his eye with the screen. "Let's share our sexual histories while I fuck you in the shower."

The retinal scanner blinked, and the double doors to his suite clicked open.

"God, you're a pig." She sneered. "No, scratch that. You're a disgusting boar."

In a flash, he cuffed a hand around her throat and slammed her back against the wall. "You forget yourself, Camila."

She closed her eyes, but that stubborn chin of hers jutted above his knuckles. "Forgive me, Sir."

The pulse point in her throat thudded steadily against his palm, but the moment he leaned in and touched his lips to her brow, he felt her heartbeat quicken.

Tenderness scared her more than cruelty. What a complicated, remarkable creature. It was no wonder she'd held his attention all these years.

Stepping back, he assessed her gaunt complexion, cracked lips, and sharper-than-normal cheekbones. She hadn't eaten or hydrated since last night, and her arms and shoulders must've been killing her from being restrained for so long. Yet she hadn't uttered a single complaint. She was a fucking trooper, and it only made him want her more.

He ushered her into his private suite, a domain that only three other people could access.

The doors locked behind him as he steered her

toward the huge balcony where a dining table waited with an assortment of *arepas* and fruit.

"Sit." He pulled out a chair.

She lowered into the seat and eyed the food. "Impressive service. A benefit of working for a drug lord?"

Something like that.

He removed a key from his pocket, unlocked her cuffs, and set them aside. As she rubbed at her wrists, a pinch of guilt sneaked up on him. He shook it off.

"Put any notions of running out of your head. The only way in and out of here is by helicopter." He flicked a wrist at the roof. "Unless you have some latent survival skills." He gestured at the endless green beyond the railing. "You can try your luck out there."

Anyone else would've freaked the fuck out at the impossibility of escape, but not her. She poured a glass of water from the pitcher, leaned back in the chair, and drank deeply.

Because she didn't intend to escape, not without getting what she came for.

She'd already guessed that he'd expected her to arrive with Van Quiso. But she didn't know the half of it.

He had a myriad of bombs to drop on her, and each detonation needed to be thought out and timed perfectly. Like the one he was about to deliver.

As she piled her plate with *arepas* and dug in, she was probably mentally walking through a plan that relied on one key component if she failed. And she *would* fail.

Dipping into his pocket, he pulled out a tiny silver box and set it beside her plate.

She froze mid-chew and stared up at him, eyes

hard and suspicious.

"Open it." He sat in the chair across from her, elbow on the table, chin on his fist. "Go ahead."

Swallowing a mouthful of ham and cheese, she lifted the lid and choked. "You fucking bastard."

Her hand shook, and the box tumbled from her fingers, spilling the smashed GPS chip and pieces of her filling on the table.

CHAPTER 10

"This is…" *Fuck, fuck, fuck.* Camila pressed her tongue against the filling in her tooth, struggling to speak amid the turbulence whipping inside her. "Why?"

"You know why." Matias leaned across the small table, hands folded on the white linen and eyes twinkling with smug victory.

Her lungs constricted, making it a bitch to breathe. She was so damn angry she didn't even know what she was asking him.

The doctor on the plane… What was his name? *Picar.* Was he a dentist? Or had someone else drilled into her teeth while she'd been unconscious all night?

"I'm not asking why you removed it." She mirrored his leaning position, bringing her face within a fist's swing of his. "Why did you fix it?" Her tongue swiped over the molar as she glared at the broken microchip beside her plate. "Why fill the tooth and let me think you hadn't found the chip?"

"There were exposed nerves that needed to be sealed before you woke." He shrugged. "I didn't want you to suffer."

Is he serious right now?

He smiled, flashing those deep dimples, and it was

like staring at a terrible distortion of a precious memory. "The dentist was a trusted associate, exceptional at his trade, and was generous enough to meet us at our layover."

"Where was that?"

"The chip was disabled before you left the States."

Of course. Tate was probably losing his shit over the dead signal. He would track her last known position—likely some shady airport near the border—and assume the worst.

She blew out a breath. The GPS chip had been a safeguard, simply a backup plan if she didn't succeed.

But she could die here. In the cartel's citadel. Tate would never find her, would never stop the depraved transactions that happened within these walls.

She was on her own. A one-woman army against a powerful crime syndicate. And it all hinged on the man sitting across from her.

Matias knew she'd preemptively planted herself here, so there was no point in pretending. Since he hadn't asked her why she did it, he either knew that, too, or he didn't care. How much should she reveal? Maybe she should just lay it all out there and demand he put an end to the slave trading.

Right. When she'd woken in the living room, he was all *This is business* and *Go human slavery!* Had he been putting on a show for his boss, or had twelve years of crime well and truly carved out his heart? She needed to find out what his agenda was, where his loyalties lay, and how easily he could be turned.

"If I hadn't been there last night, would you have come?" She poured another glass of water and drank half of it. "Or would you have bought the girl who was supposed to be there?"

"I knew you'd be there."

"How?"

"I know everything." He grinned.

She seethed. "Does Nico know about our history?"

"I keep nothing from him." He watched her steadily from across the table.

He could be lying.

But why would he?

"What about the others?" She set the glass aside. "Do you share your personal life with Frizz, Picar, and whoever else lives here?"

"Some of them, yes. Others haven't earned my confidence." His fingers laced together, thumbs brushing lazily one over the other.

Faded ink sleeved both forearms, and at first glance, the matching designs appeared to be stars scattered among leaves. She lingered over the art, her gaze tracing the shaded lines of… *Not stars.* They were five-pointed blossoms on the branches of fruiting lemon trees. The same delicate blossoms he used to pick for her and put in her hair.

Memories uncoiled, tugging at emotions she'd tried so hard to keep contained. Her stomach hardened as beloved images blotted her vision. She'd spent her entire childhood with him, elbows-deep in lemon trees. His arms had once bore the scratches of mischief and labor. Now, they were permanently branded with those treasured moments, *their* moments, to remind her of everything she'd lost.

"Remember Venomous Lemonous?" His gaze lowered, resting on his tattoos.

"*Si.*" She'd hated the old, cantankerous lemon

farmer.

She couldn't remember his real name, but he'd worked in the grove most of her life. She and Matias used to sneak under his lemon trees to have…outercourse. Hands down each other's pants, bodies grinding, breaths heaving, tongues entangled. Just when they'd reach the heat of the moment, old Venomous Lemonous would slither out of the foliage, hollering and swinging his damn stick.

"He used to tell me" — Matias deepened his voice and scrunched up his face — "keep your root in your pants, boy, or it will do to her what spring does with the lemon trees."

The memory echoed hollowly in her chest. If Matias had knocked her up, would he have come back for her? Would Van have captured her? Would she be here now, grieving her past?

"Venomous Lemonous must've put the fear of God in you." She released a heavy sigh. "Since you did…you know, keep it in your pants."

Figuratively speaking. He'd never fucked her, but she'd been intimately familiar with every hard inch of him.

"I'm not that boy anymore." He slid his tongue across his bottom lip.

"And not just because you don't keep it in your pants." Roiling heat simmered in her belly.

Hell knew how many women he'd been with, consensual or otherwise. This was the guy that, less than an hour ago, made her choose which girl he would sell into slavery. Who stood by while a woman was burned, stitched in the eyelid, and hauled away. He was felonious, toxic, heartless.

But there was something else about him, something both troubling and captivating.

He reclined in the chair, legs spread wide and hands dangling loosely on the armrests. Dust covered his fatigues, ridges of muscle strained his t-shirt, and what looked like dried blood flecked the skin on his thick neck. No, that wasn't what was unsettling her.

Was it his expression? The way he regarded her, all moody and contemplative? Maybe it was the darkness that shadowed his face. The jet black hair that was clipped close on the sides and choppy on top, the stubble on his jaw and throat, the fringe of thick, smudgy lashes, and the heavy ridge of eyebrows that made his golden eyes glow with an intensity she felt beneath her rib cage. God, how he stared at her…

That was it.

Liv had told her once that a legitimate Master could command a woman using the power of his eyes.

What Camila saw in his gridlocked glare was an indisputable leader. A dominant male. When he fought, he won. When he wanted something, he took it. And right now, he wanted her attention, her nearness, her obedience.

Something inside her clicked into place, her entire body vibrating with the pull of an unbreakable string that drew her to him. She couldn't look away, couldn't breathe or speak.

She rose from the chair and closed the distance, her insides thrashing.

Wrought iron screeched against tile as he scooted back and tapped his inner thigh. A single tap and she was there, standing in the V of his legs, waiting for his next command with equal amounts of wonder and trepidation. *What's happening to me?*

"Remove the shirt."

Ahhh, that voice. He'd always known how to sweeten it to coax her and how to sharpen it in challenge. In three words, he achieved both.

She lifted the shirt over her head and let it fall to the floor.

He didn't move, didn't blink, but his taut inhale sounded like a whip cracking beside her ear. "Now the panties."

Her breath hitched. No underwear meant no more physical boundaries. She squeezed her eyes shut, breaking the spell.

A breeze from the ceiling fan brushed across her bare breasts, hardening her nipples. He'd seen it all before, most recently on the plane, but now that he'd declared his intent to claim her, exposing her pussy would feel more vulnerable, more significant.

She stole a glance at the ruined microchip on the table. She was just one girl, raised on a poor Texas farm. Completely out of her league.

But how many Restrepo enemies had made it this far? Did the FBI, DEA, or Colombian Police even know how to find this place? *No es probable.* Yet she stood within the walls of the cartel's lair, unrestrained and still breathing.

Steeling her spine, she resolved to see this through. For her survival. For the innocent lives they bought and sold.

She hooked her thumbs under the elastic at her hips, shoved the panties to the floor, and kicked them. The urge to curl inward and cover herself made her fingers tremble, but she fought it, adjusting her stance into one that had been beaten into muscle memory. Legs wide, hands behind her neck, back straight, tits out, eyes on him.

The heat of his gaze seared her pussy, and his fingers twitched against the armrests. She wished she hadn't waxed off all her pubic hair. She felt so damn bare and unprotected.

"I miss your soft curls here." He stroked the back of a knuckle across her mound. "No more waxing."

She shivered. She couldn't help it. It was the thick intonation of his voice, a subtle trace of Colombia. When she was sixteen, she'd clung to the gravely rumble of his timbre. And now, fuck, he still had the ability to make her wet with his voice alone.

He leaned forward, his lips a kiss away from her chest, warm breath on her nipples. She stifled a gasp as fingertips grazed her hipbones and roamed over her ribs, his hands shaking.

Shaking? She reared her head back. "Are you nervous?"

His expression hardened. He stood abruptly, snatched her wrist from behind her neck, and pulled her after him. Inside, through a sitting room, and down an enclosed hallway, they went.

"Do you know why I'm here?" She quickened her strides to keep her arm attached to her shoulder.

"Because I want you here."

"No, I mean do you know why I showed up with the man in the Mustang?"

"Van Quiso?" He slammed to a halt, causing her to crash into his chest as he whirled on her. "The *hueputa* who tortured you for a year?"

Cords pulled taut in his neck. Muscles and veins

strained against the skin on his forearms, and the fingers around her hand cinched so tightly it felt like he was seconds from snapping bones.

She'd obviously hit an overprotective nerve, which was hypocritical as fuck seeing how she'd spent the last however many hours in his restraints.

"Don't hurt him." There was no love lost between her and Van, but she'd been making progress with the man.

"Give me a reason not to," he spat and turned away, yanking her into a massive bedroom.

"He's not worth your time, he loves his wife, and he doesn't give a shit about me. That's three." She glimpsed white walls, white bedding, and white woodwork before she was shoved into an all-white bathroom the size of her bedroom at home.

Oval glass tiles glittered like diamonds around the vanity on the wall to the left. Sunlight warmed her right side, spilling in through the floor-to-ceiling pane of glass that ran the length of the room. In the distance, a pair of blue and yellow macaws soared above the trees and perched in the leafy canopy. She stood there for a moment, contemplating the surrealistic beauty that enveloped her nightmare.

She was in Colombia, her parents' birthplace, with the boy she'd loved and lost—the man who'd become her enemy. The scenery shouldn't have been this awe-inspiring.

The white travertine floors cooled her bare feet as she stepped forward and followed him to the shower at the far end. But as she passed the separate toilet room, her bladder pinched.

He glanced at her face and waved a hand at the

toilet. "Go."

A year without privacy in Van's attic made it easy to sit down and pee under Matias' watchful gaze.

"You haven't answered my question." She tore off a wad of toilet paper.

"Do I know why you tortured Larry McGregor for information? Why you killed him and pretended to be his delivery?" He twisted the shower faucet on and spun back toward her with fire in his eyes. "I know everything about you, *mi vida.*"

How? A chill raced down her back. That meant Nico probably knew her plans, as well. Unless Matias was bluffing. Maybe he didn't know *everything.*

She wiped, flushed, and walked toward him, fingers twitching at her sides. "Who took my virginity?"

His gaze flew to her pussy, and his hand shot out and clutched the towel rack on the wall beside him. A second later, the brackets ripped from the woodwork, and metal hurtled through the room and crashed near the doorway.

She jumped, pulse hammering in her throat.

"Get in the shower." He thrust a finger at the walk-in enclosure.

The tiled space was large enough to wash a harem of women. She tried not to dwell on that as she stepped beneath the warm spray of multiple shower heads.

He tackled the laces on his boots, toed them off, then moved to his socks, shirt, fatigues, and…sweet God in heaven, he wasn't wearing underwear.

Maybe the steam was distorting her vision, but his cock looked so much longer, thicker, *harder* than she remembered. Where his body used to be tall, slender, and a little awkward, it was now broad, vascular, and stacked with brawn and power. Every inch of him was pure, raw testosterone.

Her knees loosened, and her skin flushed. Was it possible to sweat in water?

"Why did you tell me the GPS tracker was removed?" She gave him her back and grabbed the shampoo. "You could've let me go on thinking I had help coming."

His footsteps squeaked on the wet floor, closing in. She held her breath.

"The sooner you accept your future with me," he said, his mouth at her ear, "the easier this will be for you. Turn around."

She inwardly growled, shaking with the impulse to tell him what he could do with his orders. But she needed to pick her battles.

If she turned around, though, her brain would get all scrambled under the force of his eyes. And his cock, good God, it would be standing proud and right there between them.

Just don't look at it.

With a tight throat, she pivoted to face him.

CHAPTER 11

Warm water rained down from the array of shower heads, heating Camila's skin. Or was it anxiety making her hot and itchy? Keeping her focus above Matias' waist as she angled her face out of the spray, her gaze landed on another tattoo.

At first glance, it looked like black veins forking over his shoulder. She felt him watching her as he turned to the side, allowing her to see the full image.

The outline of a tree trunk etched across his upper back and spread into leafless branches. The piece was twice the size of her hand and crawled over his shoulder. An orange tree. She'd recognize the rounded, symmetrical shape anywhere.

A closer inspection revealed two images in one, an optical illusion of limbs curving into the figure of a woman with hourglass hips and flowing black hair. Branches formed her slender neck, the bends of her arms behind her, the dip of her waist, all of which stemmed from the V at the apex of her thighs. It was eerily beautiful, unique, and really fucking sexy.

But an orange tree? A woman with long, black hair? Surely, it wasn't…

"Me?" She looked up and froze in the prison of his

eyes.

He gave a terse nod, lifted the shampoo from her hand, and stepped behind her.

She stared at her toes in the swirl of water. He'd tattooed an image of her on his body.

That should've ignited her with outrage and confusion and sparked all kinds of questions. But dammit, her nerves were frayed, her body too tired to care. Way too tired to stop him from washing her hair, making her sigh with his distracting fingers, and massaging her scalp as the scent of citrus and lavender wafted around her.

After all these years, she still knew the feel of his strong hands, the muscles that thickened his palms, and the surety of his grip. She'd known how his mouth tasted after a long day in the sun, the way he'd moaned when she kissed that spot beneath his ear, and the intensity of his eye contact as he'd chased his orgasm.

"Tell me his name." He shifted around to her front, his hands lathered in soap.

"Who?"

"The one who took your virginity." His voice was soft, at odds with the teeth-breaking set of his jaw.

"Um…" She blinked through the deluge of water. "Oscar."

"Oscar?" He scowled, nostrils flaring. "That's not a name. It's processed meat."

"It *is* a name." She was pretty sure Oscar had been a manwhore, so maybe *processed meat* was more fitting.

"Did he make it good for you?" His tone was incisive, guttural.

"Two pumps and done."

His entire demeanor darkened. She knew what he

was thinking. *It should've been him.*

He lathered her body, his hands sluicing soapy water from her neck to her toes and everywhere between. Fingers curved around her breasts, stroking, molding. She twitched away and raised her head, her gaze entangling with the luminous gold of his eyes.

Her breathing shortened, and his touch slid lower, down her sides, around her waist, stopping to palm her ass and squeeze her flesh.

"Matias, don't." She gripped his wrists, tried to push him away.

It only made him clench harder, putting enough pressure against the muscles on her backside that pain twinged through her nerve endings. Weightless energy charged through her—an intense kind of energy that buzzed like an angry vibrator in her pussy.

Straightening her upper body, she flexed her thighs, trying to block out the sensations he stroked between them.

He seemed to be pondering dour thoughts because his caresses grew rougher and less controlled, making her cringe.

"When you escaped Van Quiso and called me…" He crouched before her, eyes on her cunt as he traced the seam with a warm, wet finger. "You were a virgin then."

"Yeah." A shiver trickled down her spine.

She was grateful to have left the attic with that one part of herself intact. At the same time, it became a burden she'd carried for months after. The label of innocence didn't quite fit after what she'd been through with Van. It'd felt like she was holding on to her virginity *because* of the abuse she'd endured.

When Oscar propositioned her in a coffee shop six

months after her captivity, she'd been more than ready to prove she wasn't a fearful victim.

"You should've fucking told me how to find you." Without warning, Matias shoved a finger inside her and used it like a hook to yank her closer.

She gasped. Trying to buck free, she smacked at his arm and kneed his chest, but couldn't dislodge his finger. "I didn't know you anymore."

He'd been led from his home by armed men, and in the few phone conversations they'd had before her abduction, he'd acted so damn secretive and shady. He'd told her nothing, refused her questions, and hadn't come back for her when she still lived in the grove.

"I didn't trust you." She twisted her hips away from his hand, going nowhere. "As it turns out, I have killer instincts."

"You were wrong." He launched to his full height and squeezed her neck as he added another finger inside her, thrusting them mercilessly and wrenching a whimper from her. "And you're wrong now. I will never forgive you for hanging up on me. For making me wait a fucking year before you called again. Making me wait while you spread your legs for other men."

There was so much pain in his voice, in the taut line of his shoulders, the glaze in his citrine eyes, the vicious drive of his fingers making her pussy ache.

"You're hurting me." She clawed at the hand around her neck.

"You hurt *me!*" He tightened his grip, holding her back against the wall. "You were mine, goddammit!"

"Yours?" Her temper inflamed, flushing her system with adrenaline. "When I called that day, were *you* mine? Were you a twenty-year-old virgin holding out for his childhood sweetheart?"

"I did wait for you!" Flexing his hand at her throat, his other withdrew from between her legs to stab through the wet strands of her hair. He yanked at the roots as he tipped back her head. "I waited until I could come back for you. Waited a fucking year. Then you disappeared, and I thought…" The anger drained from his voice, and his forehead dropped to her temple, his breath hot on her face. "I thought you were dead."

Her throat closed up, her eyes burned, and she felt an overwhelming urge to wrap her arms around him.

He's a slave trader, living in luxury that's paid for in innocent lives.

"I was gutted." He trailed fingers over her shoulder and around her breast, the hand on her throat loosening. "Consumed with rage. A nineteen-year-old kid with so much hatred eating me up. I fought and drank and killed." He pinched her nipple, squeezing painfully. "Then I fucked a whore in an alley."

Her chest caved in beneath a barrage of jealousy. And rage. So much fucking rage it seethed from her pores. He should've returned for her. Should've talked to her, confided in her, *trusted* her. Then he never would've had to stick his dick in a whore. Fuck him.

"The next day…" He brushed his lips across her cheek. "I got the shoulder tattoo."

A branding of guilt. He deserved it.

Except she understood that odious feeling. She'd starved herself for weeks after she gave her first time to Oscar. She hadn't belonged to Matias, but all of her firsts had been meant for him.

He released her throat, and when he lifted his head, his haunted eyes filled her horizon. Her brain couldn't reconcile the look on his face with the cold-hearted man auctioning off women in the living room.

Going into this, she'd known rape was on the table. She had an IUD to prevent pregnancy, but STDs were one of the many known risks. One risk she hadn't calculated was having sex with Matias. Whether it would be willing or forced, it was a threat to her heart, one that could destroy her.

He gripped her wrists and pinned them against the wall above her head. She anticipated what was coming and couldn't stifle the feelings exploding inside her. Her legs shook, and the inner muscles contracted and heated. For years, she'd imagined him between her thighs, his body a pillar to hold on to, and his groans a comforting embrace.

The lean muscles of his chest flexed, and his full mouth parted as his wet body slid against hers. He pressed his hard length against her pussy, seeking entry, his gaze feral.

He shifted her wrists to one hand and grabbed the base of his cock. Stroking himself, pressing his body impossibly close to hers, he licked the seam of her lips then kissed her like he'd waited his entire life for this very moment. His hard, frantic nips and urgent flicks of his tongue left her gasping, biting, reciprocating.

Hunger coiled between her legs, and her clit throbbed beneath the massaging glide of his length. She wished her arousal was a trained response, but Jesus have mercy, she wanted him. Wanted him in her.

She rocked her hips, needing more friction as she chased his tongue and devoured his lips.

"I've waited so long for this," he breathed between kisses, his eyes molten gold.

Without looking away, he speared his fingers inside her, spread her open, and slid his cock along her folds. Fucking her without penetration.

Just like old times.

She tried to disassociate what was happening now from her cherished memories, but the pieces of her that would always want him were breaking open and messing with her mind. As he nudged the broad head of his erection at her opening, her pleasure centers fired in excitement, and her heart pounded frantically, even as her brain screamed *no*.

He stilled, his breath cutting off as his smoldering gaze drilled into her.

Holy fuck, this was it. She couldn't breathe.

The hand on her wrists clamped to the point of pain, and his head whipped around to look over his shoulder.

"I need you in the west wing." Nico's accent echoed through the bathroom.

Heat rushed to her cheeks as she peered around Matias' stiff shoulders. What the hell was Nico doing here? In Matias' bathroom? Without fucking knocking?

"Sorry about the timing, *parce*." Nico stood a few feet away, hands in his pockets, his scowl prominent amid his dark trimmed beard. "This can't wait." With a sharp glare in her direction, he strolled out of the room.

"Fuck!" Matias released her and shoved his hands through wet hair. "Fucking fuck!"

She sagged against the wall, her body buzzing and head spinning. Just a sliver of another second and he would've been inside her. Their first time together. Connected in the way she'd always imagined. So fucking close.

She should've felt relieved. Should've been over-fucking-joyed by the interruption. Instead, her heart felt like it was shrinking.

Matias smacked the faucet, turning off the water. Then he stood there, swiping his palms down his face, his body a vibrating coil of tension.

How was he okay with Nico coming into his bathroom and ordering him around? It was either a really close relationship or an authoritarian one.

Maybe she should dry off, try to wipe away the last few minutes. As she moved to step out, he beat her there.

Wrapping a towel around his waist, he held one out for her. "Let's go."

Go? She assumed this was a business call. Would he take her with him? Hope bubbled up. She needed to get a lay of the land. *And cool off her damn libido.*

In the bedroom, he dragged on black suit pants, tucking his erection to the side as he zipped up. *No underwear.*

She bit her lip. What was she supposed to wear? She dried off and looked around.

A wall of windows led to another balcony. A king-sized bed sat in the corner of the room, draped in white fabrics. Couches and chairs formed a horseshoe in front of a fireplace. And a large column stood in the center of the room, rising up to the apex of the vaulted ceiling. Everything painted in white.

"Kneel beside the post." His voice crept over her shoulder, shockingly close.

She turned to face him. He wore a black button-up tucked into the narrow waist of his pants.

In his hand dangled a length of chain. Her stomach collapsed, and she spun back to the post. There, screwed into the wood near the floor, was a metal ring.

"If I told you I wanted to leave," she said, mouth dry, "that I wanted to go home, would you let me?"

"Never." He walked past her, locked the chain to the metal ring, and held on to the leather collar at the other end. "You want to be owned."

"Said no slave ever." She stood her ground. "But I won't try to escape. You don't need to chain me."

He widened his stance, hands clasped at his back with the short chain hanging behind him. But it was the cutting look in his eyes that made her shake from head to toe. It conjured dark enclosed places, ear-piercing screams, and bruising thrusts against the back of her throat.

Her heartbeat went ballistic, banging in her ears. He wasn't Van, but he wasn't Matias, either. The man standing before her made a living off of human pain, and his interest in her was personal.

She lowered her head, her feet moved, and the sour taste of dread flooded her mouth.

Lifting the towel from her grip, he folded it on the floor in front of his shiny shoes. Then he straightened and touched his lips to her forehead.

She cringed, eyes glued to the square of terrycloth, knowing what he wanted and inwardly fighting it.

You won't win this battle. Focus on the end goal.

Methodically, one muscle at a time, she knelt for him. Back straight, weight evenly balanced between her hips, palms facing outward on her thighs, eyes on his belt. Then she adjusted, spreading her legs shoulder width apart to allow full view of her pussy, her skin prickling with self-loathing.

"Your orgasms belong to me." He glanced at the

ceiling and the camera tucked in the corner. "I'll know if you touch yourself."

She gritted her teeth. *As if!*

"Any man can chain you to a post." He buckled the leather collar around her neck, securing it with a four-digit padlock.

The leather sat snugly against her skin, the gravity of it choking her air.

"Any man can rip off your clothes." He tested the chain between her neck and the wooden column. "Fuck your throat, call you a whore, and you might even like it. That's rough, gritty sex. But it isn't dominance."

Her heart stuttered. He'd described her experience with Van so accurately.

He glided a finger across the line of her jaw, tilting her face upward. "Dominance is when I kiss your brow and you obediently lower to the floor. Willingly. No hesitation." His eyes flashed. "It's when you kneel for me, give me the power to break you inside and out, and trust that I won't. You will surrender your vulnerability without shame, because that's what I want, and what I want, you crave."

"You're delusional." She struggled to swallow. "I'm not—"

"You're not there yet. So in the meantime, I'll settle for rough, gritty sex."

With that, he left her trembling on her knees.

CHAPTER 12

Instinct guided Camila through the next few hours. Naked and shivering with raw nerves, she'd attempted dozens of combinations on the lock she couldn't see at her throat. She'd tried to unscrew the metal ring on the post until her fingers turned red. Then she'd walked the radius, measuring the span of the chain.

With arms out, she could stretch about six feet in every direction, but the bed sat twice that far. The bathroom, couches, and built-in wall cabinets were even farther. The doors to the hall and balcony closed off the exit points. Another door, also shut, must've led to a closet. There was nothing within reach except the towel and an expanse of gleaming white marble floors.

Not that she intended to break out of this fortress, but dammit, she needed to snoop through drawers and closets to find out what Matias was hiding, anything that might explain why he was so obscure.

She glanced up at the camera in the ceiling. Was he watching her now, waiting for another reason to hurt her?

There was also a building pressure in her bladder. Probably shouldn't have drunk so much water, but *come on!* Van would've at least given her a bucket to piss in.

Restless and wary, she paced circles around the pole like a tetherball, switching directions, and pacing again. She replayed her conversations with Matias, searching every interaction for hidden meanings in his words, clues that would indicate there wasn't a monster behind those mercurial eyes.

But she recalled nothing helpful. Everything he'd said and done implied he was one-hundred-percent invested in the cartel. *And owning her.*

When she'd asked him where she'd be staying, he'd said her life was with him, diminishing any hope of disentangling her past from the present. This was no longer just a battle against slave traders. She would be fighting to protect the heart of the girl he'd abandoned in the citrus grove.

She gripped the chain and yanked. *Fuck!* How long would he keep her locked up?

God, she'd thought she was so fucking clever. Thought she could just smuggle her way into a slave ring and single-handedly take out the asshole in charge.

She didn't know shit.

How arrogant of her to assume she'd end up in the boss's bed. While she didn't want to be anywhere near Nico Restrepo, the alternative called into question some seriously conflicted desires.

She glared at Matias' bed across the room. *Forgive him. Bite off his dick. Fuck his brains out. End his life.*

No, killing him wasn't an option. To put an end to the cartel's slave trading, she needed to get to Nico. To do that, she'd have to win over Matias by any means necessary.

I'll settle for rough, gritty sex.

She could still feel his voice vibrating through her,

and she shuddered anew. Worse, he knew he affected her. He wasn't a stranger she could inveigle and trick. He could see past her act, undress her mind, and fuck her thoughts.

She tapped her fingers against her thighs and pulled in a deep breath.

When they were kids, she'd anticipated what he wanted and followed his every whim without reservation. Hell, she'd followed him around like a lost puppy. But he was also two years older.

No, that wasn't why. There had always been a captivating shift in the air around him. A dominant man stretching the skin of his prepubescent body. A Master lying in wait.

She leaned against the post and slid to the floor, tucking her knees to her chest. With a shaky hand, she traced the stiff band of leather around her neck. The texture and weight felt like Van's restraints, but the similarities ended there.

Being bound by Van had made her feel defenseless, trapped, uncared for like an insignificant nothing. But this… She pressed her palm against the leather, squeezing it around her throat. Matias' collar felt like armor, *his* armor, protecting her from the world. Why? Because they shared history? Or were his parting words messing with her?

Kneel for me…give me the power to break you…trust that I won't.

Funny thing, trust. It was so hard to give, yet easy to rip away. He'd earned her trust through sixteen years of friendship. Then he'd lost it. Not the day he left, but in the phone call that came a month after. It'd been the coldness in his tone and the furtive way he'd steered the conversation away from commitment and love. He'd chosen his future, and it hadn't included her.

She lowered her hand to the round metal tag that hung on the collar, tracing the engraving for the hundredth time. What she wouldn't give to know what it said. Was it his name and phone number like a damn dog tag? A quote from a handbook on how to destroy human lives? Or was it something personal, like his tattoos? Not likely. Dozens of his slaves had probably worn this very collar.

She sucked in a breath, hating that the pang in her chest was jealousy of other women rather than remorse for the abuse that might've occurred. Yet the idea of being owned by him, being the only one he'd ever kept, made her crave things—filthy, kinky things she'd fantasized about during sex.

It didn't matter how skilled her lovers had been, none had taken her to the depths she hungered for. No matter how much she begged, no one spanked her long enough, choked her hard enough, or left her unable to think afterward, lost to sensations. She ached to be fucked violently and loved tenderly, and for the life of her, she didn't understand why.

She wasn't one of those women who needed a man, but she longed to be the kind of woman a man couldn't live without. And while Matias' intentions hovered somewhere between terrifying and soulless, the way he looked at her made her feel treasured. Protected.

His spoken promises should've horrified her. Instead, they poked at the twisted parts of her soul that wanted things she was too afraid to ask for.

What the hell was wrong with her? This wasn't Stockholm Syndrome—she'd loved him before he was her captor. Insanity, maybe? Brain damage? Or just good, old-fashioned stupidity.

As the balcony glowed orange in the blaze of the sinking sun, interior lamps flickered on around the room. Growing more distressed about his return, she resumed pacing, which seemed to ease her irritated bladder. She considered peeing on the floor and thought better of it. Van would've pressed her face in the mess. Who knew what Matias would do?

An hour after sunset, footsteps sounded in the hall. As if compelled by the confident pace of the strides, she knelt at attention on the towel, facing the door. With shins placed against the floor, thighs vertical, and body held upright, she positioned her arms in strappado — behind her back with elbows, forearms, and wrists pressed together with imaginary restraints.

It was sick the way her pussy clenched in anticipation. She'd fantasized being taken by him — forcibly, passionately — since forever, but the circumstances were all wrong. *He* was all wrong. Her insides knotted.

Still, she kept her attention on the door, anxiously awaiting his expression upon finding her posed in presentation.

The knob turned, and the door swung open, revealing the golden flames of his eyes, motionless in a sea of crimson.

Blood spattered his face and throat and caked the ink on his forearms where he'd rolled up his sleeves. His black shirt and pants glistened with wetness, and his hands clenched at his sides as he stared at nothing.

"What happened?" Her heartbeats fell hard, her posture crumbling. "Are you hurt?"

He didn't look at her, didn't acknowledge her in any way as he stepped into the bedroom. No noticeable limping. Not a hint of physical pain or visible wounds beneath the smears of blood.

Stopping at a built-in cabinet, he opened the doors to a wet bar and poured a glass of *aguardiente,* neat, the way Colombians preferred their soft vodka.

She wanted to ask him whose blood he was covered in, hoping with every shuddering breath that the gore didn't belong to one of the captured women. "Matias?"

His entire body stiffened, the glass hovering midway to his mouth. Maybe this wasn't the best time to call attention to herself.

He swallowed back the *guaro* in one gulp, poured another, and carried it into the closet. When he disappeared beyond the doorway, she couldn't see inside, but the retreat of his footfalls hinted at the extensive depth of the room.

She pressed her lips together and sat back on her heels. Did he get in a fight? Torture someone? Stand too close to a ritualistic slaughter?

Her stomach rolled. Maybe this was just a normal day of work for him. Except the crystallized glaze in his eyes suggested that whatever happened had rattled him.

A moment later, he exited the closet, carrying a fraternity paddle, a cane, handcuffs, and a ball gag. His stony gaze landed on her.

"What're you doing?" Her pulse went crazy as she scrambled to her feet and shuffled backward until the chain snapped her to a halt. "I behaved while you were gone. I fucking knelt for you!"

Jesus, he hadn't even changed his clothes, standing

there like a blood-soaked nightmare. And his eyes... Something wasn't quite right in the shadows behind those unmoving flames.

He dropped his bundle on one of the armchairs and dragged the chair toward her, its legs squealing across marble.

Parking it just out of her reach, he stood so very still and silent, intent on watching her while her insides fell apart and her bladder screamed to spill all over the floor.

"I have to pee, Matias." Her voice wavered. "And you need a shower. I'll help you clean up."

He continued to stare, studying her in a detached way. No, not studying. He seemed to have retreated inward, mentally shut down. His hand blindly swept over the chair and picked up the ball gag.

Shit shit shit!

"Matias? Remember when I got this?" With trembling fingers, she parted the hair on her scalp.

His gaze flicked to the jagged scar above her hairline and returned to her mouth without a trace of emotion.

She was seven when she fell out of the orange tree, busting her head open and bleeding all over the place. "Do you remember what you told me?"

"An ounce of bravery is more valuable than a gallon of blood." His voice was ice grinding against rock. "Andres taught me that. Then he died a coward's death."

What did that mean? His uncle had perished in the fire that had taken her family. A conversation for another time.

"The day I got this scar," she said hoarsely, "you promised me you would never let me fall again."

If she reached out an arm, she could touch his sticky shirt. But she didn't dare.

He stood taller, his chin level with her forehead as he lifted the ball gag. "Open your mouth."

"Don't do this." She shook her head, eyes blurring. "Don't hurt me."

"If you fight me, what will I do?" His tone held no pitch or fluctuation.

Take it out on someone else.

She tensed with the compulsion to kick out a leg, knock him off balance, and lock him in a chokehold. Then what? She was chained to a fucking pole.

Her attention flew to the cane and paddle. Deep down, she believed he wouldn't kill her. Probably wouldn't make her bleed either, no matter how badly this would hurt.

She stretched open her mouth.

His lips curved, but there was no pleasure in his smile. No dimples. No emotion whatsoever as he pressed the rubber ball between her teeth and secured the strap behind her head. Thank God, his hands were free of blood, washed clean up to the wrists. Or he'd worn gloves.

"Face down." He stabbed a finger toward the floor. "Legs spread wide and pray to hell."

A punishment position, one that allowed full access to the tender areas of her body. She lost control of her breathing, her tongue pushing against the gag as her skin broke out in a cold sweat.

She must've hesitated too long, because he grabbed her hair and forced her to the floor on her stomach. With his knee digging against her back, he wrenched her arms behind her, forcing her hands in a reverse prayer position and securing them in the cuffs. Then he grabbed the long wooden paddle.

Tremors assaulted her arms and legs, and her throat sealed up. Didn't matter how high her pain tolerance, this was going to hurt like a motherfucker. She might've fantasized about Matias spanking her, choking her, and fucking her to near-death, but the truth was, she didn't *enjoy* pain. Unless…maybe…it was inflicted with love.

There's no love here.

Her reflexes begged her to fight him off, but experience had taught her that tensing muscles beneath a strike resulted in days of painful bruising. So when he removed his knee from her back and replaced it with the heat of his hand, she let her body go limp and focused on breathing deeply.

Before she drew her second breath, a whistling scream cracked the air, and the paddle made contact in a fiery explosion of broken skin.

 CHAPTER 13

Camila howled against the gag, her teeth sinking into rubber as Matias swung again and again. He'd skipped the goddamn warm up and slammed her straight into a body-twitching, skin-burning overload of agony.

Kneeling at her side with his weight braced on the hand at her back, he struck her ass and the backs of her thighs with deep, swift, penetrating thuds. Had she been standing, the first hit would've knocked her over. As it was, it felt like he was beating her into the floor.

Stop! Dios mio, es demasiado. It's too much. Her screams garbled against the gag as every hit vibrated through her like a muscle-thumping bass note, chattering her teeth and blazing fire down her legs. *Please make it end.* She wanted to curl into a ball, close her eyes, and dream all of this away. And never wake up.

The fucking wooden paddle didn't let up, its rigid width covering such a huge impact area she felt it everywhere. Each heavy, hard-hitting blow stopped her heart and lingered long after the next thud. Her vision blurred, her lungs wheezed, and her bladder felt like it was going to burst.

No más, por favor. No more!

She attempted to slow down her breathing, but she

couldn't tune out the anguish. So she tried to experience it as an observer, focusing on where each burning sensation originated, where it ended, what shape it was, and how deep it sank into muscle and bone. The exercise pushed her through the worst of it, but eventually, dizziness set in, endorphins flooded her bloodstream, and darkness invaded the edges of her consciousness.

Just when she thought she would pass out, he tossed the paddle in the chair. "If you need to pee, do it now."

He didn't move to unchain her. Piss on the floor then? Maybe he got off on that brand of humiliation, but she was in too much pain to give a fuck. Except, when she tried to release her bladder, it wouldn't relax. She concentrated harder. Nothing. Was it shock? Stage fright?

She bit down on the rubber ball and glared at him through her tears.

Caked in blood, expression vacant, eyes cold, he was death and hell and the devil that ruled it all.

Hooking a finger through the ring on the collar, he dragged her to her knees. For an ignorant moment, she thought he was finished.

Without meeting her eyes, he arranged her lethargic, aching body against the post. On her knees, back against the column, and shins bracketing the base, she felt a tug at her wrists. Heavy deadness pulled on her eyelids. She blinked, tried to keep hold of awareness, but she had no fight left.

The smack of a hand across her cheek snapped her awake, and her attention fell on his bloody shirt. *Oh God, this is still happening.*

Her breaths came in asthmatic bursts. She tried to pull her arms forward, but they remained where they were, hugging the post at her back and locked with metal rings.

Saliva pooled around the ball in her mouth and trickled down her chin as her entire body shook beneath a rush of adrenaline and whatever morphine-like chemicals her brain had released. She wished she was drugged or drunk. Or dead.

He picked up the cane, and she swung her head left and right. She couldn't do this. No more pain. *Please, Matias!*

Like the paddle, he didn't ease in. The cane flew through the air and landed on the front of her thigh.

"Noooo" ripped from her throat in a keening, indistinguishable wail.

The cutting stripe seared a trail of heat across her skin, followed by another and another.

Her chin dropped to her chest with the weight of her head, and she watched with horror as each new welt bloomed on her thighs. The cane never slowed. Ladder-like cuts formed, some of them torn and bleeding on the surface. It was if he were trying to mark every inch of skin between her groin and knees.

She'd rarely cried after those first few days in Van's attic, and she hadn't intended to now. Except this was Matias, her childhood best friend, beating her body to a pulp.

Tears coursed down her cheeks, and a heavy, helpless feeling settled in her chest. But amid the heartache throbbed something sharper, darker. Something so very wrong.

Her gaze lifted to the zipper of his pants, where the long, hard outline of his erection strained against the fabric. She looked up at his eyes and found a smoldering flicker had chased his coldness away.

His breathing lost rhythm, and his hand shook as he lowered the cane. He was turned on by this, by her responses, her body? Whatever it was, his arousal fed hers, awakening the nerve-endings in her pussy and soaking her with heat as images of him coming on her abused body flashed through her mind.

Her stomach cramped with disgust and shame. Why was she so fucked up in her head?

If he were any other man, she would've vomited against the gag. The only reactions Van had stirred in her were raw fear and rage. But Matias was deep beneath her skin, his gaze touching her everywhere, heating her from the inside out.

He dropped the cane, and it clattered across the floor.

She sagged in relief, wobbling on her knees as every welt on her body pulsed with the beat of her heart. When she caught her breath, she dragged her gaze to his.

"You're a fucking feast for the eyes, Camila." He stared down at her, no smile, but his dimples flashed.

While life seemed to be returning to his face, she could feel the last trickle of energy draining from her limbs. He caressed her cheek, and she didn't have the strength to pull away. Until his other hand opened his zipper.

Eyes wide, she made a groaning noise against the rubber ball.

His blood-soaked pants slipped down his thighs as he freed his cock. He fisted the length, gliding his hand up and down. A vein bulged along the shaft, the crown swollen and wet with precum. He tilted his head back, and his jaw looked so fucking strong, so powerful shadowed in stubble and clenching harder and harder with each vigorous stroke.

"No teeth, Camila." He pinned her with an intractable glare and released the buckle on the gag.

The instant it fell from her mouth, he thrust past her lips and hit the back of her throat.

She gagged, convulsing and drooling, but he didn't pause or slow.

"Oh fuck." Tremors skated across his thighs as he dragged his length over her tongue. "So fucking good." He circled his hips and gripped the post with one hand while holding on to her head with the other. "Goddamn, I missed your mouth."

Tears blinded her eyes. She choked and sucked air, her hands twisting in the cuffs. She had nowhere to go, couldn't move, couldn't breathe. She sure as hell didn't roll her tongue or do anything to increase his pleasure. She was just a hole pinned to post, a face to brutally fuck.

And he did, every slam of his hips adding another fissure in her memories until the rot seeped out. Van's musky scent. The coarseness of his hair against her nose. The ruthless hammer of his dick in her mouth.

"Stay with me, *mi vida*." Matias gripped her jaw with both hands and forced her eyes to his. "I know what he did to you, and that's not what this is."

Yes, it was! Only so much worse. Van had beaten and tormented her to terrify her into obedience. He'd made her powerless in her pain and humiliated by her pleasure. With Matias, her depraved desires came from a completely different place, the part of her that had never stopped loving him.

He stared at her like he could feel her anguish, as if he longed to take it away. His expression softened, his eyes watchful. *Thoughtful.* So unlike the man who just caned her. Jesus, what the hell was happening?

At least with Van, she'd known he was the enemy every harrowing hour she spent in his attic. But this man? He was the criminal who petrified her and the lover she longed to lay beneath while he did all manner of dirty things to her. It threw her off balance and made her want to lash back with burning revulsion.

Without looking away, he widened his stance, his breaths quickening and fingers tightening against her cheeks. He was close. *Please hurry.*

His body became a piston, flexing and jerking as he found his release. The next thrust sent a shock wave down his thighs. He pulled out then sank deeply, his hands shaking as he shouted to the ceiling. "Fuuuuuck!"

Salty come shot down her throat, and his cock slid free from her lips. She vibrated with a full-body shiver, her lips tingling with his taste and her pussy aching to be touched, filled, pounded.

It had been twelve years since she'd taken him in her mouth. She struggled to make sense of the man staring down at her while her mind clung to the boy who used to guide her lips to him, slowly ease his girth in and out, and encourage her with softly whispered words. The boy who never orgasmed without seeing to her pleasure first.

Now he simply stared down at her as her ass throbbed and her thighs lit with pain, with no relief in sight.

He kicked off his shoes and made fast work of stripping his bloody clothes. Fully nude and partially erect, he removed her cuffs, unlocked the chain from the collar, and lifted her off the floor.

Cradled against the damp skin on his chest, she let her head loll against his shoulder. Every shift against him made the welts on her thighs throb with heat. She couldn't bring herself to do anything but droop in his arms.

He carried her into the bathroom and set her on the toilet. Her bladder released immediately, and a wave of vertigo sent her canting sideways.

His hands caught her shoulders, his broad body crouching in front of her. "You need to eat."

"I need anslers...answers. Shit, I'm slurring." She couldn't make her mind work, every part of her over-stimulated. *Lost to sensations.*

"It's the intensity of the pain." Something slipped behind his eyes, there and gone before she could identify it. He scratched at the blood on his neck. "The adrenaline burns off quickly, but the endorphins linger, creating a *crash.*"

Rage powered through her spent muscles. "How many torture sessions did it take for you to learn that?"

He stared her down as if trying to frighten her. She wanted to smack that look right off his fucking face, but she couldn't summon the strength. So she stared right back, despite the tremble in her chin.

Rather than giving her time to wipe and flush, he scooped her off the toilet and stood her on her feet in the shower.

Soap in hand, he scrubbed them both with clinical efficiency, his expression tight with concentration.

She leaned against his chest, hating that she needed his support to stand, but the floor was tilting. The room darkened. Too dark. She couldn't see. She didn't care.

A towel wrapped around her, then his arms, and

she floated.

She must've passed out, because her eyes blinked open to a fully-dressed Matias. He wore a charcoal suit and a gold button-up that he'd left open at the neck. His dry hair spiked in chaotic strands that fell over his brow.

Lying face up on the bed, she was dressed, too…partly. A stiff, silver corset strangled her torso, and lacy black panties rode high on her ass. She looked around the room. Where were the rest of her clothes?

"I need you to get through the next few hours." His hands slid over her thighs, working a glob of ointment into the cuts.

Dread simmered in her empty stomach. "What's the next few hours?"

"Dinner." He capped the tube of ointment and grabbed her hand, guiding her to the full-length mirror propped in the corner.

"Dinner with who? Where? What am I supposed to wear?" She met his eyes in the mirror.

Standing behind her, he combed fingers through her hair, arranging the length to fall in waves around her shoulders. She'd always considered her hair black, but even semi-damp, it wasn't as dark as his. Same for her complexion. By no means was she pale, but she looked straight-up white next to him.

His frame dwarfed her, twice as wide and a head taller, and now she knew what it felt like to be on the receiving end of that strength. As if his size wasn't intimidating enough, the way he raked his sharp focus over her reflection made her want to retreat to the floor in a fetal position.

He'd shown up in her life out of nowhere, beaten her without purpose, fucked her mouth, then tended to her. He was either pathologically insane or there was something else here at play. Was he putting on an act for someone? For Nico? Or for whoever was on the other side of that camera lens? What was their hold over Matias, and how could she use that to her advantage?

She glanced down at the rows of cuts reddening her thighs. He'd hurt her ruthlessly, callously, but she'd endured the same in Van's attic. It was the slew of unanswered questions that scared her the most, and her mind raced to dissect the last twenty-four hours. But she narrowed her focus to the topic that mattered.

"I put myself here because I want to help people. Women, just like me. I thought…" Her voice wobbled, and as much as she tried, she couldn't drag her eyes to his in the mirror. "I thought you cared about me."

His chest rose and fell heavily behind her, but he said nothing.

"Stop trafficking humans. That's all I want." Her chin trembled. "Please."

"No." One word, crisp and final.

Her heart sank, but she would keep trying, keep pushing for as long as it took.

The metal tag glinted on the collar, catching her attention. She leaned forward, squinting to unscramble the reversed reflection of text.

Don't fuck with my property.

Meaningless. Impersonal. Recyclable. Was that how he viewed whatever this was with her?

"Let's go." He gripped her hand and pulled her toward the exit.

"Wait." She tugged at the corset's bust line, where it rested just above her nipples. "Not like this.

The burnish of his eyes darkened ominously.

"Exactly like this."

CHAPTER 14

Matias had done some godawful shit over the years. Theft, torture, slow agonizing fucking deaths as he brought unfathomable hell upon too many to count. But he'd never deliberately harmed Camila, not the way he had tonight.

With heavy footsteps and a strangling ache in his chest, he led her out of his suite.

Beating the ever-loving shit out of her had not only killed something inside him, it moved him in the opposite direction of his goal. But those marks on her body were necessary.

Forcing himself in her mouth, though? That had been for him.

The sight of her nude body, kneeling, collared, and trembling when he'd opened the door… Fuck! She'd stripped away her fears for him. It was the most seductive thing she could've done.

And he'd repaid her by fucking her throat raw.

Clawing branches of guilt stabbed in his gut. Not only was he a selfish fucking prick, he was pushing her too fast, too soon. All that talk about dominance and her willingness to submit had been ill-timed. While he'd passionately meant every word, he needed to earn her consent first.

Her bare feet padded along the marble as he guided her out of the east wing and through the foyer. Arms clutching her body and shoulders hunched, she seemed to be trying to hold herself together. No doubt she was exhausted, wracked with pain, and fuming fucking mad.

He would've preferred to leave her in the room, but that wasn't how things worked around here. If a cartel member stole a new assault rifle, he showed it off to his buddies. If a lieutenant or drug lord acquired a new slave, he brought her to dinner. The last thing Matias wanted was to raise suspicion, not after what had happened in the west wing tonight.

In the States, the *war on drugs* put crackheads in jail for little baggies and taught grade-schoolers how to sing jingles about the evils of marijuana. But south of the border? The war was real, and narcotics were just a drop in a cartel's bucket.

Matias covered the gamut of criminal commerce, from trafficking weapons and humans to smuggling immigrants and terrorists — all of which made his wallet fat and his dick hard, proving that he was, without question, a very bad man.

The fucked up part? He didn't give a rat's ass, and that made sweeping Camila off her feet one helluva challenge. Figuratively sweeping, of course. He could force her to her knees anytime he wanted. What he couldn't force her to do was offer her soul in supplication.

He wanted her to love every piece of him, even the most depraved and unworthy pieces. *Especially those.* In return, he would protect her soul, cherish it, and put it at peace again.

He rested a hand on the rise of her ass and slipped a finger beneath the tight cinch of the corset. As much as he enjoyed her on her knees, he preferred this — the rigidity of her backbone — as her gorgeous legs stretched to match his strides.

She wielded the kind of inner strength that would intimidate an average man. He fucking loved that about her. So much so he'd spent the last four years shifting the world beneath her feet to ensure that when she finally offered him her soul, she would do so with her integrity and backbone fully intact.

"Will you talk about what happened?" She peeked at him through her lashes as they rounded a bend in the hall. "About what upset you before you..." She pressed her lips together. "Before you came back to the room?"

The hallway was empty, and they hadn't passed another person since exiting his suite. But the walls had ears.

"No." He studied her huge disappointed eyes and reconsidered. "Maybe later."

The grooves in her forehead smoothed away, and she nodded.

Dozens of residents had witnessed his gory walk from the west wing. That kind of thing was commonplace since they frequently brought captives to the compound to be tortured. A rival gang member here. A government official there. Seemed there was always someone begging for a bloody send-off to hell.

Tonight's dismemberment, however, had been one of their own.

His hand clenched against Camila's ass, and she gasped.

He'd known Gerardo since the beginning and never would've suspected their trusted accountant of leaking information to another cartel. Valuable information, such as numbers of bank accounts, names of intermediaries, drug transactions, and payoffs to law enforcement officials. The extent of the damage was still unknown.

He hadn't felt this kind of betrayal since… His chest tightened. The day he'd learned Jhon had set up Camila's abduction. The sick son of a bitch. Matias shook with the need to kill his brother all over again.

The drone of voices and laughter filtered in from the veranda at the end of the hall. It would be a full room tonight since most of the operators were in town—forty or so lieutenants and hitmen.

Dinner was held every night on the veranda, and while business wasn't always conducted at this hour, members needed a damn good excuse to miss it.

It'd been over a decade since he'd walked in there with the slightest twitch of unease, but as the dining area came into view, his insides lit with nervous energy. He glanced down at one of the reasons.

Silken black hair, soulful eyes, and a body that wickedly sinuated the lines of her corset. Camila was the only woman he'd ever loved, and he knew—somewhere beneath her campaign to save the free world—she could love him. *Him,* not the ghost of the boy he'd been.

But he needed her to hang on to her hatred for just a little while longer.

Gripping her arm, he pushed her back against the wall of the empty corridor. She stiffened then launched into a muscle-tensing, kicking, shoving struggle. He wrenched her hands behind her and pressed his weight against her chest.

Anyone who passed by would simply see him enjoying his new slave before dinner.

He touched his mouth to her ear and kept his voice at a whisper. "I won't tell you to trust me. You're not there yet. But I want you to listen."

Her jaw tensed against his. Then she relaxed in his hold.

"Nico knows our history, as do the small few in the inner circle."

"Who's in the inner—?"

"Everyone at my table." He leaned back and watched her eyes dilate as she absorbed the information. Stifling the overwhelming urge to kiss her, he returned his lips to her ear. "The rest of that room is on a *need to know*, and they need to know you're just the slave of the month. A fresh hole to fuck. You mean nothing to me."

He released her and stepped back.

"I fucking despise you." Vicious honesty snarled through her voice and hardened her eyes.

He inwardly winced and smoothed his tone to hide the hurt. "Perfect."

Setting off toward the veranda, he didn't look back.

The cartel had never had a turncoat among their upper ranks, and that was the other reason his stomach was knotted all to hell. No matter how many body parts he'd severed from Gerardo, the only thing the snake confessed was that he hadn't been working alone.

There was another mole on the property, and it could be anyone. A maid, an armed guard, a hired whore, or one of the members sitting out there on the veranda. His opponents were many, but this was a rival cartel, gunning to take them out and steal their business.

Where Nico was the face and the name of the organization, Matias was the spine. Their enemies didn't know this, but a spy among their ranks would know where to hit and how deep to cut. If they realized what Camila meant to him, they would start with her.

Hence the barbaric markings on her legs, the slutty attire, and the hatred in her eyes. They would see an abused slave, a piece of property, and *not* a cherished pet he would trade all the secrets in the world to keep safe.

A hush fell over the dining room as he stepped onto the veranda. Eyes lifted, beer bottles froze at mouths, forks settled against plates, and heads lowered. *Respect.* After twelve violent years, he'd fucking earned it.

He gave a general nod to the congregation of men, and they resumed drinking and conversing.

Ten round tables of six filled the spacious, roofed balcony. Of the sixty seats, only a few were empty. Two or three girls knelt on the floor around each grouping, but some members had wives and mistresses who sat in chairs beside them. There were also a few non-members like Yessica, the resident madam, who'd secured a seat at a table.

As he passed Yessica's chair, she reached out and brushed a hand against his cock, her lips puckering in an air-kiss.

He couldn't hear Camila's footfalls behind him, but the sharp exhalation at his back sounded as if she were choking on smoke and ash.

Without acknowledging his slave, he weaved through the dining room, stopping every few feet to shake a coke-stained hand, pat a tattooed shoulder, and answer questions about his recent visit to the States. Frivolous questions about the weather, the watered-down alcohol, and American pussy.

Other than the wandering eyes and looks of appreciation, they seemed to dismiss Camila as his slave and nothing more. She wasn't restrained like the others on the floor, but no one would question how he kept her in check. His brutal reputation glowed in angry red welts all over her legs and ass.

She remained silent, head down, and spine straight. Her mind, however, was likely spinning off its rails, absorbing every detail of his criminal wonderland. Her thirst for information matched his own, but where he'd unearthed almost everything he needed to know about her, she was still fumbling through the dark.

If she looked hard enough around her, she'd find her answers.

CHAPTER 15

Matias took his time making his rounds on the veranda.
Amid the holstered guns and scarred faces, the usual
laid-back energy circulated through the room, making it
easy to hold a smile as he examined expressions for
deception, studied postures for restlessness, and refused
the drinks offered to him.

Camila followed, sticking close to him, but not too
close. He suspected she wasn't seeking protection from
the heated stares, but instead trying to evaluate every
word spoken and glance exchanged between him and the
other members.

He hadn't bound her hands because he didn't want
to add more discomfort to her beaten body, but she held
her arms behind her anyway. Perhaps it was her slave
training. Or maybe she was trying to keep herself from
drawing the .45 from his shoulder holster and blowing
his brains all over the linen tablecloths.

When he reached the head table, he lowered into
his chair and pointed at the floor beside him. She knelt
without hesitation, and possessive warmth settled in his
chest.

Beside him, Nico frowned at the screen of his
phone, eyebrows furrowing and releasing. The man

might've seemed disinterested in his surroundings, but he was always watching, constantly on high-alert.

Picar, Chispa, and Frizz were already seated at the table, which left one empty chair. Matias could smell Gerardo's death and deceit wafting from it.

"Someone get rid of that." He waved a hand at the vacant seat.

A man in a black suit emerged out of nowhere and carried the chair away.

Nico glanced up from his phone and rubbed a hand over his dark beard. "Taking this personal, *ese*?"

"Don't pretend you're not." Frowning, he snatched the bottle of *aguardiente* from the center tray and poured a glass.

By now, every member in the room had been briefed on Gerardo's betrayal. However, no one outside of the inner circle knew about the mole that still lurked among them.

Matias tossed a casual glance across the veranda. Men of all ages and style of dress sipped from a range of beer to hard liquor. Their preferences for jeans or suits were as diverse as their motivations. The elders tended to be content in their positions, just buying time while protecting their families — their legacies. The younger members took more risks, always searching for greener pastures, hungry for more money and more power. Like Gerardo.

With a shrug, Nico cast his eyes on Camila. "Any success on the other matter?"

Matias looked down at the swollen cuts on her thighs and felt a deep ache to pull her onto his lap. "Success is relative."

Once he owned Camila's heart, he would spend

every day of the rest of his life continually seducing her consent for his brand of fucking.

She didn't seem to be following the conversation, too frozen with horror as she stared at the man and woman on her other side.

Frizz poked a straw through the gap in the threads on his mouth, sucking from a glass filled with a thick, brown puree—probably whatever was on the menu blended into a soup. His other hand stroked the head of the Latina brunette. Tears ran down her face, her eyes dead as she cried silently on her knees beside his chair.

She was one of the slaves brought in with Camila this morning. Nico must've gifted her to Frizz, because she wore Frizz's tragic trademark.

Red X's stitched across the woman's lips, with excess thread dangling from one corner of her mouth like a drool of blood. A needle was tied to the end and swung like a pendulum with each violent shudder of her nude body.

Camila pressed her hands to her stomach. Her shoulders quaked, and she jerked her head toward Matias with accusation and tears in her eyes.

Yes, he'd told her if she fought him, he'd take it out on someone else. That didn't mean he'd protect the slaves from harm.

He bent down and put his mouth beside her ear. "*I didn't do that.*"

She gave him a vicious glare then redirected it to Frizz.

Sure, his corpse-like appearance and fetish with sewn mouths was gruesome, but she wouldn't be so quick to judge if she knew his story.

Frizz ticked his head to the side and wiggled three

fingers at her in greeting.

She choked and shot her gaze to the floor.

Dinner was delivered in courses by servers in black suits, beginning with grilled lamb *chunchullo,* followed by *sancocho,* large pieces of plantain, sliced avocado, and white rice. The rich spicy scent of the tropical stew blended with cigar smoke and the hum of laughter. Easy conversation added a low-key backdrop. Nothing seemed out of place, which made it difficult to keep his guard up.

As Nico discussed the finer details of yesterday's heroin shipment to Orlando, Matias spooned hunks of salty meat from the soup and fed Camila.

She sat on her heels, knees bent in perfect form, and opened her mouth for each bite without contest. But she couldn't hide the pain etching her face.

There was that pinch of guilt again, twisting behind his ribs.

He glanced across the table and met Picar's cloudy eyes. The old doctor didn't speak very good English, but he excelled at deciphering expressions. Gerardo's double-dealings had begun only two days ago, and it had been Picar who'd noticed Gerardo seemed shady.

Leaning to the side, Picar removed something from his bag on the floor and slid it across the table. Matias recognized the color and shape of the pill, and for a moment, he considered the possibility that it could be poison made to look like Vicodin. But Picar was a devoted husband and father. He had nothing to gain and everything to lose if he fucked over one of his own. Besides, if he'd wanted to harm Camila, he would've done it when he injected the sedative on the plane.

Matias pocketed the pill.

DISCLAIM

Between spoonfuls of *sancocho*, Chispa and Nico debated strategies on how to deal with the federal agents that hovered around the compound in El Paso. In the distance, thunder rumbled, drawing Matias' attention to the huge archways and columns that encircled the veranda.

Nightfall blackened the horizon, hushing the chirrup of cicadas, but the sound of drizzling rainfall helped to ease his nerves.

He pushed his chair back and patted his lap, watching Camila out of the corner of his eye.

She grimaced, and her mouthwatering cleavage heaved above the bodice of the corset. She could hate him all she wanted. His lap would be a fuckton more comfortable against her sore muscles than the wood floor.

With a deep breath, she rose, her legs trembling with the effort. As she stepped in front of him, she kept her head lowered and arms hanging loosely at her sides.

He turned her to face the table, and sweet mother, her round flawless backside flexed inches away. He wanted to shred the panties, bend her over the table, and sink his teeth in. Followed by his cock.

Heat surged along his shaft as he imagined how tight that little hole would feel clenched around his thrusts. He could do it, fuck her ass right here, and not a goddamn person in this room would raise a brow.

The way into her heart was without a doubt a path of tribulation. But where he put his mouth and cock wasn't the key factor in obtaining his goal. It was the ability to connect with her on a fundamental level.

Curling his fingers over the black lace on her hips, he drew her toward him and settled her on his thigh.

173

She sat rigidly, hissing from the pain, elbows locked against her sides, and legs shaking. With an arm around her waist, he pulled her back against his chest and scooted the chair forward, sliding her lower half beneath the edge of the table top.

Stiff as a board, she refused to relax against his reclined body. Her breaths sharpened, expanding her rib cage and testing the seams of the corset.

She really wasn't going to appreciate his hands on her, but anyone outside of his table would expect a public display of groping to be the only reason he moved her to his lap.

Over the years, he'd brought slaves to dinner, not for his pleasure, but for the sole purpose of tormenting them. After Camila's disappearance, he'd taken a special interest in slavery. He so badly wanted to sit her down and explain his involvement. Hell, he wanted to explain everything. But she wasn't ready.

Beneath the concealment of the table, he cupped her pussy over the panties. His other hand rested lightly against her throat as he made a shushing noise at her ear.

She drew several more breaths. Then her muscles began to loosen against his legs and chest. An eternal moment later, she let her head fall back on his shoulder. He released her neck.

Her soft hair brushed against his throat, and the heat of her body seeped through the threads of his suit. Christ, he'd waited so fucking long for this, to feel the beat of her heart against his, protected in his home, and held in his arms.

With great reluctance, he removed his hand from between her legs, trailing fingers gingerly around the welts on her thigh. His chest squeezed with regret, and hers inflated with a held breath. Shifting his hand toward his pocket, he slipped the pill between two fingers.

"Open your mouth," he whispered at her ear. "For the pain."

Her instant obedience was a testament to how much she was hurting.

He placed the pill on her tongue and traced the plump flesh of her bottom lip. Then he offered her a glass of water, which she drank greedily.

He didn't have to glance up at the room to know he was being watched. Yessica, for one, would spend the entire evening trying to gauge his interest in Camila. Others would simply be looking for weaknesses. They might work for the same team, but they would kill one another if it meant moving up in the ranks. And Matias held a covetous position.

Giving a slave a pill, however, wasn't uncommon. Ecstasy, roofies, any number of trance-like drugs made unwilling partners more malleable.

He returned her water glass to the table and slid his hand beneath the front of her panties. Her abdomen quivered, and her thighs clenched together like a vise.

"Open," he whispered firmly.

She parted her legs, and he caressed the delicate flesh, slowly, teasingly.

"So I've been thinking…" Chispa stroked the thin mustache on his lip. "We need to work on our PR."

"*Se necesita un cerebro para pensar,*" Picar muttered.

"Isn't it past your bedtime, old man?" Chispa grinned.

Picar held up a fist with his pinkie and index finger extended like bull horns. The gesture was as old as Colombia, meaning *Your wife's a cheating whore.*

Matias chuckled. Since Chispa wasn't married, he could interpret it however he wanted.

"You need to loosen up, Picar." Chispa folded his twiggy arms behind his head. "Sometimes you gotta let your ball sac hang like two cacay nuts in a wet baggie to know you're alive."

Given Picar's stony glare, his next gesture would involve making a fist shape out of his strongest hand and slamming it into Chispa's face.

"You two need to get a room." Matias roamed his fingers lazily across Camila's soft folds.

She relaxed against him, breaths even and silent and eyes lowered. He guessed most of that was an act. The painkiller wouldn't have kicked in yet, and he knew she wouldn't miss an opportunity to be as invisible as possible while studying every person on the veranda.

He turned his attention to Chispa. "What did you have in mind for PR?"

Soliciting low-rank falcons was an aggravation, but they were the eyes and ears of the streets and the best access to information on the activities of the police, military, and rival gangs. They also propagated fear. Scaring the *picadas* out of the general public kept people in line and out of the way.

Matias slid his finger through moisture. Warm, wet *arousal*. His cock hardened, suddenly and painfully. His breathing sped up as he stroked deeper, circling the entrance of her pussy without penetrating.

Her thigh kicked up and bumped the underside of the table, rattling dishes.

No one at the table spared her a passing glance, but Matias vibrated with excitement. He knew her mind was fighting this, fighting him, but her body still loved his touch.

"We need a motto." Chispa tapped a fist on the table.

"How about *Give us your shit or we'll kill you*," Nico said with a gleam of amusement in his eyes.

Her breath hitched.

"Or…" Matias stroked his other hand down her arm, smiling. "*There are some things that can't be smuggled. For everything else, there's the Restrepos.*"

"Not bad, not bad." Chispa nodded thoughtfully.

Picar swiped a gnarled finger across his eyebrow, his expression dead serious. "*Armas got?*"

"Got guns?" Chispa howled with laughter.

The entire inner circle joined in, hooting and slapping the table.

When they finally settled down, Chispa snorted. "I've got one. *The Quicker Fucker Upper.*"

The laughter began again.

Matias enjoyed nights like this. A departure from the stress of business to drink and shoot the shit. Camila appeared to be focused solely on what his hand was doing, but he knew she was listening, picking apart every word and judging the whole lot of them.

Someday she would sit here among them as his equal and join in the camaraderie. Hopefully, someday soon.

For now, he was content with just holding her while reacquainting himself with her body. As much as he wanted to sink his fingers inside her, he'd rather show her how much pleasure he could give her in private, when he could focus on only her and not on the countless others who might be scrutinizing his motivations.

Frizz reclined in his chair and whistled a song. The

table fell quiet, listening as he continued the tune.

"Is that...?" Chispa made a disgusted face. "'Dead Babies' by Alice Cooper? You want *Dead Babies* to be our motto?"

A smirk pulled at strings on Frizz's pale lips.

"Frizz..." Matias rubbed his free hand across his scowl. "Why'd you have to go there?"

Frizz shrugged.

"Moving on..." Chispa shook with an exaggerated shudder. "We also need a logo."

"I'm bored with this conversation." Nico scowled into his beer.

"Dude. All the other cartels have one." Chispa leaned forward, his dark eyes animated. "We can hand out monogrammed switchblades and put up a Facebook Fan page."

"Facebook," Matias said dryly. "What're you going to post? Pictures of dismembered corpses, status updates on our assault weapons sales, and incriminating selfies?"

"Yes, exactly!" Chispa pointed a finger at him, laughing. "Think about how many *likes* we'd get with that shit? Everyone knows mutilated bodies get more shares than adorable duckling pictures."

Because dumbass kids loved to brag about their cartel affiliations and celebrate murderous gangs like sports teams, going so far as to take time out of their midday gunfights to post photos of themselves posing with guns.

"I think we're freaking them out." Chispa lifted his chin at Camila and the Latina on the floor.

He was probably only referencing Camila, but included both women to avoid suspicion. Everyone in the inner circle knew what she meant to Matias and what his plans were for her.

"Nah." Matias tugged on a lock of her hair. "They know we're just fucking around."

She grew limper, more relaxed on his lap, probably fighting sleep. He moved his hand to her waist and simply held her. Her body had endured an intense amount of strain over the past twenty-four hours, and he needed to put her to bed.

After the last course was served, the veranda thinned out, leaving half-empty tables cluttered with full ashtrays and discarded beer bottles. It was time to go.

"Is there room on this lap for me?" Yessica's voice clawed like nails over his shoulder.

Camila roused against him, lifting her head and blinking heavy eyelids as she stared at Yessica.

"Calling it a night." Matias shifted Camila off his lap, holding on to her hips as she wobbled.

"So early?" Yessica propped a hand on her cocked hip. "Send that one off to her room" — she waved a hand at Camila — "and come have a dip in the pool with me."

"We're not dressed for swimming." He tossed back the last of his *aguardiente* and stood.

"Since when do you and I need clothes?" She tilted her head and pushed out her mouth to emulate a puffy-lipped pout.

Her duck face detracted from her pretty features.

Camila stood motionless beside him with her hands fisted at her sides and a twitch in her eye. She was upset, but it had nothing to do with Yessica. Her attention was glued to Frizz's slave, her body leaning subtly toward the woman on the floor as if she wanted to swoop in and protect.

"Goodnight, Yessica." He curled his fingers around

Camila's upper arm and dragged her away from the table.

"I'll walk with you." Nico joined his side.

They strolled in silence toward the west wing. Camila dragged her feet, seemingly losing strength with every step thanks to the painkiller.

Matias' hands flexed with the overwhelming urge to carry her. But preferential treatment wouldn't have gone unnoticed in the busy halls as residents geared up for the usual late night parties in the various sections of the estate.

When he reached the wooden doors to his rooms and found the corridor empty, he lifted her listless body into his arms. She rolled against his chest, and a night's worth of tension uncoiled inside him.

Nico stepped in front of the retinal scanner and opened the door for him. Then Nico trailed him through the expansive living space and into the bedroom.

By the time he laid her on the bed, she was out. Breaths deep and even. Eyelids relaxed. Lashes fanning over her cheeks. Gorgeous as sin.

He rolled her to her stomach and sat on the edge of the mattress to tackle the ties of the corset.

Nico stood at the foot of the bed, watching intently, his natural scowl darkening the edges of his mouth.

"Well?" Matias unraveled the knot at her tailbone and worked his way up her spine, slowly loosening the cinch.

"We still don't know if Gerardo revealed—"

Matias made a slashing gesture with his fingers across his neck and aimed a pointed glare at Camila. He was almost positive she was asleep, but the *almost* was too big a risk. He wasn't ready for her to know this secret, and the gritty details of this conversation could wait until morning.

"We'll just keep doing what we're doing." He reached the last tie on her back and wiggled the corset loose around her ribs. "If the mole knows, he or she will expose it soon enough."

"Camila's going to find out, regardless." Nico clasped his hands behind his back. "I still don't understand how you intend on keeping this from her while she's living here, *parce*."

There were so many things she didn't know, like the fact that he'd had a brother by blood or why her parents died. She didn't know the reason he'd been ripped away from her or what his role was in the cartel.

Soon, she would learn that the reason she was here was not to stop human trafficking, but to uncover the truth.

"Trust me." Matias stood and removed his suit jacket, his hands confident and mind clear.

"I trust you unequivocally with our lives." Nico's eyes flashed, his voice sharp. "That doesn't mean I have to like this asinine plan."

"As you've said for the millionth time."

"Just making sure we understand one another." Nico glanced at Camila's sleeping form, and his scowl bent into a half-scowl. "*Que duermas bien.*"

"*Buenas noches.*"

As the tread of Nico's shoes retreated and the doors to the suite shut behind him, Matias removed the rest of his clothes and locked his gun in the closet. Then he turned his attention to the woman in his bed.

Fifteen minutes later, she lay naked beneath the sheets with fresh ointment on her thighs. She'd slept through it all and continued to sleep as he removed the collar and set it in the drawer beside the bed. Then he tucked in behind her, his chest against her back, and slowly explored every exquisite bend, dip, and slender bone of her body.

Despite the ache in his cock, he was happier than he'd been since the last time he held her like this.

He closed his eyes in memory, and the grass tickled his back. The sun warmed his face. Her skin pressed against his, legs entangled, with the aroma of citrus and earth in the air.

Back then he had to worry about Venomous Lemonous chasing them apart with a stick.

He opened his eyes and brushed his lips against the delicate shell of her ear.

Now he faced a different opponent, one less tangible but far angrier. Her heart might've been locked up like a fortress, but it wasn't impenetrable.

He shut off the light and curled his body tightly around hers.

Twelve years, he'd imagined waking to the smell of sex and contentment and *her* tangled in the sheets around him. Tomorrow morning, that dream would become a reality. And after that?

He had a lot of fucking work to do.

CHAPTER 16

Camila woke to the caress of fingers on her hip and rapid breaths falling against her nape. She blinked in the darkness and held herself immobile on her side, arms hugging the pillow beneath her head, her own breath parked in her throat.

Fingertips trailed along her waist, traced the grooves of her ribs, and lingered on the underside of her breast. Her breath escaped, but she kept it slow and stable, feigning sleep. The same instinct that had *never* saved her in Van's attic.

Did she actually think she'd make it through the night without Matias fucking her? She'd hoped. Like *press my goddamn hands together and pray to whoever's listening* hoped. After he'd beaten her, fucked her face, and fed her on the floor beside a woman with stitched lips, her libido had shriveled up and died.

But she knew better than to hope. He'd already stripped her naked — the corset, panties, and collar gone. Not even the sheet covered her.

Every hair on her body stood up, screaming at her to bite, choke, kick, and run the fuck away. Could she get past the eye scanner? Slip around the guards? Hijack the helicopter? No chance in hell she'd survive the Amazon rainforest.

She was stuck here. *I put myself here.*

Her plan had been ten kinds of fucked in the head.

Masculine heat saturated her back, his legs intertwined with hers, the hard muscles in his thighs and calves flexing with his rapid breaths. And his hand shook, fucking vibrated as he cupped and kneaded her breast.

How long had he been awake? Touching her and working himself into this panting, trembling state?

Maybe his hands shook with all the women he fucked, but at gut level, she didn't believe it.

He wasn't taking. Taking would've been fingers digging, pinching, claiming. No, shaking meant restraint.

If the circumstances had been different, she would've been shaking with breathy enthusiasm. He was the one she'd always fantasized about during sex, but now that she was in his bed, her stomach knotted.

Moving only her eyes, she sought out the clock on the bedside table. *3:13 AM.*

As if the passing of minutes, days, years even mattered. Time might as well have been frozen. Like her lungs. And her life.

He lowered his hand to her hipbone, fingers curling against the juncture of her groin and thigh, reaching, stretching toward her pussy.

Her pulse sprinted, and her mouth went dry. She kept her thighs pinched together and squeezed her eyes shut. *I don't want this. God, please, I don't want to be forced.*

The welts on her skin stung each time she tensed. What if he decided to be really cruel and dig his fingers against them? She'd probably pass out.

With his hand on her hip, he ground against her in

tight, slow rolling motions. The hair below his abs rubbed against her ass, and every hard naked inch of him twitched — his chest, his legs, his swollen erection. Goose bumps shivered down her spine.

She feared him as all monsters were meant to be feared in the dark. Only he wasn't under the bed. He was in it, his breath on her neck, skin against skin, and he was hungry.

If she looked over her shoulder, she'd find a monster with eyes of golden green, wearing a face she once caressed and kissed and loved. With hair she'd stroked with intimate affection, the strands in every shade of the deepest black — the color of his soul.

"I know you're awake," he said in a rumbling voice and lowered his lips to her neck, whiskers scratching and teeth scraping.

"I don't want this." Her throat closed up, strangling her voice. "Please, Matias."

He bit her earlobe then suckled the sting. "I'll change your mind."

Not happening. Her mind hurdled along a course that ended with a punch to the esophagus, his skull slamming against the marble floor repeatedly, and castration. She couldn't escape, but maybe a chokehold would help him understand how fucking wrong it was to take an unwilling woman.

With a deep breath, she twisted toward him and swung to hook her arms around his neck.

He didn't move, but something caught her hands, holding them to the pillow. The fuck? She tried to yank free to no avail, and her pulse detonated.

The mattress bounced as he leaned toward the side table. The lamp clicked on, and a dim glow illuminated the bed.

Lying on her back, she angled her neck and spotted two skinny ropes between her hands and the headboard. Her blood turned cold.

She knew restraints intimately, had fought them and lost too many times. No amount of jerking and yanking would help her, and the ties on her wrists were the kind that constricted under pressure, the braided nylon so thin it blended with the white sheets. No wonder she hadn't noticed it when she woke.

"Don't test the knots." He crawled over her, easily restraining her kicking legs as he settled his hips between her thighs. Then he braced his elbows on either side of her head, studying her with a predator's vigilance. "They'll only cinch tighter and cut off the blood to your hands."

But her legs weren't tied. She relaxed her arms above her head, her hands curling into fists. "Why am I restrained? I'm not—"

"I want you this way."

"I have chlamydia and…and syphilis and—"

"You're clean." He rocked against her, gliding the rigid length of his cock along her mound, breaths slipping, and lids falling half-mast. "We both are."

She turned her head away. "You don't know—"

"Picar drew our blood and took swab tests on the plane." He gripped her face and forced her gaze back to his. "I've never had sex without a condom."

Neither had she, and she sure as fuck didn't want to start now.

Except she had always wanted this, with him, without anything between them.

Not like this.

"Christ, Camila, I've waited—" His fingers slid into her hair and dug against her scalp, eyes searching and voice hoarse. "I've waited an eternity for this."

Molten gold bled into emerald rings around his irises, the bones of his face sharp across his cheeks, square around his jaw, and exquisitely Matias. Women everywhere probably fell at his feet—with or without his command. How many had sampled his warm skin and tasted his firm lips?

Her heart twisted. Why did she care? She didn't, but it still hurt like hell lying beneath him and staring into eyes that had once meant the world to her. And it was only going to get worse. He was going to fuck her and make this ugly goddamn mess of feelings a thousand times uglier and more painful.

A hot ember sat in her throat. She pinched her lips together, refusing to give voice to her weakness. There was no sane reason for her to feel anything but pure fucking rancor.

Yeah, *that*. The anger, the murderous hatred… She grabbed hold of it and let it consume her. Snapping her teeth together, she crunched her abdominals and kicked a leg up and over his shoulder. With a twist of her hips, she landed a knee hard against his jaw, using his shock to drive him to the mattress and into a cry-angle choke.

But without her arms, she couldn't stop him from trapping her leg and rotating it. With her kneecap against his torso and the pressure of his upper body against his grip, her leg snapped straight, hyper-extending the knee joint.

She cried out against the unbearable agony, and the cuts on her legs protested against the strain. She slapped her hands on the bed, thrashing her arms against the rope.

When he released her, the pain ebbed. Until he tossed her onto her back and crushed her with two-hundred-plus pounds of ravenous need.

"Fighting me like that?" He buried his face in her neck. "A *huge* turn on." His hands frantically stroked every inch of her he could reach. "You're killing me."

She shook with volcanic rage. "Then die already!"

A muscle bounced in his jaw, and his eyes flickered with...hurt?

Fuck his feelings. She dug her heels into the mattress and tried to buck off his heavy-ass body.

He let her struggle for the span of a few heartbeats, while he rubbed and caressed and kissed her skin, the fucking bastard. Then without warning, he wrapped a hand around her throat and pressed hard against her windpipe, instantly subduing her.

"If you kick your legs again..." He stared at her like a nocturnal predator, a creature at home in the shadows of hell. "I'll restrain them to the bed, spread eagle."

Flashes of white blotted out his scowl. She couldn't breathe beneath his hand, couldn't speak, but she opened her mouth in a plea for air.

He let go, and she gulped, lungs heaving. She yanked against the rope, unable to pull her hands to her aching throat.

As she caught her breath, he returned his attention to her body, fingers roaming, his mouth feeding on her skin, licking and biting.

"You've always been beautiful." He kissed his way toward her pussy. "Your confidence. Your spirit. Your body." He nibbled on her hipbone. "Look at you. Fuck,

Camila. You can't possibly be real."

She deflated beneath him, and tears gathered in her eyes. She couldn't fight against his words. Why was she even fighting at all? She'd known this would happen before she left Texas.

Because it's Matias.

The same Matias who chained her to a post and caned her. And he could do it again if she continued to push his patience.

She blinked, and the tears knocked free, trickling down her temples.

His shoulders lowered between her legs, his hands spreading her thighs wide and baring her cunt for his gaze. But he didn't look down, instead holding her gaze for a long, uncomfortable moment. Then his focus drifted to the tracks of her tears.

His expression clouded with an emotion she'd never seen there, not once in the countless times he'd witnessed her cry as a child. Was it guilt? Pity?

Whatever it was softened his features and wrinkled his brow, giving him a brooding, contemplative visage. It only added to his exotic beauty, the stubble on his face dark and dangerous against a complexion that glowed like bronze in the sun. His allure was so intoxicating it was painful to look at him.

"Don't pity me, Matias." She rolled her shoulders against the mattress, stretched her fingers to grip the bottom edge of the wooden headboard, and forced her gaze to his. "It's the wrong feeling for what's happening here."

The muscles in his face tightened, all softness gone. "Pity is not what I'm feeling right now."

He dipped his head between her legs and inhaled

deeply. His fingers clamped tighter around the backs of her thighs as he smelled her, dragged his nose through her folds, then buried his mouth.

She arched her back, stunned by the assault of sensations. It took several seconds for her lower body to rouse, but when it did, her pussy throbbed hard and greedily, soaking her with a rush of arousal.

He moaned against her cunt, his tongue strong and firm as it lapped and swirled and dipped inside.

Shame coiled in her belly, and a whimper escaped her lips. This wasn't supposed to feel good. It was wrong, sick, fucked up in the worst way possible.

His eyes stayed on her, his kiss aggressive, frantic, and so damn sexual. Then his fingers joined in, stabbing, curling, and stealing her air. His muscled shoulders contracted with his frenzied movements, pressing against the backs of her legs as he bit and sucked her delicate flesh.

Each lick was a rasping whisper, liquefying everything in its path as it penetrated deep, coaxing and seducing the dark cravings inside her. She didn't want this. She didn't. Yet her entire body hummed with pleasure. It had never been this good. Ever. Not when he was younger, not with anyone, and she despised him most of all for that.

His groaning kiss might've felt like heaven, but his demon tongue was an enticement to hell. This was worse than him fucking her dry. He was turning her body against her, using their familiar intimacy to make her wet and twist her up.

Arms above her head, legs spread, and nipples erect in the lazy breeze from the ceiling fan, her traitorous body melted beneath the sensual slide of his mouth. She focused on the fan blades, watching them go round and round — *whoosh, whoosh, whoosh* — in rhythm with her heart and the throb against his tongue.

Eventually, his lashes lowered, concealing the predatory glow in his eyes. She found relief in that, until his fingers strummed against her thigh, tightening and loosening, as if he were trying to hide the shaking. He used to do that when they were teenagers, quaking and twitching his hands when he was overly excited and trying not to come.

Her chest constricted. He was a rancid poison, injecting himself into her system. Circulating through her blood. Breaking her down and rotting her from the inside out.

But the poison thinned as she climbed. He floated her up and halfway down again. The smell of his rotten intent still lingered, but underneath, she tasted ecstasy. Because he'd brought her to the cliff, and though she fought against the fall, his tongue was too talented, knew her body too well, and he pushed her over.

She moaned as blissful shocks burst across her nerve endings, spreading outward, trembling her legs, and wiping her mind. She spun through a vortex of unimaginable pleasure where she didn't need air or legs or wings, because he was there, catching her, holding her, and carrying her through the haze. He was with her, protecting. *Mine.*

Her arms twisted in the ropes as she clung to the lingering sensations, quivering and gasping to catch her breath.

When she finally came down, the weight of what just happened pressed against her chest.

He'd made her come, and it left her feeling more

alive than she'd ever felt in her life.

And raw. So fucking raw it hurt in places she couldn't identify or reach.

Why hadn't he just raped her without all the foreplay and eye contact? He could've fucked her, gotten off on whatever sick shit he was into, then left her the fuck alone to lick her wounds. She could survive physical pain. But this...this godawful ache inside her? She didn't even know where to start.

"How long has it been?" He kissed the hood of her clit and leaned up on his elbows.

"How long for what?" she snapped.

"Since someone ate your pussy."

"A week ago." She considered leaving it at that, but since he wanted to stick his fucking nose in her business... "Larry McGregor had skills."

"What?" he bellowed and shot up off the bed, his face contorted and fiery red. He swung an arm out and sent the lamp crashing to the floor, spinning the glowing light through the room. "You fucked that worthless son of a bitch?"

"No." Heart thundering, she slammed her legs together and scooted toward the headboard. "I let him go down on me so I could—" *Shit*. She'd said too much.

"So you could put him in a chokehold," he said, voice cold and deadly calm. "Same thing you just tried on me."

Technically, it was a different chokehold, but she wasn't about to point that out.

He stood with his back to her, the brawn of his ass hard and flexed like a gladiator preparing for battle. She'd seen his nude body so many times, but that was *before*. This body was so much bigger, his thighs cut and dusted with dark hair, his waist narrow and widening into defined shoulders, and his spine straight and confident.

He was power and danger and persuasion, and she was a quivering blob tied to his bed.

Scrubbing a hand over his head, he dragged it down his face, his profile angled downward as he glared at the glowing exposed bulb on the broken lamp. The heave of his back slowed, and he seemed to be reigning in his temper.

He sat on the edge of the bed, his cock still hard and jutting upward as he shifted his gaze to her. "When was the last time you had sex?"

She hesitated. Did the truth really matter? Would it reveal a weakness or some hidden psychological condition he could use against her? She didn't think so. "Four years ago."

"Four—" He choked, his head tilting and expression perplexed.

No, not perplexed. *Possessive.*

Maybe she should've lied.

He crawled toward her with a feral glint in his eyes. She tucked her legs close to her body, but he caught her ankles and dragged her down the mattress on her back.

"Four years ago," he said quietly and wedged his hips between her thighs.

The last time she'd felt his weight on her, he'd been on the thin side of sexy, but now he was stacked with compact muscle, his shoulders beautifully sculpted, and his torso a rippling slab of intimidation. It was like being pinned by a fallen tree. With eight-pack abs.

With a hand in her hair, his other reached down to

cup her pussy. His mouth parted with the acceleration of his breaths as he sank two fingers in, teasing and tormenting.

"What about you?" Her voice shivered as she tried to block out the warmth and pressure of his hand.

"I'll tell you." He brushed his lips against hers. "But not right now."

Anger sparked in her veins. Typical evasive Matias, telling her exactly nothing.

He sucked on her bottom lip, his fingers curling lazily inside her. "We always talked about our first time together, how perfect it would be."

She didn't want that memory here. It was too sweet, too fragile. "Don't do this."

"This isn't going to be perfect. It's going to be ugly and conflicted, because you can't get out of that damn head of yours, and I'm too fucking worked up to draw this out. But when I'm inside you, it will always be honest."

Honest? She buried her fingernails into her palms. "Fuck you."

"In a second." He slid his fingers out of her and gripped his cock, seating himself at her opening. Then he held her head in his hands and rested his forehead against hers. "I need you with me, *mi vida*. Forget about all the bullshit and just focus on us."

"There is no—"

He kissed her, forcibly, hungrily, his mouth rough and wet and persistent. She tasted herself on his lips, a despicable reminder that she'd orgasmed on his forked tongue.

His hips rocked, just enough to press his tip inside, and stopped. His legs shook, and his fingers curled against her scalp as if he were struggling with the need to slam all the way in.

"It's just you and me in this bed." He licked her lips and kissed the corners of her mouth. "No history. No future. Nothing but *right now* and *us*."

The intensity of his eyes seemed to say so much more than his words. His pupils pulsed, dark and bottomless but not empty. There was something there, way down deep. Something huge and profound. She peered in, all the way inside his soul, and she felt it instantly. They both did, their breaths hitching as one.

In that frozen space of time, she saw not the monster that sold women into slavery, but the boy who had kissed all her scrapes and scratches, taught her how to face her fears, and promised her he would never let her fall. The bond she had with that boy was still alive, right here in this bed. It was more mature now, scarier, stronger, but it held her just as tightly, demanding she give herself in return, and she wanted that. Desperately.

She nodded her consent, a reflex that immediately warped into regret, then panic, but it was too late.

He thrust, his head falling to her shoulder. "Ahhh, God. So tight." He worked his hips, inching through her wetness and pushing, pushing, to fill her fully. "Fuck, let me in."

Desire thickened his voice and shivered through her. She squeezed her fingers against the headboard and tried to relax her inner muscles, but he was huge, his girth stretching and invading until, finally, he was buried balls deep and panting.

"Oh fuck, Camila. Fuck." His chest vibrating with a deep groan. "Hold on."

Then he fucked her, and she did hold on—to the

headboard. Her emotions, however, were slipping through her fingers. She tried to separate, tried not to feel anything as he pounded inside her, his hands everywhere, caressing her chest, her hips, her legs. But it was the potency of his eyes, his gaze never leaving hers, that held her there, commanding her to stay.

He pressed her knees to her shoulders, deepening the angle as he hammered in and out, faster, harder, his passion unlike anything she'd ever experienced. Pleasure fired through her nerve endings, and she tried to pretend she felt nothing, tried to block it all out.

But she felt everything—every slide of his cock and curl of heat, the spasmodic quivers across her skin, and the needy grip of her pussy. Her body wanted this, and she hated it. Hated herself.

He kissed her urgently between heaving breaths, his grunts and groans unrestrained and his body a contracting tireless machine.

With his tongue in her mouth and his bruising grip on her legs, he slammed against the back of her cunt, ignoring the flinch of her body. He took her harshly, fervently, as if he were fucking her with every torment, dedication, and dream in his soul.

This was what was missing in all her one-night stands. This driving vehemence to give and take, the devastating risk to own or disclaim, to just toss it all out there, consequences be damned. She had no defense against this. No amount of shutting down or tensing up could overpower the force of his gaze or the urgency in which he consumed her.

Each drugging stroke tore at the surface of her shields, burrowing into her secret places and unleashing dark things—filthy desires of being taken, used, dominated, and...loved. Exactly like this.

The rope prevented her from moving her hands. His strength stopped her from lowering her legs. The steadiness in his gaze forced her to look at him, and in his eyes, she saw herself in a way that terrified her.

She was a powerless woman beneath a powerful man. She couldn't dictate positions and speeds or the degree of pain and pleasure. She wasn't having sex to wheedle information, control the results, or search for meaning in her life.

Yet there was power in just *being*, in letting it all go as he made the rules, led the movements, and determined the purpose. It felt...*right*. Amid the ugly, conflicted honesty of what was really happening, it was perfect.

She didn't just feel him between her legs. She felt him everywhere, ripping her apart and putting her back together in a way that served him. But somehow, it served her, too.

He kissed her, and she lost herself in the thirsty strokes of his tongue, the heat of his breaths, and the promise of his hunger. She kissed the boy who haunted her and the man who filled her with dread. And somewhere between the shadows of her past and her future, she surrendered.

Whether he saw it on her face or felt it in her kiss, he knew, his eyes sparkling with flickering fire. His hands cupped her head, his fingers shaking and hips ramming as he groaned through labored breaths.

"Swear to God, Camila. I'm trying not to come." He slammed his mouth against hers and devoured her lips with frenzied bites and licks. "I'm not stopping until you're trembling around my cock." He ground against her clit and hardened his voice. "Come with me."

197

His command triggered a swell of electric heat between her legs. He captured her moan in his mouth, kissing her deeply, assertively, and undoing her completely.

She broke the kiss with a hoarse gasp as the orgasm rolled over her in pounding waves. He rode her through it and followed her off the edge with something akin to awe widening his eyes and slacking his mouth. Without releasing her from his gaze, he came with a rumbling groan that faded into breathlessness as he slowly dragged his cock in and out, drawing out his pleasure.

Remnant vibrations twitched and jerked between them, their breaths jagged, bodies damp with sweat, and his cock still inside her. Once her pulse returned to normal and her lungs caught up, he loosened the knots on her arms and kissed each wrist with heartbreaking affection.

His tenderness made her want impossible things. Happy endings didn't exist in a cartel compound that housed slaves with sewn lips. She was here for them, not him, and he knew it. So why the devotion in his expression? Why bother giving her pleasure at all? Maybe he genuinely loved her. Or maybe he wanted to destroy her. Both options terrified the hell out of her.

She tensed to push him away, his weight suddenly too hot and heavy, but her liquid bones refused to move.

"Camila." He studied her face for a moment then sighed, and pulled out of her.

He left the bed, but didn't go far, disappearing into the bathroom and returning with a washcloth.

Numb and suspicious, she lay still while he gently cleaned between her legs. Then he tossed the towel on the floor, rolled her on her side, and curled around her possessively with his chest against her back.

Caring for her. Cuddling with her. Her chest tingled with warmth, longing for more.

It was too much. Too wrong. She wriggled and shoved. "Why are you doing this?"

He refused her the distance she needed, holding her against him with an arm hooked around her ribs and a leg wedged between her thighs.

"I've been deprived of your touch for twelve years." He found her hand in the bedding, twined their fingers together, and kissed her shoulder. "Now that you're finally here, I'll deny myself nothing."

"If I fight and tell you *no*, will you fuck me anyway? Would you have raped me tonight?"

"Yes."

It wasn't his answer that shot a violent tremor through her body. It was the way he delivered it—swift, cold, and with unwavering conviction.

"Shh. I know you're scared." He tucked her hands against her chest and massaged the blood back into her fingers.

"Because you're a raping, slave-trading monster."

"Yes, but once you fall in love with a monster, you no longer fear them."

CHAPTER 17

Sunlight warmed Camila's legs through the bedsheets. She lifted her gaze toward the glass wall and squinted at the brilliant blue backdrop. Maybe Tate or one of the others was looking up at that very moment, beneath the very same sky, thinking of ways to find her. The likelihood that she'd never see them again made her heart sink, but determination charged through it, energizing her blood.

Except she couldn't move. She could barely breathe in the solid arms that restrained her more effectively than chain or rope.

"When are we leaving this bed?" She pushed against Matias' shoulder, fingers grazing the tattooed branches.

"Someday, never," he said in a sleepy voice, pulling her impossibly closer, chest to chest.

He'd woken earlier and fucked her in the spooning position. She hadn't told him *no,* hadn't said a word when he'd roused her from sleep, rocked slowly into her from behind, and refused to come until she did. And she did come, with the same snarl of emotions as the first time.

But that was a couple of hours ago. Now he

seemed content to do nothing but hold her. It felt almost…safe. *Almost.*

The dull pain pulsing deep beneath the welts on her thighs and butt helped her remember what he was capable of.

"Don't you have henchmen to recruit and women to sell?" She lifted her gaze to his.

"You're supposed to be a slave, not a slave driver." His voice was stern, but the glimmer in his eyes betrayed his amusement.

She guessed her own expression wobbled somewhere between *go to hell* and *oh well.* Truth was, she preferred this…this mellow, amicable Matias. He reminded her of the boy she used to laze around and laugh with. If she kept him in a jovial mood, maybe he'd open up enough to talk to her. Civil conversation would be major progress after yesterday.

As her bladder twitched with pressure, an odd thought struck. "I haven't seen you use the bathroom since I've been here."

"I went while you were sleeping. Even brushed my teeth." He touched his lips to her forehead. "Are you concerned about my bathroom habits?"

"No, it's just…" With her arm resting along his ribs, she traced a finger across the bottom edge of his pectoral, which felt a whole lot like steel. "I guess…I don't know. It'd be nice to see you do something human."

"Look closer then." He lifted her chin with a knuckle and gave her a good look at the hazel swirls of life in his eyes. "I feel pain and hope and fear, just like you." He moved his hand from her face to hold up his wrist with the pockmarked scar. "To this day, I'm afraid of big black dogs. I take melatonin because I have trouble sleeping. I get indigestion when I eat too many *empanadas*."

Her heart thudded and twisted.

"And I dreamt about this, Camila." He touched her cheek oh-so delicately with the pads of his fingers. "I dreamt about waking up with you for as long as I can remember."

That was… *Wow*. He was sharing, and she liked it. Liked it so much it made her uneasy and fluttery, her lips teetering on the verge of a weird smile.

With a ragged inhale, she lowered her gaze to the dense stubble on his jaw. "Remember when we sneaked into the faculty room at school and photocopied our faces?"

"That's not the only thing we photocopied."

"That was all you." She jabbed a finger at his chest, fighting a grin. "*You* yanked your pants down and sat your butt cheeks on the glass top. My poor innocent eyes."

"You looked?" He leaned back, eyebrows arched.

"Well, um…yeah." It'd been her sixth grade year, so they'd been twelve and fourteen. She'd seen him nude as a child, but that day had been the first time she'd ogled him in all his postpubescent glory. "I don't really remember."

"You're lying." He bit her neck playfully. "You definitely remember."

A full-blown smile stretched her cheeks as she recalled her shock. He'd looked like a man to her then. All that pubic hair—black like the hair on his head. And balls that hung low beneath a cock she'd fantasized about every night for the next three years. To think, he'd waited until she was fifteen before he let her touch him beneath his boxers.

She shrugged. "Too bad we didn't save the evidence. When the Xerox machine spit out that grainy picture of your ass...Oh God, do you remember? I've never laughed so hard in my life."

"Yeah, you peed your pants." His shoulders shook with laughter.

"Down my legs and all over my flip-flops. I had to wear your gym shorts home." She groaned. "I was so embarrassed you saw that."

"Why?" His brow furrowed. "Did I say something—?"

"No, you were cool about it. You were always..." *So tender and protective and perfect in every way.* "You had my back."

She sighed, holding on to the memory and her smile.

"This is what I missed more than anything else." He trailed a finger across the curve of her lips. "You're so goddamn beautiful, Camila, but when you smile, you light up the whole fucking world."

Her lips fell beneath his finger, her chest tightening with the weight of the huge, indescribable thing between them. She couldn't pretend this bond didn't exist. It'd been there her entire life. Even through twelve years of separation, she never stopped sensing it, thinking about it, and now, it sang with his words and vibrated with his touch.

But it was also murky and distorted with ugly truths. He'd purchased her, beaten her against a post, and refused to talk about his job. He was a slave trader, yet he'd helped her dispose of the bodies of slave buyers.

Because he cared about her? He was an infuriating contradiction. As much as she wanted to luxuriate in their reconnection, doing so would be a death sentence for the women he preyed on next.

She needed to be smart about it. Nurture the bond. Manipulate it. Keep her fucking heart focused on the reason she was here. Except she wasn't a manipulative person. She was better than that, and at one time, he'd been a better person, too.

She lifted her hand and clutched his. Their fingers entwined, grasping and shooting tingles up her arm.

With a sudden shift that made her gasp, he yanked her up the bed and put them at eye level on their sides, fingers laced between them and his arm locked around her back.

"I know you felt it." He searched her face, lips parted. "Last night when I was inside you, and now. You feel *us*."

Her chest ached. She tried not to feel anything at all, gulping down her breaths to stay quiet.

"Just stop for a second." He rested his forehead against hers. "Give yourself this, Camila. Let it happen."

"I can't." She leaned her head away. "It's like dangling a prize in a trap."

She desperately wanted to reach for it, to hold him, knowing if she did he'd break her, painfully and irreparably.

"What's the prize?" He watched her intently.

"Happiness without fear. Love without cruelty." She closed her eyes, voice raw with honesty. "You without slavery."

He let go of her fingers and smothered her against him in an embrace that buried her face in his neck. She wished she could see his expression, but his deep, steady breaths told her enough.

"You like my answer." She matched the pace of his breaths as if she wasn't trembling inside.

"Mm."

"What is *Mm*? I don't understand you. You seem to want this, *us*, but you also want your disgusting profession. You can't have both, Matias. Don't you get it? As long as you're enslaving women, I will never stop fighting."

"You're wrong."

"Then explain it."

"Not yet." He pressed his lips to the top of her head.

"Why not?"

"You need to see it for yourself."

Fucking impossible. "I need to pee." She squirmed against him.

He kissed along her hairline, his thumb stroking against her spine. With her nose against his throat, the warm scent of his skin overwhelmed her senses.

She told herself he smelled like rusted chains and broken dreams. "I really need to—"

"Go." He lifted the weight of his arm with a sigh and rolled to his back. "Return to the bed, and I'll tell you what happened in the west wing yesterday."

Images surfaced of him covered in blood, a cane in his fist, and death in his eyes. The cuts on her legs twinged in memory, and she shivered so hard she bit the inside of her cheek.

She slipped from the bed and scanned the floor. Every inch of marble was spotless—his bloody clothes, the broken lamp, corset, and panties nowhere in sight.

Without anything to wear, she made her way toward the bathroom. As she walked along the glass wall that led to the balcony, she spotted another balcony jutting from a separate entrance in the curve of the building. After hiking through the compound, she had a sense of its enormity, but seeing all that exterior glass covering multiple floors and balconies, it reminded her of an extravagant hotel with a steel beam infrastructure.

A table sat on the other balcony, the same one that connected to his living room where she'd scarfed down sandwiches yesterday. Now it was covered with domed plates and pitchers of juice. Her stomach grumbled.

If someone had brought breakfast into the suite and cleaned the bedroom, they had access to come and go. Were the servants around here armed? Maybe it was someone who could be overpowered and get her past the eye scanner.

She paused at the bathroom doorway and turned toward Matias.

He lay in a tangle of sheets around his waist, the white bedding aglow against his tawny skin and black hair. With his arms folded behind his head, he looked peaceful, almost harmless. But the way he studied her, his expression covetous and his eyes roaming her from head to toe, she knew there wasn't a harmless fiber beneath all that muscle.

"How many people have access to your suite?" She held her hands at her sides, fighting the urge to cover herself. "You and…?"

"Three others. Nico, Anacardo—"

"Anacardo?"

How did they take themselves seriously with these nicknames? *Picar, Chispa,* and *Anacardo* translated to

Chop, Spark, and Cashew. Apparently, the use of sobriquets was a thing among narco-killers?

"He manages my domestic stuff—food, laundry, cleaning." His gaze rose to her face. "You're the third person."

"Me?" A flush of excitement tingled through her, quickly followed by suspicion.

No way would he make it that easy to escape. It wasn't like he handed over keys to the helicopter. Or a training manual on how to fly it.

"I can get past the scanner things?" She shifted her attention to the hall beyond the doorway. If she found a computer or phone, she could contact Tate.

"Your eyes were scanned before you woke yesterday. You have access to certain areas of the property, including my suite."

"Can I go outside?"

"Of course." With his legs spread wide and hands laced behind his head, he didn't seem to have a care in the world. "I thought you had to pee."

She slipped into the bathroom and used the toilet, buzzing with the new information. While she brushed her teeth—with his toothbrush because *fuck him* – she entertained scenarios of freeing all the slaves in the compound and leading them through the rainforest like a Rambo woman. She needed a badass rifle and a bandanna headband for maximum effect. Oh, and some survival skills, because she didn't know shit about trekking through two million square miles of jungle.

The dangers that lurked amid those majestic palms were so beyond anything she'd prepared for. Not to mention, her escape would provoke a manhunt. If Matias was willing to let her go outside, the odds of getting out were probably not in her favor.

But her goal had never been to save herself or existing slaves. She'd come here to stop them from taking more women. If she couldn't persuade the cartel to end that business, she would have to kill them.

Nausea curled in the pit of her stomach.

She rinsed out her mouth and stared at the wide brown eyes in the mirror. The anguish in those eyes was everything. Matias could be the most atrocious man on the planet, but there was no use lying to herself. She didn't have the emotional strength to end his life. Not now. Not ever. As inconvenient as that was, it loosened some of the knots inside her.

When she returned to the bed, he'd shifted into a half-sitting position, his back leaning against a stack of pillows and a tube of ointment in his hand.

As she crawled toward him on the mattress, he tracked her movements and patted his thigh. His ever-present desire to be all up in her personal space might've been a coercive tactic, but there was more to it. Maybe that was the key. She just needed to find a way to peel back the layers, starting with his obvious attraction to her.

Reaching for his waist, she dragged the sheet off with a quiver of fear darting down her spine. She pushed through it, lifting a leg over his nude lower body and straddling his partial erection.

His hands gripped her ass before she sat down, holding her upright on her knees.

Confused, she looked down at his swelling dick.

"Hold still." He squeezed a dollop of ointment into his palms and rubbed the icy balm over the backs of her thighs.

Instant relief shivered into her skin, and she swayed, dropping her hands on his chest.

"This is new." She twitched her fingers, indicating the sprinkle of dark hair on his sternum.

"So is this." He met her eyes as his caress glided over her ass, making wide circles to encompass the curves of her hips.

"Not the scrawny girl you remember?"

"You were never scrawny." The corner of his mouth lifted, and his gaze wandered over her body. "I spent the majority of my teen years hiding a chubby from you."

"You did?"

"You have no idea." He added more ointment to his hands and massaged the fronts of her thighs. "Last night..." His chest rose, fell. "The empty chair at our table belonged to a close friend."

The sudden somberness in his tone stiffened her muscles. She held still, focused on the movements of his hands, willing him to continue talking.

After a nerve-racking pause, he told her about Gerardo's betrayal, the information leaked to a rival cartel, the dismemberment, the blood, and the spy who still lived among them. His voice became rougher, angrier, with every word, leaving her cold long after he fell silent.

With the nudge of his hands, he lowered her to sit back on his thighs, his semi-flaccid cock resting in the *V* of her legs.

"There are other secrets." His jaw shifted. "Valuable secrets that Gerardo may or may not have released."

"Like what?" She liked this, him sharing, her

listening, even if the subject matter fucked with her blood pressure.

"The kind no one talks about." He looked her firmly in the eye. "In time, you'll see things as they really are, and when you do, I want you to come to me and no one else."

Warning bells sounded in her head, raising the hairs on her nape.

Maybe he was working against the cartel? Except he seemed to be genuinely hurt by Gerardo's betrayal. What the hell was he hiding? And who was he hiding it from?

They need to know you're just the slave of the month. A fresh hole to fuck. You mean nothing to me.

She'd assumed he was just being a dick last night, but now... "Is your paranoia because of the spy or are there others here you don't trust?"

"Trust is earned, and we have a process that vets members and residents. Backgrounds, ranks, and positions are factors in granting access to certain information, but a lot of it is based purely on gut."

"Is that your job? To vet cartel members?"

"One of them." His blank expression lacked all the clues she was attempting to draw from him.

"And your gut steered you wrong with Gerardo."

He nodded, and somehow that tiny admission to making a mistake made him seem more human, more Matias.

His attention lowered to the raised bumps on her thighs. "Now I'm erring on the side of caution, even if it means risking more of your hatred." He gingerly trailed a finger over the worst cut. "I can repair the pain I cause you, but I can't bring you back to life."

"Someone wants to kill me?" A chill coursed, wild and panicky, through her limbs.

"To get to me, they might try."

Did that mean last night, with the cane...? She stared down at the welts.

I know what he did to you, and that's not what this is.

Her throat thickened. "You beat me and scared me so I would look like an abused slave instead of your...your...whatever I am?"

"Yes. But don't misunderstand me." His expression morphed into cast iron and sexual heat. "I get off on bringing you pleasure while you're trembling with fear."

"What am I to you?" She glanced at the rope near the headboard and returned to him. "Am I a slave or something else?"

He cocked his head, his hands absently stroking her legs. "You're my life, *mi vida.*"

She swallowed. "Do you beat other slaves like that?"

"You're not asking the right questions."

Jesus, fuck. What questions? Like who did he beat? How? When? Where?

She looked up. "Why do you do it? Why do you capture and torture women? Is it a kinky fetish? Or is this really just a business to you?"

"Right question." His eyes hardened. "Wrong answer."

"*Qué mierda!* Yesterday, you said this is business, supply and demand, and you don't make the rules."

"It is a business and so much more than that."

"Then tell me!"

"The answer is right in front of you." He dumped her onto the mattress and stood, his voice rising to a shout. "All you have to do is fucking look!"

"I am looking, but you're a goddamn black hole." She leapt off the bed, snatched the sheet, and wrapped it around her.

He growled and stormed toward the closet.

She chased after him. "How about you give me a straight answer instead of this mind-fuck game you're playing?"

"Game?" He whirled on her and put his face in hers. "This is *real*. You and me. No games. No mindfuck. If you put aside all the other shit, you'd know with absolute certainty that every breath I take, that my fucking purpose in all of this is for you."

His choked words, stiff neck, and pained, over-bright eyes stopped her heart. He stared at her as if he were desperate for her to not only hear him, but to see what he wasn't saying.

Why wouldn't he just tell her? Was someone listening?

Her eyes widened, and she jerked her head toward the camera on the ceiling. "Who's watching us?"

"I'm the only person who has access to that feed."

"What about listening—"

"There are no listening devices in my suite."

Well, shit. She pulled the sheet tighter around her chest and met his gaze. "Fine. I'll keep looking and figure out what you're not telling me."

"Where are you going to look?" His breathing started to return to normal, the tension in his face dissolving.

"All the answers are here, right?" She touched a finger to the outer corner of his eye.

"*Muy bien,* my beautiful girl."

He bent closer and brushed his mouth against hers. Another brush and another, until his tongue swept past her lips. The gentle kiss deepened, turning breathy and earnest.

His hands sank into her hair, and his erection jabbed at her stomach. But she didn't pull away, her tongue licking his with all the hope he'd planted in her. He'd opened up, and while she was more confused now than before, he'd given her enough to believe that there was something more than a monster behind those golden eyes.

He broke the kiss and cupped her neck. "We need to get dressed and eat. Then I'll give you a tour of the property."

Her pulse kicked up with excitement as he led her into the closet, activating a sensor light in the ceiling.

Rows of clothes on hangers and cubbies lined the walls on the left and right. Straight ahead was another door, this one with an eye scanner.

"What's behind that door?" She nodded at it.

"Skeletons." He grabbed a pair of jeans and pulled them on.

Her mind conjured a torture chamber with dead slaves hanging from chains on the walls. She shuddered, cursing her overactive imagination. "Do I have access to your skeletons?"

"Not until you're ready." He waved a hand at the racks of clothes on the left wall. "That's your side."

Kicking at the sheet that draped her body, she investigated the extensive wardrobe. Cocktails dresses, casual wear, and lingerie filled the space, all with tags and in her size.

She mentally ran through the last twenty-four

hours. She'd spent most of that time in this suite.

"When was all this brought in?" She narrowed her eyes at him.

"Does it matter?" He slipped a blue t-shirt over his head.

"Yeah, it really does. Was it here before I arrived?"

"What does your gut tell you?" He touched a fingerprint scanner on a small safe in the wall, unlocking it and removing the Glock he carried in his waistband.

"My gut tells me…" She studied his face, watching for a reaction. "You expected me to show up as a slave with Van."

He seated the gun in the back of his jeans and stared at her, eyes and mouth giving nothing away.

"I can't figure out how, though." She snatched jean shorts from a cubby and held them up with a questioning brow.

"You can wear what you want during the day, but I choose your attire for dinner."

Fair enough. "The thing with Larry…that was all kind of up in the air." She dropped the sheet and slipped on the first bra and panties she found—white lacy things—then the shorts. "I followed him for months, knew he was involved in the trade, but I didn't know exactly how I was going to infiltrate until I tortured him."

He leaned against a shelf, legs crossed at the ankles, arms folded over his chest, regarding her with an unreadable expression.

"You must've been watching me for a while." Her stomach clenched with that realization. "But you couldn't have known my plan until I called you that night to pick up Larry's body. And even then, I don't know how you knew." She put on a brown tank top while keeping her focus on him, examining every twitch in his body. "That would've given you two days to stock the closet with clothes in my size, which is really creepy, by the way."

And immensely satisfying. How many men had that kind of attention to detail?

Stalkers did. And serial killers. Oh, and psychopaths.

She rubbed the back of her neck. "So am I warm on any of that?"

"You're hot." A panty-soaking smile filled his face. "Really fucking hot."

"You're not going to make this easy on me, are you?"

"The best rewards are the hardest to earn." He straightened and held out his hand. "Let's eat."

Thirty minutes later, she swallowed down the last bite of egg soup and leaned back in the chair on the balcony. It was the best *changua* she'd ever tasted, filling every crevice in her stomach with rich, milky warmth.

A temperate breeze stirred the humidity to a comfortable level, and the landscape pulsed with the sway of large fronds and the bellow of frogs. But the high-pitched, repeating shrills in the distance sounded like something was dying.

"What's that noise?" She reached for her coffee mug.

"Tinamous." He wiped his mouth with a linen napkin. "Mountain hens. They lay freaky alien-looking eggs with an unusual iridescent shimmer that changes color at different angles."

"So basically they lay eggs that scream, *Hey, look over here! Eat me!*"

The corner of his mouth curled up.

"Are they safe to eat?" She wasn't still considering going Rambo, but a backup plan wouldn't hurt.

"The birds or the eggs?"

"Both?"

"Yes." He studied her for an unnerving moment. "Finding food would be the least of your worries out there."

"Same could be said for in here." She pushed away the soup bowl and met his eyes. "You never carry a phone, yet you always answered when I called."

"I don't need one anymore." His timbre deepened. "You're here now."

He'd only carried a phone for her? She folded her arms across her chest, refusing to be sucked in by the sentiment in that.

"Every device on this property is locked down." He touched his fingers together like a steeple. "To make a call or access the Internet, two-factor authentication is required — a pin number and fingerprint scan."

Fuck, there went that idea. She pushed her shoulders back. "I want to call my friends and let them know I'm alive."

"Not yet."

Her pulse jumped. "Does the *yet* mean there might be a *yes*?"

"Yes."

"*Gracias.*" Now for the hard question. "Can I get a private meeting with Nico?"

"No." His tone was final, his direct eye contact impenetrable.

"Because you're afraid to ask him or because you don't want me to talk to him?"

"Neither."

Interesting. He'd said the inner circle knew about her history with him and that he kept nothing from them. Maybe he just didn't want to be left out of the meeting. Damn men and their egos. She couldn't think of another way to go about this, though. It wasn't like she could snuggle up to Nico's chair at dinner and demand a meeting from the kingpin. Not without drawing the attention of forty scary-as-fuck hitmen.

"Okay." She sipped her *tinto,* savoring the syrupy cinnamon-coffee concoction. "I want an audience with you and Nico. In private. No one needs to know about it."

He leaned forward, chewing a bite of bacon, studying her. "Why?"

"To present arguments against human trafficking. Offer alternatives. A different perspective."

"You think you can win him to your way of thinking?" His eyes squinted, lit with an inner glow.

"I want the opportunity to try."

Determination and heart—that was what she was made of. If she could interest Nico in the cause, it might distract him from the effect.

If not, she'd paint the glass walls with his blood.

"All right." Matias leaned back in the chair with a pensive look softening his features. "I'll think about it."

"Today?"

"Later."

Later didn't come when he gave her a tour of the property and made her kneel in a corset beside his chair at dinner on the veranda. There was no later when he fucked her against the post, in the bed, and any damn place he pleased.

The wait for later plodded into days. Days twisted

into unbearable impatience. But time was inconsequential, so she bade it by being a timid little slave when they were outside of the suite, watching and analyzing. When they were alone, she shared her past with him and didn't push when he refused to discuss the present and future.

Later ended up being two weeks later, but the wait paid off.

He took her to meet with Nico.

CHAPTER 18

Matias strode along the path on the east side of the property, his boots crunching gravel and an anxious hum in his veins. The gray sky chased away some of the afternoon heat, but the humidity hung on, pasting his thin Henley to his skin.

He released the buttons at his neck and glanced at the woman walking beside him.

A sheen of perspiration glistened on Camila's adorable nose, her eyes sharp and focused on the path ahead. Her long strides exuded self-possession, though her rigid posture suggested she was beating herself with a thousand over-analyzing thoughts.

He hated the distance between them whenever they stepped outside of his suite. It was necessary, but she took it to the next damn level, refusing to look at him or acknowledge him unless he commanded it.

With an irritated huff, she pulled on the thick leather collar around her throat. While it was there as a statement for others, every time he put it on her, it made his dick hard. Even so, he always removed it when they were alone. Someday, she would choose to wear one, a permanent one—for her and him only, fuck everyone else.

"Camila."

The command in his tone lifted those huge soulful eyes. He remembered the way they'd smoldered this morning, dazed with desire, glassy with uncertainty, her thighs trembling and hips rocking as he licked her cunt and fingered her to orgasm.

"I assume you have a speech prepared for this meeting." He clasped his hands behind his back, head forward, and watched her at the edge of his vision.

Her eyebrows pulled together as she gazed back at the estate, zeroing in on windows near Nico's rooms. "Isn't Nico's office that way?"

She scanned the perimeter of trees, pausing on each of the three armed guards who trailed out of earshot. There were five more chaperons she couldn't see. If she knew they were following, she didn't let on.

Matias' suite offered the most privacy, but he wanted this meeting to take place in his personal, most cherished location on the property. He'd never led her this deep into the jungle. She had no idea this little piece of heaven existed.

He'd debated whether or not it was too early to show it to her, that maybe he was revealing his hand too soon. It was her rejection he feared the most. If she didn't give him the reaction he longed for…

He'd man the fuck up and keep working on her.

"We're meeting him off-site." He steered her to the left at a fork in the trail, leading her deeper into the shadowed jungle.

The gravel thinned to dirt, softening their steps, and the thick canopy of smooth oval leaves created a cool shade. He'd taken her all over the property since she'd arrived, never leaving her side when they stepped out of his private rooms. She'd sulked about that for the first few days, as if she'd expected him to give her security access to the entire estate and just let her roam free.

As long as there was still a threat living among them, she wouldn't be leaving his sight.

He stepped closer to her, resting a hand on the curve of her lower back. "Did you prepare a rhetoric of bullet points and pretentious language for Nico?"

The neckline of her t-shirt had slipped off her shoulder, exposing her bra strap. He wanted to set his teeth in the delicate dip between the collar and her ear and bite down just to hear her breath catch.

"I couldn't pull off pretentious if I tried." Her jaw clenched, released. "Never received my high school diploma, remember?"

Several times over the last two weeks, she'd spoken late into the night about her captivity with Van Quiso. Though Matias had learned the details years ago, she didn't know that. It killed him to hear the specifics of her abuse all over again, especially whispered in her soft voice, but he'd held her tightly in bed, absorbing every word, every shiver and teary-eyed glance she shared with him.

She'd also told him things he hadn't known, like how she completed the remainder of her high school curriculum on-line and lamented the fact that she couldn't receive a diploma since she was still considered missing.

While her tenacity never ceased to impress him, it twisted a hellacious knot in his stomach. No matter what she said in this meeting, Nico was going to challenge her.

To what end would she go to succeed in her mission?

"You're going to wing it, then?" His chest thickened with all the things he wanted to tell her.

"I'm going to stand before him as a slave, not a politician."

"That's your strategy? Persuade him with your heart?"

"I know it sounds illogical. I mean, he's the Restrepo kingpin, for fuck's sake." She rolled her lips between her teeth. "But he's also a person, and people aren't rooted in logic. We're creatures of emotion, bristling with selfish wants, preconceptions, and brutality. But inside every man is possibility." She lifted a stiff shoulder. "I'll just talk to him in terms of what he wants."

While everything she said was smart and fascinating and maybe even partly correct, it sat in his gut like a red hot coal.

He slammed to a stop. "You didn't take that approach with me."

"Because you already had what you wanted." She spun toward him, with a finger hooked under the collar and resentment in her eyes.

He grabbed her throat. "*This*"—he squeezed the leather against her neck—"is fucking window dressing, and you know it. I want the real thing, Camila. I want your submissive soul, sighing and replete, in my hands."

Her face paled as she gasped and clawed at his fingers around her throat. "I can't…I won't survive that."

Goddammit, how could her brilliant mind get this so fucking wrong?

"Not only will you live, you'll be more alive than you've ever been." He withdrew his grip and strode up the path without waiting for her.

When he reached the stone wall of their destination, she caught up with him, arms crossed over her chest, gaze lowered, demeanor subdued. Scaring her hadn't been his intention. Or maybe it had been. Either way, he wanted the light to return to her eyes.

He paused at a heavy wooden door, watching her closely. His hands felt sweaty, his throat parched and scratchy.

"What is this place?" Her gaze skittered along the eight-foot-high rock wall, tracing the length left to right where it faded into the jungle in both directions.

"Go ahead." He gestured at the retinal scanner that was bolted into the stone. "This is the only entrance. The wall keeps out most of the critters, but we still have problems with monkeys and large birds."

His pulse hammered as she leveled her eye with the security panel. He rubbed his palms on his jeans as she pushed open the door. Then he followed her in, clinging to her every movement as she gazed upon the landscape that had taken him a decade to recreate.

Her hands flew to her chest, her gait faltering mid-stride beside the first row of orange trees. Her head swung right, toward the acre that housed kumquat, tangerine, grapefruit, and lime trees.

"Holy shit." Her mouth fell open, and her steps sped up, still unsteady but her excitement palpable.

She walked beneath the limbs, her hand reaching upward. He remained at her side, devouring the bright glow of her eyes, the tremble in her chin, and tentative way she brushed her fingers over the leaves as if she couldn't believe they were real.

She halted suddenly, her attention directed straight ahead on the lemon grove. Her breath cut off. Then she gulped raggedly, again and again, her hand lifting to cover her mouth as the other reached out, blindly searching for his.

He caught her fingers, lacing them with his own, and inhaled the deepest, fullest breath he'd ever taken.

Four hundred flowering trees spread across the secluded five-acre grove, infusing every particle in the air with tranquil memories. There was only one scent as sweet as the fragrance of citrus blossoms, only one sight as beautiful, and she was finally here.

Her wide, unblinking eyes took in the delicate buds, the vibrant colors of the fruit, and the fertilized soil, and he knew she appreciated the labor and passion in a way that had connected them since they were small children. She appreciated his tribute to her.

"How did you—? You did all this…" She stepped toward the nearest lemon tree and gripped tighter to his hand, pulling him with her as she studied the healthy branches. "They're… God, they must be ten years old?"

"Yes." His voice broke, and he cleared it. "Yeah, I've been at it a while. But I've had help. Hired one of the best citrus farmers in Florida about eight years ago."

"Nico let you do this? I mean…wow. There must be four or five acres here."

"Five acres. Four hundred trees. And Nico…" A smile pulled at his mouth. "He questions everything I do."

Most of his arguments with the other man had been over the necessity of the eight-foot wall.

She didn't let go of his hand as she entered the lane between two rows of lemon trees, scattering the bees that hovered around the blooms. Twisted branches arced over the path and tangled together, forming a living trellis of deep green foliage and dangling fruit.

When she tilted her head upward, a tear glistened on her cheek. She swatted it away with a soft smile on her lips.

"It's just like home. The planting pattern. The archway. Every detail." She stopped walking and turned toward him, her gaze on the inked leaves on his forearm, her fingers squeezing tighter around his. "You did this because you missed it?"

He lifted her chin with his free hand and held her gaze. "I missed *you.*"

She pulled her head back, and her focus slipped away, seeking the trees, the ground, their entwined hands. When she returned to his eyes, hers were wet with regret. But there was hope there, too.

"A five-acre grove recreating our childhood. Because you missed me." She touched his jaw, the line of his throat, her gaze following the movement. "I understand you were taken by the Restrepos, and I assume you didn't rise to the top-level in the span of a year. So you must've started as a lackey? Is that why you didn't come back for me?"

"Camila—"

"I was there, Matias. Right there in that grove waiting for you for a year before..." She swallowed. "Before it was too late."

"I couldn't." He released her hand and crushed her against him, holding her face to his chest as his insides rioted with invidious memories. "The men who found me—"

"*Found* you?"

Fuck. He should've chosen a different word. "The people who came for me that day made threats."

"What kind of threats?"

She tried to lift her head, but he held her in place so she wouldn't see the vulnerability in his expression. He was having a hell of a time evening his voice.

"They threatened everyone I cared about." He pressed a kiss to her head. "Specifically you."

She stiffened against him. "Why? What did they want?"

He couldn't explain that part without unraveling every fucking thing he'd tried so hard to protect her from. "Camila, there are things I can't tell—"

Her fist slammed against his abs, not with any kind of force, but hard enough to break free of his hold. She spun away, her face emblazoned with rage.

"You knew about my family." She balled her hands at her sides. "The day I called you, when I escaped, you told me not to contact them." Her eyes narrowed. "Why didn't you tell me they were dead?"

"Lower your voice." He folded his hands behind his back and widened his stance.

She glanced around, but the rows of trees blocked her view of the wall. "Is someone here?"

"No one has access to the grove besides Nico, the caretaker, you, and me."

"Is Nico meeting us here?" She pulled on her ear nervously, her attention darting through the branches, as if she were torn between pursuing this conversation and focusing on her end goal.

"He's waiting for us in the gazebo." He turned and pointed down the path through the lemon trees. "Just through there."

"We probably shouldn't keep him waiting then." She moved to walk past him but paused, her gaze lingering on his face.

She'd spent the past two weeks watching everything and everyone around her. There were slaves on the property, in her periphery, kneeling beside her at dinner, all of them gagged in her presence to prevent communication. But just as he'd hoped, the bulk of her searching had been focused on him, on what he knew and what he was hiding.

He needed her to not only see the truth for herself, but to see *him,* the man she was meant to love.

"Your uncle died in that fire, with my family." With trembling fingers, she brushed the tattoo on his forearm.

It wasn't a question, so he remained still and quiet beneath her rare touch.

"I'm sorry." She dropped her hand, letting it hang at her side. "I've been so angry, so suspicious about what happened to them, I've lost sight of the fact that you lost him, too."

He didn't have a regretful bone in his body with regard to that old man. But as far as she knew, his parents had died when he was an infant and the uncle who had raised him on the grove was the only family he'd had. None of that was true.

With an arm raised in the direction of the gazebo, he waited for her to move then followed behind.

Her jean-clad legs carried her out of the lemon grove, the subtle sway of her ass unintentionally seductive in her determination. Despite the confident way she carried herself, he suspected each step twisted her up with nerves. He wished he could carry her out of there and save them both a lot of potential pain.

They turned the corner, and the gazebo came into

view. Seated at the table, Nico glanced up from his phone, his brows heavy over dark eyes and mouth turned downward in his usual relaxed expression.

She looked back at Matias, her brown eyes hesitant. Then she blinked, and her focus cleared, her features hardening.

He molded his face into something that resembled self-assurance. He was ninety-nine percent certain he knew how this would end. But it was that one-percent that sank his stomach with dread.

CHAPTER 19

A swarm of bees took flight in Camila's stomach as she stepped into the gazebo and met Nico's demoralizing glare. He rarely looked into her eyes, as in not once since she arrived in Colombia. But sometimes she sensed him watching. Like it was his job to watch her without her noticing.

His elusive observance was so much better than this in-her-face staring.

"Matias' little happy place suits you." Nico's gaze subtly skimmed over her body and returned to her eyes, his Colombian inflection falling flat. "You're much more enticing than the fruit."

Okay, that drained her blood straight to her feet. It was a joke, right? Nico might've kept tabs on her, but he'd never given her so much as a glimmer of interest.

His apathy was frightening, and he exuded it as if deliberately playing it to his advantage. Even now, his arms hung limply at his sides, his posture relaxed behind the wrought iron table, almost bored, as his gaze wandered away.

"She likes the grove." Matias stepped around her and pulled out an empty chair, gesturing for her to sit.

She loved the grove. Loved it so much, in fact, she

didn't want Nico anywhere near it.

Sitting as directed, she entertained a silly thought about plucking one of the ripe fruits and traipsing the endless maze of paths through the trees. It was how she'd spent her childhood, letting the twisty arms of the branches guide her, never without a juicy snack in her hand.

"I should hope so, *ese*." Nico focused on an errant crease in his black suit pants, smoothing it with a thumb. "You spent an embarrassing amount of time and money growing shit that can't be injected, smoked, snorted, or smuggled."

"That sounds dangerously close to complaining." Matias lowered into the chair beside her, putting her between him and Nico. Folding his hands on the table, he leaned in, eyes on Nico. "You done?"

"I haven't decided." Nico shrugged.

Both men grinned, sharing a cryptic moment of silence. As their smiles faded, they continued to stare at one another. Communicating? Whatever it was hinted at a strange kind of simultaneous trust between them. Their postures remained at ease, their eyes bright. Until Nico shifted to her.

"So you wanted to meet with me to discuss the cartel's affairs?" His tone dripped with censure, expression hardening in a blink, erasing all traces of humanity.

Just like that, he looked every bit the kingpin. Her insides churned.

He didn't belong here in this magical place, where the trees fluttered with vitality, trilling with birds, and saturating the air with the quiet, aphrodisiac sweetness of orange blossoms. Matias had created a miniature version of her beloved sanctuary, knitting her memories into the soil and coaxing them to life. The resurrected ambiance filled her with a sense of innocence, an unexpected warmth of heart that made her want to turn to him with openness and affection.

And hope.

He could tell her a million times he wanted her, needed her, that her disappearance had gutted him, whatever. It was just words. But this…this nostalgic place was infinitely more moving. It was a proclamation that couldn't be cheated or faked.

The maturity of the trees alone proved that a decade had been dedicated to growing it, to nurturing something much too wistful for a cartel compound. Sure, he hired out the labor, but his touch was in the tiniest details, such as the planting patterns, the types of fruiting trees, the yellow twine her *papá* had used to support the saplings, and the unusual way the secondary limbs were pruned — exactly how Venomous Lemonous had taught them.

No one else could've replicated her memories with such painstaking and sentimental precision. She knew without a doubt Matias had been here since the plants germinated and participated in every step of their life cycle.

Because he'd missed her.

It left her feeling groundless, dizzy, and utterly seduced by the idea of *him and her*, by the beauty and promise it bestowed. She could envision living here, being whatever Matias willed her to be, if it meant spending time in this place, recreating stolen moments with him, and cultivating dreams.

Because she'd missed him, too. So fucking much it

made her chest hurt.

Maybe that was why he'd chosen this location for the meeting. To bewitch her so thoroughly she'd forget the reason she was here.

Tightening her muscles, she angled her body to face Nico and gave him strong eye contact.

"You might see me as just a slave, but I'm not controlled by fear." She crossed her legs at the knees, the position pulling the jeans tight across her ass as she rested her hands on the table. "I've killed people, and I'm intimately familiar with human trafficking." She paused. "Can I call you Nico?"

"Please do." His eyes flickered, and it might've been curiosity.

"I'm not an accountant, Nico, but I find it hard to believe the slave trade yields as much profit as, say, your drug smuggling ventures. First off, the slaves I've seen on the property are my age. Some are even older. I doubt any of them are virgins."

He exchanged a look with Matias, and she would've given anything to know what was going on beneath their blank expressions.

"Not that I'm suggesting you capture young girls." Her foot twitched restlessly. She stilled it. "I'm just questioning why you capture and sell people at all."

"Tell us your theories," Matias said. Elbow on the table, he rested his jaw on loosely curled fingers, the liquid gold of his eyes sharp around the edges.

Twisting her thoughts to that of a criminal, she voiced a cut and dry hypothesis about how they sought to gain market share and remain competitive against rival gangs and drug lords. She talked out of her ass while trying to keep her opinions on a cohesive level, brainstorming ideas they could relate to, and maintaining an eager, unbiased tone, like she was a fucking marketing consultant for the cartel.

It was ludicrous, listening to herself suggest how they could broaden their drugs and weapons smuggling to other countries, like Australia. But in her desperate mind, smuggling those things were a lesser evil than selling innocent lives.

Neither of them interrupted her long-winded pitch. Matias nodded at some of her points and lifted his eyebrows at others. She avoided those hazel eyes, though, as well as the symmetrical beauty of his flawless face. She tried not to glance at him at all for fear he'd derail her, command her with a look, and make her want things that didn't belong in this conversation.

Focusing on Nico wasn't any easier. He was dangerously handsome, or at least, he would've been if he didn't look so scowly and disinterested all the time. Didn't matter where he was or what he was doing, he gave the impression that he wanted to be somewhere else, like he was too goddamn important for the world around him.

Other than the night Van delivered her to them, Nico always wore a suit. The crisp black fabrics and collared shirts that opened at the neck projected an urbane, cultured persona that was only mildly intimidating if taken at face value. It was what he hid beneath the casual arrogance that had her carefully choosing her words.

Was she talking to a psychopath? An empty soul? A man who didn't rationalize his own behavior? If he was a man at all, then somewhere in there was a heart.

Steeling her backbone, she changed gears without

segue and launched into her experience as Van's captive.

"He locked me in a coffin-like box for the first twenty-four hours, wearing only rope around my hands and feet and a ring gag in my mouth."

Her cheeks twinged in memory at the godawful stretching, and sweat beaded between her breasts. With a waver in her voice, she told them how Van fucked that ring gag over and over in the days that followed, how he beat her, spit on her, and stripped her of every ounce of hope and courage, all while refusing to speak to her beyond the bark of his commands. *Kneel, open, suck, cry…*

"I was there a week before Liv stepped in." Camila folded her trembling hands on her lap. "She introduced herself as a deliverer and said I was to be trained as a slave and sold as a piece of property."

She rushed on, giving voice to the worst of her time there. The whips, the rules, the stifling loneliness, each harrowing memory blooming heat behind her eyelids. "You can't comprehend the depths of human depravity until you experience it on your knees, in the dark, your body broken and throbbing, your mind pulling away in an attempt to protect, to endure. But no matter where your thoughts go, there is nothing or no one to cling to. It makes you question the very reason for life, like what the fuck are we even doing here and why are we the cruelest to our own kind?"

Matias stood, fingers sliding into his pockets, and stepped out of the gazebo. He strode away with a wide gait and strong posture—shoulders back and chest out, but she hadn't missed the stark pain in his eyes.

Her pulse quickened. She'd already given him the full unpolished recitation of her year with Van and Liv, hoping to soften his insistence for slavery. Maybe she was finally getting through to him.

Except he wasn't the one she needed to convince.

Nico stroked a finger over the shadowed edge of his thin beard as he watched Matias walk the path to the far side of the grove, fringed by rows of lemon trees.

Matias sat on a stone bench out of hearing range, elbows braced on knees and profile angled so that he could still see her.

For the span of several heartbeats, Nico didn't move or speak, his vacant eyes on Matias as if gazing down a long dark road. Then he blinked, straightened in the chair, and turned his attention to her.

"You know what I see when I look at you?" His tongue slid over straight white teeth. "With your tight body and your anti-slavery campaign? I see a hardcore submissive in deep denial. A well-trained cliché, trying to top from the bottom, all the while telling yourself you want no part of it. Stubbornness and fear have driven you to fight against your nature, but you're only one hard, violent fuck away from surrender. Am I right, Camila Dias?"

Her stomach bottomed out. "No, you're—"

"Those dark desires you try so desperately to hide beneath your quivering victim act? I see the hungry, dirty slut." His accent thickened into a rolling drawl. "Hell, every man here sees it. And wants it."

Ice filled her veins. This motherfucker was either blowing smoke up her ass or he paid attention a hell of a lot more than he let on.

"I'm *not* a slut." She jutted her chin, hands fisting on her lap, and eyes burning with angry tears.

"You're a slut in the most desirable way possible. How many men have you fucked, *chiquita*? How many dicks have left your pussy clenching for something harder, crueler, and more powerful? All those sloppy, monotonous hookups with strangers, while searching for the one who will pound you into submission, searching for anyone who will fuck your convictions into broken meaningless pieces. A search that took you all the way to Colombia, shackled as a slave in a slave trader's bed."

Fuck him to hell! She shook with unholy rage, her gaze skipping across the grove to Matias. He tipped his head in her direction, elbows propped on his knees, but he was too far away to make eye contact. Too far away to hear this fucked-up conversation or to stop Nico. Not that he would. A twinge of hurt stabbed through her.

"You don't know me," she said to Nico while keeping her gaze trained on Matias.

"No, I don't. But Matias does, and he tells me everything."

Her hackles went up. Matias told him all of this? Why would a cartel boss even entertain a conversation about her?

This discussion had taken a turn into Insanityville. She should've brought a pillow so she could bury her face in it and scream. Everything about this felt off. Yet she couldn't stop Nico's comments from sinking in, itching beneath her skin, and sparking a pang in her chest.

She sucked in a serrated breath. Matias should've been sitting beside her, not on the other side of the grove like a goddamn coward. It was as if Nico had waited until he had her alone to unleash his crazy. But why wait? He was the fucking capo. He made the rules, could do whatever he wanted, and didn't have to explain himself to anyone. None of this made sense.

Throwing Matias a frigid stare, she returned to Nico. "Would you have said all of this in front of him? I thought you two were friends."

"I prefer your genuine reactions, not the ones influenced by him as he breathes down your neck." His tight grimace strained the tension in the air. "I want to talk to Camila Dias, not the woman who's Matias' slave."

"No one influences my...anything." Her voice came out small, weak. She strengthened it with a deep inhale. "No one owns me."

"No one owns your soul. *Yet*. But a voluntary captive lives deep inside you, craving to be claimed, used, and fucked in every way imaginable."

"That's slavery, Nico." She seethed with indignation. "A violation of basic human rights. It was a monstrosity two-hundred years ago in the south, and it still is, here, now, no matter how sexy you try to paint it. But clearly, you and Matias and your damn profit margins—"

"Now you've ruined it." His scathing stare made her wilt. He didn't even need to raise his voice.

"Ruined what?" Her throat closed up.

"Your proposal."

"Were you actually considering it?"

He continued to glare, but now that she looked closer, there was something missing in it. The hard lines of his jaw, dark furrow of his brow, flat line of his lips—it was all there to appropriately communicate his displeasure. Deep behind his inky eyes, though, she didn't see the heat or the passion she'd expect in an outraged man.

Maybe she was just imagining it. "Tell me what you want, what to say. If you'll reconsider, I'll take back whatever I said and—"

"See, you were doing so good there. You were respectful of our business and made suggestions for improvement. You initiated trust by sharing your weakest moments with Van Quiso. Then you blew it with your self-righteous, preachy judgment. If I wanted a homily on moral values, I'd visit my mother."

Shit. Fuck. Okay, she could recover from this. "What do you want?"

He leaned in, and the potency of his cologne chased away the perfume of orange blossoms. "I want you."

CHAPTER 20

"You want *me*?" Camila widened her eyes, her insides shriveling from throat to gut.

"You," Nico mouthed, his face a breath away. "In my bed, riding my dick, and wearing my collar." He flicked the lock at her throat.

A vise gripped her chest, squeezing her air. She couldn't breathe, couldn't think past the words burning through her heart.

"In return, we'll pull out of the slave trade." He sniffed. "We'll stop capturing women in your hometown. We'll stop enslaving humans altogether."

Her muscles were so locked up she couldn't move, but her head shifted, seeking out Matias on the other side of the lemon grove. His attention was on her, his ass still seated on that bench.

"Eyes on me." Nico's bark jerked her focus back.

His straight nose, even breaths, and dark gaze betrayed nothing. His features were so empty, in fact, she decided he was probably a very good liar. That sucked considering every answer she needed was concealed behind those eyes.

She lowered her head, trying to reason through his offer. "I become your willing slave and you end the slavery of all others. That's what you're proposing?"

"Yes."

"If you wanted me, you could just take me, with or without a deal."

"That's not how this works."

Because of Matias? Or something else? The proposal was irrational. He knew Matias had claimed her. Why would he destroy their friendship or risk Matias' loyalty? Her mind whirled to decrypt the undercurrents. There was more to this. Something he wasn't saying.

"I want Matias in this conversation." She met his eyes.

"No." He bent closer, hands dangling between his spread knees and lips inches away. "This is between you and me."

"Does he know you're making this offer?"

His head turned, and she followed his line of sight across the grove. Matias stared back at her for an endless moment and looked away.

Her heart sank. *He knew.* He knew, and he was letting this play out.

Because he chose his job over her.

"Decide, Camila." Nico's rhythmic accent grated across her skin. "The offer's about to expire."

She wanted to kill him. Strip his golden skin right off his face and smother him with it. But she couldn't.

After two weeks of residence in the cartel's headquarters, she'd watched and learned and come to a glaring realization that attempting to murder the capo would result in an epic failure for two reasons. One, he was never without guards. Even now, she knew Matias was armed and would protect his boss with his life. Two,

Nico would be replaced, likely with Matias or someone else in the inner circle. Someone who would continue the slave trade.

Nico's offer was her best choice. Not that she could trust him to follow through on his end of the deal, but it would put her in his bed and potentially in his heart. It would give her an advantage, the ability to persuade him, an *in,* that she didn't have with Matias.

But there was one very muscular, dark, and deadly problem.

Fire trickled behind her eyes and burned through her sinuses. "What about Matias?"

"Disclaim him. Choose your crusade over the man who has caused you so much torment. Is the decision really that hard?"

The lump that was lodged in her throat burned hotter. "He'll kill you."

"Do you honestly believe he cares more about you than he does about me?" He arched a brow.

Logic and reasoning said *no.* Matias sat his fucking ass on the other side of the grove knowing what Nico would offer.

She'd put herself here with the very real possibility of death. *To end slavery.* Now she had what she'd come for — the cartel capo, the top fucking guy, telling her she could stop their human trafficking with her surrender. How could she *not* do this?

Something didn't feel right. Deep in her gut was a discomfiting suspicion that she was being set up. And crowding that suspicion was her stupid sentimentality. Did she care more about saving slaves than she did about Matias? Than the boy she grew up with? Than the man who rebuilt her citrus grove?

Could she willingly have sex with another man?

"Time's up." Nico tilted his head, his fingers playing with the short black hair on his jaw. "I need an answer."

"No." The strength of her voice rose from a place of besotted resolve, but it was resolve nonetheless.

With her heart in her throat, she pushed away from the table, strode out of the gazebo, and took the path through the lemon grove, heading toward Matias. There would be a shitload of introspection in her near future, like was that decision ever really hers to make? But she knew with certainty, no matter what happened, she would never regret choosing Matias.

He lifted his head at the sound of her steady footfalls, and when he stood, the relief etching his expression sent her heart racing. And her feet.

Hands behind his back and stance wide, he stared at her without moving, forcing her to take every last step toward him, sealing her future with him. Her choice solidified as she ran, and when she reached him beneath the canopy of leaves, she looped her arms around his neck.

He stood still for a moment, his rigidness choking her heartbeats.

Slowly, confidently, his arms wrapped around her back, smothering her against him. His chest felt hard, burning up through the thin material of his Henley. A vein bulged in his brow, the sinews in his neck strung tight. She stroked his throat, making his breath catch.

"*Gracias*," he said in a raspy rumble and touched their foreheads together.

Her entire body trembled as she slid her fingers along his softly shaved jawline and stabbed them through his hair. "I'm scared, Matias." *Scared of him. Scared Nico will take her away from him.*

"I know, *mi vida*. I know." He kissed her with a glide of lips and warm gasps. "Thank you for facing your fears with me."

He kissed her again, this time with force and urgency, his tongue sliding against hers and his fingers digging along her spine. Then the kiss was no longer a kiss. It was his lips whispering into her heart and his breaths caressing her soul. He was hers in his citrus grove, and she was his in any manner he wanted.

It was a dream, one that would take a lot of work and even more answers. But for now, she savored it, tasting and licking his mouth. He was hunger and passion, his tongue tangling with hers with a ferocity that curled her toes.

He swung her around, and hard wood met her back. She lifted her gaze to a ceiling of leaves and ripe yellow lemons. Laughter burst from her chest, shaking her against the tree trunk and breaking the kiss.

His hand swept through her hair as he studied her intently, smiling. "What?"

"Kissing me in a lemon grove, Matias?" She shook her head, grinning wider. "I guess if it worked the first time…"

"And the time after that." He kissed her. "And the next time." Another kiss. "Every time, Camila. You've never denied me in our grove."

"No. I suppose I haven't."

The crunch of shoes on gravel sounded behind him, and he sighed, resting his lips against her brow.

"Guess she likes you better than me." Nico stepped off the path, stopping a couple feet away, hands in his pockets and a strange look on his face.

She untangled herself from Matias and shifted away from them.

"You knew what he was going to offer me," she said to Matias.

"Yes." He held his hands behind his back.

"What if I had agreed?" She kept her tone quiet, more curious than accusatory.

His eyes slid to Nico, and they shared one of those unspoken looks she couldn't begin to decipher.

These assholes had planned this, all of it, to test her. More specifically, *Matias* had set it up. Why would Nico go along with it? What did he gain from it? Something about their relationship niggled, and she couldn't put her finger on it.

She backed up a couple steps so she could study them side by side.

Nico was a hard one to decode with his shroud of suits and disinterest. He was a couple inches shorter, maybe ten pounds smaller than Matias, and around the same age. Nico's complexion was a shade fairer, his scowl a hundred times darker, and he was intimidating in the mysterious way he was always inconspicuously watching, always present. *Like a guard.*

Contrarily, Matias was jeans and guns and hot-blooded temper, but he didn't carry the vigilance of a sentinel — which she assumed was one of his jobs. In fact, he had a slew of guards that followed him everywhere.

"Why do you need armed chaperons?" She narrowed her eyes at Matias.

"I know things."

"What things?" She ground her teeth.

"Important things that require security."

"You give me answers that tell me nothing." She rubbed her head. "What is your job in the cartel?"

Nico cleared his throat, drawing her gaze. He looked away, and she swore a smile touched the corner of his mouth. That was weird. And why was his shoe scuffing the ground?

Because Nico's not who he says he is.

"All this time, I thought he was your boss." She pointed at Nico with her eyes on Matias. "But he's not."

"Not exactly." Matias scratched the back of his neck. "We're close."

"Close like besties? Or brothers?" She watched them carefully, looking for reactions. "Lovers?"

"No," they said in unison then laughed uncomfortably.

She turned her attention to Nico, who was just standing here instead of hurrying off to run the cartel. Hell, the man spent the majority of his time up Matias' ass. And Matias walked around like he owned the joint, building citrus groves and silencing rooms just by stepping through the door. Then there was his extravagant suite that only a few people had access to. She'd never entered Nico's personal space, but from the outside, it looked like Matias' wing was the prime real estate with the best views.

Nico appeared to hold authority over everyone who lived here, barking orders and sending people scuttling. But when he was alone with Matias, the dynamic between them flipped.

Like now. The three of them stood there, as if waiting for instruction, for someone to say *Let's go.* Naturally, she looked to Matias.

But so did Nico.

Light bulbs went off in her head, and her mouth dried as she aligned the pieces. "Who owns this property?"

"Hector Restrepo built it." Matias leaned a shoulder against the tree trunk, his timbre as steady as his eyes.

She'd heard stories about the old capo in the news and whispers in the halls during her stay here. Apparently, he was a brutal bastard. *Was.* Hector was dead.

"You're not Hector's son, are you?" She directed the question at Nico, but holy hell, she was certain she knew the answer.

He glanced at Matias.

"See, he's looking at you!" She turned to Matias, heart hammering. "Because you're the one making decisions around here." She fisted her hands on her hips. "Who are you?"

"You already know." Matias stared at her, his unblinking gaze knocking the air from her lungs.

He's the boss.

Matias is the goddamn kingpin.

What better way to protect the capo than to make everyone think someone else was the capo? How had she missed this?

"If you're not the second in command..." She glared at Matias then looked at Nico. "You are."

"Told you she'd find out." Nico scrubbed a hand over his head and scanned the surrounding trees.

"I need to hear you say it." She swayed as her stomach bucked in denial. "Say it, goddammit."

"I'm Matias Restrepo." The name rolled off Matias' lips with mellifluous possession.

Her face numbed with icy prickles. "You're Matias *Guerra*."

Matias Guerra, the boy she'd spent her childhood with. Camila Guerra, the name she'd doodled on all of her school folders.

Her mind swam, and her pulse spiked. Christ, she'd grown up with a Restrepo family member? And he'd inherited this estate? This business?

"I'm Nico Bianchi." Nico held out a hand. "Matias' adviser, personal guard, and decoy."

Decoy echoed through her head. She stared at his offered hand, refusing to touch it, her muscles too stiff and heavy.

Her chest heaved as she peered up at Matias through her lashes. "You're the capo."

"Yes." Matias' tongue darted out, wetting his bottom lip. "This is my cartel."

CHAPTER 21

A massive weight evaporated from Matias' shoulders, replaced by a warmth of sunlight that broke through a rip in the clouds. He licked his lips and swore he tasted joy, tasted *her*, the beauty of his *vida*.

Camila paced in front of him, working herself into a sexy mess. Her nipples pebbled beneath her damp shirt, and denim molded deliciously to her tight ass. He wanted nothing more than to strip her bare and fuck her under the blooming branches, just like he'd been meant to do twelve years ago.

But not with Nico here and not while her huge brown eyes were searching for answers.

She'd turned down Nico's offer, surrendered the easier path, and abandoned herself. *For me.*

Just the thought of what that meant left him breathless.

"All these years…" She wandered a short distance away and returned, her eyes cloudy, distant. "You were the boss since the beginning."

Not exactly, but close enough.

Withholding who he was had haunted him since the day he left her, but numerous safeguards needed to be implemented first, with Nico's proposal being the last measure. Eventually, she would understand the prudence in his secrecy.

"This is madness." She raked her hands through her hair and closed her eyes. "I have so many questions I don't even know where to start." Her head snapped up, and she scanned the grove with a startled whisper. "Who else knows?"

Nico raised a brow in an expression that somehow made his frown look pleasantly surprised. He'd had his doubts about her ability to keep secrets, but Matias had always known that when Camila Dias gave her loyalty it was fiercely deep-rooted.

"The upper-ranking lieutenants and hitmen know who their real boss is." Nico watched her, his hands hanging loosely at his sides. "As well as some of the staff and hired whores on-site. But the cartel's thousands of underlings and countless opponents scattered across North and South American? They have no idea."

She cut her eyes to Matias, every muscle in her body radiating anger. "Why didn't you tell me?"

"I don't think she's ready for this conversation." Nico pulled a pack of cigarettes from his pocket.

She clenched her hands. "How about you let me be the judge—"

"Camila." Matias infused his tone with steel. "I couldn't tell you anything about the cartel over the phone. As for why I didn't tell you the past two weeks..." He pointed a look at Nico.

She followed his gaze and chewed her lip. Then her lip started to curl. "You wanted me to think he was the boss so he could offer me that deal?"

Matias nodded, waiting for the explosion.

Spinning toward Nico, she leaned forward and

stabbed a finger in his direction. "Your proposal was complete bullshit."

Nico approached her, slowly, dispassionately, and put his face in hers. "Respect me."

His quiet command held a lethal edge that made her breath catch.

As long as Nico didn't put his hands on her, Matias wouldn't interfere with how Nico managed his relationship with her going forward. She needed to adhere to the boundaries Nico had already set and treat him like a superior in front of others. The spy might've known who the true capo was, but no one outside the inner circle knew who Camila was. Once Matias caught the son of a bitch, she and Nico could battle it out all they wanted.

"You said you wanted me to ride your dick and wear your collar." She swatted at a fly near her ear, her complexion red-hot and sexy as hell. "You called me a slut."

"I gave him a script." Matias braced for a Camila-sized fist in his direction. Even he knew his approach had been slightly depraved.

"You what?" Her voice shook, but she didn't swing.

"Give me a little credit here." Nico lit a cigarette and exhaled a puff of smoke. "I improvised some of that. Very well, I might add."

"Let me get this straight." She paced again, which was really distracting because her ass looked damn good flexing in those jeans. "You told Nico to say those things, to *humiliate* me, all to force me into making a choice? You could've just skipped the damn meeting and talked to me like a normal person."

"Then I would've missed your delightful conversation," Nico said dryly, a gleam of mischief in his eyes.

She shot him a glare and returned to Matias. "If I would've chosen him and his offer, you would've what?" Her voice grew louder, her steps falling harder, faster. "You would've told me it was all a game, beat me with a paddle, and sent me to bed without dinner?" She stopped in front of him, her entire body frozen as she seethed. "It's really fucked up that you engineered this just to know what I would choose. Because guess what? I might've chosen you, but I will *not* stop fighting for those women."

There was her backbone, and goddamn, it made him hard as hell.

"She really gets wrapped around the axle." Nico cocked his head, watching her.

"To the point of paralysis." Matias flattened his lips to hide a grin.

"I don't...argh!" She flung her arms up. "I'm trying to make a point."

"She's still going, spinning round and round." Nico took a drag on the cigarette. "She's probably going to rip out her hair."

Matias couldn't stop his chuckle from escaping. Nico laughed, too, and it was crazy to see him drop his facade so quickly in front her. The man had spent the last decade perfecting the cold, psychopathic mask he wore every day. It had become so much a part of him he struggled to shed the act. He must've truly liked her.

She stared at them as their amusement faded, hands on her hips and tension flaring in her shoulders and neck. "Laugh it up, but the joke's on you. I passed your little test, and in the end, I *will* win the game."

He drew in a deep breath. They were just teasing her, but he needed to cut her a break. She wasn't emotionally or mentally in the same place he was. She'd chosen him, but she still saw him as the enemy, the man who beat her, raped her mouth, and sold slaves.

There were several crucial things he was keeping from her. He could spill it all right now, prove that she was fighting the wrong opponent, and she would fall to her knees, overwhelmed with wondrous glee. Okay, maybe he wouldn't get *that* reaction, but she would certainly look at him through a different lens.

That scenario terrified him.

He didn't want her to fall in love with his agendas or crusades. He needed her to love him the same way she'd loved him twelve years ago — truly, madly, deeply, without argument or thought, with a passion that stemmed from an instinctual, unquestionable place inside her.

He needed her to love him the same way he loved her.

"This isn't a game." He stepped toward her until a sliver of space separated them and lifted her chin with a knuckle. "I didn't stage the meeting with Nico because I wanted to know what choice you would make. I did it so that *you* would know."

She studied his face, her pupils dilating with a thousand seeking thoughts. She could think whatever she wanted as long as she was looking at him, *seeing* him.

Gripping his wrist, she pulled his hand away from her chin, but she didn't let go. Her fingers slid over his, absently caressing his knuckles as she stared at him.

"For the record" — Nico flicked ash from his

cigarette, eyes narrowed on her—"I meant everything I said in the gazebo, except the part about being in my bed. If I touched you, Matias would rip me from limb to limb."

"True, but I wouldn't enjoy it." Matias smirked.

"*Me importa un culo.*" Nico glanced behind him. "I'm gonna head back to the house. Guards will be stationed outside of the wall."

Then he strolled away, puffing on his cigarette. When he vanished from view, Camila ambled in the opposite direction, fingers tucked in the back pockets of her jeans and her steps soft and aimless. Matias trailed behind her, keeping a few feet between them to give her space.

She stopped at a small patch of grass between two lemon trees, kicked off her sandals, and lay down on her back, just as she'd always done as a child, with her gaze on the overhang of leafy limbs.

"Why do you need a decoy?" She glanced at him and looked back at the tree cover.

He sat beside her and removed his boots and socks, his chest tightening with all the things he needed to tell her.

"I'll start at the beginning." He lay on the lawn, his shoulder brushing hers, the ground soft and cool against his back.

"I'd really appreciate that." She reached for his hand and laced their fingers in the swath of grass between them.

"My mother was Hector Restrepo's mistress."

She kept her gaze skyward, her brows pulling together. "When did you find out?"

"The day the cartel came for me." He closed his

eyes against the memory — the fear and confusion, the unholy shock of it all. "She fled to the States when she became pregnant with me. Didn't want me to be raised among criminals. But Hector knew I was his. And he knew how to find her."

"I assume her name wasn't really Maria and she didn't die in a car accident?"

"It was Natalia." He opened his eyes and pulled Camila's hand to rest on his chest, where he hurt the most. "Hector captured her, held her somewhere in Texas until I was born, then had her killed."

Her breath hitched, and she rolled toward him, aligning her body along the length of his, with her cheek on his shoulder. "I'm so sorry."

He wrapped an arm around her back, the other bent beneath his head, and grounded himself in her. She was the honeyed scent of orange blossoms, the light that shone through the trees, the very air he breathed. Hell knew he didn't fucking deserve her.

"To this day," he said, "I don't know if Hector thought I was unworthy to be a capo's son, if he felt guilty for killing my mother, or if he was trying to protect me, but for whatever reason, he kept my existence a secret and gave me to Andres to raise."

"Andres was your mother's brother, right? Or was that a lie, too?"

"He wasn't my uncle or any blood relation. He was just a guy, trafficking drugs for Hector." He paused, letting that settle in with the heave of her breaths.

It took him several years to accept that the man who'd reared him had been nothing more than a lackey doing a job. While Andres had effectively filled the role of disciplinarian, Matias had been deprived of a mother and all the nurturing softness and affection that came with that. But he'd had Camila.

"Did my parents know?" she breathed against his neck.

"Yes, they knew all of it." With his arm around her back, he held her tighter. "Camila…"

She lifted her head at the grimness in his tone.

"Your parents worked for Hector. With Andres' help, they used the citrus grove as a cover for their narcotics trade."

"No." A vehement whisper. "That's not possible. I would've noticed something." She rose up on her elbow, eyes wide and glistening. "We both would've known. No way that was happening under our noses without us stumbling on—" She gasped. "Did you know?"

"I didn't learn any of this until after I left. They used the shack in the woods to store shipments."

"The cannibal shack?" Her hand flew to her mouth. "But it was abandoned."

"Not always."

"That's right." She dropped her arm. "It used to be all locked up. Windows covered. Creepy as hell."

He nodded. As a kid, he hadn't given much thought to it beyond the stories they made up about a reclusive cannibal. "Andres and your father built that metal barn on the south side of the grove when we were older, remember?"

"The one packed with boxes of fertilizer and plant food and…"

"Some of it was legit. Most of it wasn't. When they outgrew the shack, they used that barn."

"*Mierda*." A dark cloud shifted over her expression, stiffening her jaw. "My parents were simple people. They never would've wanted any part of that."

He placed a hand on the side of her face, stroking his thumb across her sharp cheekbone, fully aware of how hard this was for her. "Hector smuggled them out of the poorest region in Colombia and set them up with a productive business in the States. He handed them a dream."

"In exchange for a lifetime of servitude." A frown appeared on her forehead.

"Yes."

Trailing his fingers around the shell of her ear, he followed the graceful lines of her jaw to her neck and lower, beneath the edge of the leather collar. Her breath quickened, and her hand landed softly on his chest.

"The fire wasn't an accident, was it?" Her fingers twitched against him, and her lip trembled. "They're gone because of their involvement in your cartel? My sister, too?"

"Yeah. I hate this for you. Wish I could protect you from it." He caught the metal ring at her throat and used it to gently pull her face to his.

She let him, but the arm against his chest was stiff, ready to fight. "Did they witness something or do something related to drug trafficking?"

His stomach hardened. Her parents had definitely done something, and it had nothing to do with drugs.

He evaded the question by answering one she hadn't asked. "The night of the fire, I wasn't the capo yet, but Hector was already dead. Died a year earlier from lung cancer."

She searched his eyes, her expression suspicious, and she had every right to be.

"Jhon was running the cartel when your family

died." His pulse swished in his ears.

"Jhon?"

"My older brother. Jhon's mother was Hector's wife. Murdered when Jhon was young by a rival cartel."

"You have a brother." She caressed his face, fingers tentative.

"*Had* a brother." He relaxed beneath her touch. "The night Hector died, he handed down the empire to Jhon. The next day, Jhon came for me."

"How did he find out about you?"

"Hector spoke about me on his death bed, delirious and apparently regretful." His throat tightened. "The only two people in the room were Jhon and Nico."

Nico was the only reason Matias knew any of these details.

Her gaze turned inward, no doubt trying to connect the dots. "What happened to Jhon?"

As much as he disliked the topic of conversation, it loosened the knots he'd carried for years. He'd dreamt of this, the ability to talk and share with her again. She'd always been a good listener, the only person he could open up to about anything. This was how it was supposed to be.

"Jhon was a cold-hearted bastard, Camila." He pulled in a thick breath. "He took me from my home, from *you*, when Hector died. He was so fucking narcissistic he wasn't content to just own the cartel. He had to own everything and everyone around him, especially his only brother. So he came for me and controlled me by threatening your life." He shoved a hand in his hair. "Christ, I was just a sheltered, eighteen-year-old kid. I know it's no excuse, but he had a goddamn hold over me, one that kept me fearful and quiet about who I was."

"He didn't want anyone to know you were Hector's son?"

"No. The secret stayed buried the year under Jhon's reign. He treated me worse than a lackey, made me do things…"

He shuddered in memory of the torture, his and others. The metallic taste of blood in his mouth, the endless beatings, the helplessness and anger. So much fucking anger. He'd lost the soul of the boy he'd been and replaced it with a bloodthirsty savage.

"When I talked to you on the phone after you left…Jesus, Matias." She touched his cheek and slid her fingers to his jaw, lingering on his bottom lip. "You were protecting me? From him?"

"Yes." He met her eyes. "Until I didn't."

Her face paled. "Jhon arranged my abduction?"

Jhon hadn't been the only one, but he couldn't bring himself to break her heart. Not here in their grove.

"I'm sorry, Camila." He pulled her against him and wrapped his arms around her back. "So fucking sorry."

"It wasn't your fault." Her breath trembled across his neck.

"It *was* my fault. I pissed him off. My relationship with Nico…" Fuck, he'd been so careless, so fucking naïve. "Nico's father was Hector's best friend. When his father died, Hector took Nico in and protected him like a son. Jhon resented him, viciously, and the feeling was mutual."

"You were close to Nico back then?"

"He was the only friend I had, and other than Jhon, he was the only person who knew I was a Restrepo. We bonded instantly in our mutual hatred for Jhon. Nico covertly fed me information, secrets about the cartel and what Jhon was doing, all in an effort to take him out. In return, I saved Nico's life."

"Jhon tried to kill him?"

"Repeatedly. I watched Nico's back, stopped multiple hits on him. Instead of killing me, Jhon turned his outrage on you."

She lifted her head, eyes welling with tears. "You killed him, didn't you?"

"Six weeks after you disappeared."

A bird chirped somewhere in the foliage overhead, the grass soft and supportive beneath their entwined bodies. The warm air stirred with their breaths as he lay in silence, pondering the hell that had brought them to this point.

"With Jhon dead, why didn't you come home?" Pain and confusion choked her voice.

"You were already gone." He kissed her softly.

She nodded, and a tear fell down her cheek. "When I called you after I escaped, you could've told me all of this. We could've been together."

"In that year you went missing, I did horrible things in my search for you. Slaughtered countless people. Used every brutal weapon in the cartel at my disposal. Somewhere along the way, I gave up. Gave up on you and myself and surrendered to this life. I became worse than the man who captured you."

She went rigid against him, and he knew she was thinking about the slave trade, a conversation he didn't want to have right now.

"My hunt resulted in more enemies than the cartel had ever faced." He coiled a lock of her hair around his finger. "I couldn't rationalize bringing you into it."

"So you kept me in the dark, made me fear and distrust you, which kept me away."

"Yeah." His chest panged with regret, but hindsight changed nothing. It'd been the right thing to do.

"If you have so many enemies, why in the hell would Nico agree to be your decoy?"

"He owes me his life." He huffed a laugh. "The past decade hasn't been a total hardship for him. I shoulder all the stress and decisions while he struts around with more power and wealth than he would've ever had as a lieutenant. He's been more than compensated for the risk."

She rolled to her back and gazed up at sweeping arms of the trees. "Thank you for telling me. For protecting me from it all these years. I get it. I don't like it, but I understand why you couldn't tell me until now, when you could trust me with the information and protect me from those who want your secrets."

He gripped her hand and held tight as a light breeze rippled over them, rustling the leaves and brushing his skin. Somewhere in the distance, a macaw squawked.

He was so close to winning her heart and yet so far. She seemed to be trying to look past the monster she thought he was, but she still hadn't accepted the real reason she'd come here. Submission and bondage were such dirty, shameful concepts to her. She fought against the healthy, consensual aspects of it by focusing on only the ugly illegal kind of slavery.

She pulled her hand away and touched the collar at her throat. Her nostrils flared, her muscles tensed, and he knew she was preparing an argument.

She sat up and pivoted toward him with a stubborn set in her jaw. "You make the rules around here, which means you have the power to end the suffering of all those slaves. I know" — she hardened her husky voice — "I *know* that with the snap of that one command you would make me happy. So fucking happy, Matias, that I would give you my heart and soul and whatever else you desired."

His stomach twisted and soured. "I don't want your fucking negotiated affections, Camila."

He lurched up and gripped her hips. She yelped as he dumped her on her back and fell on top of her.

With her chest rising and falling against his, she gave him her best glare. "Then what do you want? What can I do?"

He had been inside her pussy every day she'd been here, and other than his massive fuck up when he took her against the post, he'd only bound her with lightweight string. Most of the time, he hadn't restrained her at all. He hadn't spanked her, whipped her, or done anything to cause her physical pain since that first day.

He wanted her willing and begging for bondage. While she hadn't once fought him during sex, her participation had been dubious, as if her body was submitting while her mind screamed *hell no*.

All of this was expected. He knew it would take a lot of time and patience, but it didn't make it any easier.

"I've already told you." He shackled her wrists with his hands and pinned her arms against the grass above her head. "Stop focusing on what you think you know and look at me, at *us*. What are you really after? What do *you* need?"

"The prize." Her eyes flashed. "You without

slavery."

"Slave has more than one meaning. Open your mind."

"You're talking about what Nico said to me?" She yanked her arms against the grip of his hands. "My supposed search to be owned and dominated?" At his nod, her gaze widened. "Are those women...? Holy shit, are they here willingly?"

"No." His heart pounded with frustration. "They definitely don't want to be here."

Flickering shadows spread over her face. "I don't understand."

"Try."

She regarded him for a long moment then blinked. "You want me to trust you."

"It's a very good place to start."

She breathed in, out, and again. Then muscle by muscle, she slackened beneath him. Her arms went limp in the grip of his hands. Her legs widened, knees falling open to accommodate his hips.

His nerve endings stirred everywhere their bodies touched—hands, chests, thighs, and...fuck, her cunt burned hot against his cock. Excitement surged through him, coiling like a fist around his shaft. He couldn't stop himself from grinding, his breaths shortening and control unraveling.

Eyes damp and overly bright, she started to tremble, her voice reedy. "One hard, violent fuck away from surrender?"

The words he'd given Nico sounded so fucking erotic whispered from her quivering lips. Surrender didn't come without fear, and she was there—the perspiration on her brow, the ashen coloring in her cheeks, the irregular pace of her breaths. He was going to fuck her and make it hurt, make her scream. But he knew that somewhere deep inside her, she was going to enjoy it, and that probably scared her the most.

"Remove your clothes." He shifted to his knees and tackled his belt.

She hesitated, her gaze locked on the strap of leather he folded in his fist.

"Camila."

She looked up at his cutting tone, and he gave the command again, not with his voice, but with the full force of his eyes.

Her inhale fluttered, fingers curling in the grass. Then, with a nod, she obeyed.

CHAPTER 22

Matias tightened his hand around the leather belt, unable to stifle the shaking in his fingers as Camila stood and reached for the hem of her shirt. He could no longer hear the drone of bees, feel the sunlight, or smell the citrus in the air, yet the atmosphere had never been more alive than it was now.

Balancing her weight on the heels and balls of her bare feet, she pulled the shirt over her head. Her slave training was evident in the way she held herself—legs straight, knees unlocked, gaze trained on him. But despite the darkness of her past seeping in, her brown eyes shone through it.

Fuck him, but he loved her inner strength, loved how her chest lifted and arched, her shoulders squared, and how her attention homed in on him as if the movement of her hands was merely reflex. He felt her submission at a molecular level, every cell in his body gravitating toward her, his muscles hungrily aware and throbbing to take what was his. But he remained where he was, three feet away, and devoured her every move.

Keeping her face and chest angled toward him with her chin drawn in, she slowly and gracefully removed her bra, jeans, and panties. Then she straightened, the alignment of her head and neck vertical, arms hanging at her sides without stiffness, and let him stare.

He stood frozen in the wake of her beauty, absorbing her nudity, her willingness, in the place he'd meticulously rebuilt, amid the trees he'd planted and cared for, every seed, yard of dirt, and precious memory put here for her.

Long black hair fell over the slender lines of her shoulders, framing round, perfectly-shaped tits. The curl of her fingers against her thighs drew his gaze to the feminine curves of hips, the flat expanse of stomach, and the shadow of hair that had grown back between her legs.

A growl escaped his throat, and he grabbed himself through the jeans, running a palm against his aching cock. She was built for him, every dip, arch, muscle, and bone, all his to worship and protect.

He prowled toward her, soaking in her quickening breaths and the way her gaze tracked him as he circled her. When he stopped behind her, her toes flexed in the grass. He took his time examining her sinful ass and strong, sinuous backbone before dropping the belt and sweeping his hands down her arms.

The marks had faded to yellowish bruises, and he hadn't needed to cut her again. The first time had been a strong enough statement, and she exuded the timid slave act like a pro.

"Matias…" She shuddered, and it wasn't an act. "I'm afraid."

"Afraid of me? Or this?" He hooked an arm around her and squeezed a nipple, hard enough to make her whimper. "Are you scared to want this?"

"Yes." Her voice wavered. "All of it."

He put his nose in her hair and slid his fingers around the sides of her breasts, the dips in her waist, and lower to cup and stroke her pussy. A rush of warmth chased his pulse, his erection bent painfully in his jeans. His fingers quaked and stiffened in his desperation for her.

"What did I tell you about fear?" He pressed his dick against her ass and lightly caressed her damp folds.

"It will haunt—" She cried out as he pinched her clit, but she kept her hands at her sides and didn't pull away. "It will haunt me until I step inside and show it my teeth."

"I'll be right here with you. Always."

The thudding of his heart beat in sync with the pulsing in his cock. She had no idea the power she held over him, didn't know how dry his mouth had gone or that his insides heated to a fevered level of dizziness. Nothing or no one had ever affected him the way she did. She was it for him, his past and future, his weakness and strength, his meaning for everything.

Brushing her hair to the side, he tiptoed fingers up and down her abs, inching close to her pussy without touching, and back up, lingering beneath her tits before dipping down again. With his mouth at her ear, he nipped her skin above the collar, flicked his tongue, and inhaled her warm scent until her head dropped back on his shoulder, breaths catching.

Her face rolled toward him, and she rubbed their cheeks together, her parted lips searching. He captured her mouth in a collision of gasps and hungry tongues that was neither soft nor gentle. He chased and hunted and fed, his fingers sinking between her legs, thrusting hard, and coaxing a moan from deep within her.

Her lower body clamped around him, her neck angling her closer as she tried to deepen the kiss. Her urgency spurred him on, making him hotter, greedier, more frantic.

"Matias, please." She arched into him, her ass grinding against his painful cock.

He tore his mouth away, his heart tripping at a dangerous level.

"Bend forward." He kissed her shoulder and stepped back, keeping his tone silken, yet inflexible. "Hands on your ankles. Spine straight."

She followed his command to perfection, and he swallowed a groan. Yanking off his shirt, he used it to wipe the perspiration from his brow. Then he tossed it and knelt behind her.

He tried to start slow, his hands exploring her ass and legs, but the more he touched the more he needed. Her skin was so tight, so fucking smooth he wanted to lick and bite every inch of her. So he did, gliding his tongue and teeth across the backs of her thighs as he teased her soaking cunt with his fingers.

The hitch in her breath amped his pulse, but he kept his movements slow, sensual, savoring her goosebumps and the flex of her muscles as she anticipated the path of his lips. She was so fucking responsive he couldn't wait any longer. He buried his mouth between her legs.

"So damn wet, *mi vida*. Such a hungry slut."

With her head hanging upside down, she snarled through clenched teeth. "I'm not—"

"A slut, my gorgeous girl, is brave enough to pursue her own definitions of pain and pleasure. She's willing to explore and search for what she enjoys rather than shun her desires like a dirty secret." He bit the delicate skin between her legs, wrenching a yelp from her. "You welcome sex with open legs, because you understand the benefits, the ecstasy it brings."

"Okay, when you put it that way," she said in a throaty voice.

"*My* slut." He licked her from ass to pussy, his tongue probing in both holes with abandon.

She panted and shook, her tits swaying and head lifting to accommodate her breaths, but she held her bent position with flawless grace. A reminder that she'd endured a year of hell to master that composure. Anger simmered through his blood, but he pushed it down, refusing to let it ruin the moment.

When her moans grew shorter, faster, he knew she was peaking. He stabbed his fingers inside her, and in two hard drives, she came with a choked-off scream, her inner muscles spasming against his hand. Fucking beautiful.

He eased out of her and helped her straighten to her full height, pulling her chest to his as she wobbled.

Lifting her chin, he submerged his gaze in hers and saw unspeakable desire in the watery depths. Love was there, too—the love they'd always shared—but it seemed stronger now, pummeled and tested and resuscitated back to life. And in the strength of that love, he saw the tiniest glimmer of trust, the kind of trust that only a submissive could offer.

As far as she knew, he hadn't done anything to earn her trust, yet she was handing it over, instinctively, bravely, and the only explanation was because she loved him.

He took her mouth, and the instant their lips touched, the fusion was frantic and visceral, hitting him right in the stomach. He felt her in his skin, every gasp, bite, and voracious lick connecting to an emotion that had endured the torment of time.

Her beautiful tongue flicked, twirling in greedy euphoric circles and following his lead as he demanded everything and took even more. She dragged her short nails down his back, bursting his nerve endings into a thousand frenzied pieces.

He pressed his lips to the corner of her mouth then kissed a path to her ear, whispering, "Do you want to come harder next time?"

Eyes beckoning, she nodded, shook her head, then let out a husky laugh. "Will I live?"

"For the first time in your life." He reached up and tested the strength of the thickest branch. "Hold onto this."

Lifting her heels from the soil and stretching her arms, she curled her fingers around the limb.

He snagged her bra from the ground, checked it for wires and found none. "Stand flat on your feet."

When she lowered, she was still able to hang on. He used the strip of black lace to tie her hands to the branch.

"Comfortable?" He kissed her mouth softly.

With a glance at the belt in the grass, her expression tightened, but she gave him a jerky nod.

"How did you get into this…this kinky stuff?" Her voice cracked, and she cleared it. "You've done this a lot?"

"I'll answer your questions, but first, tell me why you abstained for four years."

Her eyes darted away, and she bit her lip. "I slept with a lot of men after I escaped, trying to prove to myself that I was the one in control of my sexuality." She looked back at him. "I was also looking for…I don't know. A connection? But after a while, I decided I had better luck with my vibrator."

Exactly what he'd thought. He clenched and relaxed his hands.

"I did the same thing, fucking my way through countless women." At her wince, he cupped her face and pressed so close he felt her heartbeat pound against his chest. "I was searching for something, too. Anything that might resemble what I had with you. I never found it."

"I hate—" She bit back a strangled noise, and a twitch flickered her eyelashes. "I hate that all those women know you in that way."

He wholeheartedly sympathized with the pain in her eyes. "No one knows me the way you do."

The corner of her mouth bounced. "Smooth talker." She slackened against him, almost as if trying to snuggle with her arms restrained over her head. "None of those women know what your fourteen-year-old ass looks like on a copy machine."

"Or my ass at any age on a copy machine." He chuckled into another long, delicious kiss.

She hummed against his mouth as her tongue traced the seam of his lips.

He brushed his hands through her hair. "What I discovered in my fumbling attempts at happiness is that bondage and pain have the potential to make sex more intense and intimate. People fuck all the time without conversation, commitment, or any emotional connection. But when I tie up a woman and beat the living hell out of her, there's a crucial responsibility that comes with that, one that involves clear communication and acceptance — hers and mine. Those very things enhance sexual pleasure." He paused. "Because it requires trust."

"But the slaves you—"

"I've never fucked a slave."

"Oh." Her brows drew together then released with the flash in her eyes. "But you hurt me without communication or acceptance."

"Tell me why I did it."

"You wanted me scared." She swallowed. "To protect me from your enemies."

"Yeah." His throat thickened. "I'll hurt you again, Camila, and I'll be the one to soothe it. Only me." Lowering his hand, he trailed his fingers over the bruises on her ass. "I'm going to give you a different kind of pain. The kind that comes with acceptance." He felt the heat of her lips brush his. "When trust surpasses that pain, the result can feel incredibly profound."

"Okay." Fear threaded through her voice.

"Imagine what it will be like for us. We already share a connection no other two people have. Our memories, our regrets, and this." He kissed her hard and deep, with the entirety of his soul. "*Us.*"

"You think this is what we've both been searching for?" She subtly rubbed her pussy against the zipper of his jeans.

"Yes." He was certain of it. "Listen carefully. If I hit you too hard or overstep your limits without explanation, you need to trust that I'm doing it for you."

"No safe words?"

"No." He laughed and shoved a hand through his hair. "I'm not running a high-end glitter club here. I'm a fucking cartel capo who hangs people in chains to kill them, not to tickle them with a flogger. Dangerous and crazy is the way I operate, Camila."

"Basically the opposite of safe, sane, and consensual." Her eyes narrowed.

He refused to abide by anyone's rules, but… "I want your consent."

"Jesus. Everything you said was so fucking wrong." She stared at him, absently digging her toe through the grass. "But I don't feel a pressing need to kick you in the nuts."

"You normally feel that need?"

"Maybe." Her mouth flattened, but a smile touched her eyes.

"When I restrain you, it's just you and me." He glided his hands up her arms and squeezed the elastic strap around her wrists overhead. "No safe words. No rules. Have we reached that level of trust yet?"

"I'm trying." She licked her lips. "I want to."

That was closer than she was two weeks ago. His pulse kicked up.

Sliding his hands back down her arms, he rubbed her tits, pinched her nipples, and moved to her ass, her thighs, her pussy. He touched her everywhere, keeping his gaze on her parted mouth and the peek of her tongue as she wet her lips.

The rhythm of her breaths led the pace of his strokes. As she panted faster, harder, he added pressure and speed to his caress. Soon, she was trembling, gasping, ready.

As he adjusted his cock to relieve the agonizing pressure, he grabbed the belt from the ground and folded it in half. She tracked him with half-lidded eyes, her expression aglow more with curiosity than fear. He didn't need to tell her how to breathe and relax into the strikes. She'd been mercilessly beaten against her will more times than he cared to think about.

With a steady inhale, he let the strap swing, landing the initial hits on her thighs and ass. He didn't go easy on her, but he knew he wouldn't. He'd pounded his fists against men to the point of bloodshed and death, and while he didn't hit her with anywhere near that kind of strength, he wasn't a gentle man. Nor was she weak.

Her head fell back on her shoulders as she gasped and whimpered. He worked over her body, striking without pause and watching for swelling and broken skin. But more than that, he studied her eyes, thrilling in the dilation of her pupils beneath her glazed expression of lust.

Good God, she had a high-tolerance for pain. As hard as he was hitting her, she didn't scream or shift her feet. Not even when he reached his groove, his arm swinging with speed and agility, muscles loose, and attention focused.

He walked a circuit around her, slamming the leather against her legs and ass, listening to the tempo of her breaths, and devouring the red blooms across her skin. His heart pounded like it had the first time he'd kissed her fifteen years ago. It was finally alive and beating, no longer lost. It had come back, here, to her in their lemon grove.

Inflicting pain wasn't what made him hard. It was one-hundred-percent about the power in trust. She was giving him this, letting him hurt her while trusting that he wouldn't destroy her.

He returned to her front and struck her tits,

alternating between them. She keened, her eyes wide and staring upward as tremors rippled up her legs. He knew she'd hit that altered state of consciousness, where time distorted and pain ebbed. She looked like she was floating, peaceful, high as a fucking kite.

Hands slick with sweat, he moved the strap lower, thwacking lightly over her stomach. When he reached her pussy, he landed a vicious blow against her clit.

"No!" She snapped to awareness, screaming and writhing, knees buckling. "I can't...not there—"

He hit her again and again, pummeling the sensitive nerves, testing her.

"You...sona...fuck...ye...pleee..." Tears skated down her cheeks as she gulped for air, glaring at him and bellowing between sobs.

She'd reached her breaking point, and broken was a place he never wanted to take her.

He tossed the belt.

"Fuck you, Matias." Her voice didn't hold a trace of heat as she slumped. Then she gave him a shaky smile. "That wasn't too bad."

Goddamn, he loved this woman. He released the button and zipper on his jeans, shoving them down as he closed the distance.

With shaking hands, he gripped her hair and claimed her mouth, his tongue probing, caressing, and taking. She tasted like citrus and desire, her lips soft and yielding and *his*. She kissed him with the same urgency, her breaths warm and erratic as she hooked a leg around the back of his.

His balls tightened, and his cock throbbed to the point of pain. He gripped himself, aching to fuck her, brutally, possessively, and if he waited much longer, he was going to come before the first fucking thrust.

With his jeans hanging beneath his ass and a fist around his shaft, he lined himself up and rammed hard, missing completely in his pressing need to be inside her.

"Need help?" She laughed and bit his jaw. "I can—"

He smacked her hard on the ass, and she choked on another laugh. Christ, she made him crazy. He kissed her again, and this time, with a bruising grip on her hip, he slammed inside of her, buried to the hilt.

"Fuuck!" Pleasure shot through his cock, and his forehead dropped to her shoulder.

"Oh, God." She groaned and wrapped her other leg around him, giving him all of her weight and the full use of her body.

Adjusting his stance, hands on her waist, he fucked her with every inch of his soul. She tightened her fingers around the branch and threw her head back, crying out with each unapologetic drive of his hips.

"Look at me." He couldn't get close enough, deep enough, couldn't taste enough of her, or wrench enough cries from her seductive lips.

She gave him her eyes, and he held her there, sliding her up and down his length and jacking himself off in her tight sheath. She felt so fucking good he couldn't stop shaking, couldn't catch his breath.

Without breaking eye contact, they moved together as one, the rock and kick of her hips matching the force of his. They were wild and electric, a violent landslide of grunts, slippery skin, and thundering hearts.

His lungs caught fire, and his pulse hammered as fast as his thrusts, everything inside him simmering, building, pressurizing. The whole damn world felt like it was going to explode, and he didn't care. He couldn't stop. He was so fucking lost in her he didn't want to find his way back.

They were both panting so hard they couldn't keep their mouths connected, but he tried, chasing her lips, licking and sucking and swallowing her breaths as he fucked her.

Her tits bounced with the slam of his hips. Her exhales came in short bursts. Then she was coming, screaming, her eyes wide and fixed on him as if blindsided by the sensations. She shuddered and twitched through it, and when she finally settled against him, he pulled back, slipping his cock free and teasing the tip around her opening. She groaned.

"Again?" He bit her nipple, her collarbone, her lips, then sank back inside her. "Yeah, you can do that again."

"I think...maybe... Yes, please." She smirked, eyes half-mast.

Reaching down to where his jeans had fallen around his knees, he removed the switchblade from the pocket and cut her hands free.

Her fingers flew to his hair, and her mouth attacked his, wet and hot, eating at his lips and licking his tongue.

He flung the blade near his boots, kicked off the jeans, and rolled her to the ground beneath him. With the solid support against her back, he let himself go, fucking her ruthlessly, powerfully.

Holding his gaze, she moved her body in a sensual dance with his. Her hands glided across his back, their chests heaving together, and legs entwined. Shock waves descended down his spine, gathering at the base of his cock. He tangled his fingers in her hair, his hips caught in a desperate tempo. He wanted to last longer, but knew he couldn't.

There would always be later, and tomorrow, and forever.

"I'm going to come, baby." Spasms gathered behind his balls. "You're coming with me."

Her eyes flared with concentration. "Kiss me."

And he did, vigorously, passionately, while fighting the agonizing impulse to release. She flexed and strained beneath him and released a strangled shout against his lips. He stared into her eyes, captivated by her orgasmic bliss, and followed her over.

He came violently, pounding her into the ground, his body convulsing with a series of contractions that pumped deep inside him, ejaculating, filling her up, and the pleasure… Fuck, the pleasure was unimaginable as he groaned and thrust and stretched it out as long as he could.

As their breathing evened out and their bodies went limp, a fog of numbness tingled through him. But he kept his hips moving in slow, satisfied strokes, his gaze centered on his favorite brown eyes.

"That was pretty good." She pursed her lips.

He continued to lazily thrust, didn't want to stop, didn't want to leave the drenched clasp of her pussy. "As sloppy as your cunt feels, I think it was better than pretty good."

Her expression softened, and she ran her hands across his jaw and into his hair. "It was perfect, Matias."

Rolling them to their sides, he kissed her tenderly, achingly, with every ounce of love he felt for her. Her arms twined around his neck, and his cock softened inside her, but she didn't seem to want him to pull out, so he held her closer, kissing her as the sky darkened with the approach of dusk.

They lay there for an eternity, nude, in a bed of grass, surrounded by lemon trees, and he knew. He'd finally succeeded in his pursuit for happiness. Then again, he'd always known that this was how it should be.

She watched him as he watched her, seemingly just as content, but something lurked in the back of her eyes.

He spread a lock of her hair in the grass, snaking it around like a black river. "What are you thinking about?"

"Your spy problem."

He didn't expect that, and his heart lurched excitedly. "What about it?"

"Well, you haven't caught this person."

He arched a brow. "Are you questioning my competence?"

"Yep."

"All right." His chest filled with pride. "I'm listening."

She leaned up on an elbow, and the twin peaks of her pink nipples drew his attention.

"Up here, Matias."

He flicked his eyes to hers and found a glint of amusement there.

"You've been monitoring every outgoing transaction and message?" She cocked her head. "Even phone calls?"

"Everything. Nothing is getting leaked or discussed. We're on virtual shutdown. We've flown in all of our technical geniuses and highest-ranking members to the property and haven't let anyone leave. We have every able and trusted person hunting for this person."

She nodded, her expression contemplative. "Have you considered the possibility that Gerardo might've been lying?"

"The man was in a world of pain when he confessed." His heart skipped. "He lasted through hours of slicing and severing and—"

"He was loyal to this other group then. Loyal enough to endure that kind of torture." She glanced away, scrunched up her nose in concentration, and looked back at him. "What if he was trying to distract you from something? What if he wanted you to congregate your cartel?"

Dread sank his stomach, and his blood pressure skyrocketed. "Fuck. No, that's... Shit, we've focused all our efforts here, searching internally. And we're all together, pulled all of our resources to one place."

"The enemy is out there, doing hell knows what, while your attention is centered on yourselves." She sat up and stared over the trees. "If someone were to...I don't know, drop a bomb on this place, every important member would be blown to bloody pieces. Would the cartel die with them?"

Yes, it absolutely would.

CHAPTER 23

A week later, Camila stretched on a lounge chair on the balcony outside of Matias' private living room, listening intently to the drone of voices around her. Not really hearing the words as much as evaluating inflections, pitch, and volume of one voice in particular.

Twilight blushed the sky and cast a radiant glow across Matias' stern expression. Sitting at the wrought iron table cluttered with bottles of beer and *aguardiente,* he strategized and argued with the men in the inner circle.

His timbre was calm and even, but the Texan drawl he tried so hard to hide slipped through, barely there, pulling on some of his consonants. Was he worried? Scared?

He hadn't let her out of his sight in over a week. Whenever he left his suite, he took her with him, to his meetings, to walk the perimeter of the property, to dinner on the veranda. Given the current topic of conversation, she doubted he would be leaving her side any time soon.

Other than the potential danger that threatened his life — as well as hers — she didn't *want* to care if the cartel perished or survived. She needed to focus on the horrors Matias kept imprisoned in the west wing. She'd counted at least fourteen slaves since she'd arrived, and who knew how many others weren't being paraded through the halls like dogs on leashes.

A slaughtered cartel meant less slave traders in the world. She tried to feel enthusiastic about that, but instead, it sank a heavy feeling in her stomach. Did she actually like these guys?

Other than her first day here, the inner circle hadn't treated her like a slave, never even raised a brow when she voiced her opinions or asked questions in the privacy of Matias' suite. Of course, Matias had told her multiple times that his four closest men knew who she was and why she was here.

But she couldn't ignore their depravity. The evidence was etched into the horrified faces of the slaves they kept.

Except every time she looked at Matias, she didn't see a man who wanted to profit from women's suffering. She saw a man who adored her so deeply he would sacrifice everything for her.

It didn't make sense that he loved her while doing the one thing that hurt her the most. But rather than fight him, she watched him, tried to understand his motivations and trust that there was something he wasn't telling her, something important.

If I hit you too hard or overstep your limits without explanation, you need to trust that I'm doing it for you.

Was there another message beneath his words? Something below the threshold of her understanding? Because dammit, his involvement in human trafficking did overstep her limits, and how the fuck could he possibly be doing that for *her?*

She wanted to trust him, which was huge and

terrifying and really goddamn hard on her heart. It shattered every night at dinner, every time she saw a sewn mouth, a shackled hand, or a fearful set of eyes. She was reaching her limits on trust.

"What about the north wall?" Matias leaned back in the chair, his hand resting on his thigh. "Have we added more cameras?"

Chispa jumped in with a technical report, and Matias asked more security questions, his thumb moving restlessly, sliding over the pads of the fingers on the same hand, back and forth, again and again.

There was so much power in those fingers. They could be cruel, fucking brutal in his passion, but they could also be tender, gentle on her skin in his affection. Whether he was whipping her, caressing her, or fingering her into mindless bliss, those fingers inspired strength and dominance, left her craving more, wanting more of him, needing him to be the man she trusted him to be.

He flicked his eyes to her, to his lap, and back to her face. Her heart raced, her entire body pulling toward him as her feet slid to the floor. She stood, straightened her shorts, and crossed the balcony.

Nico, Chispa, and Picar continued the conversation, but all eyes were on her as she lowered onto Matias' lap. Frizz's watchful gaze was the hardest to meet, but she forced herself to hold his stare and not let him intimidate her. Of all the men in the inner circle, his eyes were softest, a strangely-innocent shade of blue. She couldn't help but morbidly wonder about the mystery he kept trapped behind those threaded lips.

A shiver raced through her, and she tried not to wriggle on the hard bulge pressing against the zipper of Matias' jeans.

For the next hour, she sat sideways on his lap, resting against his chest with her head on his shoulder. She indulged in the vibration of his voice as he rumbled on about security, debating the idea of leaving the property and going into hiding.

If they fled the compound, she wouldn't use it as an opportunity to escape. Maybe she was determined to the point of self-destruction, but she needed to see Matias' slave trade through to the end.

But it wasn't just that. The mere thought of being separated from him twisted her insides into panicky knots. That fear alone trumped the accumulation of every fear she'd ever felt. He was the only person who had ever made her lungs stretch, heart sing, and mind dance. No way in hell was she giving him up.

He slid his knuckles up and down her inner thighs as he talked to his men. One might've assumed it was mindless fidgeting, but the swollen proof of his awareness jerked persistently against her hip.

She sighed. If there was one thing she'd learned in her three weeks here, it was that she loved his cock. She loved the thick girth, the veins that ran along the underside, and the little freckle just beneath the crown. Her pussy clenched as she replayed the way he'd woken her this morning—his dick in her mouth, his musky scent in her nose, and his salty come in her throat.

She'd never considered herself a slut, but after he'd framed the term with admiration, she'd spent the better part of the past week learning how to be more honest with herself about who she was and what she wanted. While his beautiful cock consumed her thoughts, she'd become more receptive to him as a whole, and the biggest piece of that was his dominance.

Sitting on his lap like this filled her with belonging. The strength and power in his body coupled with the tenderness of his touch and the warm scent of his masculinity felt like home and permanence, instilling in her a sense of security. All that searching with other men had been such a wasted effort. No wonder losing Matias had hurt her so much. *He* was where she should've always been.

Nico rolled up the sleeve of his shirt. "All I'm saying is we need to be—" A phone chirped on the table, and he grabbed it, glanced at the screen. A second later, he straightened, his eyes lifting and landing on Matias.

Matias stiffened against her, prompting the same reaction in her muscles.

"They found more." Nico's usual scowl vanished amid the starkness of his unblinking eyes.

"Found what?" She sat up and turned to look at Matias.

His hand went to her face, cupping her jaw, but his focus remained on Nico. "Where?"

"Three hours north by helicopter. *Permítame un momento.*" Nico stood, lifting the phone to his ear as he strode to the far end of the railing.

She touched the hand on her cheek. "Matias? What's going on?"

His lips formed a pale line, his hazel eyes sharp as he stared at Nico's back and lowered their hands. She searched the other faces at the table—Frizz, Chispa, Picar—and found the same expressions, all of them watching Nico, rigid in their chairs as if bracing to leap up.

"Does this have to do with Gerardo's betrayal?" Her breaths quickened. "Did you find spies?"

Matias gave her a stiff shake of his head, and Nico ended the call.

With a strong, urgent gait, Nico returned to the table, eyes on his capo. "We can make it there without a refuel. Burd will drive us the rest of the way."

"And you trust Burd?" Matias shifted to the edge of the chair.

"We've used him a dozen times. He's a good falcon. But I recommend waiting a while. Maybe next week—"

Matias slammed a fist on the table, stopping her heart and knocking over several beer bottles. "We're not fucking waiting." He launched from the chair, taking her with him and catching her around the waist to support her stumbling steps. "Set up the appointment for tonight. Get the helicopter ready. We're leaving immediately."

"Tell me what's going on." She folded her arms across her chest, shivering against the tension in the air.

"What about the plan we discussed?" Nico scowled.

"Get everything lined up." Matias grabbed her hand and turned toward the door.

"Hey, boss." Chispa stood, rubbing the back of his neck as he lifted a chin in her direction. "Maybe you should sit this one out. We can do this—"

"No fucking way." Matias pulled her into the interior living space.

Her scalp tingled. "Hold up!"

"Are you bringing her with us?" Chispa chased after him. "What if something happens while—"

"She's going."

"Matias!" She slammed to a stop, only to be yanked forward again by his strong grip. "Are we in danger?"

    "No. We're in a hurry. Pick up your fucking feet."

CHAPTER 24

Matias pressed his back into the plush leather of the helicopter chair. The seven-passenger light twin was built for luxury and comfort, but he was far from comfortable.

Squeezed into the cabin with the entire inner circle and battling for leg room, he felt like rubber bands were wrapped around his chest. Guns at his lower back, shoulder, and ankle dug into his skin. His hands slicked with sweat, and the woman sitting next to him glared daggers at the side of his face.

The past hour had been a whirlwind of weapons collecting, safety planning, and route mapping. Camila had followed him around his suite, huffing and demanding answers, but he'd been too focused and rushed for a sit down with her.

Now that they were in the air and heading out of the Amazon basin, he had three hours to tell her where they were going and what he'd been doing for the past ten years.

A jittery ache kicked through his stomach, and it had nothing to do with the flight. The twin engines purred quietly, and the smooth rotor system propelled the aircraft fast and seamlessly through the atmosphere. With a sticker price of eight-million dollars, he'd more than paid for a shudder-less ride.

"I thought it would be louder in here." Camila leaned over his lap in their rear-facing seats and peered out the window into the dark sky.

"There's a capsule between us and the airframe, and the dual-pane glass helps."

Two rows of three seats filled the cabin, configured to face each other. The cockpit was behind him and Camila. Nico sat on her other side, talking quietly with Chispa and Picar as they bent over the tablet he held between them, studying a digital map.

Frizz sat directly across from Matias, head resting back on the seat, eyes closed, and complexion paler than usual. Matias wished the guy wouldn't participate in these jobs, knowing how they affected him. But like Camila, Frizz was haunted by his own experiences and motivated to retaliate.

"I'm trying to be patient." She sat back and drummed her fingers on Matias' thigh. "Like really trying here."

He hadn't envisioned telling her like this. Of course, showing her had always been the plan, but he would've rather sat her down in private, when she was ready, and explained it all.

His stomach hardened. Fuck, what if she wasn't ready?

He'd removed her collar last night after dinner, and she didn't need it now, not where they were going. She wore jeans, a long-sleeved shirt, and tennis shoes, just as he'd instructed. Everyone in the cabin donned the same look—casual, a little rugged, with footwear that wouldn't slow them down if they needed to run.

Maybe it would be better if she went in blind. With

an actual blindfold, because she would never be able to unsee what they were about to walk into.

"Why aren't you telling me where we're going?" She pressed her nails into the denim on his inner thigh. "And why don't I have weapons like the rest of you?"

His breath hitched as hope warred with suspicion. Did she want to shoot him or… "Would you fight alongside us?"

"Yes." She lifted her chin. "I mean, as long as we're not headed to some meeting place to pick up more slaves."

Chispa coughed into his fist, and she whipped her head toward him. Matias clenched his teeth.

"Sorry, it's…" Chispa gave her a sheepish look. "It's the stale air in here. Makes my throat tickle."

Motherfucker. Matias schooled his expression, and she looked back at him, shaking her head with wide eyes.

"Tell me that's not what we're doing. You wouldn't…" She searched his face, voice reedy. "You're taking me on a slave run?"

A swallow caught in his throat. It was the moment of truth, a moment of courage, the testing point of her instinct, her trust, and her love.

He held himself still and confident as his stomach flipped inside out. "What does your gut tell you?"

She glanced around the cabin at the guys, and none of them made eye contact with her.

"Look at *me*, Camila." When her teary eyes returned to his, he said, "What do you see?"

Her hands balled against her thighs as she stared at him, long and hard. "I see a man…the man I—"

"Sir!" the pilot shouted from the cockpit behind him. "We're being tracked."

"Who?" Matias twisted in the seat and scanned the glowing panel of gauges. "Something on the radar?" He didn't have a clue what he was looking at.

"I have it." Chispa bent over a tablet on his lap, gaze focused on the screen. "There's a jet above us. Probably Colombian military."

"Or American." Nico rubbed a hand over his scowl. "We can lose them. It's the helicopters and puddle-jumpers below and around us we need to worry about."

As predicted, it didn't take long for the first helicopter to buzz by, swooping and circling. Matias' pilot outmaneuvered and outran it, allowing a few minutes' reprieve before the next one showed up.

Despite his strung-out nerves and heart palpitations, Matias kept his breathing tempered and mind clear, watching Chispa as the man stared unblinking at the radar on his screen. They'd been through this countless times.

But never with Camila in tow.

Her hand clung to his leg, her complexion bloodless beneath a sheen of perspiration.

"Who are they?" Her voice was strangled.

"Deep breath. Good girl. Now another one." He laced their fingers together on his lap. "We're flying over rival territory, so it could be another cartel. Or the military. They're always looking for us, waiting for us to come out of hiding."

"What the hell, Matias?" Her knee bounced wildly against him.

"This is Colombia, baby." He clamped a hand on her leg, stilling her. "The conflict between armed groups like us and FARC and governmental forces has been ongoing for the last fifty years."

"What happens if we don't lose them?"

"They'll track us until we land and try to take us into custody." *Or kill us if it's another cartel.*

"You weren't kidding when you said you had a lot of enemies." She offered him a strained smile.

"No." His mind went through the worst-case scenarios, all of them ending with them getting shot out of the air and her body burning in an inferno of metal and debris. "But I bought this helicopter for its speed. We always lose them."

Two hours and several reroutes later, they slipped beneath the radar and landed out of sight in a sweeping field of darkness.

A collective sigh breathed through the cabin as Nico opened the rear clamshell door. The guys filed out, leaving Matias alone with Camila. He unlatched his safety belt and crouched before her to remove hers.

As he rose to lead her out, she grabbed his hand. "Wait."

He lifted a questioning brow and lowered to a crouch before her. "Camila—"

"Let me just say this." She slid a hand over her collarless throat, her expression deep and serious. "There's always a basis for justifying an action and an outcome for that action. A motive and a result. You told me, in not so many words, that I might not like the result, but to trust the reason you're doing it."

His heart slammed against his ribs as he nodded.

Nudging him backward, she slid off the seat and knelt before him in perfect form—spine erect, shins flat against the flooring, arms behind her, and head held proud. His pulse went crazy.

"I'm giving you the power to break me inside and out, and I trust that you won't." She stared into his eyes and pulled in a jagged breath. "I'm scared, Matias, fucking terrified of where you're about to take me, but I'm relinquishing that to you, surrendering my vulnerability without shame, because that's what you want, and what you want, I crave."

Tingling weightlessness filled his chest as he pulled her against him and crushed his mouth to hers. He kissed her frantically, devotedly, for as long as he could, but not long enough. When he pulled back, she gazed at him with unfettered trust.

"When I look at you, I see the man in the boy I loved." She brushed a finger over the dimple in his cheek.

"I fucking love you." He kissed her again, smiling like a lovesick asshole.

"Wanna know who I love?" She returned his smile and pointed at his chest. "That guy."

"*Gracias, mi vida.*"

"Now where's my gun?" She held out her hand and arched a sexy brow.

He laughed and gave her the 9mm from his boot. "I trust *you* to not shoot me in the ass."

CHAPTER 25

Camila held tight to Matias' hand as a leathery-faced man named Burd drove them along a dirt road in a black sedan. Ice-cold dread swelled in her stomach, and she couldn't swallow past the clot in her throat. She still didn't know where they were going, but that was the point of her trust, right?

However naïve or insane, she did trust him. The thing was, she'd squandered so much time focusing on the slaves at the estate that she'd only seen Matias as a monster. But when she looked at him, really looked hard into his eyes, she saw a monster that would never hurt her without reason.

Alone in the backseat with him, she rested her head on his shoulder and tried to absorb some of his calm strength. Nico sat in front with Burd behind the wheel. Chispa had stayed with the helicopter pilot to wait for a refueling truck.

Headlights bobbed in the rear window. Burd had brought two armed soldiers in ski masks—lower ranked cartel members according to Matias—who followed behind in a separate sedan with Frizz and Picar.

Outside the window, tiny villages twinkled by. Despite the ramshackle sheds and the bleakness of poverty, the communities seemed tranquil beneath the full moon, scattered across the mountains and surrounded by cultivated fields.

During one of her late night conversations with Matias, he'd told her about these poor rural populations. These indigenous people bred their chickens and labored in their fields of corn and coffee. Their children attended the nearest schools, sometimes hours away, and played with dolls and footballs like any other place in the world.

But it was a hard life. Land was expensive, and the whir of bullets and helicopters were a constant invasion. While the people were resigned to it, the buzz of rotors always sent them running for cover, often forcing them to abandon their farms and move elsewhere until the violence ended.

She'd thought about this when Matias' helicopter had landed in the field of an impoverished village. How many families were cowering in their homes, waiting for Matias to leave? How many other gangs were prowling this area right now?

"This is it." Nico's heavy accent rose above the hum of the engine.

The headlights behind her went dark as Burd pulled into a long gravel driveway. A porch light glowed at the end of the drive, illuminating the front door of a rickety house. Several cars parked out front. Overpriced luxury cars that didn't belong in this poor village.

Prickles raced down her spine. "What is this place?"

Nico pulled on a ski mask and twisted in the front seat to toss another mask to Matias.

Her mind flashed with images of the night Van delivered her to them. "I hate those fucking masks."

Matias eked out a sad smile then slipped the ski mask over her head, covering her nose, mouth, and neck. "You'll stay with Nico."

"Why?" Her throat sealed up. "Where are you going?"

"Just until I get through the door." He adjusted the itchy fabric on her face until only her eyes peered out.

He exchanged a look with Nico, and while they both exuded calmness, there was an undercurrent in their confidence. Not fear or worry. Something akin to grief.

What was this place? Why were they here? Her mouth dried, and she grabbed the 9mm on the seat beside her, having no idea why she needed it or who she would be aiming it at.

Halfway up the drive, Burd turned the sedan around and parked, with the headlights shining in the opposite direction of the house. The second car was nowhere in sight.

Burd shut off the headlights but kept the engine running. "I wait here in car." He crammed the words together with a thick Colombian accent.

"Where's the other car?" She anchored her gaze on Matias.

"They'll come in on foot." He touched his lips to the material over her mouth in a whisper of breath.

Every cell in her body sighed then snapped tight as Matias pulled away and stepped out of the sedan. The interior lights remained off, and the door hung open, letting in the rhythmic chirp of insects.

In the next breath, his silhouette melted into the darkness. She felt like she was going to be sick.

The crunch of his boots on gravel faded in the direction of the house. He had about a hundred feet to walk before he would appear beneath the glow of the porch light. If the other guys were sneaking onto the property, this must've been some kind of ambush. Who the hell was in that house?

Nico exited the sedan and stopped by her door, his whisper muffled by the mask. "Keep quiet."

With the 9mm in hand, she climbed out into the balmy night air. She didn't hear people nearby or vehicles in the distance, much less see any signs of civilization other than the house. But she felt something, a prickly unrest crawling through the black landscape.

Was someone out there? Watching them? Maybe it was the skeletal shapes of the surrounding trees or the fact that she couldn't see Matias, didn't like her hearing hindered by the mask, and didn't want to be alone with Nico. Whatever it was, this remote place gave her the fucking creeps.

She leaned toward Nico, closer than she was comfortable, to speak low at his ear. "Why isn't Matias wearing a mask?"

"Someone has to show their face at the door," he whispered, eyes darting to the house and back to her. "I'm too recognizable." He removed a huge handgun from his waistband and flicked off the safety. "This is how we always do it. He'll be fine."

Always do it. She searched the eye opening of his mask and found his gaze more alive than ever and tinged with deep emotion. Whatever was about to happen, he seemed uncharacteristically affected by it. That only made her stomach cramp harder.

With a crook of his finger, he beckoned her to follow him up the driveway.

She switched off the safety on the 9mm and

gripped it with both hands. Her finger trembled beside the trigger guard, and her breath huffed heat against the mask, wetting the material. Stepping softly through the grass to match Nico's steps, she trailed behind him toward the house.

The only assumption she had to go on was they were breaking up a slave ring. If that was the case, wouldn't they want to make sure she didn't accidentally shoot an innocent? Maybe there weren't any slaves in that house.

Rather than leading her to the porch, he ushered her along the side of it. As Matias climbed the short flight of steps to the front door, Nico kept her in the concealment of the shadows ten feet away. She ducked behind an overgrown bush beside the railing just as Matias knocked.

A mewling noise sounded from the darkness on the far side of the porch. Then it mewed again in a harrowing appeal for mercy — the weak cries of a dying animal.

Her breath came in gasps, and the hair on her nape rose. Nico gripped the juncture of her neck and shoulder with warning pressure.

Matias turned toward the cries, and the muscles across his back visibly stiffened. What did he see? A cat? Dog? She tried to block the mewling out of her head by focusing on Nico's grip.

Matias shifted back to the door as it opened. Nico dropped his hand.

She angled her neck, peering through the branches to see whoever stood just inside the house, but Matias' broad shoulders obstructed her view.

A handgun was tucked in the back of his jeans.

Another one sat in a noticeable shoulder holster. His hard-packed body flexed beneath his t-shirt, but in the next heartbeat, his entire demeanor changed.

His hips loosened and his stance relaxed in a picture of suave arrogance. He crossed a foot over the other and propped it on the toe of the boot. With a forearm braced on the door frame, he lifted the other to slide his thumb over his bottom lip.

Wearing a sexy as fuck smile, he rumbled the Colombian greeting. *"Qué más pues, señorita?"*

"My, my, aren't you a handsome one?" a woman purred in Spanish.

Tension shot through Camila's shoulders and neck. Was he here for this woman? To capture her? Seduce her? Maybe this was a brothel of slaves.

Trust his reasons and keep him alive.

"I have an appointment." He continued in the native language.

"I might be more your flavor, no? Spend some time with me and find out, *viga.*"

Her Spanish was so thick Camila struggled to translate it. *Viga?* She thought it meant *superior muscles.*

"I have particular tastes, yeah?" Matias moved his hand toward the vicinity of the woman's chest as his eyes swept past her.

Scoping the place?

His fingers stroked something on the woman, something Camila couldn't see but had no fucking trouble imagining. She felt her damn eye twitching and couldn't stop it.

Nico gripped her wrist. Without looking at him, she nodded and forced herself to relax. Matias had said he needed to get through the door. Evidently, that required fondling another woman's tits.

He continued the flirtatious conversation in Spanish, telling her how sexy she was, how *bacano* her tits felt, and that her lips were more deadly than his .40 cal. He wooed and winked and charmed the panties right off her skank ass. Hopefully, not literally. Camila still couldn't see her beyond the door.

Camila kept her finger off the trigger and her breaths steady, but Nico didn't let go of her arm.

"I have an appointment." Matias rolled the syllables in Spanish.

An appointment for what? A prostitute? The idea of him fucking other women was ridiculous. Saving them, though? That made so much more sense. But who was he saving them from? Whoever had arrived in those luxury cars? An icy chill rushed through her core and chased the heat from her limbs. She glanced at Nico, but his attention was locked on Matias.

"You're no fun," the woman said. "This way."

Matias followed her in and closed the door behind him.

"Fuck," Camila whispered, shoving Nico's hand away. "Are there slaves in there? Is this a whore house?"

He launched to his feet, dragging her with him, and pivoted toward the side of the house.

A second later, a solid dark shape darted around the corner from the backyard. Ski mask. Slender build. Large knife in hand.

Frizz. She recognized the metal buckles crisscrossing his black shirt.

"Back door?" Nico asked the other man in a hushed voice.

Frizz shook his head, blue eyes glowing in the dim

light from the porch. Jesus, he looked different with his stitched lips hidden and his crazy hair tucked away. He looked…normal. Young. Really fucking young, like late-teens. He was just a baby.

Had he been rescued from slavery himself? If so, why would he torment the slaves at the estate?

He held up two fingers and pointed across the yard at the shadowed tree line. Identifying the location of the men Burd had brought?

Holding down three fingers and a thumb, he pointed his knife at the house.

Nico nodded and turned toward her, whispering, "Three men and a woman inside. Shoot anyone you don't know. Try not to kill the female."

What the fuck? The gun rattled in her hands. "Why would I kill anyone when I don't know who they are?"

Those people could be undercover DEA or FBI or just a family trying to survive amid the violence. They could be the good guys.

What if that wasn't it at all? Maybe Matias' cartel captured women who ran slave rings and sold them as punishment. Her heart pounded. Could she hope for such a possibility?

Nico lifted a hand to touch the mask on her face and stopped before making contact. "You're about to find out."

Frizz slipped around them and crept onto the porch, his steps silent and movements graceful. Nico followed, and she stayed on their heels.

They froze at the sound of a wane cry coming from the dark corner of the stoop. Definitely a dying animal.

Frizz moved first, slinking toward it. Thank fuck, the boards didn't creak, but she braced for it, tensing for any noise that might give them away.

She stepped where Frizz stepped and stopped beside him, her eyes straining in the absence of light as she tried to make out the floating shape.

A lamb. She sucked in a breath through the mask.

A newborn lamb, hanging upside-down by its back legs. Its front legs scissored weakly, reaching for the floor but not quite touching. Its mewls were so frail and brittle it must've been hanging there for a long time.

Manic energy surged through her blood, begging her to help it. But Frizz beat her there, knife out and cutting it down before she took the first step.

When he lowered it to the floor, she whispered inanely, "Why?"

"Dinner." Nico turned back toward the door.

Dinner? Fine, then fucking eat it. Don't torture it first. What the fuck was wrong with people?

She moved to follow Nico, but her gaze was glued over her shoulder.

Frizz squatted beside the poor thing, petting it and making shushing sounds. It didn't even try to move or run away. Probably too weak. Or maybe it didn't know any better than to trust a guy who sewed up women. Maybe this was an alternative reality, and *she* didn't know which end was up. Whatever was going on, watching him soothe that lamb made her chest so tight she couldn't breathe.

She joined Nico at the door, and he held up a closed fist, signaling her to stop. His other hand gripped the knob, but he didn't turn it, didn't move.

Her pulse spiked. They'd already used up thirty seconds with the lamb. What if Matias needed back up for…whatever the fuck he was doing?

Another count of too many seconds stretched by before a scream penetrated the door from within. Nico swung it open, and she followed him through, gun pointed toward the floor and her pulse pounding in her stomach.

A woman lay unconscious on the floor, bleeding from her temple, but it was the heavy thumps and whimpers coming from the back of the house that slowed Camila's gait.

Frizz swept around her and knelt beside the woman as Nico took off down the long hall that led toward multiple closed doors, his pistol trained and ready. He slipped into the first room and shut the door. Grunts immediately sounded through the wall, followed by something crashing.

With wobbly steps, she moved in that direction, but a hand gripped her ankle, causing her to stumble. She whirled and met Frizz's wide gaze where he knelt on the threadbare carpet. He shook his head frantically and pointed at the floor beside her feet.

He wanted her to stay? But Matias was back there. What if one of those grunts was his? She didn't even know who was in those rooms. Slaves? Being forced at that very moment? Oh God, she hoped she wasn't right.

Her hands shook around the stock of the gun, palms soaked in sweat as she inched toward the hallway.

A different door opened up ahead, and a fat naked Caucasian man stepped out, his penis fully erect beneath his jiggling belly. Her heart stopped.

He looked at her and narrowed his eyes on the gun she pointed at him. "Who are you?

The mask protected her identity, and Nico had told her to shoot anyone she didn't know. But on what grounds? Because the man's dick was hard? Maybe he'd been jerking off. Completely naked? No fucking way.

She steadied the iron sights on his chest. "Who are you?"

CHAPTER 26

Camila kept the 9mm leveled on the naked man's torso, her chest heaving, knees wobbling. She wet her lips, and her tongue brushed against the mask as she slid a finger over the trigger.

A pained male voice bellowed from the back room, followed by a succession of crashing sounds. The naked man widened his eyes, glanced over his shoulder, and darted that way, toward the last door where the screaming came from.

Her pulse thundered in her ears as she pointed the gun at his back. Fuck, she'd never forgive herself if she killed an innocent man, but he if touched that door knob, she wouldn't hesitate to squeeze the trigger.

"Stop or I'll shoot!" She ran after him.

The next few seconds flashed in the span of two anguished breaths. She passed the fat man's room in the first breath, glimpsed a baby doll on the floor, a bare mattress, and the lopsided pigtails and tear-soaked eyes of a girl no older than nine huddled nude in the corner.

No no no no! Her second breath came with an explosion of fire as she aimed her horror-stricken fury on the fat man, trained the gun a few inches higher, and sprayed his brain matter across the wall.

Her next breath died in her throat as she screamed in horror. But nothing passed her lips. Not a sound. Not a breath. Every living thing inside her was sobbing in the room with that little girl. This wasn't shock. She stood frozen in a place she wasn't sure she could come back from.

The remaining two doors opened at the same time. Her arms moved on reflex, the gun swinging left to right as she waited for another naked dead man to step out.

Nico emerged first, eyes scowling through the ski mask and red dots peppering his gray shirt.

"Camila." Matias stepped out of the last room, wearing a mask of blood. He raised red-smeared hands and took a limping step toward her. "Lower the gun."

What was in those other rooms? She wanted to ask, but her voice had left her. Maybe she already knew the answer. Her brain felt fuzzy, and she shook. Fuck, she shook from head to toe.

Nico stood nearest to her. Close enough to reach out and grip the barrel trembling in her hands. She let him take it.

Matias glanced down at the fat man and lifted his eyes to her, wearing a blood-speckled smirk. "You're so badass."

She stared at the body blankly, didn't feel a twinge of regret.

Favoring his left leg, Matias slowly erased the distance with his arms stretched open. She walked into his embrace and dropped her forehead on his blood-soaked chest.

He pulled the mask off Camila's head and held her against him as footsteps sounded behind her. Tiny cries trickled from the three rooms, and his arms tightened.

More little girls. She fought back the rising, burning need to sob and glanced over her shoulder.

The men who had arrived with Burd strode through the front room. Nico and Frizz stepped aside, their tight expressions no longer hidden by masks.

The soldiers pulled off their own ski masks, revealing feminine faces and long hair. Not men? The rest of their womanhood remained hidden beneath fatigues and loose shirts.

Matias shifted Camila out of the way as the women split off into separate rooms. A moment later, Picar shuffled in, carrying a medical bag.

A tidal wave of questions and confusion slammed into her. Two women and a doctor. Presumably, there were three young girls in those rooms, and two more dead pedophiles. All of this had been planned out and executed with one goal. Matias had come here to save those girls.

She struggled to stand upright against the pounding, overwhelming barrage of emotions. Working her throat, she couldn't separate the numbness from her voice. "Can I...do something?"

What could she do? Comfort the girls? Play nurse? Clean up the bodies? Fuck, she wasn't emotionally fit for any of that. She needed to sit down.

Matias turned her toward the front of the house. "You need air."

She needed to know he was okay. With a surge of determined concentration, she shifted back to him and crouched to examine his leg. Her fingers slipped over blood in the ripped part of his jeans on his thigh. "How bad?"

"I'm fine." He pulled her up and nudged her

toward the door.

As she crossed the front room, she glimpsed worn wood paneling on the walls, ratty furniture, dishes piled on a counter in a kitchen that was more like an extension of the front room with a stove, sink, and fridge shoved against a wall.

A little pink backpack and a fuzzy stuffed rabbit sat the corner. Her fingernails pierced into her palms.

The woman lay on the floor, eyes blinking rapidly, face streaked with tears, and lips sewn shut. *Just like the slaves at the estate.*

Camila froze as the last three weeks started to click into place.

"Who is this woman?" She stopped a few feet from Frizz.

His lips rolled behind his own stitches as he looked to Nico, who stood in the front doorway, smoking a cigarette.

"That woman," Nico said through a puff of smoke, "is the girls' mother. Ages nine, eleven, and twelve. The same girls she offered to sell to our slave ring."

His eyes shifted to the hallway. Then he turned away.

The same girls she'd pimped out to those dead men.

Camila's vision turned red with murderous rage. "Why is she still alive?"

Blood surged to her arms and legs, her hands fisted, and her pulse screamed through her veins. She flung herself toward the woman, claws out, teeth bared, desperate to scratch eye balls, rip out hair, and ram something sharp and lethal down that vile gullet.

Matias caught her around the waist before she

reached the despicable waste of life.

"Shh." He turned her to face him.

"The slaves at the compound…" she choked. "They're not innocent?" A wave of chills swept through her, followed by a rush of heat as her mind assembled the pieces. "You torture slave traders. Then you sell them."

"Oh, I kill them, too, like the one in the back room." He stared into her eyes, his face splattered with blood and the hazel depths of his gaze stark with sadness. "But every woman and man we capture and sell deserves a fate worse than death. Some traffic humans. Others are like her, sell or whore out their own children."

Her stomach swooped and flipped. The ages of his slaves, his complete lack of sympathy for them, his reason for doing it…

The answer is right in front of you. All you have to do is fucking look.

He'd wanted her to see a man who loved her so much he would never become a slave trader. A man who loved her to the ends of hell and back as he tracked down the worst kind of monsters and stopped them from harming others.

She swayed with dizziness, her eyes burning with the onset of tears. "I need to sit down."

He moved her outside to the porch, and she instantly glanced at the dark corner, searching for the lamb. It was too shadowy, too quiet, so she stepped in that direction.

"Frizz wouldn't have left it there." Matias' timbre caressed the rawness of her nerves.

"Oh." She frowned. "Do you think…?"

"He ended its suffering?" He nodded. "And moved it somewhere you wouldn't see it."

She stared out into the gloom of their surroundings, probing for the little lamb's body. Her stomach squeezed painfully. It was silly to care about a dead animal considering what she'd just witnessed. She must've been stretched thin on heartache.

"Sit with me." He held out his hand.

She joined him on the steps, where they sat side by side and gazed at the vastness of the black sky. A moment later, Nico brought out a couple of towels and returned inside.

Welcoming the distraction, she focused on cleaning Matias' face, wiping the sculptured edges around his strong jaw, stern brow, and the strands of his thick black hair. His gaze never left hers as she used the corners of the cloth to clear away the splatter around his eyes, perfect nose, the creases in his ears, and his dimples when he smiled gently.

Then she used the clean towel to dab at the knife wound in his thigh.

"Picar needs to look at this," she said with an achy voice, her mind spinning in a million different directions.

"He's busy." Matias grimaced when she pressed too hard. "Frizz can stitch it."

"Frizz!" she shouted over her shoulder. When he appeared on the porch, she lifted the towel. "Need you to sew up a stab wound."

His eyes glimmered, and he rushed back into the house. When he returned moments later, he carried an armful of bandages and supplies that he'd probably swiped from Picar's bag.

He cut Matias' jeans away from the injury and set to work, cleaning and preparing the wound.

She lifted Matias' hand and used one of the

bandages to clear away the blood. "How long have you been doing this?"

"Ten years." His fingers curled around hers.

"A year after I was captured."

"Yeah. It took some time to organize."

"Jesus, Matias." Her heart panged. "You could've told me this during any one of our phone calls. I would've joined your efforts and helped you." *We could've been together all these years.*

He shook his head. "I was in a bad place those first few years. I killed more slave traders than I captured. So fucking reckless and dangerous and *angry*." He lifted his chin at Frizz. "This guy kept my head on straight."

Frizz paused during a stitch and stared at the ground.

"You've been doing this with Matias since the beginning?" she asked Frizz, studying his youthful face. "How old are you?"

Frizz closed his eyes, opened them, and reached for the knife beside his knee. Then he lifted the blade to his mouth and cut each stitch, one by one, pulling away the threads as he went.

Matias squeezed her hand, and she squeezed back, her insides twisting in knots.

"I was eight when Matias found me." Frizz's voice cracked, soft and chalky with disuse.

Her heart clenched.

He glanced toward the house, but his gaze turned distant. "He pulled me out of a place just like this. My old man…" He cleared his throat, his inflection gentle and distinctly American. "My father used to sell me to men like those in there. The men wanted to hear me cry and beg. When I wouldn't do it, my father hurt me very badly."

An ache pressed against the backs of her eyes and seared through her chest. She wanted to reach for him, hold his hand. Matias looked as if he wanted to do the same, but didn't move, so she followed his lead.

"I like to sew my mouth." Frizz licked his bottom lip. "So I won't forget."

"So you won't forget…?" The lump in her throat burned painfully.

"I'll never give them what they want." He stared at his unmoving hands, fingers clenched around the needle. "They'll never hear me beg, never force…themselves in my mouth again."

She tried to keep the tears at bay, tried not to look at him with pity. All she could think about was an eight-year-old boy, abused and molested, living with a cartel and following the capo around while he slaughtered predators.

Maybe it was the best form of therapy. Hadn't she done the same thing?

"What happened to your father?" She had a damn good guess.

"Matias castrated him." Frizz smiled. "And cut out his tongue. He removed other organs, too. *Then* he killed the bastard."

Her stomach curdled. "Is there anything left of the man in the room you were in?" she asked Matias, nodding at the house.

"Pieces." Matias looked over at her and shrugged. "I have a really sharp knife."

"Good." She lay her head on his shoulder. "Did the little girl…did she watch that?"

"I sent her to the closet the second I charged in."

He tensed, relaxed. "Those girls will be removed without witnessing the gore."

She traced the ink on his forearm, following the branches with a finger. "Okay."

Frizz sewed up Matias' leg wound in silence. Then he restitched his lips without a mirror, his fingers expertly moving the needle through the existing holes. She watched through a new set of eyes and no longer saw a scary freak. As he poked the needle through his flesh, she thought of it as a lip piercing, a rebellious expression of self. A *fuck you* to dear old dad.

When he finished, he gathered the supplies and strolled into the house, whistling a cheery, unfamiliar tune.

She sat alone with Matias for an endless moment. The heavy hush between them bled into the darkness, dampened by the buzz of winged insects.

"When we get back, I'm calling my friends, Matias." She slid her hand over his thigh. "They need to know I'm okay."

"Anything you want." He turned his face toward her and put his lips on hers. Slightly open. A tiny gliding movement. Then he kissed her nose.

"Why didn't you tell me about the slaves three weeks ago?"

"I wanted you to love me despite this." He pulled away, bracing elbows on his knees, and stared straight ahead.

"I would've loved you no matter what. It was inevitable."

"Through all your one-night stands, what would you have done if one of those men told you he saved child slaves? Would he have become more to you than just a hookup?"

She rubbed her forehead and stared at him sidelong. "That's such a crazy *what if.* I don't know." But she did know. She would've clung to that connection.

"Your heart beats for the end of slavery. If you found that same passion in someone else, *anyone* else, your heart would've cemented you to him." He met her eyes. "I didn't want to be just anyone. I wanted to be *your* one, passions and pursuits aside. I wanted you to choose me for *us.*" He looked back at the landscape. "So I let you see whatever you wanted to see at the estate and waited until you saw *me.*"

She swallowed thickly. "The amount of fear and doubt and fucking dread I've gone through over the past few weeks…"

"Vulnerability has to happen for love to be real."

Profound and really smart, but also… "This is crazy." She scrubbed her hands over her hair. "You could've just told me your slaves were horrible people, and bam, you would've had me just like that."

"Too easy. You're not getting it." He shifted to face her and gripped her chin. "I refuse to settle for anything less than what we had as kids. You loved me when you were sixteen for no other reason than because your gut told you we were meant to be together. But age and experience fucks with our instincts. Our minds get in the way and try to reason and rationalize every goddamn emotion." He released her chin. "I stripped those rationalizations away and forced you to focus on what you really felt, not what your mind told you to feel. And you believed. You believed in us without seeing…this." He gestured at the house.

"Faith," she whispered.

"Faith in *us*." He focused on her mouth and leaned in, kissing her in that tender way that always made her melt.

"Seems like you went through a lot of trouble for such a blurry concept," she said against his lips, her vision smudging with tears. "Who does that?"

"People have been killing each other because of faith for hundreds of years." He smoothed a hand across her cheek.

"Because of religion, Matias, which is based on control and fear."

"But it starts with faith. Some believe strongly enough they die for it." He leaned in and touched his forehead to hers. "You took that step tonight. You believed in us so passionately you walked into that house and risked your life."

"You're insane." She wrapped her arms around his wide shoulders and sighed. "I love it. Everything you said was wild and inconceivable and could be argued until the end of the burning sun, and that's why it makes sense." She kissed him, softly, deeply. "Every reason, justification, and argument leads us to the same result. We're together because that's where we belong."

He pulled her into his arms, and they settled into a cradle of silence. Voices and footsteps trickled from the house. The constant noise of whirring life echoed around them, and a thickening mantle of sorrow and relief smothered the air.

"How are you doing with this?" He nodded at the door.

"I experienced that whole thing way, way down deep." An unreachable shiver jolted inside her. "All those feelings are still there, lodged somewhere between my heart and stomach. When they decide to resurface, it's really going to hurt like hell." She rubbed her face. "Those girls, Matias…God, I can't…I just can't think about it."

"Don't." He kissed her cheek, brushing his nose against hers affectionately. "It gets easier, I promise. And I'll be right at your side every step of the way."

Golden fire, kindled in a Texan citrus grove and forged in a decade of hell, burned in his eyes.

She drew him close and touched her lips to his scruffy jaw. "What happens to them now?"

"The women will take them to a foster home, one of the many I vetted and trust. I fund every step of their recoveries. I also put the fear of God in those foster families to ensure they provide the best environments for the children I send to them."

"There's my crime boss." She stared up at the sky and smiled to herself. "You're a good man, Matias."

"Then I haven't scared you enough." He lowered his mouth to her shoulder, pressing a kiss there while never taking his eyes off her. "I'll have another chance to do that before we head home."

"What do you mean?"

"The Córdoba cartel is waiting at the helicopter to ambush us."

Her face went cold. "What?"

CHAPTER 27

"What do you mean? Why are we just sitting here?"

Matias felt the worked-up rasp of Camila's voice like a hungry tongue on his cock. "We have time."

"Time for what?" She sprung nimbly to her feet and stepped off the porch.

Dark jeans stretched over her sexy curves, paired with a plain black t-shirt that molded to her perfect rack. Illuminated by the glow of the porch light, shiny black hair framed her gorgeous face and hung in windblown waves around her shoulders. There wasn't a square inch of imperfection anywhere on her.

The savage need to claim her in front of God and everyone stirred in his blood. *Wrong fucking place and time.*

She stood in front of his perch on the steps, putting them at eye level. "This better not be one of those I-ask-you-don't-say-shit conversations."

He combated her glare, but goddamn, she made him hard as a rock. "We're catching a different ride home." His annoyance with the deal Nico made coiled tension into his shoulders. "I lost my favorite helicopter."

"Wait. Hold up." Brown eyes full of spark, she anchored her hands on her hips in the feisty pose he'd loved since they were kids. "You said there's another cartel waiting to ambush you?"

"Yes. Los Córdoba."

"How do you know this?"

"I set it up."

"You *what*?"

He smirked, enjoying the angry flush in her cheeks.

She cast her gaze heavenward. "*Santa Madre de Dios*, give me the strength to *not* strangle this man."

The crunch of tires on gravel sounded in the distance and grew louder up the driveway just as Nico stepped out of the house.

"We're on our way," Nico said into the phone at his ear. Ending the call, he strode down the steps past Matias.

As the black sedan pulled up behind Camila, she pointed at Matias. "Keep talking."

"In the car." He moved off the porch, toward the driveway, and opened the rear door for her.

Burd relinquished the driver's seat and headed into the house. As a lower-ranked member, he'd been vetted for the vigilante portion of this trip, but not for the next part.

"Are the others coming with us?" Camila stared after Burd as she slid into the backseat.

"Frizz and Picar will stay with the girls for a couple days." Matias latched her seatbelt, trailed a finger across her bottom lip, and shut the door.

He met Nico's eyes over the roof of the sedan. Matias preferred to be the fake bodyguard and chauffeur—the guy no one paid attention to or targeted. But as Nico climbed into the backseat beside Camila, Matias reconsidered the whole decoy thing.

It was purely an emotional reaction after a godawful night. He didn't want anyone else protecting her or sitting by her. He sure as hell didn't want people thinking she belonged to Nico.

Fuck, that sounded ridiculous, even in his head.

Wiping a hand down his face, he lowered into the driver seat, cranked up the A/C, and drove away from the house. He only had about ten minutes to prepare her before they reached their rendezvous point.

"Last week, you gave me an idea." He adjusted the rear-view mirror and found her steady brown eyes. "I decided that we didn't have a mole, but we needed one."

"I'm not following." She shook her head.

Nico powered on his tablet, and the glow from the screen brightened her face.

"We know Gerardo leaked information to a cartel." He eased onto a dirt road, watching the side mirrors for other vehicles. "We just didn't know who he worked with or if he exposed our two biggest secrets."

"I assume one is your identity. The other..." She frowned in concentration. "The location of your headquarters?"

"Yes. For the past week, I kept all our lieutenants congregated at the estate and inconspicuously beefed up security, all while giving whoever was watching our business activities the impression that we were still focused on finding a spy." He hit the gas on a straight empty road surrounded by fields. "We kept our ears to the ground, listening for whispers about an attack against the estate, and uncovered nothing. Not a peep. The location of our headquarters remains a secret, but..." He propped an elbow on the console. "The information Gerardo leaked put our smuggling routes at risk."

"They're going to attack your supply lines?"

"The most profitable ones. Our rivals want that business more than anything." He clenched his jaw. "I've let them think we're too distracted to notice what they're planning. And I gave them a different distraction—another Gerardo."

"You gave them a mole? Inside your cartel?" She leaned forward, watching him in the mirror with wide eyes.

"A fake one." *Mierda,* he loved her interest in his business. "Chispa sent out feelers, making contact with our enemies under the guise that there was unrest within our ranks and he wanted out. He dangled valuable secrets, trying to lure the group that turned Gerardo."

"I bet your enemies crawled all over themselves trying to recruit him."

"Of course. But only one cartel could confirm their involvement with Gerardo." Matias drummed his fingers on the steering wheel.

"Los Córdoba?"

He nodded. "They know things only Gerardo knew."

"That's the group you set up to ambush you?" Her voice pitched with disbelief. "Why the hell would you do that?"

"*Oiga,*" Nico said. "He's getting to the good part."

"Chispa made a deal with Los Córdoba." Matias veered onto another dirt road. The lights of the nearest town glimmered on the horizon, but he made another turn, driving away from it and into the darkness of barren landscape. "In exchange for their protection, Chispa gave them the names of our liaisons and security details on the narcotics business we run through our El

Paso compound. He gave them everything they need to steal that operation from us."

"What?" She gasped. "You forfeited your entire El Paso division?"

"To convince them to trust Chispa." Matias shrugged. "The Feds are days from taking it anyway. Los Córdoba doesn't know that. Besides, someone suggested we start looking at new smuggling routes like Australia."

She flopped against the seat back and groaned. "Me and my fucking mouth."

"Love fucking your mouth, *mi vida*." He held her gaze in the mirror.

Nico cleared his throat. "Turn right at the fork up ahead."

"I'm still waiting to hear about this ambush." She raised her brows.

"Mm." Matias squinted at the road, watching for the turn off. "Chispa contacted Los Córdoba when we left him at the helicopter. Told them where he was and that Nico Restrepo would be returning soon. Perfect set up for them to trap us. I'd be really surprised if the Córdoba capo isn't there just to watch Nico get killed."

Her gaze darted to Nico, her mouth hanging open. "Okay, we're obviously not returning to the helicopter." She looked back at the mirror. "When you don't show, they'll know Chispa set them up." She narrowed her eyes with suspicion. "You did something, didn't you? Did you assemble your own surprise attack on *them*?"

"Love the way your mind works." He grinned.

"I have a contact on the Colombian police force," Nico said.

"Not an ally." Matias spotted the fork and turned off. "Just a guy Nico makes deals with."

"Oh my fuck." Camila touched her throat, her gaze flickering between him and Nico. "You sent the police to ambush them? What about Chispa? Won't they take him into custody?"

Nico powered down the tablet. "I negotiated the release of Chispa and Don—the pilot—in exchange for the location of this ambush."

"But the police are keeping my fucking helicopter." Matias gritted his teeth.

"I should be getting a call anytime from my police contact," Nico said. "Hopefully, they'll have Álvarez"—a glance at Camila—"he's the capo, in custody and put this headache behind us. Los Córdoba won't survive without him."

"Jesus." She slumped in the seat. "What if Álvarez isn't there?"

"Then he got a very strong message from us." Matias spied a helicopter-sized blob in the field up ahead.

"Don't fuck with the Restrepo cartel?" she breathed.

"Exactly." Nico removed his seatbelt and leaned forward to speak low in Matias' ear. "You're out of time, *parce*. You need to tell her."

"Tell me what?" She unlatched her belt, her gaze skittering over the field and landing on the helicopter.

The moment Matias parked beside the twin-engine, Nico swung open his door and stepped out.

"Camila." Matias shut off the motor. "This is the helicopter I keep in Bogota. I had one of my guys fly it here along with someone—"

"Oh my God." She stared out the passenger window, breaths quickening as her hands fumbled with the door latch. "Is that…?"

He followed her gaze to the man hopping out of the aircraft. Muscled physique, dark blond hair, arm sleeved in ink. Yep. "Tate Vades."

She flung her door open and ran. Had they been on a busy street, she probably would've leapt over cars in her urgency to reach the bastard. Matias rubbed the bridge of his nose and followed her.

With her arms wrapped around Tate's shoulders, she lifted on tiptoes and pressed her cheek against his neck. "What're you doing here?"

Matias flexed his fingers and forced his feet to remain planted a couple yards behind her.

Tate met his eyes, expression tight. "You didn't tell her?"

Expecting the piercing anger in the question, Matias lifted a shoulder. "I ran out of time."

She stepped back, staring at Tate then glaring at Matias. "Why is he here?"

"You had three weeks!" Tate threw his arms up.

"I've been wooing her." Matias straightened, clasping his hands behind his back.

It'd been critical that she didn't know about Tate's role until she'd given herself to Matias fully and completely. That hadn't happened until she knelt for him and told him she loved him on the other helicopter only a couple hours earlier.

"*Wooing?* Is that what you call it?" Camila held his gaze as she stabbed a finger toward Tate. "Explain this."

The pilot started up the helicopter with a squealing whine of the engines. The tail rotor and blades turned, spinning faster and ruffling her long hair.

"Hash it out in the air," Nico shouted as he strode by with his nose buried in his phone. "We need to go."

Matias and Nico quickly changed into the clean clothes the pilot had been instructed to bring, and twenty minutes later, the helicopter reached coasting altitude.

The cabin was comparable in size to the other one and refurbished to enable passengers to talk without headsets. But it was older and made for wear, reminding Matias of the interior of a commercial airliner. That was fine since it was primarily used by his lieutenants and hitmen.

Nico and Tate sat with their backs to the cockpit, facing the bench seat Matias shared with Camila.

"They got Álvarez and most of his top men." Nico held up a text message on his phone, grinning. "Chispa and Don are going to lay low for a few days before we send for them."

Los Córdoba is finished. Now Camila could safely wander the estate as his equal.

Matias closed his eyes in relief and reached over to clasp her hand. When her soft fingers closed around his, he knew that everything would be okay. They were headed home, and while she was probably ready to chew him a new asshole over Tate, she was here, holding his hand, her thumb stroking his. Because she loved him. Best fucking feeling in the world.

"Are we worried about being tracked again?" she asked.

"Not till we get closer to home." He took in the beauty of her profile—long lashes, high cheekbones, supple lips—and drew a deep breath. "I met Tate four years ago."

She glanced at Tate, who nodded.

Her eyes closed. "I assume that wasn't coincidental." She cast a sideways glare at Matias. "How did you find us?"

For the next few minutes, he explained how he'd arrived to collect Van Quiso's body the day Liv Reed shot him, and how Van, bleeding and barely alive, led him to Liv, who unknowingly took him right to Camila.

She tipped her head as she listened, and when he fell quiet, she didn't blow up or rush him with questions. She simply waited.

"I watched you for a couple of months. Determined your patterns, your goals, who you were closest to." He lifted his chin at Tate.

Her former roommate sat directly across from her, his knees brushing against hers.

"Matias approached me at a bar." Tate bent forward and gathered her hands in his. "He told me your history with him, how you guys grew up together, that he was the one you called to deal with the bodies, and that he loved you. So I knew you trusted him to some degree." His leg bounced. "He told me he was the boss of the Restrepo cartel and that he was the kind of guy who took what he wanted. But he couldn't take you because you'd been captured before. He couldn't just rip you away from your life because he'd never win you that way." He smirked. "He pitched this crazy fucking plan to me, Camila."

"What plan?" She pulled her hands gently from his.

Next to Tate, Nico put in ear buds and reclined in the seat, closing his eyes. He'd heard this story so many times, had been there through it all. Matias didn't blame him for shutting them out.

Tate gave Matias a questioning look, and Matias gestured for him to continue. It would be better for her to hear this part from him.

"There was a slave ring in Austin. Just a couple of local guys. Not affiliated with anyone. Those are the guys you initially started tracking."

"Oh, God." She ran a hand through her hair. "I can totally guess where you're going with this."

Matias put a hand on her thigh, and she didn't push it away. She didn't touch it, either.

Tate gave her a small smile. "Matias told me that night he intended to kill off that slave ring and replace it with his own people. He would continue to operate it, except the slaves would be fake. Actresses. All of it staged to draw you in. And he needed my help."

Her face turned white.

Matias tried to hold his breath, but he couldn't. He needed to make something very clear. "I know you would've taken down that operation within weeks. You're so damn tenacious and brave those motherfuckers didn't stand a chance. But I was selfish. I wanted you fighting at my side, in Colombia, against some of the worst slavery on the planet. I needed you."

She rubbed her forehead and closed her eyes, her expression giving nothing away. Then she looked at Tate. "So you went along with this?"

"Not immediately. I left the bar with my goddamn head spinning." Tate pulled her arms down and forced her to look at him. "A month later, he flew me to Colombia and took me on one of his raids. It was a fucking barn…" He swiped a hand over his mouth, his blue eyes darkening with memories.

A shiver raced through Matias as he recalled that night. He'd never been enslaved, but the depravity he'd witnessed over the years had deeply connected him to her cause. All the effort she invested — the spying, planning, and risking her life — meant as much to him as it did to her. She was *his*, and he was wonderstruck by her ambition. She hadn't let her own captivity ruin her life. She was too strong a woman to hide in fear. Instead, she used her knowledge and experience to save as many lives as she could.

She would've eventually expanded her campaign beyond Texas, and it was his responsibility to be there, protecting her when she did. There were so many predators in the world, breeding the kind of horrors she fought against. Like the barn.

"There were children," Tate whispered, "naked and shackled, being auctioned off." His shoulders shook, and he met Matias' eyes. "Matias saved every one of them and left an unholy massacre in his wake."

"You fell in love with him that night." The stubborn set of her chin eased as she studied Tate's face.

"Uh." Tate laughed and raked a hand through his blond hair. "As much as a straight guy can appreciate another man, I guess. I was willing to do whatever he asked of me."

At some point over the past four years, Matias developed a soul-deep respect for the guy. Deep enough that he would kill anyone who tried to harm Tate.

"Your heart beats for the end of slavery." She echoed Matias' words to Tate. "You found that same passion in Matias."

It was exactly the thing Matias needed to hear her say. She understood him in a way no one else could.

"For sure." Tate wiped his palms on his thighs, avoiding Matias' stare. "By the way, he was dead set on capturing Van and Liv and selling them into slavery."

"What?" She froze.

Matias still wanted to punish them, but... "Tate filled me in on how they were coerced into human trafficking, so I made an exception and spared them."

"Thank you." She played with the ends of her hair. "I'm still reeling over the fact that you and Tate know each other." She eyed Tate suspiciously. "Four years ago, you left for a week to go on a soul-searching road trip across the States."

"He was with me in Colombia," Matias said. "After the raid at the barn, he stayed at the estate for a few days."

"Why did you involve Tate at all?" she asked.

"He was the closest I could get to you." Matias' stomach sank just as the helicopter dipped and recovered altitude. "He watched over you, protected you, and called me every day, letting me know every detail of your life, including the things you confided in him."

"What things?" she growled, shooting a glare at Tate.

"This is why I wanted you to have this conversation before I arrived." Tate frowned at Matias as he leaned back and folded his arms across his chest.

Matias caught her chin and touched her mouth with his, quick and chaste. Then he released her, but kept his face close. "You told him your sexual cravings. Your desire to be held down, controlled, fucked hard—"

"Okay, stop." She leaned back. "I know what I told him." She turned her glare on Tate. "Not cool, man."

Without Tate's intel, it would've taken Matias a long damn time to figure out she was a sexual submissive. He knew she leaned that way as a sixteen-year-old girl, but she'd also been young and innocent.

After her abduction, he'd been shocked as hell to learn that her submissive cravings had only deepened.

"He told me things, Camila." Tate cocked his head. "*His* sexual preferences. You were both in my fucking ear. Him wanting to dominate you. You wanting to be dominated. I knew, without a doubt in my mind, you were perfect for each other. So I helped him out."

"With his plan," she said. "And that was…?"

"To get you to come to me willingly." Matias paused as the helicopter shuddered through turbulence. "I knew, eventually, you would try to infiltrate my fake slave ring disguised as a slave—"

"Oh, no." Her face turned ashen. "OhGodOhGod, I tortured and killed Larry McGregor."

"He was a legit scumbag," Matias said. "At first, you were tracking a real slave ring. I took those guys out, trickled you a few leads, planted people in your path, but after four years, you weren't biting." He smiled. "You were really cautious, and I'm fucking proud of you for that. But I was growing impatient. So I hand-selected Larry McGregor, a bona fide kidnapper. He'd never murdered anyone. Still, it was a risk I didn't like. Tate ensured me you would go back to his house and immediately choke him out." His nostrils flared. "Except you decided to—"

"I had to get him in that chokehold." She straightened and lifted her chin.

"Wait." Tate widened his eyes. "Tell me you didn't fuck—"

"I didn't." She sniffed. "What about the girl in Larry's barn?"

"An actress," Matias said. "I placed her in Larry's path."

She stared out the window as the helicopter vibrated and swooped with sideways movements and occasional rapid changes in altitude. He already missed his smooth-gliding Bell 429.

"I was making a difference in Austin," she said quietly. "So why do I feel like such a dumb, predictable pawn?"

He didn't want her to think he'd used her passion against slavery to trick her. Nor did he intend to belittle her extraordinary accomplishments.

His stomach hardened as he formulated his words. "You took down Van Quiso's operation, did you not?"

"With help."

"How many of your freedom fighters volunteered to infiltrate a slave ring as a slave? Look at me." When she did, he rested his forehead against hers. "The only predictable thing about you is your prowess. Frankly, I'm blown away by your badass-ness, Camila Dias. As a capo, I can't *not* recruit you. As the man who loves you, I can't *not* be at your side while you put yourself in danger."

She drew in a ragged breath. "You manipulated me."

"And you manipulated me, sneaking your sexy ass into my cartel with the intention of removing my head from my body."

"Well, yeah." She laughed nervously. "I…uh, decided that was a terrible plan."

"Thank fuck for that."

The helicopter wobbled, and she leaned away, tilting her head as she stared at Tate. "How did you get to Colombia so quickly?"

"I've been in Bogota since you left," Tate said.

334

"Waiting for this guy to fly me to you."

"Oh." Her eyebrows drew together. "Do Liv and Van and the others know?"

"Yeah." Tate picked at a hole in his jeans. "I filled them in after Van dropped you off."

"Bet you had a good laugh when I had that chip put in my tooth." Her jaw hardened. "That damn thing cost me a lot of money."

Tate grimaced. "Sorry about that."

She blew out a breath. "This is a lot to take in."

"You wouldn't have come to me any other way." Matias gripped her hand. "I couldn't capture you, couldn't chain you to my bed and force you to love me. It would've created a huge ugly thing between us. So I devised a plan that would bring you to Colombia, one that wouldn't put you in a situation where you'd be consumed with trying to escape."

"Wow," she whispered, staring at their entwined hands. "Fucking brilliant, really. I never once tried to escape. My interest was solely on you and your slaves."

Exactly.

Tate angled his body toward the window and closed his eyes as a smile played on his lips.

"You looked past my criminal activities." Matias traced her fingers where they curled around his. "The weapons, drugs, torture, my position in the cartel — all of it. You wouldn't have accepted any of that had I knocked on your door and explained it to you."

"You're right." Her grip tightened, and the vertical lines between her eyebrows deepened. "I probably would've stopped calling you if you'd told me you were a capo. But that doesn't mean I'm not angry about your secrecy."

"I'll make it up to—"

The soft weight of her hand covered his mouth.

"You're going to make it up to me by stepping out of my way when I take over your anti-slavery operation." She raised her brows in challenge.

He pulled her hand down and held on to it. "How about a compromise? I'll stand by your side while we run this thing together. It'll be one of my priorities, but I can't leave the cartel. I have too many enemies. If I walked away from this life, I would lose the protection and resources it gives me. It would be a life on the run, and I wouldn't be able to keep you safe the way I need to. Believe me, *mi vida*, I will chain you to my bed before I sacrifice your safety."

For the first time since she stepped onto the helicopter, her eyes shone bright.

"I never asked you to leave this life, but sometimes…" She leaned up and peppered his mouth with quick electric kisses. "Sometimes I might ask you to chain me to your bed."

CHAPTER 28

The next morning, Camila stood in Matias' closet — *their* closet — and stared at the door that hid skeletons. It'd been a low priority on her list of things to puzzle out, and he'd said she would have access when she was ready. She wasn't sure she'd ever be ready.

She continued to stare at the mysterious door as she dressed for the day. A simple white sundress. Flip-flops. No bra or panties, since he had a habit of ripping them in his haste to remove them. And no collar because she didn't find it in its usual resting place beside the bed.

He always removed it at night — a thoughtful thing to do since the stiff leather was uncomfortable to sleep in. But she felt naked without it. Disconnected from him.

He wasn't around to ask about it. A few hours earlier, he'd left her utterly exhausted and satisfied after waking her with his mouth on her pussy. As she'd drifted back to sleep, he'd kissed her and told her to find him when she was ready for the day.

She smiled as she strode out of the suite and wandered the halls, searching for him. She passed dozens of guards and other cartel members, and no one gave her a questioning look as to why she was collarless and strolling alone. Had he made some kind of announcement?

Twenty minutes later, she found him on the terrace by the pool, deep in conversation with Nico and Tate.

Tate.

Seeing him here really fucked with her reality. In a good way. Her worlds had collided, but instead of everything crumbling down around her in a fiery crash, it all just kind of…gelled.

Even so, she'd had a long talk with him and Matias on the flight home about how all their planning behind her back was the same as lying, and lying was the opposite of trust, and if they pulled that shit again, she wouldn't be as forgiving.

On the far side of the terrace, Matias sat with his back to her. As she emerged from the interior living room, he turned immediately, like he had some kind of internal radar tuned in to her location.

His white t-shirt pulled across his muscled shoulders and put his gorgeous ink on display, giving him a rough and dangerous look that made her heart shiver. He was powerful and infuriatingly domineering, but he was also so deeply sentimental she felt like a cold-hearted bitch in comparison.

He gave her a wink that liquefied her insides. Then he turned back to his conversation.

A quick scan of the terrace revealed two paths to reach him. One would take her around the left side of the lounge chairs. It was a few extra steps out of the way, but far more appealing than the other choice.

If she took the direct path alongside the pool, she would pass Yessica and the bevy of giggling women in string bikinis. Since she hadn't left Matias' side over the past three weeks, his presence had served as a buffer between her and these women. A conversation with them was overdue.

She looked at the safer path longingly.

Don't wimp out, Camila. Show them your teeth.

Squaring her shoulders and straightening her spine, she chose the path of most resistance.

The giggling stopped as she approached the lounge chairs, and four pairs of mascara-caked eyes locked on her.

"I heard Matias removed your collar." Yessica fingered an olive out of her martini—*at ten in the morning?*—and popped it in her mouth.

So Matias had made an announcement, but it could've been anything. *The slave is off her leash. The slave was never a slave. The slave is my life, and I'm going to marry her and have lots of babies…*

She sighed. How to reply?

Touching a hand to her naked throat, she went with honesty. "I miss it already."

Matias sat some thirty feet away, his upper body twisted in the chair and hands gripping the armrests as if moving to stand. She gave him a sharp shake of her head, and he relaxed, but didn't turn away.

A warm wind rustled across the terrace, rippling the water in the pool and producing a backdrop of whooshing noises. She doubted he could hear her from where he sat.

"Don't get too comfortable." One of Yessica's friends, a pretty blonde, adjusted the strap of her red bikini top. "He's not a one-woman kind of man."

"Oh really?" Camila kept her tone light and playful as her stomach boiled with acid. "How's that?"

"Well, we've all fucked him." The blonde gestured

at the other three women. "He visits lots of beds. Never sticks around." She shrugged. "He's the boss. Too important to be tied down."

Camila tried to ignore the twitch in her eye and the pang in her chest as her smile strained her face. She focused on the fact that this woman had casually mentioned Matias' role as the boss in front of his supposed slave. Now she really wanted to know the specifics of his announcement.

"But he seems to prefer Yessica." Another blonde plucked an olive from her bloody mary and tossed it in Yessica's modest cleavage.

They all laughed as Camila tried her damnedest to keep her fists from bloodying their noses.

"He makes his rounds, but he always comes back to me." Yessica stretched in the lounge chair, her tiny swimsuit revealing far more of her Latina curves than it covered. "I'll just hang out here until he comes in me...I mean, comes to me again."

"Huh." Camila gave her a thoughtful look. "When was the last time he came *in* you?"

"It's been...Oh, you know." Her eyes darted away, and she grinned, but it was taut at the corners. "He holds out for a while then he comes to me all pissed off and sexy. Sweet Jesus, that man gives good angry sex."

Camila's stomach threatened to hurl. She felt Matias gaze hot on her face, but she refused to look at him. It was crucial that she establish her position here without his dominating interference.

"And good gifts, too." Yessica's eyes sparkled. "He always gives me dresses and pearls and makeup—"

"Does he give you the belt?" Camila asked sweetly. She really didn't want to hear this answer, but she needed to understand if Yessica had been just an orgasm to him or if she was one of the women he'd shared a more intimate relationship with. The kind that involved pain and acceptance and trust.

"A belt?" Yessica pursed her lips. "You mean, does he beat me?"

"Yes. Did he whip your ass with a belt?"

She snorted then exaggerated a full-body shudder. "No, sweetheart."

"Interesting."

"Why is that *interesting?*" She narrowed her eyes.

Her friends found interest in their fingernails, drinks, and the grout in the tile flooring.

"Any woman can get dresses and pearls and makeup, but only the special ones get his belt." Camila leaned over Yessica's chair. "I'll say this one time, and this goes for all of you." She waved a hand, indicating the collective whole of prostitutes. "Do not touch him, invade his personal space, or proposition him. Do not do anything that disrespects me. If I get a whiff of it—and trust me, ladies, I'll know—I'll have your asses removed from this estate. I have no problem with the services you provide around here, but going forward, Matias is no longer a client. Are we clear?"

Paralyzed silence.

Camila sighed. "I asked a question."

"Yes." Yessica ground her teeth. "We're clear."

"Cool." She gave them a cordial smile. "*Chau pues!*"

She turned and headed toward him, her steps lighter, easier. As she closed the distance, however, jealousy tried to work its way into her resolve. She pushed it back with the reminder that she'd fucked countless men, causing Matias the same amount of pain.

When she reached his table, she moved toward the empty chair, but he gripped her arm and pulled her onto his lap.

"Do I want to know what that was about?" He brushed his lips against her ear and nibbled.

Tate angled toward Nico, distracted by whatever was displayed on Nico's phone.

"No more gifts for Yessica." She twisted to look at Matias.

"I don't shop for her." His eyes glimmered. "I receive all kinds of shit when I travel to the States. Presents from my business partners. I give her the girly stuff to divide among the whores."

Relief settled through her. "Well, maybe just give that stuff to a homeless person or something."

"I can do that." He nuzzled her neck. "What else?"

"They won't be propositioning you anymore. Hope your ego can handle that."

"I'll live." He nipped the skin beneath her ear.

She shivered with pleasure. "What did you announce this morning?"

"I briefed my lieutenants on your status and had them run the update down their chains of command. Everyone who stays here now knows you're my equal."

"Your equal?" Her heart slammed against her rib cage.

"My life," he said matter-of-factly.

A wave of heat gathered between her legs. As significant as his statement was, it also carried an undertone of need. Every interaction he shared with her was sexual in its delivery. He knew how to arouse her with his growly timbre, a look in his eyes, a caress of his breath against her skin. He didn't even have to touch her to satisfy her. It was his demanding hunger—that of a confident, dominant man—that she responded to, lifting her face to the rumble of his voice, offering herself to his desires.

She held her mouth against his, touching, not touching. Teasing. "I have two requests."

"I'm listening," he breathed against her lips.

"I want…" She touched her throat. "I want my collar back. Or better yet, I want something permanent and comfortable and *ours*."

His body went hard a millisecond before he gripped her neck and captured her mouth with his. The kiss was potently seductive, possessive, and consuming, stealing her air and awakening every cell in her body.

Too soon, he pulled back, breathing heavily. "The other request?"

"I want to see the closet."

CHAPTER 29

Matias led Camila into the closet of their private suite and angled her in front of the retinal scanner. His breaths quickened as the lock disengaged. What waited behind that door, the pieces he'd been holding back from her, were the knots of guilt he'd carried for years.

"I'm nervous about this." He stepped behind her and wrapped his arms around her chest, kissing her shoulder and savoring the feminine scent of her, bathed in the clean bite of citrus and lavender. "I'm not one of the good guys. I've done things for which there might be no forgiveness."

"I disagree. You've eliminated bad guys far worse than yourself for over a decade." She touched his inked forearm and turned her neck to press her lips against his bicep.

"Hold on to that thought for the next few minutes." He let go and nudged her through the doorway.

She looked up at the ceiling as motion lights flicked on then turned in a circle, scanning the shelves of the small second closet. "Boxes? Plain, non-threatening cardboard. Definitely not what I expected."

He went to the top shelf on the right and pulled

down his two favorite boxes.

"We'll start with these." He passed her one and carried the other into the bedroom.

They placed the closed boxes on the bed, and he stepped back, hands in the pockets of his jeans.

"Open them." His pulse accelerated, and a damp mist formed on his brow.

She flashed him a concerned look and opened the first box. Gasping, she removed picture frames filled with her and him, her and her sister, Lucia, and even photos of the old stray dog, Rambo. The citrus grove was the backdrop in most of the images.

"How did you get these?" Her hands trembled as she flipped through bundles of loose pictures.

He'd grabbed what he could that awful night, leaving behind the photos that included her parents. "There's more."

Eyes glistening, she darted to the second box and pulled out a slingshot fork from an orange tree, her favorite raggedy doll as a child, and his denim jacket— the one she'd stolen from him when she was fourteen and refused to return.

His heart hammered in his chest. There were a dozen more boxes of memorabilia in the closet. He'd gone through them so many times over the past eleven years he knew the contents by rote. He used to think he'd found comfort in them on his loneliest nights, but looking back now, he realized those memories had only made him lonelier.

"Matias…" She wiped the back of her hand across her cheek, erasing a fallen tear. "I thought all this stuff—" A sob rose up, but she choked it back. "I thought it was lost in the fire."

His eyes felt gritty and hot, but he didn't look away.

She pulled the jacket to her nose and inhaled deeply. "It still smells like you." Her gaze turned inward, and little lines formed on her brow. "Did you go back there after I disappeared? Did you see my parents before they died?"

Yes, yes, and fuck those motherfuckers to hell.

With a heavy breath, he sat on the bed and patted the spot beside him.

She set the jacket down and joined him, her shiny eyes searching his face. "You're scaring me."

Perhaps he would always scare her, but she wasn't a runner. She would fight him, maybe even kill him someday, but she would never leave him. He found a strange sort of comfort in that.

"Six weeks after your disappearance, I killed my brother, Jhon."

She gripped his hand and kept her teary gaze on his.

"A few weeks after that," he said with a tight throat, "your sister disappeared."

"Lucia?" Her voice whipped through the room.

"I had some guys watching the grove. I was in full-time-guns-out search mode, pulling every resource I had, trying to find you, hoping you'd show up there. When Lucia didn't return home from work one night..." He insides clenched with guilt. He should've been watching her sister, protecting her. "I knew."

"What did you know?" A lethal chill spiked her tone. "Where is she?"

"She's gone. I'm sorry, Camila." Pain stabbed through him. "She was abducted. Killed."

Her hands flew to her mouth, her eyes wide and wet.

"I prayed to hell I was wrong." He pulled her against his chest and stroked her hair. "Weeks went by, and your parents never reported her missing."

"She would've been…nineteen." She gripped his t-shirt. "She was an adult—"

"She was a missing person, Camila. *Missing*, and no one was fucking looking for her."

"No." A keening noise sounded in her throat. "I can't hear this…"

"You have to hear it." God knew, he needed to put this to rest. They both did. "Jhon was dead. Nico was the new face of the cartel. But Andres and your parents knew who I was, knew I was a Restrepo and the real capo. So I paid them a visit."

Her tears soaked his shirt, her cries silent beneath the rush of her breaths.

He held her tighter, running a hand through her hair as his chest squeezed painfully. "Your parents denied any involvement in her disappearance. Said she ran away, she was trouble, and more bullshit on top of bullshit. Goddammit, I was so fucking pissed. And desperate. I had their houses bugged and their phones tapped. A few days later, I got my answer."

Her breaths cut off, her shoulders hitched around her ears. Her entire body froze as if waiting to hear what he knew she'd already figured out.

"When Hector and Jhon died, they left behind an army of loyal men in my cartel. Men loyal to *them,* not to me and certainly not to Nico. This insurgency tried to overtake the cartel, and it took me months to root them all out."

Her chest began to heave again, and her fingers dug into his arm. Having lived at the estate for a few weeks, she knew enough about cartel politics and understood how easily an uprising could occur in the wake of a fallen leader.

"These men who wanted to take over..." She gazed up at him, eyes tinged pink. "They went after you by going back to the place you grew up? To threaten your loved ones?"

"Yes. Except the only one I loved was already gone." His insides tightened. "Camila, your parents..."

"They negotiated, didn't they?" Tears skipped down her cheeks.

"They didn't want to lose the grove or their lives, so they gave up Lucia in exchange for protection."

"Why?" She reared back, teeth gnashing, and voice angry. "If my parents knew you were the capo, they would've come to you. And who the hell did they need protection from?"

"They needed protection *from me*."

She sucked in a sharp breath. "I don't understand."

He angled toward her, shifting as close as possible with his thigh pressed against hers and his hands cupping her neck. "I was hunting through my ranks, torturing and killing those who were involved in *your* abduction. That's how I learned that Andres and your parents..." He paused, closed his eyes briefly, then looked at her. "They gave *you* up to Jhon to save their own lives." When her face crumbled, he rushed on. "When I killed Jhon, they knew I would come for them."

The brokenhearted look on her face and hitching sound of her cries sent a sharp bolt of agony through him. He pulled her onto his lap and held her for an endless moment as her shock morphed into full-body trembling. He rocked her and shushed her, his own eyes burning with so much goddamn remorse he couldn't catch his breath.

Eventually, she settled into soft sniffles, and he moved the boxes to the floor to lay with her on the bed. Side by side, faces inches apart, she stared into his eyes as hers became clearer, more lucid.

"How did you kill them?" She balled her hand in the bedding between their chests, but sympathy flooded her expression.

He pulled in a dry breath. She knew her mother had been the only mother he'd known. While her parents had never really accepted him, never thought he was good enough for her, it still killed something inside him when he pulled the trigger.

His rage, though… That had made it easier. It was such a deadly emotion, rising up from a dark place and taking over without logic or attention to consequence. His anger had been pure passion—raw, vindictive, and his only friend that night.

"Bullets. One shot each. Quick. Andres included." His voice was scratchy, hoarse. "Then I gathered your personal things. Set the fire. Covered my tracks."

"Where's Lucia?" Her voice was so small and hesitant he knew she didn't want the answer.

"She wasn't in that fire, but she's still gone, *mi vida*." He'd give anything to return her sister to her.

She lifted up on an elbow. "Where is her body? Do you have that proof?"

"No, but I have an investigation that proves her death. Every trail I followed, every name of every person involved is in one of those boxes in the closet."

"Show me." She jumped off the bed and straightened her white dress over her legs as she headed to the closet with way too much hope in her steps.

He couldn't bring back Lucia, but he could help Camila through the healing process as she grieved her sister all over again.

Two hours later, he sat with her on the bed amid papers, maps, printed photos of locations and slave traders—the entire portfolio of his two-year investigation. An investigation that ended with Lucia inside a transport that crashed in Peru. No one survived in the cargo full of trafficked slaves.

Camila stared at a newspaper clipping, her eyes glazed as if not really seeing it. "She's gone."

Her cheeks were sunken in, face pallid, and the paper trembled in her hand. She needed to eat, rest, take a fucking step back from this, and let her heart breathe.

He gathered the papers and started boxing everything up. "Tate asked about Lucia years ago then again this morning. He doesn't believe me and wants to retrace my steps, see if he can find something I missed."

"Really? Why?"

"I think he's just being a competitive asshole. Honestly, I don't understand his motivation, but he can take a stab at it if he wants. There's nothing to find that I don't already know."

She smiled sadly. "Guess he has a lot of free time now that he doesn't have to babysit me."

"He never looked at it that way." He softened his expression. "If I hadn't threatened his life four years ago, I'm pretty sure he would've gone after you for himself."

"I always wondered what his deal was." She shook her head. "I'm still trying to process the last four years."

She watched him put the box with the others on the floor, her eyes narrowing as he sat beside her on the bed. "What else are you keeping from me?"

"You have all my secrets now." He rubbed a hand up and down her arm, reflecting on her comment about the last four years. "But there's one question I never answered."

"I don't…" She blinked, and blinked again, lips parting. "What question? My brain is crap right now."

"That last phone call you made to me four years ago…"

"To collect Van's body?"

He nodded. "It changed my entire world, Camila. Following Van, finding you, approaching Tate, my plan to win you. During those four years, you were all I thought about. In my head, you were already mine, and I was yours. After that phone call, I remained one-hundred-percent faithful to you."

"You didn't…" She bit her lip as the corners of her mouth tipped up. "You didn't have sex for four years?"

Neither had she. It'd been an unknown connection between them, both of them abstaining as if fate had already intervened, pulling them together.

"I didn't touch or look at another woman," he said. "Whatever Yessica told you—"

She gripped the back of his neck and kissed him, putting every ounce of her grief and love into the vibrating hum of her lips. When she touched her tongue to his, his brain ignited, and heat spread from his chest, loosening the coil of remorse in his gut.

He broke contact and pressed his forehead against hers, his breaths erratic as he caressed the line of her jaw, kissed the soft skin there. Never had he felt so loved, so wanted. And deep beneath their connection was something more, something darker, sexual and potent, and he knew. It wasn't just his desire he sensed. It was hers.

"I'll be right back." He carried the boxes to the closet, making several trips, and returned to her with a smaller box, wrapped in black velvet.

Sitting cross-legged at the center of the bed, she reached for it, her eyes swollen from crying and nose pink. Her fingers trembled with the latch as she stared at him with a glint of excitement peering through the shadows on her face.

"Go ahead." He sat beside her, his breaths cut short. He'd waited for this moment for so long.

She lifted the lid, lips separating with a ragged exhale as she touched the platinum, double-link chain inside. "It's beautiful. When did you get it?"

"Years ago." He kissed her mouth. "I've *never* collared another woman. The leather collar was intended to be a statement to others and sturdy enough to be used when I restrain you." He ran a thumb along her wet bottom lip. "And I *will* restrain you."

She leaned into his touch, her eyes shutting for a moment then opening to stare at the collar in her hand. He removed it from the box and held it up so that she could read the inscription on the round platinum tag hanging from the *O*-ring.

Su vida.

"His life," she whispered and blinded him with a teary smile.

Then she lowered her head in offering. With shaky fingers, he fastened the lobster clasp at her nape and felt his whole world click into place.

"Gracias. Te amo." She wrapped her arms around his shoulders and pulled him to lie beside her, resting her cheek on his chest.

"I love you, too. *Más que nada."*

She squeezed him tight, and her grip on him alone told him she was happy to be with him, that she trusted him. Didn't matter how they arrived at this point, they were here, folded together, him holding her close to his side, and her closing fingers over the tag at her throat.

His heart sang beneath her cheek, his body vibrating with each breath they drew in sync. He internalized every twitch across her skin, the brush of her eyelashes against his shirt, the scent of her hair in his nose.

He tipped her face up and put his mouth on hers. She melted into him, snuggling in, and they stayed that way, wrapped up in each other for the rest of the day. When he had lunch brought in, they moved to the balcony where they ate *arepas* and curled up together on a wide lounge chair.

As the sun sank behind the vivid green landscape, they shared stories, painful stories, of their time away from one another. The men they'd killed, the nights they'd spent alone, and the searching, always searching for *this.* At some point they fell asleep, entwined together beneath the warm blanket of the black sky.

He woke with her sitting on his lap, leaning over him with her thighs straddling his hips, and a look of intent sparking in her eyes. The timer on the bedroom lights had clicked on, illuminating her white dress in an ethereal glow.

Pulses of heat charged sharp and low in his pelvis. He never would've imagined she'd want him so soon after the news he'd shared with her today. But this was Camila, his fighter, his backbone, a woman of carnal flesh—a yearning, determined, courageous woman. And she loved him.

She bent forward and propped an elbow on his chest, balancing her chin on her knuckles. "What if I asked you to just lie there and let me ride you for a while? Think you could handle that?"

Her husky voice curled around his cock, instantly turning him into iron.

"Yeah, I can—" Hunger strangled his words and shot through his veins, hot and restless.

Straightening, she pulled the dress over her head and dropped it. Her tits lifted with her inhale, peaked with hard rosy nipples, and her body gloriously nude except for the silver choker at her throat.

"I've never seen anything more beautiful." He breathed her in and smelled the sweetness of her arousal.

His pulse hammered, and his blood simmered, begging him to take her, to bury himself inside her. His hands flew to the button on his jeans, fumbling in his urgency.

She helped him, her fingers moving over the zipper, her breaths growing louder as they tackled his clothes, stripping off his shirt and pants. When she straddled him again, her hand closed around the swollen heat of his erection.

A groan pushed past his lips, his hips rocking, thrusting his cock into the vise of her fingers as he stared with wonder into her eyes. She stretched over his chest, fusing her mouth to his, and he was lost. Floating, reaching between her legs, stroking her wet pussy. He battled her tongue, moaning with garbled demands that she keep stroking him, kissing him.

"Ride me, Camila." He bit her lips and smacked her ass. "Sit on my cock and fuck me."

And she did, sinking down and shuddering around him. He grunted as she eased up and down, slowly, tenderly, hips circling and hands planted on either side of his head. He stroked her tits, leaned up to suck on her nipples, his balls tightening with blissful pressure.

His eyes never left hers as she moved over him, her cunt clamping down and stealing his thoughts, his breaths, and every tormented ache inside him. In that exquisite moment, there was only her and him, the tight warm clench of her body, and the glorious sight of her riding his dick.

He reached for her hands and held them against his chest, held onto her gaze. "You want to be owned."

"By you? Forever. Promise me."

His heart swelled. *"Sí prometo."*

When she came, she took him with her in a detonation of electricity that left him with no doubt who owned him, body and soul.

CHAPTER 30

Four months later...

The reek of cigarette smoke and the clinking
sounds of china swirled around Camila, mingling with
the gentle breeze that drifted across the veranda. Her
insides vibrated with the murmuring voices of forty
men — dangerous men — but none as powerful as the one
stroking her thigh.

Matias Restrepo owned every person in the room,
but she was the only one who owned his heart.

She reclined in the chair between him and Nico,
her belly full after an exorbitant five-course dinner, and
pulled a long draw from her beer. She looked forward to
these gatherings now that she didn't have to spend them
on her knees. In fact, no one knelt on the floor anymore.

At her request, Matias had banished all of the
imprisoned slave traders to the west wing. There, Frizz
could sew up their orifices and Matias could sell them off
at will. She supported whatever punishments were
inflicted as long as she didn't have to look at it while she
was eating.

That wasn't the only change that had happened
since Matias had announced her as his equal.

As it turned out, Yessica hadn't been able to keep

her hands to herself. Two weeks after the conversation by the pool, she propositioned Matias in the hall with her hand on his cock. He told Camila about it after he transferred Yessica — along with every resident prostitute he'd ever fucked — to his compound in Mexico. Sadly, that left only a couple women at the estate.

Camila was working on rectifying that. She'd recruited her old roommates in Texas to join her here. Now that she'd taken over Matias' anti-slavery operation, she needed more people she could trust. Her friends were hesitant, but considering the offer.

Tate sat across the table from her, listening to Chispa enthusiastically explain how to make a woman squirt. With a chuckle, Tate slid his eyes to her and winked. She shook her head, smiling.

He'd visited her a couple times in the last few months, but this time, he was just stopping by on his way to Peru, where he intended to follow up on Matias' investigation into Lucia's death. Her heart punched full-speed toward hope, but Matias tried to keep that reined in. He didn't want Tate's confirmation to bring her more grief.

She glanced at the man who protected her soul as much as her body. His muscled arm lay across her lap, his thumb stroking the denim on her inner thigh. In his reclined position, his brawny chest stretched the cotton of his black t-shirt. A foot rested on the knee of his opposite leg, drawing her gaze to the delicious way his jeans cupped the bulge of his cock.

When she looked up, his eyes were on her, invading, pressing deep inside her, into places only he could reach. Places that feared him as much as loved him. But she no longer had to carry those vulnerabilities alone.

He wanted all of her, cherished every one of her weaknesses and strengths. And whenever she offered herself to him, put herself fully into his hands, he silenced her doubts and insecurities.

The expression he wore now looked as if he wanted to invade her in a different way. His gaze heated with golden flames, his arms and torso flexing, seemingly restless. Wide shoulders, trim waist, hard abs—it was all there, one layer of clothes away from stealing her breath.

Without warning, he stood and threw back the last gulp of his *aguardiente.* "*Buenas noches,* guys."

Then his hand was around hers, dragging her away from the veranda. She jogged to keep up, her pulse sprinting with excitement. Damn his dangerously flirty *fuck me* eyes, but she couldn't get back to their suite fast enough.

He didn't release her until they reached the bedroom. She made a beeline to the bed, stripping her clothes as frenzied need stretched inside her, heating under her skin and throbbing between her legs.

She dropped her blouse, jeans, and removed her undergarments, her back burning from the heat of his gaze. But he hadn't followed her?

She turned. The sexy bastard leaned against the wall by the door, arms crossed over his nude chest and a bare foot hooked around his ankle. He'd removed his shirt and boots, but the jeans remained, the zipper partially lowered to reveal the dark patch of hair around the root of his erection—which was bent downward and tucked beneath the denim.

Her pussy contracted, and her nipples hardened. "Are you going to—?"

"Stand with your chest against the post. Hands

above your head."

It was never a request with him. He commanded, and she obeyed. In the bedroom, with that aggressive look firing in his eyes, she wouldn't have it any other way.

She lingered for a moment, unable to avert her gaze. Inky black hair lay in haphazard spikes and fell across his brow. His expression was dark and severe, but his dimples were there, reminding her of the boy who'd stolen her heart.

The muscles in his torso were flawlessly defined, layered in ridges that were honed in combat. Whether he was training for a raid or running into a gunfight, he was built for this life. His job still scared the bejesus out of her, but she was confident in his ability to stay alive.

She resisted the urge to cross the room and put her hands all over him, because seriously, no man should look that good. With a sigh, she faced the post and reached her arms toward the ceiling.

His footsteps approached, and her breaths picked up. His masculine scent attacked her senses as he stopped behind her, crowding into her space in the possessive, overbearing way she loved.

"I'm going to hurt you," he breathed in the space beside her ear.

She shivered.

"Then I'm going to replace the hurt with something else." His chest slid against her back, his hand closing over the chain around her neck.

"With your cock?"

"Yes." A smile teased through his rumbling voice. "With my cock."

"I accept."

"I'm not asking." His hand lowered to her pussy, cupping and squeezing. "This is mine."

"Oh, you arrogant ass. You want me willing—"

He slammed a palm against her backside, shooting fire across her skin. Her breath left her so quickly and thoroughly she was still struggling to catch it when he disappeared in the closet and returned again.

With leather cuffs and a string of chain, he locked her wrists to the eye bolt in the post above her head. Stepping back, he simply stared at her. Patient. Watchful. He just…stared. After a long, unnerving moment, he grabbed the cane from the floor.

Then he hurt her. Holy fuck, he hurt every inch of her ass and thighs.

She screamed and writhed and cursed him to hell, tucking her hips against the post and trying to keep her lower muscles loose beneath his strikes. She begged him to stop, but those tattooed forearms persisted, welting her skin with hard, erratic blows. Beneath the searing pain, however, something else bloomed, something stronger, deeper.

Trust.

She believed he wouldn't take her too far, wouldn't give her more than she could handle. It was trust that had connected them as children, and it linked them now, more intimately than she'd ever bonded with another person. Her entire body followed his movements, shivering with the rapid gusts of his breaths and giving beneath the drive of his strikes.

It was trust that aroused her pleasure, igniting heat between her legs and damping her inner thighs. He was hurting her to remind her that she trusted him with her whole heart.

He dropped the cane and pressed his chest against her back, soothing her with shushing noises. She melted against him, rolling her head back on his broad shoulder and savoring the heat of his body.

His lips glided along her jaw with caressing licks, his fingers sliding between her legs, stroking and working her into a panting, hungry animal. She ground her sore ass against the opening of his jeans, sending bites of pleasure and pain through her body.

He ran his palms over the backs of her thighs, rubbing the hurt there, tracing the creases between her legs and butt. He groaned as he dragged an invasive stroke up the crack of her ass. Then he released her shackles.

Carrying her to the bed, he chained her hands to the headboard and removed his jeans.

He didn't make her wait when he settled between her thighs and notched his cock against her pussy. The instant he claimed her mouth with his, he thrust.

Pleasure lifted her off the bed as he hit deep with long, stroking stabs, shoving a moan from her throat. With his elbows braced on either side of her head and his biceps the size of her thighs, he moved his cock inside her, never looking away.

"Love you," he mouthed.

"Love you." She pulled her arms against the chains, aching to touch him.

Eyes burning bright with the ferocity of his love, he reached a hand over her head and laced his fingers with hers.

He'd finally captured her, enchained her, and she never wanted to escape.

The **DELIVER** series continues with:

DEVASTATE (#4)
Tate's story

TAKE (#5)
Kate's story

OTHER BOOKS
BY PAM GODWIN

LOVE TRIANGLE ROMANCE
TANGLED LIES TRILOGY
One is a Promise
Two is a Lie
Three is a War

DARK PARANORMAL ROMANCE
TRILOGY OF EVE
Dead of Eve #1
Heart of Eve #1.5
Blood of Eve #2
Dawn of Eve #3

STUDENT-TEACHER ROMANCE
Dark Notes

ROCK-STAR DARK ROMANCE
Beneath the Burn

ROMANTIC SUSPENSE
Dirty Ties

EROTIC ROMANCE
Incentive

ACKNOWLEDGMENTS

To my Freedom Fighters — You're the best street team in existence. I'm so incredibly lucky to have your support and friendship. I would be lost without you.

To my alpha and beta readers — Amber Bauswell, Lindy Winter, Ann White, Jill Bitner, Lindsey R. Loucks, Kathryn Sparrow, J. Andrew Jansen, Myra Stark, Shabby Arora, Shea Moran, Ketty Beale, Kristine Hannaford, and Michelle Tan — There are so many other ways to pass your time, yet you spent hours, days, weeks with me in this gruesome world of anti-heroes and human trafficking. You encouraged me, showed me ways to improve, and held me to a spectacular bar. Thank you for believing in me.

To my proofreader, Lesa Godwin — A typo-free narration is the only kind of book worth publishing, and that's what I have — because of you. I love you.

To the Founders of Starbucks — Jerry Baldwin, Zev Siegl, and Gordon Bowker — Your coffee fueled me for several sleepless months, kept me focused, and helped me publish this book on time. Nothing wires me quite like a cup (or twenty) of your delicious dark roast.

To my family — Chad, Jaedha, Leighton — You're my whole, my universe, my everything.

ABOUT THE AUTHOR

New York Times and USA Today Bestselling author, Pam Godwin, lives in the Midwest with her husband, their two children, and a foulmouthed parrot. When she ran away, she traveled fourteen countries across five continents, attended three universities, and married the vocalist of her favorite rock band.

Java, tobacco, and dark romance novels are her favorite indulgences, and might be considered more unhealthy than her aversion to sleeping, eating meat, and dolls with blinking eyes.

EMAIL: pamgodwinauthor@gmail.com

36634287R00224

Made in the USA
Middletown, DE
17 February 2019